A MEMORY WORTH DYING FOR

A NOVEL

JOANIE BRUCE

AMBASSADOR INTERNATIONAL
GREENVILLE, SOUTH CAROLINA & BELFAST, NORTHERN IRELAND
www.ambassador-international.com

A Memory Worth Dying For

This is fiction. Names, characters, places and incidents either are the product of the author's imagination or are used fictitiously. Any resemblance to actual persons, living or dead, events or locations is entirely coincidental.

© 2014 by Joanie Bruce

All rights reserved. Printed in the United States of America. Except as permitted under the United States Copyright Act of 1976, no part of this publication may be reproduced or distributed in any form or by any means, or stored in a data base or retrieval system, without the prior written permission of the publisher.

ISBN: 978-1-62020-253-1
eISBN: 978-1-62020-353-8

Cover design and typesetting: Hannah Nichols & Joshua Frederick
E-book conversion: Anna Riebe

AMBASSADOR INTERNATIONAL
Emerald House
427 Wade Hampton Blvd.
Greenville, SC 29609, USA
www.ambassador-international.com

AMBASSADOR BOOKS
The Mount
2 Woodstock Link
Belfast, BT6 8DD, Northern Ireland, UK
www.ambassadormedia.co.uk

The colophon is a trademark of Ambassador

A MEMORY
WORTH DYING FOR

Zippy + Bonnie –
Best wishes and
may God bless!
Joanie
Bruce

I would like to dedicate this book to my loving husband, Ben, who supports me in everything I do. He's my biggest fan. Thank you Sweetheart.

I love you.

Acknowledgement:

I would like to thank my Lord and Savior, Jesus Christ for giving me the ability to share His love with everyone who likes to read.

PROLOGUE

Carson City, Texas

Marti gripped the car seat in front of her with rigid hands and wondered why she let her brother-in-law drive her car.

"Please, Vinny, slow down or let me out."

"Aw, come on, Martha. Don't be such a scaredy-cat. I know what I'm doin'. I'll have you to the hospital in no time."

Vinny's wife, Angela, grinned and turned around to glance at Marti in the back seat. "His NASCAR reflexes are still there, hon. He can make a car do amazing things."

Marti leaned back in the seat and tried to relax. Tucking an auburn curl behind her ear with one hand, she massaged her stomach when she felt the baby kick with the other. She swirled circular patterns on her stomach and yearned to be anywhere but in this speeding car.

Up ahead, a crooked stop sign balanced halfway between a vertical position and the pavement. Instead of slowing up, Vinny's foot forced the gas pedal further down to the floor.

"Watch me beat that old rattle-trap, Angie darling."

Marti's stomach clenched. With tightness in her throat, she watched a beat-up red truck plowing toward the intersection. The truck was traveling too fast. They weren't going to make it to the stop sign first. She inhaled a stale gulp of air and watched in horror as the truck barreled toward them.

Marti closed her eyes. If she ignored the truck, maybe it would disappear.

What a ninny! It wasn't going to disappear.

Lord, please make it disappear.

Dread forced her eyes shut, but terror opened them up again. The truck was still there, and it wasn't slowing down. The driver couldn't see them through the willows blowing on the side of the highway.

She held her breath as Vinny sped through the intersection, foolishly ignoring the proximity of the two vehicles. The front bumper of the truck passed within inches of the back corner of their car.

A long horn blared behind them as the truck flashed by—the sound hollow and metallic in the humid air. The tires of the truck squealed briefly, and Marti's imagination supplied the smell of hot rubber.

She watched the red truck round the sharp corner behind them and disappear. A gulp of air cooled her parched throat, and a sigh of relief made its way to her lips. She turned to the front. "Vinny, please—"

Suddenly, she felt the car slide on the muddy road and hydroplane on top of the puddles of water. Her brother-in-law let out an expletive before he wrenched the wheel to the left.

Inside the car, Marti had the surreal feeling of being suspended in a boat on top of frothy waves. The car skated steadily sideways until Vinny lost control, and the right side of the car lifted into the air. Marti experienced a floating sensation and braced her hands on the car frame.

Lord, please help us.

The car tilted. Hard metal met her body as she was thrown against the side door. Broken glass scraped her arms and face.

The car tumbled. She crossed her arms over her stomach and tried to protect her baby from the blows. Screams filled the night air, and she heard crunching . . . metal ripping apart. The car beat at her whole body. A heavy blow to her arm was the last thing she remembered before something hit her in the back of the head, and the whole world swirled into oblivion.

A pain in her stomach woke her. Groaning filled the air around her until she realized it was coming from her own throat. The taste of her lips was bitter, but wetting them was impossible. Her mouth was parched, and there wasn't enough moisture to keep her tongue from sticking to the roof of her mouth.

Towering over her, a strange woman gazed down at her. Marti stared up at the blurred face.

"Who . . . who are you?" Marti's voice was just above a whisper.

The woman hovered over her. "Don't you know who I am, Martha?"

Marti shook her head before another pain in her stomach doubled her over, and the woman moved to help her.

"Don't worry, honey. I'll help you. You're gonna have this baby right here, before the ambulance gets here, aren't you?"

"What h-happened? Where's my husband?" Marti grabbed the woman's hand as another contraction filled her body with agony.

"Just relax, honey. I'll take care of everything."

ONE

Landeville, Tennessee

Three years later

"And I will restore to you the years that the locust hath eaten." Joel 2:25a

No! Not here!

Marti Rushing gawked at the coffee-colored hair of the man standing fifteen feet to the left of her. He was pointing out the brush strokes in one of her paintings.

Chills immobilized her heart and muscles for what felt like a full minute. It took that long for her feet to respond to her brain's command—*Hide!*

She slipped behind a rotund man gesturing wildly about his life as an architect and peeked around him at the man who caused her initial panic.

Daniel Rushing—her ex-husband.

First surprise and then shame raced through her head before being washed away by the next emotion filling her heart—fear.

Why was he here? Had he chased her down to torment her further?

Memories of their last argument three years ago threatened to emerge from deep within the crannies of her mind. She pushed them out of her thoughts. No! She would not think of that now. She'd ignore him. She could do this. Her jaw tightened, and she took a deep, shaky breath. This was her big day. After working for months to prepare for this exhibit, she would not let the appearance of one man ruin it by his mere presence.

Even if it was Daniel.

"Marti, here you are." Her friend and gallery owner, Sandra Wellington, put her lace-covered arm through Marti's and pulled her over to a couple sipping punch from a vintage crystal goblet.

"Mr. and Mrs. Samson, this is Marti Rushing. Marti, the Samsons are buying your Blue Mountain landscape."

Sandra's calming British accent soothed Marti's angst, and she forced a mega-smile at the couple. Trying to keep the shiver from her voice, she spoke. "That's wonderful. I'm so glad you like it."

Mr. and Mrs. Samson smiled and held out their hands to shake hers before Mr. Samson bobbed his head into her space.

"Like it? We *love* it. My wife came in every day this week, hoping no one would buy this painting before today's opening. It's so nice to finally meet such a talented artist."

The smile Marti gave the couple felt genuine, but her face felt like it would break into pieces. She looked at Mr. Samson as he spoke, but out of the corner of her eye, she watched Daniel and the back of an elegantly dressed female in a satin gown standing a few feet from their circle.

Marti's eyes strayed to his lean form as she watched the back of his wavy hair, her breath shallow and tight.

"Marti?" Sandra's voice prodded, and Marti jumped.

"Oh, uh . . . I'm sorry. Would you please excuse me?"

She forged a straight line to the back of the gallery and barely made it around the corner before she collapsed on the chair sitting inches inside the door of the tiny kitchenette. Her breath came in gulps. She struggled for each breath. Numbness traveled through her body, and she recognized the first signs of a full blown panic attack.

No! Not now!

She hadn't had an attack in months. Her eyelids felt heavy as she concentrated on the advice the counselor had given her.

Relax! Breathe deeply.

Stop thinking about the stimulus—*Daniel*.

Repeat the coping words.

"I'm fine. Everything is fine. I'm fine. Everything is fine."

"Marti, what's wrong?" Sandra's voice sounded like it came from a deep hole.

Marti covered her eyes with her hands and concentrated on breathing.

Sandra placed a hand on Marti's auburn hair. "What's the matter, love?"

Marti shook her head. "Sandra . . . that man . . . he's . . ."

Sandra's blond head leaned back around the corner. Surprise registered on her face, and she turned to Marti.

"Is that Daniel?"

Eyes squeezed shut, Marti nodded jerkily. Her face felt cold and clammy.

"Should I ring 9-1-1?"

Marti shook her head. "No, it's been three years. Surely by now—"

"What's he doing in Tennessee? Do you know?"

Marti shuddered. Tears burned the back of her eyes. "I'm fine. Everything is fine."

Sandra placed an arm around Marti's shoulders in a supporting hug and waited until her breathing slowed and her trembling lessened.

"Marti, you need to go in there, look him in the face, and demand to know what happened between you three years ago."

The shake of Marti's head moved auburn tendrils of hair into her eyes. "No. Absolutely not."

"Well, this is certainly at sixes and sevens. What are you going to do?" Sandra blew out a pained breath. "You can't hide back here all evening. It's your show, for goodness sake. Do you want me to tell him to leave?"

Marti's eyes popped open. Normally Sandra's British expressions brought a smile to her face, but not this time. Leaning her head against the wall behind her chair, she looked up. What should she do? She had to go back in there. If he came here to taunt her, he would have sought her out by now.

She stared at the kitchenette's wispy blue ceiling she and Sandra had painted and decided to hold fast to the life she had created for herself during the last three years.

"No. I'll go back out there. I don't care if he's here or not. I'll ignore him. I can do this."

She summoned a look she hoped was filled with determination and spunk. "I will *not* let him ruin my life—not again."

"That-a-girl. Remember, fear exists only in your mind."

Marti stood on shaky limbs. "I'm fine. Everything is fine."

She took another deep breath and slowly rounded the corner. Daniel and his companion were nowhere in sight. She blew out a relieved puff of air, gave Sandra a faltering smile, and turned to meet her customers.

After fifteen minutes of dealing with several interested shoppers, she completed the sale of two paintings and three signed prints. She also had a portrait commission pending after the first of the following month.

When Marti finished handling the sale of her last painting, she turned around and suddenly found Daniel towering over her.

His nearness spiraled her back into the past and stirred up pleasant memories of sawdust and basswood. Her eyes rose to meet his like magnets. She felt her soul being pulled into the brown depths, and she could only stare.

Daniel held out his hand, took her trembling hand into his, and shook it.

"Hi. Are you the one I need to see about buying a painting?"

When his hands touched hers, shock exploded across his face, and questions filled his eyes. He pulled his hand back immediately. After masking his own surprised reaction to her touch, he crooked his head slightly.

When the meaning of his question dawned on Marti, her eyes widened in incredulity.

"What?"

"Uh . . . I'm interested in buying the landscape at the end of that wall, if you can give me a price." He pointed to one of her larger paintings. It was a landscape of mountains she painted from memory—of the mountains outside their former bedroom window.

"You've got to be kidding." Marti's breath was coming fast. "Daniel, why are you doing this?"

"I beg your pardon? You know my name?"

The world was crumbling around her. Daniel acted as if he didn't know who she was. She couldn't pull her gaze away from his, and she could read confusion in the brown spheres.

He doesn't know me. He really doesn't know me.

The thought chilled her. How could you not remember someone after living together four years as husband and wife? She clutched her stomach and tried to breathe.

Sandra hurried up to them and turned toward Daniel. "I'll help you, sir."

Marti backed off—never taking her eyes from Daniel's face. The tan skin and rugged features sent a wave of longing through her that made the breath catch in her throat. Her feelings for him were still strong—the truth screamed at her. In spite of what he had done, she still loved him. She could feel it all the way to her toes.

The realization hit her between the eyes, and her eyes filled with tears.

After three years of separation, anyone would think the tingle his presence evoked would diminish, but the gravitational pull between them was as strong as ever.

She turned to force herself away from the claustrophobic space and came face-to-face with Daniel's companion—the red-headed woman dressed in a green satin Armani.

"Veronica!"

Veronica Duke raised her head in total shock, obviously surprised to see her. Veronica veiled her eyes and raised her brows in a victory salute as she linked her arm in Daniel's and gave him an affectionate squeeze.

Marti shook her head and turned in desperation toward the back room. Her head throbbed as she took the steps two at a time to her apartment above the gallery. She plunged onto the comforter stretched across the bed and buried her tears in the pillow.

All the pain, the deep sorrow, the loneliness that plagued her for the last three years came gushing from her heart to her eyes. She thought she was over the devastation, but one glimpse of the man she loved brought it all back in full force.

Her heart yearned to stomp back into the gallery and confront him—to hear the truth of what happened that night three years ago in Texas. But the superior look on Veronica's face stopped her. Veronica's possessive claim of Daniel's attention spoke more than words could say. She obviously had stepped in and claimed Daniel as her own when Marti left.

Marti sat up slowly and reached for the tiny gold chain she wore around her neck. At the end of the long length was a miniature horse's head—carved from wood with intricate detail. A shiny emerald in the horse's mane glittered in the light. It was one of a matching set. Daniel had carved them for her as a gift for their third anniversary. The rest of the set had been left behind when she was forced to leave Daniel's home. She rubbed the tiny horse's smooth surface as tears once again burned through her thoughts.

TWO

Marti rallied when she heard Sandra climbing the stairway at the end of the apartment.

"Marti, love? Are you okay?"

Marti sat up in bed and sighed. A headache pounded between her temples.

Sandra came in and sat down beside her. "He's gone."

Marti nodded—a whole universe of hurt burned in her eyes. "His eyes were blank—like he didn't recognize me at all, and I don't believe he was pretending."

Sandra shrugged. "What are you going to do now?"

Marti rubbed her eyes with her fingers. "Go on with my life."

"The counselor said confronting your fear is the only way to heal, Marti. Go talk to Daniel. At least find out what happened between you."

"No way. I can't handle it." Marti's shook her head. "Sandra, I can't remember everything that happened that day in Texas, but I still have nightmares about the hours in the hospital—the pain, the depression, waiting for Daniel to come to me after the accident. He never came. And the things he said when I returned home still torture me in the wee hours of the night."

Marti trembled uncontrollably.

Sandra patted Marti's arm comfortingly. "Sweetie, you told me Daniel sent you away, but you never said why. Do you know?"

Marti shook her head. The loss and pain of the accident were hard to live through but were nothing compared to the shocked agony over Daniel's surprise welcome home.

"I thought it was because I was to blame for the accident. But he called me horrible names and never gave me reasons why." She took a tremulous breath. "A policeman picked me up from the hospital and took me straight to the police station in Carson City. When they realized I couldn't remember anything about the accident, they took me home. The funeral for Daniel's sister and her husband was that day, and when I got home, Daniel was furious. He shouted at me to get out. He said he . . ." Marti sobbed and took deep breaths so she could continue. "He said he never w-wanted to see me again. When I tried to argue with him . . . he . . . he slapped me." Marti's hand automatically touched her cheek as if she could still feel the searing pain of the blow.

Sandra drew in a shocked breath, and her eyes widened. Marti stood up and paced the room.

"Daniel blamed me for the accident that killed his sister and brother-in-law. Then his father came in. Gerald said the same thing . . . only in much stronger language. My head nearly vibrated when he shouted, 'You're a disgrace to this family. Nothing can ever undo what you've done. Leave this house and never come back.'"

"Oh, Marti."

Marti sat back down on the bed and hung her head in her hands.

"Is that when you left?"

Marti nodded. "I got a hotel room in town until after the judge's ruling. I didn't know what else to do. I couldn't remember anything about the accident. That's what hurt—the accusations they hurled at me might have been true."

"Oh, love, I doubt that. You're too sweet a person to do anything beastly. I can't believe for a minute you'd do anything to shame anyone."

Marti shuddered. Even after three years, the heartless claims pulsed inside her like the pain of a sore tooth.

"They didn't give you any kind of reason? No facts?"

"I don't know, Sandra. I can't remember. I was so devastated. I can hardly remember that day—only that the one who promised to love me 'in sickness and in health' didn't anymore. Instead, he stopped loving me that day and ordered me to leave the only home I'd ever known since the orphanage."

Sandra frowned and shook her head. She waited patiently for Marti to continue.

"I packed my clothes and walked out the same day. My eyes were so blurry from crying that I could hardly see, and my heart was broken into a million pieces. I left with nothing but a suitcase full of clothes and the car Daniel gave me for a wedding gift, and I wouldn't have taken that if I'd had any other way of leaving. I even left my wedding rings behind—sitting on the bedside table."

"What about this woman, Veronica? Do you think she had anything to do with Daniel's rejection?"

Marti shook her head. "No, but I do remember her being at the house the day I came home from the hospital. She and her mother brought food after the funeral."

"What's her connection with Daniel?"

"She and Daniel were neighbors; the ranches connect on the back fence line. Both their parents raise quarter horses, and they spent a lot of time together growing up. After Daniel and I married, Parker, the Rushing's butler, told me Shane and Mary Duke had pushed Veronica and Daniel together every chance they could, knowing it was Veronica's dream to marry Daniel one day."

"But you came along and swept Daniel off his feet."

Marti sighed and leaned back on her elbows. "We met at a regional rodeo. Immediately, our feelings for each other blossomed into something more than friendship. He never left my side until our wedding a year later."

"Did that upset the Dukes?"

"They never seemed to be upset. Even Veronica had someone make us a handmade quilt for a wedding gift. Shane and Mary gave us a silver tea set from Germany."

"Don't you think it's time to go back and confront him about the accusations? Find out why he called you those horrible names?"

"How can I do that when he doesn't even remember who I am? I know I've changed some in the last three years, but surely I'm not unrecognizable."

"Surely he remembers what happened three years ago. You need to ask. You just admitted you left without finding out why he sent you away. I can still see the circle of pain in your eyes, Marti, and it's growing like a festering sore. You need to lance the wound so the pain will go away. Maybe you were too distraught back then to get to the bottom of the wedge that tore you apart, but you're strong enough now to handle it."

Marti shook her head and shuddered. "What about my stalker?"

"Do you still think Daniel was the one stalking you?"

Marti frowned. "I don't know."

"I thought you told me the investigating officer in Alabama said Daniel couldn't have been involved because he was overseas during those months. Why do you still think it was him?"

Marti shrugged. "I guess because Daniel showed me a side of him I didn't know existed when he threw me out of the house. In our four years of marriage, I never saw him angry. Not once. And, just because he had an alibi doesn't mean he didn't hire someone to make those calls and to vandalize my apartments and my car. What a nightmare—flat tires on my car, all the mirrors broken in my apartment, furniture vandalized in my bedroom. Wherever I moved, it was the same. I tried to run, to hide from him, but no matter where I went, he found me—in four different states. And the phone calls . . ." She shuddered.

"You never told me about the phone calls."

Marti stood up and paced across the room and back.

"That's because it scares me to death to think about them. They were horrible, abusive—ragged breathing . . . threats. He threatened the people around me if I told anyone—all my new friends. I couldn't think of anyone that mad at me—enough to actually threaten me—except Daniel. He was so mad when he banned me from the house—I thought he was behind it all." She covered her face with her hands. "He threw me out of the only home I'd ever known." Her voice broke, and she sobbed.

Sandra led her to the bed. She wrapped her arms around Marti's shoulders.

"It's okay, love. Keep your spirits up. The threats stopped when you moved here, so you don't have to worry about them anymore. If the constables said they can prove Daniel wasn't involved, maybe you should believe them and go back and talk to him."

Marti sniffed.

"It doesn't matter now, anyway. Talking to him won't do any good. There's nothing I can do."

Sandra propped her hands on her hips. "Rubbish! Martha Anne Rushing, that doesn't sound like the woman I know. It's not like you to give up. I've heard you say a million times you'd like to talk to Daniel. Now when you have the chance, you run in the opposite direction." Her tone softened. "You still love him, don't you?"

Marti nodded miserably. "The orphanage director, Mrs. Timms, used to tell me that one day I'd find my match—my amigo del alma, she called it. I knew it was Daniel the first time I saw him."

Sandra raised her brows. "Amigo del alma means . . .?"

"The friend of my soul," explained Marti.

"Sweet Marti. Don't give up. Fight for him. Go talk to him. He's probably still in town. Find out why he forced you to leave Texas. You'll never heal until you do."

"How can I fight when I can't remember any of what he's accusing me of?" Marti stood and walked to the open window.

"Well, find out what he *says* happened, love. Who knows? If you get it all out in the open, you might work things out between you."

Marti clenched and unclenched her fists.

"No. He had his chance. I kept waiting for him to call me and say he was wrong . . . to say he was sorry . . . to ask me to come back."

"You didn't exactly stay in one place long enough for him to find you now, did you?"

Marti felt frustrated. "I guess not. I kept roaming around—trying to forget. When the stalker's calls and vandalism began, I ran—out of terror. I was convinced it was Daniel."

"Maybe Daniel tried to find you, and you didn't know."

Marti balked, and the anger built inside her like a windstorm. "Don't stand up for him, Sandra. If he cared, he would have found me. As far as I'm concerned, he can have Veronica if he wants her. He deserves her. Daniel and Veronica grew up together, but he won't know what hit him if he ends up married to her. She's a chameleon—changing according to whomever she's with. In front of Daniel, she's this shy, agreeable, pleasant angel, but when he steps out of the room, she's a scheming, manipulative, selfish witch." She fumed a minute before adding, "They're perfect for each other. Daniel will be miserable married to her, and he deserves her." She crossed her arms and looked at Sandra defiantly.

Sandra moved to stand beside her and gave her a hug. "You don't mean that, love. I hear a touch of denial in your voice, but it's your call to make. I still say you're making a mistake. Why don't you come with me and Vivian to the art exhibit in Vick this weekend? You've worked so hard—you deserve a little time off—time to think, and maybe pray about what to do."

"Yeah, right, like that's gonna happen." Marti laced her words with sarcasm. "You know what I think about praying. Hashtag: pointless."

Sandra gave Marti a look but didn't say a word.

"It might be nice to get away for a while. Do you think your sister would mind if I tagged along?"

"Of course not. Hashtag: the more the merrier—to quote your little Twitter language. Teaching you how to tweet has sure made life interesting." Sandra smiled and changed the subject. "I have some Yorkshire pudding downstairs. Are you hungry?"

"Not now. Maybe later."

After Sandra descended the short flight of stairs, Marti turned to stare out the open window, wishing things were different. Wishing with all her heart she could go back and confront the problems between her and Daniel but knowing it was impossible.

There was nothing she could do about the past, but she *would* control her future. She'd made a life for herself and was moving on.

"My happiness will never again depend on a man."

And that was one promise she intended to keep.

As she spoke to the stars twinkling in the night sky, a shiver traveled down her spine. Without warning, goose bumps popped out on her arms. Eyes from somewhere in the darkness watched her—like before. She could feel their intense gaze. She jerked the shutters closed and peeked through the tiny slits. Searching the darkness for a face and finding none, she stepped back away from the window. Was it her imagination?

Something crackled in the air, like the wind of the first frost. The simple decision to ignore her past and embrace the future was about to change her life. She could feel it.

Hashtag: warning.

THREE

The red stub of a cigarette glowed and ebbed as the man standing in the shadows watched the wind blow the curtains in the upstairs window across the street. A cell phone was pressed against his head, and he waited for his contact to pick up.

"Yeah?"

"I found her."

"Great. Now, I have another job for you to do."

His disgusted grunt preceded his growl. "I thought I already took care of our little bargain."

"You did, but if you do this, I'll make it worth your while . . . say maybe half of the insurance money."

Silence filled the space. He was definitely interested. "Half, you say? That's a good chunk o' change. I want it all in cash—just like before."

"All right."

"What do I have to do this time?"

"Same as before."

"Why? What's happened?"

"Never mind. Just do it. I don't want her back in Texas, and she might have reason to think about coming back again."

"She's nowhere near Texas now. Why the panic?"

"Just do it, and don't ask questions. I'm paying you—that's all you need to know. Do what you have to do to keep her moving around and out of Texas. And this time, no mistakes. You almost got caught last time. Stick to the plan."

"I knew what I was doin'. She didn't go back to Texas, did she?"

"Okay, okay."

"How far do you want me to go?"

"This time you'll have to make it a little more plain. Go as far as you need to."

His voice grew harsh. "Even if it means—"

The person on the other end of the phone interrupted. "Shut up! You don't know who might be listening. I don't want the whole world overhearing our plans, do you? Just do what you have to."

"You got it, pardner." The whisper in the phone almost sounded gleeful.

"And stop calling me that. I'm not your pardner."

"Yeah, right."

"Don't forget . . . you get caught, you're on your own. If you try to implicate me, you know the dirt I have on you—it'd be a shame if the police got hold of it."

"Right to the point . . . like always. 'Night, pardner."

He slammed his phone shut.

"You're on your own," he mimicked toward the stars with clenched teeth. The stub of his cigarette fell to the ground, and he stomped out the glowing ember with his shoe. That remark infuriated him. Just because he'd served time in prison for murder didn't mean he'd let himself get careless again.

The night was as silent and as black as a tomb. He plodded down the street and grumbled. His lips twisted in a look of anticipation. Murder was always messy, but he could handle it if necessary.

FOUR

Marti was sure her laughter could be heard tinkling through the warped windows on the rundown brick building and out into the street, but she didn't care. It felt good to laugh.

She brushed the last stroke of polyurethane on the wooden sign propped against the inside wall of the building and dropped her brush in a jar of paint thinner. The words, *"Landeville's Haven for the Homeless"* gleamed across the front of the sign in glossy black paint.

In the same room, a petite blonde descended a stepladder, swiped at a loose strand of hair, and turned to Marti.

"That's funny, coming from you, Marti. You know I couldn't paint a stick figure if my life depended on it."

"Alana Holbrook, you're just using flattery so I won't quit in the middle of painting this mural and leave you and Jaydn high and dry. Hashtag: desperate," Marti teased as she walked across the room and grinned at her friend.

Alana's laughter echoed in the empty room. "You and those hashtags! But you're right; we'd be lost without you. Staying so busy at the orphanage, Jaydn and I would go crazy if we didn't have you to help us get this place up and running. And your suggestion for the mural was a great idea. I love the neighborhood approach."

Marti picked up a small artist's brush to finish the details on the wall mural and stood back to look at the neighborhood scene on the wall. "Thanks, Alana. I wanted this wall to symbolize the American Dream. You know . . . a house, a family, a dog, a friendly neighborhood filled with kids playing basketball, washing cars, and mowing lawns. I want to infuse every homeless person who comes in here with enough drive to grasp that dream for themselves—encourage them to strive for a home of their own one day."

Alana looked happy. "You have a big heart, Marti."

Marti shook her head. "Not as big as yours and Jaydn's. I think it's great what you're doing. Opening a homeless shelter here in Landeville has to be a huge undertaking, especially when you donate so much to the orphanage in Bishop."

"Jaydn and I decided a long time ago that the money God blessed us with would always be used for helping others. This homeless shelter was a dream of my mom and dad's, and we don't care how much work it takes or how much money it costs to get it up and running; it's something we're both determined to complete."

Alana blew out a satisfied breath and swished her paint brush around in the water vat to wash off the paint. "I'm done here. The guys are gonna love this. I think the color on this wall brings out the colors in your mural. Wise choice, my dear."

Marti stretched her back then studied the maroon color of Alana's wall and how it bounced off the colors of the mural. "I think you're right."

"I'm always right."

They both giggled.

"I'm wise and you're right. What a combination."

Marti turned and looked at the floor to ceiling mural she was painting. It was almost done—just a few touches here and there.

"Hey! How did your exhibit go yesterday?"

Marti's smile slipped a little, but she covered it with deep breath. "It went good. I sold several paintings and have a couple of portrait commissions coming up. Hashtag—"

"I know," Alana interrupted and laughed. "Hashtag: success."

"Right." Marti smiled at her friend.

"Good. You deserve it. You're a talented artist." Alana glanced at the clock on the wall. "Oh my! Look what time it is. My babysitter will be wondering if I got lost on the way home." Alana laid the clean paint brush on the table covered with various painting paraphernalia and pulled the tarp over the top.

"How's sweet little Dean doing these days?"

"He's cutting teeth, and that makes him a little cranky. Other than that, he's growing like a weed. Next week he'll be ten months old. He's already taking a few steps. Before we know it, he'll be walking everywhere and getting into all the mischief he can . . . just like his daddy."

Marti laughed and took a deep breath. A quiver rose in her voice. "I'm going to finish this wall tonight, Alana. Then I might take a break for a few days."

Alana cocked her head. "You going somewhere, Marti?"

Marti nodded. "Yep. I thought I might go to the Tennessee Equestrian Competition in Vick next week."

"I didn't know you were interested in horses."

Marti shrugged. "I used to ride a long time ago, but I haven't ridden in years. Sandra and her sister are going to a big art sale at a gallery in downtown Vick. When I found out about the horse competition, I thought it'd be fun to go along and check it out."

"That's neat. I've learned something interesting about my new friend." Alana grinned as she put her arm around Marti's shoulders.

"Yeah, well, even though I don't ride anymore, it's still fun to watch."

"Okay . . . if I don't see you before you leave, have a good time. We'll be taking a trip too, in about three weeks. We're headed down to Texas."

A sudden shiver traveled through Marti's veins. "Texas?"

Alana nodded. "There's a fundraiser for the orphanage in one of the towns in east Texas. I forget the name, but Jaydn knows. We promised to show up and sort of prod the fundraising efforts. I guess I'll see you when you get back." She leaned over and hugged Marti. "Don't be gone too long now. I'm counting on you next month to help serve our grand opening luncheon."

Marti let out a relieved sigh. "You can count on it. I'll be back long before then."

Alana picked up her purse and keys from the table by the door and waved as she stepped outside.

A shaky breath followed a sigh as Marti stepped over to the heavy metal door and turned the deadbolt.

The faint orange glow of the evening sky faded into darkness while Marti put the finishing touches on the brick house in the middle of the mural.

When Marti laid down her brush, the silence of the night crept into her awareness. She raised her head and swallowed as the darkness filtering in through the tall glass windows at the front of the building seemed to wrap around her body. Shivering, she hurried to gather her tools and get home before the clock spun around to midnight.

She stored her tote full of brushes in the cabinet and slung her purse over her shoulders. The lock opened easily, and the heavy door swung open. She stepped outside and reached back in to flip off the building lights before turning the key in the lock. When the lights went out, the darkness enveloped her, and fog clung to her like a shimmering spider web.

"I'm fine. Everything is fine," she repeated twice.

She desperately sought a tiny sliver of moon—anything to soothe her unrest. She stood on the top step of the shadowed porch and stared into the darkness. A faint glow coming from an upstairs window down the street was barely visible in the middle of the fog.

Why in the world had she stayed so long? Her apartment above Sandra's gallery was two blocks away and over on the next street.

She had two choices: Backtrack the long way around the end of this street over to the next, or cut through the two-hundred-foot alleyway separating the two blocks.

Filled with dumpsters, old newspapers, and other trash, the dark alley wasn't a fun place to visit—especially at night—but it would get her home fifteen minutes sooner. And although it made her feel creepy to walk through, she'd never encountered anything unpleasant there before.

She flipped open her purse and felt for the tube of pepper spray she kept there. A smooth round surface met her fingers, and she took a deep breath. If she ran, she could make it through the alley in thirty seconds flat.

Squaring her shoulders in determination, she started down the sidewalk at a fast pace. It seemed the whole town was already asleep. No sounds preceded her down the street. No voices. No barking dog. No children's laughter filtered through the damp air.

Halfway down the street, a creeping sensation overcame her when she looked up. For the first time since their installation, the nightlights the town had installed six months ago were dark. Had someone disabled their bright glow, or had the automatic timers malfunctioned?

She stopped dead and turned to look at the Haven for the Homeless building. Should she turn back and call for the policeman on duty to escort her home?

And tell him what?

That she was a baby and scared of the dark?

Hashtag: humiliating.

Embarrassment made her turn and continue toward the alley. Calling the police was a ridiculous idea.

When she reached the edge of the alley opening, she paused and glanced around her—half expecting to see a dark figure creeping toward her.

There was no one—only blowing shadows of trees in the distance and foggy swirls through bushes outside the stores and apartments. The cool spring breeze felt good on her hot face, but she shivered anyway. Memories of someone following her every move during the first months of her exit from Texas tried to choke out her reasoning, but it had been over a year since she'd been harassed. She was determined to forget those days and look forward. Taking a deep breath, she turned once again to stare at the dark alley.

Inside the narrow pathway, she could just make out faint slivers of light coming from nightlights in the back windows of shops lining the alley. Whispering pulses of electric meters lining the wall sounded like snakes hissing in the darkness.

She could see the buildings on the next street through the opening at the other end of the alley. If she could reach that opening, she'd be almost home. So close . . . yet it seemed so far.

She took a firm step forward, and put her hands around the comforting tube in her purse. If someone came at her, he'd be sorry. One firm spray in his face and he wouldn't be able to function for a long time.

One minute, she told herself. One minute, and she'd be home.

That's only if you run, Marti.

She picked up her speed and went from a fast walk to a jog, then a run. Halfway through the alley, she tripped on something and fell hard against the damp cement. Winded, she sat up and tried to get her breath. She felt around on the oily cement for her purse. The contents had scattered in a circle around her. She was scraping everything together and into her purse when a sound made her heart freeze.

A step—not thirty feet away.

Her hand snaked out and found the thin round tube. Pulling it into her fingers, she searched the darkness for a face—hoping with everything inside her it would be someone familiar.

Instead she saw a black figure: black clothes, a black cloth where eyes should be.

A scream hung in her throat. She pushed herself off the slippery cement and jerked herself into a run—all the time squeezing the metal tube in her hand.

She only made it five steps before a hand grabbed the back of her shirt and jerked her to a stop. Rough hands shoved her to the ground all in a single movement. Her face hit the wet cement, and a nasty taste filled her mouth. She screamed and pushed at the ground, but the man behind her mashed her into the grit.

She twisted and fought with the figure behind her, trying to get away. He roughly jammed his knee in the small of her back. His hands pulled her left hand behind her and propped his knee on her wrist. She felt something in her elbow pop, and pain swept through her body.

FIVE

Texas

The theatre lights flashed three times, and Daniel touched Veronica's arm. "Come on, Nikki, they're closing the building. It's late."

Veronica frowned at Daniel and finished her conversation with her friends, laughing for the second time at a simple joke.

Daniel propped himself tolerantly against the wall of the theatre and crossed his arms. His patience was wearing thin after the last several hours.

Veronica had insisted he take her to the International Jewelry Exhibition before the show at the theatre. That was certainly a mistake. She did nothing but hint, maneuver, and solicit conversation during the entire exhibit about how beautiful and stylish the contemporary wedding rings were. The subject of weddings seemed to be interjected into many of their conversations lately. She'd been hinting for two weeks about combining their schedules, their vacations coming up in the summer—even moving some of their breeding stock together in a common pasture between the two farms.

Agitation, uncertainty, and dread were perfect words to describe how he felt about what seemed to be imminent—a marriage.

Was he ready for that next step? Daniel's first attempt at marriage had ended in disaster, and he'd only been married four years. He wasn't sure if he was ready for another attempt. He liked Veronica and was comfortable with her, but how would he feel if marriage was in their future? He wasn't sure.

He shrugged and followed Veronica and her boisterous friends as they exited the theatre. The valet handed him the keys to his car, and Daniel put a bill in his hands. The man's eyes lit up at the size of the tip, and he bowed. "Have a nice evening, sir."

Daniel smiled and opened the door for Veronica, who finally said goodbye to her friends. She raised her nose in the air and slid into the seat.

When he got into the car, Daniel could feel the frostiness emanating from her stiff posture.

"I told you not to call me that disgusting name . . . *Nikki*. Honestly, Daniel, you would think since we are so close you would make some sort of effort to please me. You know I hate that nickname, yet you insist upon using it. Can you not think of a more dignified name? *Nikki* sounds so . . . so childish. Don't you think the name *Vera* sounds much more sophisticated?"

"I've called you Nikki since we were little. Why break tradition?"

She leaned back, closed her eyes, and sniffed. "Well, break it anyway." Then she leaned forward and touched his hand lightly. "You love me, don't you?"

"Of course."

"Then do it for me because it's what I want, darling."

Daniel didn't answer but watched her eyes flirting with him. He slid the car in gear and pulled out of the lot toward home. The bugs swarming around the streetlights touched a chord of melancholy in his heart. His life seemed a lot like theirs—always revolving around one bright thing. His bright light was Veronica. Everything he did lately circled around their time together, just like the moths circled around the streetlight. Were the moths happy, or did they feel the pull of freedom tugging at their hearts?

He frowned. He was tired—that's when crazy thoughts entered his head.

After he dropped Veronica off at the Duke ranch, he drove the rest of the way home at a slower pace. Not a car was in sight as he made the two-mile trip home, and it gave him time to think.

His dad didn't like Veronica—at least, he didn't like their dating each other. Growing up, Gerald had encouraged their friendship, but since Daniel's loss of memory, his dad had taken a strong disliking to Veronica. Gerald said he didn't think Veronica had Daniel's best interests at heart. Since that time, when Daniel talked about Veronica, his father moped around the house with a frown on his face.

Daniel always respected his father's opinions, but his dad didn't understand the relationship he had with Veronica. Daniel was ready to settle down, and his father needed to understand.

He walked the pathway from the garage and saw the lights in the den shining brightly. It was after midnight. Surely his dad wasn't still up. He must have gone to bed and left the lights on again.

Daniel reached inside the den door to flip the switch when he heard his father's voice.

"Daniel?"

"Dad, what are you doing up so late?"

"I couldn't sleep, so I came down to look at some old photos."

Daniel sat down on the sofa beside his father. "What do you have there?"

The aged photo of his mom still revealed her beauty. Sitting on a horse, she wore bright red riding boots with a cowboy hat perched crazily on her head.

"She was beautiful, wasn't she, son?"

"I was thinking the same thing."

Gerald's deep breath came out on a long sigh.

"You really miss her, don't you, Dad?"

Gerald nodded. "Yep. Our marriage was a rare and special thing—just like your marriage to—"

"Dad . . . don't start, okay?"

Gerald placed the photograph back in the old photo album and closed the book. "All right, Daniel. I know you don't want to talk about it, but Veronica is—"

"You're right, Dad, I don't want to talk about it. Good night." Daniel stood up.

Gerald rose with him but froze when a newer photo fell from the pages of the book. Daniel bent to pick it up and hand it back to his father. The picture was of another horse and rider, but the young woman in the picture wore the same color boots and hat as his mom.

"Who is that?" Daniel asked as his father grabbed the photo and glanced at it before sticking it back in the book. He slipped the book under his arm and turned toward the door.

"Just a friend of the Rushing family. I'm tired now, son. I think I'll go to bed. Will you slide the rest of those albums back in the closet and get the lights?"

Daniel rubbed his chin and watched his dad leave the room. He picked up the photo albums on the floor beside the couch, but when he stuck them back on the shelf in the closet, he noticed a wooden box sitting on the back of the top shelf. For some reason, a wave of warmth filtered through him.

He vaguely remembered his dad showing him some of the contents of that box after he'd come home from Iraq. It was full of memories—memories of his marriage and his ex-wife. Memories he'd blissfully forgotten after the IED explosion.

Curiosity had him reaching for the box, but a nervous charge traveled through his body. Secretly, he wanted to explore, but he was afraid it would bring back painful memories—memories he might be glad he'd forgotten. He laid it on the table and stared at the polished oak containing a direct path to his heart. Even if he couldn't remember the keepsakes, the impression they made on his heart might linger. He reached for the box and opened the lid decisively.

The first thing he saw was a small jewelry case with a ring inside. The two-carat diamond sparkled back at him as if trying to shed light into his dark memories. He laid the box aside and pulled out a velvet cloth folded into a square. Lifting each corner, his hand shook when he opened the last corner. A set of four miniature horse-heads lay in a pile on the velvet. They were carved in wood with a variety of jewels set in the mane of each horse.

He must have carved the set. His father had reminded him of his woodcarving hobby. A small white tag was attached to the velvet.

> *To Matty, the sweetest wife a man could ask for.*
>
> *Symbols of our wedding vows: Purple amethyst for honor, blue sapphire for trust, yellow topaz for joy, green emerald for forgiveness, and red ruby for love.*
>
> *I'll always love you, darling.*
>
> *Daniel*

He felt as if he'd been punched in the stomach. What a joke—four years? Always?

But there were only four horses. The horse with the emerald was missing. He scrambled around in the box, looking for the fifth horse, but it wasn't there. His wife must have taken it with her. The green emerald was supposed to symbolize forgiveness.

Yeah, right—like that's going to happen.

He dropped the pile back into the box and slammed the lid tight. Tossing it back on the shelf, he mumbled. "That's enough of this nightmare back into the past."

Forgetting his marriage was the best outcome of losing his memory. It was time to leave the painful past and look forward to the future.

SIX

Tennessee

Marti struggled to breathe with the knee of her assailant pressed into her back and left arm, forcing the air from her lungs. The tube in her right hand burned her skin as she squeezed it tighter and prepared to use it on her attacker.

When he reached for her right arm, she twisted her shoulder and aimed the pepper spray toward his face. The spray spewed out in a steady stream. His surprised jerk back gave her enough time to struggle out from under him and scramble to her feet. She took off at a run, but almost as soon as her feet hit the ground, she could hear footsteps pounding behind her. She lowered her head and with everything inside her, she forced one last burst of energy into her racing steps.

The light from the lamppost at the end of the alley was only a few feet away. Blood pumped into her legs, and they burned as she pushed them to the limit. She felt the pounding of the man's feet behind her, gaining ground.

Suddenly, hands grabbed her shirt from behind. The man jerked her back until her collar cut into her throat and she couldn't breathe—couldn't scream. The tube of pepper spray tumbled from her hands, and her purse slid as it hit the ground. Gloved hands threw her back up against the brick wall, and a muscled body pinned her close.

She looked up and faced black mesh covering the man's face. Globs of red and orange liquid were sprinkled and heaped across the front of the mask.

Screams welled up inside her throat. She opened her mouth, but before she could release a sound, his gloved hand covered her face—clamping down tightly over her nose and mouth. He jammed her head against the hard brick wall. In his other hand flashed a knife.

"Shut up or I'll end it here and now. You understand?" The voice was nothing but a low growl—rough and raspy.

She jerked her head up and down and tried to breathe through the hand over her nose and mouth.

The man placed the blade of the knife in his right hand against her throat then slowly took his left hand off her mouth. When she didn't make a sound, he wound his hand in her hair and gave a tug. She whimpered as the knife in the other hand pressed into the skin of her neck.

"I'm only saying it once. *Stay out of Texas!* If you don't, you'll be sorry. Art galleries make good kindlin'. It'd be a shame if your friend didn't make it out of the flames."

Marti sucked in a horrified breath. He was threatening Sandra.

"Remember, I'm watching."

"Why are you doing this?" Her whispered voice threaded with fear.

He didn't say a word but pulled her body away from the wall and then slammed her head against the bricks. She saw stars and slumped to the ground as the sound of running footsteps faded into the distance.

She collapsed on the damp cement. Tears blurred her eyesight. The pounding in her head beat in harmony with the throbbing in her chest. Her throat clenched with each breath, and tears burned her cheeks. Closing her eyes, she tried to inhale small calming breaths.

"I'm fine. Everything is fine."

A popping sound in the alley made her eyes snap open. Was he coming back? Thoughts of the man returning propelled her muscles to move. Summoning strength from somewhere, she rose on shaky legs and searched both ends of the narrow passage.

Nothing.

She felt around on the ground for her purse and staggered to the end of the alley. Trudging up the fourteen steps to her apartment, she pushed the key into the lock with trembling fingers and slipped through the door. Falling against the weathered wood, she slid both locks until they were shut tight. Emotion then consumed her, and she slid to the floor against the wall and sobbed.

Not only was her life once again in danger, but Sandra was being threatened as well. Sandra and Wade were her best friends in the world. She couldn't stand the thought of them being in danger because of her.

What was it about Texas? The only connection she'd ever had with Texas was Daniel. Was it Daniel behind the threats? Did seeing her at the reception revive his anger? Rage at the unfairness churned inside her until common sense told her that was impossible. Daniel wouldn't be threatening her for returning to Texas when it was obvious she'd settled permanently in Tennessee. Whoever was threatening her wanted her to stay out of Texas for another reason. Would he leave her alone if she stayed in Tennessee, or would she have to move again?

She laid her head on her knees and cried until her eyes hurt.

There was only one thing she could do—stay put. She lived for three years without knowing the truth about the night of the accident—it wouldn't kill her to live the rest of her life without knowing. Sandra and Wade were too important to her. She couldn't risk their lives.

She would stay in Landeville and forget about Daniel. She did it once; she could do it again.

Stay away from Texas, and she was safe. Go back to Texas to confront Daniel, and everyone would suffer. As badly as she wanted there to be a choice, there was none.

SEVEN

Texas

Shane Duke pulled on the lead rope attached to Prince's head and slowed the horse to a walk. The horse shook his head and pranced around the ring adjacent to the stable, but he did exactly what he was supposed to do. Shane smiled in satisfaction. Today's workout had produced perfect results. Prince's will was broken but not his spirit. He'd obeyed the commands Shane had given him, but still showed the essence of a strong character.

Shane tugged the rope one more time, and Prince stopped. He slowly walked up to the horse and patted him on the neck. "Good boy. Mary said you'd learn quickly." Remembering the day his wife first saw Prince drew his lips into a frown. When he'd unloaded that special bunch of colts he purchased from a farm in Wyoming, Mary picked Prince out of the group and said he was her favorite. She named the horse Prince because he had more "class" than all the others. That memory hurt because it was the day before they found out Mary was ill—brain tumor, the doctors said. After that diagnosis, she gave up on her family, their thirty years of marriage, and living. She died soon after.

Shane wiped the moisture from his eyes. "You'll make Veronica a fitting mount—just like Mary planned," he said to Prince.

"Did I hear you say my name, Daddy?" Veronica stepped into the wooden corral and stood right inside the gate.

Shane didn't answer but looked at her jeans and satin shirt. "I thought you were riding over to Daniel's house."

"I am, in a little while. I wanted to ask you something first." She waited while Shane led Prince through the gate into the pasture and pulled off the halter. The horse snorted and galloped through the field toward the creek.

When Shane turned back toward Veronica, she stood in the corral with him. Wrapping her arm through his, she leaned in close as they walked out the gate and back to the house. "I saw a gorgeous wedding gown in the bridal magazine I bought last week in town. I wanted to see if I could talk you into buying it for me."

Shane froze in his tracks. "Wedding gown? Is there something you're not telling me, sugar?"

Veronica veiled her eyes and flashed a smile that would have any man quivering in his boots. "Well, Daddy, I'm sure Daniel's getting closer to proposing. Yesterday, he insisted on taking me to the International Jewelry Exhibit, and he spent a lot of time looking at wedding rings. Toward the end of the show, he disappeared for a while. I'm sure he went back to buy one." Her voice was infused with excitement.

Shane's stomach did a flip. "That's wonderful news, honey. I'm happy for you. Your mama would have been so proud." His vision blurred, but he was determined not to show his tears. He glanced down at the ground. "I guess Daniel finally realized Martha wasn't the right woman for him."

"Well . . . he doesn't actually remember Martha."

Shane turned toward her and held her hands in his. "He doesn't remember her at all?"

Veronica shook her head with a cocky smile on her lips. "No, and I like it that way. I've told him all he needs to know about their farce of a marriage, and he's ready to move on—without his memories. He said yesterday he'd rather not remember her anyway. She was a hussy and a tramp, and—"

"Hey, wait a minute, baby. Did Daniel actually say those things about Martha, or did you plant the seed in his head?

Veronica looked guilty, but she shook her head. "I didn't actually call her names, but I told him the facts. If he calls her those things, it's not my fault. Besides, Mama told him what Martha did, and he knows she would never lie—neither would the state patrol."

Shane's throat tightened. "Okay, honey, but make sure you don't push. This has to be his idea, or it won't work between you. Be patient, and Daniel will come around."

Veronica pouted and gave him a petulant frown. "All right, Daddy. I won't push, but will you buy me the dress anyway?"

Shane felt a "yes" bubbling up inside of him—no matter what the dress might cost, his Veronica deserved the best of everything. She lost her mama, and her mama had done everything she could to make Veronica happy. That meant he had to take Mary's place and fill the void losing her mama had caused.

Before he could answer, a rider galloped through the barnyard. Veronica scowled. "What's Jordan Welsh doing here?"

Gerald watched as the man slid off his horse and tied the gelding to the corral fence.

"He asked about buying some of the horses I rejected from the last bunch I bought—the ones I don't think'll make the cut."

"I thought he moved to California or something after Vinny died in that car accident."

"I, uh . . . I think he came back recently to open up the old ranch."

Veronica sniffed and raised her nose in the air. "He acted like he cared about Vinny when he died, but after the funeral, I got the impression it was the ranch and the money that he really cared about. Remember how fast he wanted Vinny's will read?"

"Hush." Shane whispered as Jordan walked in their direction. Jordan shook hands with Shane and ignored Veronica.

"Shane."

"Well, Jordan, how did you like the horses?"

"They were tolerable . . . just tolerable. It's possible we can make a deal. How about throwing in that bay I saw you working with over there?"

Shane blew out a laugh. "Hardly. That one's definitely not for sale."

Jordan looked him in the eyes. "We'll see. I bet we can come up with some kind of agreement."

Shane hardened his eyes and shook his head. "Not for sale."

Jordan shrugged. Then he sauntered to his truck parked beside the barn. "I'll be in touch."

As Jordan drove off, Veronica fidgeted beside her father. "I'm going in, Daddy, to get ready for Daniel."

"Okay, sugar. I'm headed over to the cemetery to have a little visit with your mama."

Veronica looked at him with a frown. "Again? You spend a lot of time at Mama's grave."

Shane gave his daughter a wounded look. "She likes the company, honey."

"But she . . ." Veronica shrugged her shoulders. "All right, Daddy. I guess we can talk about that little dress matter later." She kissed him on the cheek, and with a smile on her face, she turned and strutted back to the house.

Shane watched her go and swelled with pride. He had a beautiful daughter who deserved everything she wanted—the best horse in the state, Daniel as a husband, and, of course a stunning, gorgeous wedding dress. As a matter of fact, she deserved everything Mary had wanted her to have, wedding dress and all. Mary wasn't around to make sure she got it, but he'd do everything within his power to make sure it was possible.

EIGHT

Tennessee

Sandra Wellington stopped dusting the picture frames and stepped into the hot rays of sun filtering through the front window of the gallery. She let the warmth from the shaft of light caress her arms even as the central air vent flipped hair around her face. Basking in the sun was something she hardly had time for anymore.

As she stood there soaking in the warmth, she saw her husband park his patrol car out front and pull something from the back seat. He slammed the door and entered the gallery.

"Sandee?"

Sandra leaned forward around one of the free-standing exhibit walls and waved. "I'm over here, love."

Wade came around the corner carrying a large bag with black foam board sticking out the top. His black hair, barely graying around the temples, was tossed awry from the wind, and a crooked grin sat plastered on his face. "I expect a big hug and my favorite supper tonight."

Sandra jumped toward him and planted a long kiss on his lips. "You found them. Jolly good! Where in the world did you find that many pieces?"

Wade plopped the pile of foam board on the floor next to the wall and placed his hands on her shoulders. "Remember last month when Greg had a sale at the hardware store on that bunch of Swiss army knives he bought at a flea market? I remembered he used tons of this blackboard for the displays in the window, so I asked if he had any left he didn't need. He was glad to get rid of the stuff."

Sandra grinned. "That was a doodle for you, wasn't it?"

"A doodle?"

"A breeze . . . a cinch . . . you know, easy."

Wade laughed and held her tight. "That British slang of yours is why I married you, you know."

Sandra gave him a kiss. "Thank you for remembering my blackboard. Leave it to you to remember a small detail like that. Now I can finish the preparation for next month's space exhibit." She kissed him on the cheek. "Details and dependability! That's what makes you a good chief constable."

He held her for a moment until a loud noise from the apartment above startled them both.

"What's Marti doin' up there? Rearranging the furniture?"

Sandra shook her head. "I hope she's packing."

Wade stood back and crossed his arms. "Do you really think she'll go?"

"If you mean to Texas, I doubt it. She seemed okay with it last night, but today . . ." She shrugged. "She seems determined to forget Daniel, and she won't even think about praying over it."

"She needs to let God back into her heart, Sandee. He can help her find the answers."

Sandra shook her head. "That's something she'll never admit. Basically, she hasn't forgiven God for not protecting her new faith."

Wade rubbed his hand through his hair. "I told her I'd check into the accident and Daniel's accusations, but she won't let me."

"You know she needs to hear it from Daniel himself. Only he knows what happened that day. If she won't go to Texas, I'm hoping she'll come with Vivian and me to the art sale. If she can get away by herself and have time to think, she might see how lonely it is without God in her life."

Wade leaned over and kissed her on the lips. "That's why I love you so much. You're as wise as Solomon."

She grinned. "Thanks." Another loud bang from upstairs made Sandra pull back. "I think I'll run up to her flat and see if I can help her pack."

Wade nodded. "And I have to get back to the station. We're having trouble with the new street lamps we installed. For some reason the sensors aren't working all the time. If I knew I had to be an electrician when I took this job, I might have turned it down." He grinned at her and turned toward the door.

"Bangers and mash for supper."

Wade licked his lips. "*Mmm, mmm,* sweetheart! Remind me to do something special for you more often."

Sandra smiled at him as he walked through the door but frowned when another bang filtered down from upstairs. "Guess it's time to brave the lioness in her den."

She stomped up the stairs leading to Marti's apartment. Getting Marti excited about a trip to Texas was as easy as getting a turkey excited about Thanksgiving. Yet Sandra knew Marti needed the trip . . . for her own peace of mind . . . for her future . . . and possibly Daniel's as well.

When she reached the top step, she gaped through the open door of the apartment at Marti on her tip-toes—perched on a wobbly step stool. She was punching and prodding a small suitcase, trying to wrestle it into a larger bag sitting on the highest shelf of the closet.

"Marti? Do you need help?"

Marti half-turned to glance her way.

"I've almost got it." One more shove and the luggage rocked against the wall. The small suitcase nestled down inside the larger one, and they both balanced on the shelf. A black overnight bag sat by itself on the floor of the closet.

Marti blew out an exasperated breath and stepped off the stool. She turned off the closet light, pulled the overnight bag and step stool out of the closet, and closed the door.

Sandra propped her hands on her hips. "I know I shouldn't ask, but why are you putting the suitcases back in the cupboard when Wade just got them down for you yesterday?"

Marti looked down and avoided Sandra's eyes. "You shouldn't have gotten them out in the first place. I told you I wasn't going to Texas," she said as she slid the folded-up stool under the bed.

Sandra puffed her cheeks as a flow of air escaped her lips. She sat down on the bed and patted the comforter. "Sit."

Marti shook her head. "I have things to do."

"Sit!" This time, Sandra's voice was a little more forceful.

Marti frowned and perched on the edge of the bed.

"Okay. Let's have it. Why won't you go?"

"I don't want to talk to him—"

A loud "Fiddle sticks!" burst from Sandra's lips. "Like you expect me to believe that. Come on, Marti, what gives? Yesterday when you left for the homeless shelter, you were open to the idea. What changed your mind?"

Marti gave Sandra a scared look before her lips tightened and her gaze swept toward the window. The white curtains couldn't have been any whiter than Marti's face, and her eyes looked far away. Her hands rubbed up and down on her jeans, as if she was remembering something she wanted to forget.

Sandra softened her tone. "Come on, Marti. Talk to me. I'm your friend. I only want to help. Yesterday, you promised you'd think about going to see Daniel. What happened?"

Marti couldn't keep back the tears any longer, and they rolled down her cheeks. Sandra leaned over and pulled Marti into her arms.

"Marti, love, what's the matter?"

Marti sobbed against her friend until the whole story of being chased and threatened the night before burst from her lips. As Marti talked, Sandra's fury stewed inside her. Wade would hear about this. Maybe he could find a clue in the alley to pin down this bloke.

When Marti told her the stalker threatened Sandra, Wade, and the gallery, Sandra's anger hissed out in her next sentence. "Of all the nerve. Who does he think he is, threatening us? And Wade's the chief constable. Marti, don't you listen to this barmy rotter. He's just trying to frighten you. Wade can take care of us. You do what's best for you, and we both know that means talking to Daniel."

Marti stood up and walked to the window. She stared out at the morning sky. "No, Sandra. I can't do it."

Sandra leaned back against the wall. "Why not?"

Marti didn't answer, just stared out into the street. Sandra frowned. She'd seen that stubborn look before. It wasn't going to do any good arguing about it. It was plain that Marti had made up her mind.

Sandra stood and shook her head. "Okay, sweetie, this is your call, but at least go with us to the art sale. It'll do you good to get away for a couple of days."

Marti picked up the overnight bag and smiled a trembling smile. "That's why I left this out—in case I decided to go with you. There's a horse competition in Vick at the same time. I thought I might go by there one day and check it out. I think a little time away might be fun."

Sandra smiled and gave Marti a big hug. "Jolly good. We'll have a do. That's the way I like to hear you talk."

"A 'do'?"

"A party."

"Hashtag: a girl's night out."

Sandra grinned and nodded. When she left, Marti was staring out the window. Sandra would have to put her thinking cap on and figure out a way to persuade Marti to make that trip to Texas.

It meant everything to Marti's future.

NINE

Texas

Sixty-year-old Gerald Rushing jumped when the back door slammed. He was sitting in the office of his rambling ranch house in Carson, Texas, when he heard Daniel's call through the hallway.

"Dad?"

"In here, son."

Daniel's steps pounded on the kitchen tiles then entered the wide hallway leading to the office.

Gerald squirmed in the antique chair sitting behind the office desk and frowned at the ancient computer keyboard. When Daniel entered the room, Gerald looked up. Frustration pulled his face as tight as a drum.

"What's wrong, Dad?"

"This crazy computer lost my file again. Why in the world I let you talk me into putting the farm bookkeeping on computer, I'll never know."

Daniel grinned then scooted around the desk behind his dad. He punched a couple of keys, clicked in the open folder, and the file Gerald was looking for magically appeared on the screen.

"How did you do that?" Gerald's eyes opened in surprise.

Daniel hid a grin and moved to the side of the desk. "You've gotta stop pushing the 'delete' key instead of the 'enter' key, Dad."

Gerald shook his head. "Well, they're too doggone close on this tiny little keyboard."

"I told you before—you need to get one of the newer keyboards. The keys are further apart, and it's much easier to type. I don't know why you keep that one anyway. The keys are always sticking and the *R* key stays down half the time. That's tough when your name has two *R*'s in it."

Gerald grunted and pressed the "enter" key to save his file then looked up and pretended he hadn't heard. "Were you lookin' for me, son?"

"Aren't you going to the town meeting about the wildfire?"

"Wouldn't miss it, but it's been rescheduled—two hours from now. The fire chief was waylaid checking the fire damage. Bud said the wildfire overran the firebreak on the south side wall—that means it's headed our way if we don't get it stopped. Hopefully, the state fire marshal will offer resources he can contribute. Is that what you came in here for, son?"

Gerald watched a furrow grow between Daniel's eyes. "No, uh . . . I have something to tell you. I . . . I guess Veronica and I finally made a decision."

Gerald tilted his head to the side and waited.

"We discussed getting married."

Gerald never moved, but his chest deflated inside his ribs, and his blood felt like it turned cold in his veins. "What do you mean . . . you discussed it?"

"Well, she's ready, and I guess I am too."

Gerald leaned back in the groaning chair and studied his son's face.

"If you ask me, you don't look too happy about the whole thing."

Daniel plopped down in the chair opposite his father and ran his hand through his hair. His eyes blinked rapidly.

"It all happened so fast. One minute we're walking through their stables looking at her horses, and the next thing I know, she's talking about adding stalls in our barn for her horses after we get married."

Gerald knew he had to tread lightly. Saying the wrong thing could only push Daniel in the wrong direction. "Daniel, do you love her?"

Daniel rubbed his forehead with his fingers. "I care for her."

"But, do you love her?"

"We've been close for so long, Dad. This is the next step, don't you think?"

"No, son, I don't. You need to at least wait until your memory comes back. Two months ago, you could hardly remember Veronica. Two years ago you were still getting over—"

"No, Dad. I don't want to talk about my ex-wife. Veronica says she was nothing but a slut and an alcoholic."

"Daniel! Just because she—"

"Stop, Dad! We've been through this before. I don't want to talk about it again. Every time I think about the past, it reminds me of Angie."

Gerald blew out a pained puff of air. "Daniel, your sister wouldn't want you to grieve. Angie would be the first to tell you to let it go and get on with your life. She'd want you to be happy. I'm just not sure Veronica—"

"Enough, Dad." The strained tone of those two words quieted Gerald.

"My marriage was over a long time ago. It's because of her that Angie's dead. I want to forget the past and move on with the future. That means giving Veronica and me a chance. She's the only one I remember from the past. I've known her my whole life. We're comfortable with each other. Our marriage will have a lot better chance of surviving if we've been friends for this many years. We like the same things. Besides, Veronica's right—little Chris needs a father. Today he begged me to be his daddy."

Gerald started. "What do you mean, his *daddy*?"

"Well, I know technically he'd be my brother-in-law, but it wouldn't make a difference to him until he's older."

Gerald's heart was heavy. He recognized that it was probably Chris who was pulling Daniel's heartstrings instead of Veronica. Daniel's eyes lit up when he talked about Veronica's three-year-old brother. Shane and Mary Duke had adopted little Chris, and exactly two years later, Mary had died of a brain tumor. Shane was so devastated by his wife's death that Veronica took over the mothering role for Chris.

"Have you prayed about this, Daniel?"

"Dad. I told you, I don't remember all that praying stuff. We never prayed when we were growing up—how am I supposed to remember it now? You might like all that religion, but I want no part of it. Just because you say I 'got saved' doesn't mean I feel it in here." Daniel placed a fist over his heart.

"You don't have to feel it to make it real, Daniel. Just pray, and God will bring it all back to you."

Gerald grimaced as Daniel shut down the conversation with a frown. "Veronica and I are getting married in a month." With a wave of his hand, and an end-of-discussion look, he walked out the door. Gerald slumped in the chair, defeated.

"Well, Lord, what do I do now?"

He leaned his head back against the chair and thought about Martha. If only she were here, she'd be able to show Daniel what it felt like to be in love.

Suddenly, he sat up. Quickly he pulled open the top drawer and rubbed his face between his thumb and fingers. He should have done this months ago.

TEN

Gerald said a quick prayer when his neighbors grew restless in the sweltering auditorium. Anger was not the solution. They had to work together in order to solve this wildfire problem.

"Hold on, hold on!" The face of the Sander County Fire Chief, Bud Greeson, flushed red as he held both hands in the air and waved them at the men filling half the auditorium. The white shirt of his uniform was dark and sweaty around the armpits and collar.

He waved his right hand and tried to get the attention of the angry crowd. "Please, calm down. I called this meeting to assure everyone that we're fighting this wildfire with everything we have. Losing your tempers is not the solution."

Shane Duke stood up and raised his voice to be heard over the others mumbling in the background. "Well, anger is all we have right now, Bud. You said you're fighting it with everything you have, but that isn't enough. The fire's growing every day. It'll be at Gerald's in a week or two if we don't stop it or the wind don't change. If the wind changes, my farm will be next—or the Mayberry's. We thought the state fire marshal was coming in to bring us reinforcements. Now we hear he didn't even care enough to show up."

Bud drew in a deep breath before he spoke. "I told you Shane, his plane had engine problems. He'll be here in a day or two."

Gerald cringed as the crowd grew more restless, then he stood and pushed to the end of the aisle. "Look, Bud. We know you're trying, but next week might be too late for some of us. Even if the wind changes, it'll still sweep across somebody's farm. And a lot more is at stake than a barn or a bunch of sheds—our livelihoods and our homes are in danger. Can you assure us it'll be stopped before it destroys our lives?"

The crowd mumbled in agreement.

Bud looked tired and deflated. Gerald felt sorry for the man. It looked as if he knew he couldn't offer a solution. "We're doing the best we can." He held his hands, palm up, as if defeated.

Shane's protest was subdued but firm when he stepped back into the conversation. "Then you need to get men in here from other states for backup. Our men are tired, and that fire is spreading. Not only are our farms in danger, but if the fire spreads outward, the town itself could be burned. Our men can't fight twenty-four hours a day, Bud. They need rest. Can't we ask neighboring states for mutual aide? Maybe some of us should step in and help where we can so we don't feel helpless standing around watching our homes and businesses burn."

"Hold on a minute!" Bud pushed around the podium and walked to the edge of the platform. "That's unacceptable, Shane. Don't panic and do something you might regret. You're not trained firefighters—neither are your men. We don't want people getting lost in the middle of a wildfire, getting hurt . . . or worse. Let us do our jobs. Please."

Several of the men started arguing among themselves.

Max Gibson, a small, muscled-looking man with a long white beard, stepped forward. "I'd like to say somethin', Mr. Greeson; I've been Mr. Gerald's stable manager for over thirty-two years.

It's all I know how to do. If we don't get this fire under control, not only will Mr. Gerald lose his barn and his home, but all of us stable hands will lose our jobs. We'd be willin' to help if we can."

The crowd mumbled agreement.

Bud planted his feet on the ground and looked over the crowd. "Max, I know you're worried about your job. Shane, Gerald, I know you and a lot of other farm owners here are frustrated and worried about your farms, but we're gradually beatin' this thing. It's better than it was yesterday, in spite of what you think. We have it thirty-five percent contained—yesterday it was only ten percent. A couple of our firemen have been on vacation and are returning early to help."

Gerald watched as Shane stood deliberately to his feet. The crowd listened silently as he spoke.

"All right, Bud. We'll give you a couple more days. But, if things don't change by then, we'll be talking about other options. We can't stand by without a fight and watch our farms go up in smoke."

Agreements traveled around the room as they all stood on determined feet.

Gerald and Max walked over to Shane Duke, and the men shook hands.

"What do you think, Gerald? Think they'll get it stopped before it hits your back two hundred acres of alfalfa?"

Gerald shook his head. "I hope so. I have an equipment shed that's even closer than the back two hundred. If that goes, it'll hurt."

"Maybe you should go ahead and move out the equipment."

"Already did." Max spoke up. "Got it stored in an old hay barn there behind Mr. Gerald's house."

Gerald nodded. "I told my men to take the hay plows out tomorrow and dig a fire break across the back side of the alfalfa field. I'm hoping it'll help stop the fire at the line."

Shane perked up. "Yep, that's a good idea. We talked about burning off some of the back fields to keep the fire from jumping to the woods closest to the house. If the fire reaches that field, and it's been burned, it might burn itself out."

Gerald nodded. "That's a good idea too. Maybe that's what we need to do."

"Anything I can do to help?"

The men turned to see Jordan Welsh standing right outside their circle.

"Jordan. I didn't know you were back in these parts." Gerald's surprise was evident as he shook Jordan's hand. Something in Jordan's eyes seemed hardened and unsettled.

"Yeah. I figured I may as well get back here before the ranch completely went to the dogs. Vinny and Angie put so much work into it; I hate to see it abandoned."

Shane held out his hand. "It's good to see you again, Jordan. I hope you've been well."

"Tolerable, I reckon. It's hard without Vinny. He was my life, you know."

Gerald's stomach felt sick. He knew the feeling. When Angie died in the wreck that killed Vinny, he thought time would heal that sick feeling he felt when he thought of losing his only daughter, but time hadn't healed the wound—only made it easier to bear.

Jordan turned to him. "I'm headed up to Tennessee for a couple of days, but when I come back, I'd be happy to help anywhere I can. My farm's not in danger of the fire, but I can sure imagine how I would feel if it was."

"Thanks, Jordan. We'd welcome the help. We were talking about digging fire breaks and burning off some of the back fields closest to the fire, hoping that would at least slow the fire down if not stop it completely."

"I guess it depends on how strong the wind is, but two fire breaks are better than one, I reckon," Jordan said.

Gerald nodded. "I'll probably start first thing Monday morning. My place isn't that close to the fire yet, but it wouldn't take long if the wind gets up. If you wanna come by when you get back, I'd appreciate the help."

"I'll be there." Jordan nodded and left.

"See you on Monday, Shane, I'll be starting bright and early." Gerald said as he shook Shane's hand. He waved at a couple of neighbors and walked out of the building. He looked across the parking lot as Jordan got into his car. The man had aged and seemed weaker than he remembered. Jordan's hair had practically turned to all white since leaving Carson three years ago. Gerald shrugged. He probably had a few more white hairs himself. This fire wasn't helping either.

ELEVEN

Tennessee

Marti stepped out of the Landeville City Post Office and bumped into a tall man standing outside the door.

"Excuse me, sir. I'm sor—"

Shock stopped her in mid-sentence. Standing in front of her was Jordan Welsh.

Seeing the father of her dead brother-in-law, Vinny, shocked her into silence. Jordan seemed much older, and his weathered features reminded her of the pain he'd suffered when Vinny and Angie died. She never saw him after the accident, but she heard he had taken their deaths very hard. She dreaded facing him now.

The veiled look in his eyes made her squirm under his gaze. He tilted his head and spoke.

"Well, Martha. This is a surprise. Now I know where you disappeared to. I heard you moved away and didn't tell anyone where you were going. 'Course, I moved too and sort of lost touch with everybody there in Carson."

Marti stood still, not knowing what to say. Finally, the silence made her uncomfortable. "Mr. Welsh. It's good to see you. I hope you've been well."

Jordan nodded. "As well as could be."

"What are you doing in Tennessee?"

"I . . . uh, still travel around for the quarter horse competitions, and I decided to attend the one in Vick."

"Oh."

"Are you living here now, Martha?"

She nodded. "For the past year. I've been working at an art gallery here in the city."

"I see."

The pause that followed was uncomfortable for Marti, so she backed up a little and said, "I guess I better be getting back. I ran over to get the mail for my boss. It was good to see you again, Mr. Welsh."

Mr. Welsh put his hand on Marti's arm. "Wait, Martha."

She stopped and half-turned toward him. The hand on her arm gave her an uneasy feeling.

"I just wanted to say that . . . I don't hold any ill feelings toward you." His eyes shifted to stare at the ground.

The breath she was holding came out quickly in a relieved sigh. "Thank you, Mr. Welsh."

"I know things happen sometimes that are out of our control, and . . . well, I just wanted you to know." The smile he gave her was strained but she hoped it was sincere.

Marti turned toward him then and fingered the chain around her neck. "Thank you, Mr. Welsh. I know it was hard losing Vinny, especially right after your wife died. I'm just sorry it had to happen."

For a second, his eyes met hers, and then he shifted, and his gaze spiraled downward. "Yeah, same here." His voice was so soft she could hardly hear the words. He squared his shoulders and spoke. "I'll let you go now, Martha." He nodded and turned away.

She stood still and watched him cross the street to the courthouse. His lanky figure looked strong, but his legs were still tall and painfully thin. A small twinge started in her stomach and spread to her heart. Reminders of that accident always popped up somewhere. She wished there was a pill to take so she could forget everything in her past.

She shook her head and flipped through the mail while she walked in the other direction but froze when she saw a familiar address label.

Carson, Texas.

A pain hit her in the chest so hard it made her dizzy. Who would be writing her from Daniel's address? How did they know where she was?

She stared at the letter, torn between two decisions. Should she open it? Should she throw it in the sidewalk trash can and not give it another thought?

What if it was important?

She ripped open the envelope before she could talk herself out of it.

Gerald's scribbling popped off the page. Suddenly, her legs wouldn't hold her up. She collapsed on the post office steps. The rest of the mail slipped from her hand to the ground as she stared at the words on the white piece of paper.

"Daniel is dying. Please come back so he can see you before it's too late."

The first three words were the only words she saw, and they pulsed inside her brain with each heartbeat.

Daniel is dying. Daniel is dying. Daniel is dying.

A burning pain twisted in her heart, and she struggled to breathe.

"No. Please, no." The words came out in a whisper. She closed her eyes—daring the words to remain on the page when she opened them again. Even though she'd decided to forget Daniel, her heart wasn't listening. Now, the sharp pain she felt when she read those three words wouldn't go away. It kept stabbing her heart into little pieces, leaving deep wounds that would never heal.

Now going to Texas had a whole new meaning. She needed to see him—even if it was just to say goodbye.

She looked at the letter again. Gerald was begging her to return quickly. A cold chill washed over her when she remembered the man in the alley. Those threats were real and made returning to Texas a scary thing.

What was she going to do? If she went to Texas, Sandra and Wade would be in danger. The stalker had threatened to burn the gallery. No matter how hard Wade tried to keep them safe, he couldn't be in two places at one time, and he couldn't keep Sandra with him the whole time Marti was gone.

One bullet was all it took, and their lives would be destroyed. And hers.

If Sandra or Wade were killed, she would never forgive herself for caving in to the selfish desire to see Daniel one last time.

Crowds circled around her, and she realized people were staring. She gathered the gallery mail and stood up on shaky feet. The steps home were slow and deliberate. She watched the birds flitting from one power line to the next, wishing she had as few worries as they did. The Bible said God took care of the birds. She wished she could count on Him to take care of her as well. But she had learned long ago that His watchful care was selective, and she wasn't one He favored to protect.

When Marti reached the gallery, the door opened by itself. She understood why when Sandra popped around the open door and pulled her inside.

"What in the world's wrong with you? I've been watching you since you left the post office. You look whiter than the mail in your hand. Who was that man you were talking to? Is something wrong?"

Marti said nothing but handed Sandra the letter.

When Sandra was done, she looked at Marti with clouded eyes. "You have to go, love. You need to see Daniel and get this settled between the two of you before it's too late."

"I'm scared."

"Hon, you need to trust the Lord for guidance."

Marti swallowed a painful lump in her throat. "I can't hear Him anymore, Sandra. I don't know what He wants from me. As soon as I gave Him my life, He left me. All those horrible things happened, and He ignored me. How can I trust that He'll lead me in the right direction now?"

Sandra pulled Marti to the loveseat situated near the front door of the gallery and sat down beside her.

"Marti, I know you feel like God pushed you out on a limb and let it fall when you stood up for Him in front of your family, and I know it's hard to understand why He let your family turn away from you, but I know He had a reason. The Bible says 'all things work together for good to them that love the Lord.' The world is a beastly place, and wickedness touches our lives even if we are God's children, but God will never . . . ever . . . abandon you. God stays the same. If we feel far from Him, it's because we've moved—not Him."

Marti's tongue felt numb. She couldn't say a thing. Deep down inside her heart, she knew what Sandra said was true, but once you've been hurt, it is almost impossible to trust again.

TWELVE

Texas

The atmosphere at the Marvel County Clinic in Carson, Texas, buzzed with static as Lydia Barnes, the oldest nurse in the clinic, stared up at the face of the demanding woman standing in front of her. "What do you mean you want the key to Mary's office?"

The tall nurse, Clara Watting, stood to attention and faced the other three nurses in the small reception area like a sergeant in front of a group of boot camp trainees. Her blue nurse's uniform was starched and perfectly pressed with creases in all the right places, and she looked down her wire-rimmed glasses at the women staring at her in awe.

The other two nurses, Cynthia Morrison and Skyler Rountree, scurried from the room and disappeared into the filing room next door—trying to get out of the line of fire. Lydia frowned at their retreating backs.

Leaning over the edge of the reception desk, Clara seemed ten feet tall. She glared at Lydia sitting in front of the computer and barked at her again. "Since the board has promoted me from temporary head nurse status to a permanent position, I mean for things to be done more efficiently around here. Now, I said it once,

I'll say it again—find the key to Mary's office. If I'm to be in charge, I'll need a bigger space." Her spine stiffened, and she threw her shoulders back—showing she meant business.

Lydia discreetly waved her arm to dispel the strong whiff of powdery perfume emanating from the determined nurse.

"But, Clara—"

"Call me Nurse Watting now."

Lydia Barnes lowered her head and rolled her eyes. Her voice was low and controlled. "Shane Duke said to leave that office locked until the board approved the change."

"I don't care what Shane Duke said. He declared the room off limits because it was his precious *Mary's* office. It's been a year since she died. It's time he got over his superstition and let us alone. Now, give me the key."

Lydia bit her lip and pulled a large ring of keys from a deep drawer in the reception desk. She found a key with "Head Office" written on the ring and separated it from the rest.

"All the patient files in Mary's office were removed already, Clara . . . er . . . Nurse Watting, but there may be some of her personal things in the drawers that her family hasn't picked up yet."

"*Humph.* Well, it's too late now. They'll all go in the trash if I have my say."

When Nurse Watting left the small reception room, Skyler, the youngest of the nurses at the clinic, stuck her head around the corner and searched to see if Clara was gone.

"Is the coast clear?" she whispered.

Lydia watched the back of Nurse Watting as she fumbled with the lock in the door at the end of the hall and pushed her way into the office. She nodded at Skyler. "She's gone."

Cynthia followed Skyler back into the reception area. "What's got her nose out of joint this mornin'?"

Lydia rubbed her temple. "Beats me. Ever since the board named her head nurse, she's been all uppity and thinks she's better than everyone else. She's just showin' her real self this morning. I thought we were doing fine like we were—everyone sort of on the same level, you know?" She blew a puff of air up toward her graying hair to push the wispy bangs away from her eyes.

Cynthia laughed. "I guess the board didn't think so. I thought maybe her hair was pulled up too tight in that bun on the top of her head, and that's what was making her grouchy. She's in a mood for sure this morning."

"Well, she'd better not be throwing nothin' of Ms. Mary's away. If she does, she'll have to answer to me." Lydia sniffed and tightened her fists on the desk.

Cynthia laughed again. "Yeah right! You'll stand up to her like you did a few minutes ago, huh?"

Lydia frowned at the young woman and turned to finish her report. She might not be much of a fighter, but she sure wasn't going to let anything of Ms. Mary's be thrown in the trash.

"Ms. Barnes?" A bellow came from the office down the hall, and it was followed by footsteps.

Cynthia and Skyler scattered again when they heard Clara roar.

Lydia wrinkled her nose and scowled.

Chickens.

THIRTEEN

"Yikes! Listen to her holler. What's her problem, anyway?" Skyler leaned across the records desk and coveted the dangling earrings Cynthia was wearing as she bent over to straighten the shoestrings on her nursing shoes. She had to admit—jealousy was as much a part of her nature as breathing. She'd love to know where Cynthia found those three-tiered, gorgeous gold rings.

A snort burst from Cynthia's nostrils. "You and I both know what has her nose up in the air—that promotion. She thinks she's better than everybody else now."

Skyler concurred. "She always did have a better-than-thou attitude, but I think being voted 'Top Nurse of the Year' last year added fuel to her snobbiness."

"*Hmph!* If the board knew what I know, they wouldn't have made that decision. A couple of months ago, I saw Ms. Top-Nurse-of-the-Year taking drugs from the locked medicine cabinet. Then later that day, I was grabbing more gauze from the storage room when I saw a man in a top-of-the-line suit meet her around the back of the clinic with a large yellow envelope in his hand. He handed her the envelope, and she handed him a shoe box wrapped in a shopping center bag. What do you wanna bet it wasn't shoes, neither?"

Skyler pulled a piece of gum out of her pocket and stuck it in her mouth. "You think she was selling drugs?"

Cynthia shrugged. "Figure it out for yourself. I'm just saying that Ms. Top-Nurse-of-the-Year might not deserve to be at the top of anything."

"Why didn't you tell somebody what you saw?"

"And lose my job over something I couldn't prove? No way. She'd have said she was selling him some of that perfume she peddles all the time."

"Well, she's helping with the orphanage fundraiser this year—she can't be all bad. I think she's actin' this way 'cause of the head nurse position. She'll probably settle down."

Cynthia shrugged and sat down in the filing cabinet chair. "I hope so. Are you gonna do a painting of one of the houses on tour this year for the fundraiser?"

Skyler paused to blow a bubble and pop it with her teeth. "You mean the plein air competition? Wow, I don't know. Last year my painting sat there forever before someone finally made the first bid. Then it sold for a piddly ten dollars. Of all the paintings in the auction, it brought the least amount of money. It was kind of embarrassing when one painting sold for over six hundred dollars."

"Yeah, I know. Mine sold for only fifty dollars. Even the small amounts add up though. I'm sure they appreciated the effort. I'm really not very good at painting, but I wanted to help the orphanage."

"I know. Wasn't that trip we took to Tennessee last year fun? All those sweet kids." Skyler's gaze strayed to the window and a far-away look filled her eyes. "Jaydn Holbrook and his wife Alana are an amazing couple. You can tell the kids love them to death. Can you believe they have over five hundred orphans living all under one roof?"

"You're kidding! I had no idea there were so many."

"That's what Alana told me last year at the auction."

"I guess I'll try another painting this year, but I sure wish we had a real artist to encourage participation from some of the other towns around this area. Our amateur paintings aren't going to bring a whole lot. It's a shame we're lacking in talent here in Carson. The cause is such a good one."

"Yeah, I hate it for the orphanage. I'm sure it takes lots of money to feed and clothe all those kids." Skyler placed the last file in the metal cabinet. "I've run out of records to file, so I guess I'll head back."

Cynthia grabbed Skyler's arm before she could head out the door. "Wait a minute! Have you forgotten Ms. *I-want-things-done-my-way* is still out there?"

"Oh, yeah. I forgot." She peeked around the doorway, and shrugged when she saw Clara still at the front desk.

They both went back to straightening the files until the alarm alerted them to an ambulance backing up to the emergency door of the clinic. Time to get back to work.

FOURTEEN

It took Clara Watting all day to get everything cleaned out of filing cabinets, the tiny closet in the office, and three of the desk drawers. When she pulled out the top middle drawer of the desk, she found it was full of pens, paper clips, notepads, and staples. A picture of Mary and her daughter was pushed up into the back corner of the drawer inside a small picture frame. Clara pulled it out and looked at the smiling face of her former boss.

Mary was standing beside Veronica in front of a six-star cruise line ship. Their luggage was spread around them, and they both looked extremely happy.

Clara felt a pinprick of jealously stab her heart. It was easy to be happy when you had money. If she had the money to take her own daughter on a cruise—maybe Tara would start speaking to her again.

Clara shrugged and laid the picture on the desk.

She emptied most of the contents of the top drawer into a box and pulled out the drawer to dump the dust and scrap pieces of eraser into the trash. As she turned the drawer upside down over the trash, a tiny corner of paper stuck out from under the drawer. Carefully, she laid the drawer on its top and pulled on the sheet of paper. The tape that held it firm was old and gave way easily.

When she unfolded the piece of paper, she glanced at the title—trying to make sense of the contents.

She tilted her head to one side and rubbed her forehead. She walked to the other side of the room and then returned, still staring at the paper in her hand. What did it mean?

An idea occurred to her, so she left the large office and entered the room where the archived files were stored. A thorough search produced exactly what she was looking for. She carried the papers back to the desk in her new office and sat down, trying to make sense of the two identical pieces of paper . . . what it *could* mean . . . what it *would* mean to her future, if she had anything to say about it. A slow smile crossed her weathered lips, and she stood—pushing up her sleeves with precise movements.

She picked up the papers and slipped into the storage room. A peek around the corner told her what she wanted to know—the others were busy with new patients trickling into the clinic. Carefully, she placed the papers on the copy machine, one at a time, and pressed the start button.

Scared the others would hear the whir of the motor as it scanned the documents and prepared to print, she closed the door quietly, lifting the door slightly to keep the hinges from squeaking. When the copies were made, she pulled the papers from the machine and slipped back into her office.

The original documents fit into a pocket of her briefcase, and she placed the copies in an envelope and slid it into her bag. Then she picked up the phone and paused—the picture of her old boss stared up at her from the desk. Mary always did everything by the book and never thought about doing anything dishonest. Was what she was thinking about doing dishonest? Maybe so, but it wouldn't hurt anybody, would it? She straightened her back and dialed the number on the phone. She was not Mary, and she needed the money.

When the call was picked up, she spoke softly.

"I need to see you, sir. No, it cannot wait. I have something you need to see, and I think you'll be sorry if you don't agree to meet me. Yes, I can meet you in thirty minutes at the town park."

Clara hung up the phone and smiled. If this meant what she thought it meant, it was a windfall for her. Now, maybe things would finally go her way.

FIFTEEN

Marti was terrified. She glanced at the navy blue truck in her rearview mirror. It had been following her for miles, and now she wondered if she had reason to worry. She was sure leaving Tennessee would not go unnoticed by the person stalking her, but Sandra had insisted she make the trip and wouldn't take no for an answer.

"You can follow me when I leave to meet Vivian, and if your stalker's around, he'll think you're going to the art sale with me. Then when we get to my sister's house in Vick, you can keep on going. I mean, it's on the way, isn't it? And only about five hours from my sister's house. You can go see Daniel, have your conversation, and be back before this beastly bloke even knows you're gone."

The simple decision to drive to Texas in a day had turned into a scary dream. Now someone was following her, and her fear ballooned into something monstrous, making it hard to breathe. Was it her stalker or just some stranger—glad to have company on the lonely road?

She swerved right onto the next gravel road, and the truck kept on going. A sigh of relief relieved the tense silence in her car. To be safe, she took the next two left turns, and after driving for a couple of miles, jerked her car into a small rundown restaurant nestled in the middle of a huge stand of tall Texas pines. She sat staring down the smoky road she had come from. When nothing stirred up the dust on the lonesome road, she took a shaky breath and pulled out her cell phone.

The drumming of the rings wore on Marti's nerves until Sandra finally picked up the phone.

"Sandra? Are you all right?"

Marti heard a heavy sigh. "Marti, this is the third time you've called me today. Will you stop worrying? I'm fine. I'm here with my sister at the art show. So stop worrying. Wade's keeping an eye on the gallery in Landeville, and everything's fine."

Marti slumped in the seat. Her face relaxed.

"I'm sorry. I thought someone was following me, and I guess I'm a little paranoid."

"I know you gave up on God, Marti, but if you'd turn to Him—"

"Stop, Sandra! We've had this discussion before. I'm not ready to trust Him again."

"All right, Marti. But, try okay? He really is there for you."

Marti ground her teeth. "I have to go. I'll call you when I get there. Be safe."

Marti hung up the phone. Sandra was never going to give up. *Hashtag: tenacious.*

She glanced around the parking lot. Only four cars sat in the small lot of the restaurant, and everything was quiet. She grabbed her purse and hurried inside the restaurant, keeping her eyes on the road.

She would get something to eat, and maybe by the time she left, the blue truck would be miles away. Shakily, she sat down and ordered a hamburger and fries. When the meal arrived, it tasted like sawdust. The french fries stuck in her throat, and she didn't even attempt to force the rest of the burger down. She asked for a to-go box before heading to the check-out counter to pay for the food.

"How was your meal, sugar?" The hostess smacked on a piece of gum and smiled at Marti as she pulled out her money. The woman's bright red hair was a chocolate brown at the roots and was pulled back into a loose ponytail. Gold earrings at least three inches long jangled as she made change from the antique cash register.

"Fine. It was fine."

The cell phone beside the cash register rang and vibrated across the counter. While the hostess turned to answer the call, Marti searched the parking lot for a dark blue truck. The smoke filling the parking lot and surrounding area had increased, and Marti strained to see the mountains through the gray haze in the air.

The redhead hung up the phone and barked out a loose cough. She turned back to Marti. "I'll be glad when they get this wildfire under control. Ten miles is too close for me. All this smoke is rough on my asthma."

Marti tried to make polite conversation and ignore the sense of uneasiness filling the air. "I heard about the wildfire on the radio. How many acres has it burned?"

"I think about five thousand so far. It burned a couple of farms plumb to the ground. Sure is sad." The waitress shook her head and handed Marti her change.

Marti tucked her to-go box under her arm and peered out the door. It began to rain during her meal, and a brief downpour spread dust as each drop hit the dry ground. She carefully searched the area before running to her car.

As she fumbled with the keys and slid into the seat, thoughts of the man's threats in the alley popped into her head. She would have pulled all her teeth to keep from returning to Texas and putting Sandra and Wade in danger—at least until she opened that shocking letter.

Now, she touched the same crinkled letter in the seat beside her, and once again numbness crept into her veins when she absorbed the meaning of those three words.

Daniel is dying.

The word *death* left her cold, but the sentence rattled around in her brain until it finally took root in reality. After a divorce and three years of silence, it was surprising that Daniel's father would ask her to return. She wondered if the request had come from Daniel.

Thinking back to the art reception two weeks ago, Daniel's odd behavior at the gallery now made sense—could he have treated her like a stranger because of a terminal illness?

In spite of his detachment that day, she still felt the agonizing pull of the chemistry between them.

And Sandra, the little bully, had forced her to make this trip. Sandra had packed Marti's bags and had them sitting beside her own suitcases when Marti returned home from the gallery. After that, she took Marti to her car and showed her a twenty-gauge shotgun named "Betsy" lying across the backseat. She assured Marti she could protect herself and promised to keep "Betsy" with her all the time at her sister's house in the country. And Wade promised to be extra vigilant and keep an eye on the gallery while they were both gone.

So, with a good deal of trepidation, Marti had climbed into her little rundown Chevrolet coupe and pointed the car toward the southwest—right behind Sandra's Buick. With a wave goodbye to Wade and the warning of Gerald's written insistence in her head, she raced down the road—telling herself the faster she arrived, the faster she could return, store Daniel's memory in the back of her mind, and get on with her life. Seeing him again would tear her heart even further, but concern for him forced her to concede to Sandra's persistence and agree to make the trip back to Texas.

Facing Daniel after the things he'd yelled at her that day three years ago sent shivers through her body, but she needed to know what she had done to make him so angry. They were gloriously happy until the accident.

"I can't go back." She repeated through tears, until the words seemed to mock her.

She had to go. She wouldn't have another chance to fill in all the blanks.

During the three long years away, she tried to forget the results of the accident that caused the loss of not only Daniel's sister and brother-in-law, but her own newborn son. She had been told the accident was her fault. Not being able to remember left her ashamed and devastated.

The first year after leaving her home was a complete blur of numbness and depression, until Sandra bounced into her life.

Sandra and her husband Wade had pulled her out of the desolation by introducing her to the world of art. Gradually the horrible memories were pushed to the back of her mind, and slowly she established a new life for herself. One of Sandra's friends, a psychiatrist, revealed ways to cope with the devastation, and the pain that was all consuming before, now only raised its head occasionally.

Seeing Daniel again at the Landeville Gallery resurrected that pain.

But now... *Daniel is dying.*

The thought tore her heart in two. Her mind, body, and spirit would always belong to him—even in death.

Worry that he still blamed her for the accident wrapped around her chest and caused a physical pain. Being accused of something she couldn't remember burned inside her heart. Shame, regret, and determination all rolled around in her head. Seeing Daniel would be hard, but she vowed to fortify her heart and forget the agony she felt in his presence—for her own peace of mind.

There was another hurdle for her to overcome: Veronica.

The memory of her satin-clad arm draped on Daniel's and the look of victory in her eyes burned a hole in Marti's memories. Veronica would surely be there as well. Veronica, with her barbed comments and vocal accusations. Meeting Veronica would not be a pleasant experience, even if it was only for a short time.

Sweat trickled down her neck, and yet her skin felt cold.

How can I go back?

The letter from her father-in-law crackled in her hands, and she knew there was no option. She had to return.

The Texas sky brightened quickly, and the short rainstorm was over. The blinding sunlight pierced its way into her sorrowing heart and filled it with hope. She could do this. She had to. The decision to follow Sandra's prodding and return to Texas, the most difficult of her life, had come after a period of toggling back and forth, but it was the decision she was now determined to stick with.

Twenty-five more miles and she would arrive at the winding driveway that led to her father-in-law's mansion in the country.

She slid her key into the ignition and cranked up the car. Ten miles later and back on the main highway, a blue Ford truck pulled in behind her . . . riding close on her bumper. A cool wave traveled down her body. She pushed the gas pedal down a little more and glanced back. His speed matched hers.

Frustration burned inside her. Was this the same guy who was stalking her before—the one who attacked her in the alley? What was his problem? He'd left her alone for a year—maybe because he thought she wouldn't return to Texas if she was settled and running a gallery with Sandra and Wade. What changed to make him think differently?

She squeezed her eyes briefly to fight the tears gathering there, when she experienced a sudden, jerky thump. The truck hit her bumper.

She increased her speed and struggled to see the shadowy face in her rear view mirror. The cloudy sky and tinted glass made getting a clear view impossible.

She held her breath as the blue truck pulled up directly behind her, and this time the impact jerked her head backward.

Oh no! Lord, are you there?

SIXTEEN

Clara Watting paced back and forth across the pathway leading down to the playground. Three children were playing on the swingset, and their mother pushed each one in turn. The rest of the park was empty. A flock of pigeons covered the ground between the picnic benches and the small pond, making cooing noises as they pecked in the grass for scraps of food picnickers had dropped on the ground. Spent magnolia blossoms covered the ground under the huge tree and gave off a sour stench.

When Nurse Watting saw the man she was looking for, she glanced around furtively and then walked toward the painted bench positioned halfway between them. She pulled out the envelope that held the copied papers, set it on the seat, and turned away.

The man looked at her with a question in his eyes and turned to the envelope when she motioned toward the bench. An angry glare crossed his face before he picked it up and pulled the papers out into the open.

Nurse Watting stood barely breathing—waiting for the significance of the papers to dawn on the man. He stood perfectly still—as if he was reading the daily newspaper. Could she have been wrong? Was it all a misunderstanding?

She knew immediately when he realized what he held in his hands. His shoulders stiffened, and he turned a lighter shade of pink.

"Where did you find this?"

"It doesn't matter where I found it. It only matters what you're willing to pay for it."

Surprise crossed his eyes, which then narrowed to slits.

"Are you blackmailing me for two stupid pieces of paper?"

"Oh, but what important pieces of paper they are! We both know how much trouble those papers could be in the wrong hands, and I'm sure it's worth a lot of money to the right person. They're not just any old 'stupid pieces of paper.'" She tilted her head and waited until he looked at the ground. "Now, do we deal, or do I take my business elsewhere?"

Fury emanated from him before a caged look entered his eyes. His gaze darted from the paper to the street.

"They're only copies, of course," she said with a strong emphasis on the word *copies*. "I have the originals tucked away where only one other person can find them . . . *if* something happens to me, that is."

Fury bubbled inside the man's gaze, and she could tell he fought to control his temper. "I'll think about it."

"Don't think too long. I'm not a patient person." She ended the warning with a smile that didn't reach her eyes.

He grunted and squeezed the paper in his hand. His stomp toward the crosswalk was labored and deliberate. His back was straight, but his head was down. His gait seemed defeated, and that defeat made Nurse Watting's heart stutter. Was it right what she was doing? Of course! A person had to watch out for herself, even if what she was doing was a little underhanded. This was too important to let slide. If she made money off the whole thing . . . well, that money could improve her relationship with her daughter.

She straightened her shoulders and headed back to her car. She had one stop to make at the post office before going home for the day; then everything would be in place. After that, she could sit back and watch her life get a whole lot easier.

SEVENTEEN

Marti glanced at the steep winding curves ahead. A shiver traveled down her spine. She had no doubt the man in the truck behind her wanted her to plummet off those curves. Instantly, she made a decision. She had to stop before she reached the deadliest curve on that road.

Pressing her foot on the brake pedal, she pulled her car closer to the right shoulder and slowed her car to a crawl, hoping the man would pass. She fumbled in her purse for her throw-away cell phone.

Instead of passing, the truck pulled up beside her and lingered, matching her speed.

It was him—her stalker. She felt it with every fiber of her being.

A knot balled in her stomach, and her pulse rate switched into overtime. What should she do? There was nowhere to hide. Nowhere to go. If she stopped, she didn't have a chance. She opened her phone and tried to dial 9-1-1. By this time, they were rounding a long steep curve on the right. As she punched the first button, the truck veered toward her and firmly pushed her car onto the shoulder of the road.

Blood pounded in her ears, and the cell phone flew from her hands into the far corner of the floor on the passenger side. She fought against the wheel and tried to pull her tires back into the right lane. Dust flew up into the air as her tires scattered the gravel on the side of the road.

The descending landscape beside the road came into sharper focus and made her heart stop as she watched her car get closer to the edge of the cliff.

This is not fair! Her little car didn't stand a chance against a monster supercab.

Jamming her foot on the brake, she watched in horror when the truck pulled in behind her and nudged her bumper.

Her car tires squealed as the brakes skidded on the loose gravel, but the navy blue truck gave her car a determined shove, pushing her a little faster. Her brakes screamed. At the same time she fought to turn the wheel toward the center line, but it did nothing to slow her progress toward the heart-wrenching drop. Her veins turned to ice as her elbows locked and her hands clamped tightly on the steering wheel, tingling with panic.

"No! Dear God, help me." Her voice sounded hollow and weak inside the panic-filled car. Even though she cried out in panic, she felt God would never answer her uncustomary prayer.

Unexpectedly, another truck rounded the curve ahead, coming toward them at an alarming rate. The unsuspecting vehicle plowed toward them, and before he could stop, its rusty red hood loomed directly in front of them.

The Ford pulled up close behind her and slammed his car into her right bumper, swinging her car uncontrollably around in the road. She circled on the wet pavement for a dizzying few seconds, barely missing the red truck careening toward her. Her car landed, balanced on the edge of a thin sliver of ground falling away to a jagged ditch.

The red truck blew its horn as it swerved and came dangerously close to nudging her over the edge of the precipice. The navy truck pulled over in front of her and stopped.

The red truck rounded the curve behind her then disappeared in her rearview mirror.

Fear tightened its hand around her throat as she sat close to the edge of the abrupt incline. She stared at the Ford, expecting the door to open any second. He promised he would kill her if she returned to Texas, and that's exactly where she was.

She opened the door and fled down the embankment. When she looked back, she saw the door of the blue truck lurch open.

Marti turned and fled toward the small stand of trees a hundred feet to the right of the ditch. If the man came after her to finish the job, it was the only place to hide. The trees growing at an angle on the side of the steep hill to the right mocked her as she inhaled gulping breaths and ran, hoping the man would not follow.

The sound of a motor made her turn. The old red truck came chugging back around the curve where it had disappeared from view.

As soon as the old rattle-trap made an appearance, the door of the blue truck slammed shut. The man revved his motor and took off.

Marti blew out a relieved sigh and sank down onto the bristle grass and tried to breathe.

"Ma'am, are you all right?"

She looked up the embankment into the face of a young country farmer. He wiped sweat from his forehead with a red cloth and pulled nervously on his overalls. The blue jean material was dusty as if he'd just stepped out of the field.

"Yes, I'm fine," she said. Shakily, she climbed back up the slope and pulled herself up beside her car.

"That crazy driver ran you off the road. Weren't no license plate. You sure you're all right? You took off like a covey of quail at the first gunshot."

Marti straightened her shoulders. "I'm fine. I . . . uh . . . was afraid it might explode."

The farmer chuckled. "No ma'am. I think you're safe in that respect."

Marti turned to him and put her hand on his arm. "Thank you so much for coming back."

The farmer laughed. "Yes ma'am. My mama always told me, 'a gentleman never leaves a lady in distress.' And, I figure you were in distress." He walked back to the body of his truck and pulled out a long chain. "Now, let's see if we can get you back on the road."

Marti tried to summon a smile. The farmer could get her out of this mess, but who would be around the next time her stalker showed up? He knew she was in Texas now. And, it was too late to go back.

EIGHTEEN

The next six miles crawled by slowly. She had one eye on the landscape and the other on the road behind her—watching for a dark blue truck. She was anxious to get away from her pursuer but nervous about her uncertain destination. Before she was ready, the driveway loomed ahead.

The pompous brick columns beside the road were flanked with luxurious landscaping. In the evening sun, flowers of all colors stood at attention as if they were afraid to stand at ease.

Before she turned into the driveway, a faint whiff of smoke burned her nostrils. Gray smoke filled the sky on the eastern horizon behind her father-in-law's land. Must be the wildfire they were fighting. It seemed awfully close.

She pulled up to the security gate and stared at the code pad. Was the entry code the same? Should she ring the bell or try the code to gain entrance?

In the past she had entered with confidence, knowing it was where she belonged. But now she was an outcast, entering where she no longer had a right to be.

With a trembling hand, she pushed the gold visitor button. Static filled the intercom and a voice boomed. "Yes?"

"I'm Marti Rushing, and I'm here," she said simply.

No one answered, but the black iron gates rattled and slowly opened.

The driveway was wide and curved sharply to the right through a thick stand of trees. After three hundred feet, it cut to the left and opened up into an enormous front yard surrounding a two-story, sprawling stone mansion. Memories flooded her heart until she thought it might drown as images flashed back to happier times.

Games on the front lawn. Horseback riding on trails beginning at the stables on the right. Picnics under the massive oak trees on the edge of woods surrounding the grounds. Boat rides and swimming contests in the gentle waves of the private lake on the back of the property.

She pulled her small car to the cavernous garage area and parked it behind an empty bay. No need to park inside. She wasn't planning on staying long. Leaving open the option of retreating was a must. The thought gave her enough strength to open the car door and step out onto the pavement. Should she ring the back doorbell? Or go around to the front entrance? Maybe they would come to her.

"I'm here," she announced to the house, though there was no one to hear her. She waited, head hung low and eyes closed tightly in silent dread. The wait was unbearable until the whooshing of a door opening made her glance up to see a man stepping down the wide back door steps.

Jim Parker.

The air rushed from her lungs in relief when she saw it was the tall butler who worked for the Rushing family. Her lower lips stretched into a half-smile, and she nodded.

"This way, ma'am. Mr. Rushing gave instructions to bring you to his sitting room suite." His words were respectful, but in the depths of his eyes, she could see a reserved sensor.

She shrugged in confusion, then let the meaning of his words sink into her thoughts. A slight irritation ballooned in her chest. So Gerald possessed the same arrogance and demanding tone that always infested him. How dare he summon her to his suite as if she were a servant!

But the air trickled out of her chest when she realized her limbs automatically obeyed that arrogant command. Some things would never change.

As she followed the butler through the house, she noted changes in the arrangement of the furniture and décor. Most of the old furniture was gone. Smaller, more compact furniture was in its place. The wheelchair in the corner explained why. A feeling of compassion and fear for Daniel pumped through her veins. Determination propelled her heavy feet forward.

Marti paused at the bottom of the stairs that wound up to the bedrooms and searched desperately inside herself for strength. Smells of spicy wood cleaner, chimes of the grandfather clock in the den, even the feel of the wooden banisters under her trembling fingers brought back an onslaught of painful memories.

The butler, reaching the top of the flamboyant staircase, turned to wait impatiently for her to climb the stairs—his arm indicating the first door on the right.

She gulped and searched the butler's face for confidence to proceed. Although his facial features remained the same, his eyes flickered with an emotion she was scared to analyze.

She mounted the stairs with boldness and resolve. When she reached the top, Parker nodded toward the door and walked back down the stairs. Marti turned toward the room and stopped in the doorway.

The room had not changed. There was still an oppressive heaviness floating around the oversized furniture, and it landed on Marti's shoulders.

An imposing cherry wood desk turned toward an open window sat in the left corner of the sitting room outside the bedroom. The perfect place for the "tyrant of the kingdom." Behind the desk were built-in shelves made of matching cherry—full of books and souvenirs from many trips abroad.

Three plush chairs and a table sat prominently to the right and circled an oval rug in a comfortable conversational area. Through the door at the back of the room, she could see the same massive four-poster bed that had always occupied the master bedroom.

She took a deep breath and stared at the aged man sitting at the desk as he glowered at the ledger in front of him. His hair was tinged with white.

Gerald Rushing had aged tremendously.

She felt a flicker of compassion when she remembered what this man had been through. The loss of his only daughter and her husband. The dissolution of his son's marriage because of accusations and scandal.

Then she remembered the way he had thrown her out of the house, and she straightened her back to quell any feelings of tenderness for this man.

Immediately, Gerald stiffened as if he sensed a presence in the room. His hands froze. He sucked in a deep breath and slowly lifted his eyes. Seeing her standing in the doorway seemed to rouse more emotion than he could handle, and he slumped against his chair.

Marti waited quietly without moving. It was he, after all, who summoned her to this place.

He gently waved her further into the room. Her feet felt heavy as she drew closer.

"You've come," he stated quietly.

"I came because of Daniel." Her voice cracked.

"Daniel's not here right now. But, before you see him, there's something I must say first. Please," he indicated a plush upholstered chair on the right side of the desk, a few feet from his side, "have a seat."

She gaped at him for a minute, then slowly approached the chair and perched on the edge.

"I don't understand. You said Daniel is dying. Where is he?"

Gerald paused and seemed to be gathering his thoughts. "He's away at a horse auction, Martha. There's something important I needed to explain first, but I'd like you to promise one thing before I do."

Marti's head jerked up. A horse auction? She stared into Gerald's eyes. They were the same stone gray color, but there was an unaccustomed softness there. She frowned—confused.

"I'm not sure what you want from me."

"I want you to hear me out—to promise you'll hear everything I have to say before you leave—no matter how you might feel."

Even more confused, Marti stared at his eyes for several long seconds then slowly nodded. "I promise."

Gerald looked briefly down at his hands before raising his eyes to hers. "I told you in the letter Daniel was dying, but . . . that's not true."

"What?" Marti's back straightened, and her shoulders tensed. "You lied to me?"

NINETEEN

Marti sat gawking at the man in front of her—not believing he had lied to her.

"If I'd ask you to come back for any other reason, would you have returned, Martha?"

Hearing him call her "Martha" brought back throbbing memories of him shouting that name in disgust. She gritted her teeth and mumbled, "People call me Marti now."

He continued without commenting. "Very well, *Marti*, would you have come back for any other reason?"

She sat in silent indignation, her thoughts swimming with confusion.

"It was the only way I could get you to come back to help me . . ." His sentence trailed off.

Marti stared at him. His words finally penetrated the wall of protection she had erected.

Daniel was *not* dying.

The same Daniel who had turned his back on their marriage.

The same Daniel who had thrown her out of this house and blamed her for the death of his sister and her husband.

The same Daniel who . . .

Tears filled her eyes as she turned to glare at the old man.

"I don't understand. Why would you do this?"

He focused his gaze out the window and watched the wind blowing the one-hundred-year-old oak between the house and the lake.

"I need to ask your forgiveness for the way I treated you when . . . when you left here three years ago."

She saw his mouth moving, but the shock would not let her comprehend his words.

Marti's eyes narrowed. "You're saying you're sorry?"

To say an apology from the imperious Gerald Rushing bowled her over was an understatement. Gerald Rushing never apologized.

He blamed.

He excused.

But, he never apologized.

"Yes. I should never have sent you away, no matter what you did. I'm sorry for everything I did to hurt you. I should have let you explain . . . at least tried to understand. I was wrong, and I hope you can forgive me, Martha . . . uh, Marti."

When she got over the shock of his apology, she looked at him in confusion. "I don't understand. If Daniel's not dying, then why did you feel the need to lure me here? You could have apologized in the letter or on the phone."

Gerald lowered his head and swallowed twice to gather his words. They came out stilted and wooden, almost as if he were reading a script.

"About two months after you . . . left . . . Daniel joined the army. Eventually he was assigned to a special operations unit. After he completed the individualized training, he was deployed overseas for a year to conduct secret operations in Iraq. During the last month of his deployment while on his last scheduled mission, something went terribly wrong. They were ambushed. Daniel sustained life-threatening injuries as well as a severe concussion that left him in a coma for almost six months. The doctors gave us no hope he would wake up at all."

The air slowly seeped out of Marti's lungs and her face paled.

Gerald paused for a minute to collect his thoughts—his next words soft and exact.

"I tried to trace your location to let you know, Marti, but you were always one step ahead of the detective I hired."

She nodded, lowering her head, her voice just a whisper. "I traveled a lot—not staying in one place very long until recently. I was trying to run from everything."

Gerald's eye's squeezed shut. "I'm sorry, Marti. I know we hurt you terribly. We were cruel and unforgiving. I'm so sorry we couldn't find you to let you know about Daniel's injuries. He might have died during that time. He came close several times. That brings me to one of the reasons I wanted to bring you here."

Marti waited patiently with shallow breaths.

Gerald paused as unexpected tears filled his eyes.

"During that time . . . I turned to God for help. The same God I'd ridiculed you for believing in three years ago. Thanks to your witness, I had a God I could believe in and trust."

Marti blew out a doubtful breath. Trusting in God had not gone very well for her.

Gerald, oblivious to her thoughts, continued. "I didn't want to lose Daniel just like I lost Angie . . ." His voice broke, but he recovered. "Losing Daniel would have been devastating. I made a deal with God. If He saved Daniel, I would somehow find you and ask your forgiveness for my part in breaking up your marriage. I also wanted to encourage Daniel to contact you and reconcile. When Daniel woke up the very next day, I knew what I had to do—keep my promise."

Marti stared at the pale rugged face. Gerald wanted forgiveness, but that was not something she could give on command. It would take time. Even though she knew harboring bitterness only made life harder, forgiveness was not an easy thing to achieve.

She slid her purse strap onto her shoulder and stood. "So, now you've fulfilled your promise, and I can go. I don't need to see Daniel at all. He's okay, and you've apologized."

"No . . . wait, please." Gerald sat up in his chair. "That's not the only reason I called you back. Let me finish. You promised."

She reluctantly nodded.

"When Daniel woke up, he had no memory of the last few years. He still doesn't remember anything after his high school graduation. That's why I didn't contact you immediately when I found you living in Tennessee."

Marti's back straightened. "You mean he doesn't remember . . ." Her voice trailed off.

Gerald shook his head. "He has no memory of you at all, Marti. Nor does he remember being married—except what I've told him."

The air rushed out of Marti's lungs, and she sat back down stunned. "That's why he . . ."

Finally it all made sense. Now she understood his reaction to her at the gallery.

"The doctor says his memory might return naturally. It might come back quickly, or it may never come back. He encouraged us to subject him to familiar surroundings, situations, and people in order to help prod his memory. The problem is . . ."

He paused to gaze at her knowingly and continued.

"*Veronica* has her own plans for Daniel. This situation—his not remembering you—is her dream come true. Somehow, by using Daniel's vague remembrance of growing up with her, she's made Daniel believe they've always been crazy about each other, and now they're engaged. I can't seem to stop that nonsense."

"Then why did you send for me? You have what you always wanted. He can't remember me, so that should make you happy.

He can marry your precious Veronica." The sneer in her voice was not like her at all, but she couldn't hold back the derision.

Gerald's head hung low. Grief, guilt, and shame all circled like a cloud around his bowed head.

"No, Marti. That's not what I want at all. I admit I played a major part in Daniel's decision about the divorce, but I have to acknowledge the fact that during the four years you were together, Daniel was the happiest I've ever seen him. Veronica and Daniel always enjoyed a close friendship growing up, but marriage between the two of them . . ." He shook his head. "It just wouldn't work."

"I know he loved you, Marti. After you left here, he wasn't the same. He was moody and walked around with a scowl on his face. He was miserable and made everyone miserable around him."

Marti sat up even straighter, barely breathing. Gerald had made it no secret he disapproved of their marriage from the beginning, but he had never been so vocal until she had given her life to Christ six months before the accident.

Marti looked at him now. He seemed a broken man. He must be at the end of his rope if he was asking her to help. A tiny flame of compassion flared in her heart, and she knew forgiveness would not be far behind. That thought scared her to death. Completely forgiving someone for ruining her life seemed almost impossible.

She tried to grasp the situation, her breathing raspy and broken.

"So what do you want from me?"

"I . . . I need you here to help Daniel remember those happy times. To discover his memory again and hopefully the closeness you once felt for each other."

Gerald's eyes once again roved to the window before he continued. "I know I have no right to ask, but I'm hoping if Daniel sees you, his memory will return. After almost losing him, I just want him to be happy."

He paused and looked into her eyes. His eyes filled with unaccustomed tears. "With you, I know he will be. With Veronica, well . . ." He waved his hand weakly.

Marti shook her head and walked across the room, staring out the large windows. "It won't work. He already saw me at an artist reception in Landeville a couple of weeks ago. Didn't he tell you? He didn't recognize me then. What makes you think he'll remember when he sees me now?"

"Yes, Marti, Daniel told me about the reception, but I didn't realize it was you he saw until later. I'm hoping your being around him consistently will gradually bring back memories that are familiar."

"Let me get this straight. You want me to stay here for a while so Daniel will remember his life without Veronica, and realize he's not in love with her?"

Gerald nodded. "Yes. If he's around you every day, he might remember snatches of your marriage. I'm hoping he'll see the difference between how he feels when he's with Veronica and how he feels when he's with you. He loved you once. I'm hoping and praying he can find that love again."

"Why don't you just tell him he was married before? Show him pictures. I'm sure you have them around here somewhere."

"I tried that, Marti. I showed him several photographs of your wedding and of the cruise you took on your honeymoon. I prayed so hard it would help him remember, but it didn't. It only made him angry, so I quit trying." Gerald's lowered his eyes, and failure deflated his posture. "I'm afraid Veronica has exaggerated stories about your marriage with Daniel, and that has him spooked. He said if he suffered through a divorce, then there must have been a reason."

Marti sat back down in the chair and covered her eyes with her hand. "If he sees me now, don't you think he'll recognize me from the photos?"

"No. You've changed since then. Your hair's a little lighter and a good bit shorter. You're also much thinner than you were during your marriage. And, it's been months since he saw the pictures. I'm sure he's forgotten your face by now."

"What about the accident? If he regains his memory, he'll remember that as well. You know how angry he was when . . ." Her voice trailed into nothingness.

"We'll cross that bridge when we come to it, Marti, if you decide to stay."

"If he doesn't remember who I am, how will you explain me being here?"

For the first time since she set foot in the room, a hopeful gleam quivered in Gerald's eyes. He smiled at her timidly.

"I told you I hired an investigator, Marti. He finally found you last year, and he tells me you've become quite popular in the art world. So, I had an idea. I mentioned to Daniel that I hired an artist to paint a portrait of him to hang in the den with all the other family portraits. Painting his portrait will not only give you cover for being here but a perfect reason for spending time with him. The more you're together, the more it will prod his memory."

Marti's thoughts swirled around in her head when she realized what Gerald was asking her to do.

"I can't." Her breath came in short gasps. Seeing Daniel every day in such a relaxed setting would be unbearable. Painting a detailed portrait of Daniel's facial features would be torture. Close and yet so far away. And the intimacy of spending hours in his company would chip away at her newly found self-control.

TWENTY

"I don't think I can do this." Marti grasped for any excuse that would justify her leaving. "I don't have my paints or any of my materials."

Gerald slid off the black leather chair and headed toward the door.

"Come with me, Marti. I have something to show you."

Marti fearfully trailed him down the hall where he stopped in front of two tall windows laid into the end of the paneled hallway. He motioned to a solid wooden door on the right side of the massive hall. She glanced shakily at the door nestled in the opposite side of the hall and preceded him into the room. When she stepped through the doorway into the corner suite, she jolted to a stop.

There in front of her was a whole artist's studio—complete with several sizes of canvas, a palette covered with numerous tubes of oil paint, a state-of-the-art studio easel, and the most important thing for any portrait artist—floor to ceiling northern exposure windows. Both bristle and sable brushes poked out the top of a wooden basket hanging off the right side of a large wooden taboret, and a huge selection of artist pastels filled an open wooden box on a bench beside the taboret. A double paper towel holder completed the work station.

She gasped and stood with her mouth open.

"I hope I've remembered everything. I had a gallery owner in town order everything you might need. If you can think of anything else, it's only a phone call away."

She turned to stare at the short, crafty man. He must have been sure she could be talked into staying. He pointed toward a door at the back of the large room. Through it she saw a bed with a quilted comforter in patterns of blue and maroon, and just as many windows graced the bedroom wall. Double patio doors identical to the ones in the studio led out to the same balcony.

"This will be your suite if you decide to stay. I had it decorated with all your old furnishings." He shrugged and raised a hand listlessly. "I hoped it would help Daniel remember if he saw you in the same setting."

Marti's swallow was dry and hollow. "What if this doesn't work? What if he marries Veronica in spite of all your effort?"

Gerald sighed. "Then I will have done my best to correct what I had a part in. If the worst happens and he insists on marrying her, I'm hoping I can persuade him to wait until at least some of his memory returns. But, no matter what happens, we have to try. I have to correct the horrible mistakes I'm guilty of contributing to—for Daniel's sake . . . and for yours."

"I don't know what to say."

"I know you still love him, Marti. I can see it in your eyes. Please think about what I'm asking you to do. You can have the night to think about it if you like. Daniel won't be back until tomorrow evening. If you decide to leave, you won't have to see him at all. I'll understand."

He paused and said, "Please pray about it, Marti. I remember when you first got saved how excited you were about living the Christian life. It irritated me then that you never made a decision unless you prayed about it first and knew it was God's will for you. I understand that feeling now, and that's all I'm asking. Pray about it, please."

He turned toward the door and gestured to the bedroom. "I had Parker put your luggage in your room, and I'll have him bring you a supper tray if you like. Take all the time you need. You can let me know when you've decided. And, Marti . . . I hope you can forgive me in time."

Gerald walked out of the room and left her standing in awe. What should she do? She turned and walked to the front of the crystal clear windows to stare at the hazy blue mountains in the distance. Peaceful and serene, this valley had always calmed her spirit, but now the mountains in the distance seemed to mock her and shout the truth.

How can you stay and meet Daniel when he believes you caused his sister's death? When his memory returns, he'll still blame you and send you from this house again.

Thoughts swirling around her head were overwhelming. There were so many questions begging for answers.

If she stayed and painted Daniel's portrait, she would invariably see Veronica. If the beautiful redhead had done as Gerald stated and lied her way into Daniel's heart, she most definitely would not want Marti around to help bring back his memories. And yet, she knew Daniel would be miserable with Veronica. His personality would be stifled by her manipulative character—for the rest of his life, if they married.

This line of thought brought her back to Daniel's caring, loving face. He was too special to be saddled with someone ramrodding him through the rest of his life.

If she stayed, she risked losing her heart. If she left, she risked Daniel losing his. The choice was unbearable.

She pulled fresh clothes from her suitcase and entered the bathroom. A beautifully tiled shower was placed immediately across from double sinks nestled in marble countertops. There were more spray nozzles in the walk-in shower than she'd ever seen in her life. Luxury and comfort came to mind as she soaked in the pulsating jets and tried to forget the decision that plagued her mind. The rhythm of the jets pounded her tense muscles, and helped her relax.

When she stepped back into the bedroom, a tray sat on the desk. Lifting the lid revealed turkey, dressing, sautéed squash, and broccoli casserole. An apple, banana, and fresh slices of pineapple filled a bowl on the side. Beside the fruit sat a small plate that contained a generous slice of chocolate cake.

She pinched off a piece of the chocolate cake and let it melt on her tongue. *Wow*! She'd really missed Stella's cooking. Planning meals for one person was never fun, and she'd skipped meals when her heart wasn't in the preparations.

She took her tray onto the balcony and watched the sun set behind the mountain while she ate. The darkness came fast, and before she knew it, the sun's orange rays had disappeared behind the mountain.

With a mood of melancholy, she stood at the balcony rails watching the flickering lights on the mountains in the distance. The twinkling lights had a calming effect—almost enough to make her forget the threats.

Almost.

The words of the man in the alley popped into her thoughts, but she tamped them down. She would not think about that now—not here.

Here in this setting, she could feel God's presence. She wondered if it hurt God when she turned away from Him. How she missed being able to ask for His guidance. She wanted to feel that closeness again—to feel His fellowship and love. How could she make this monumental decision without Him?

Just this once, she wished she and God were still on speaking terms.

TWENTY-ONE

Marti turned over in bed, but dread kept her eyes closed. Something nagged her into believing today was going to be a terrible day. When memory stirred, her eyes popped open. She was staggered with the decision she had to make—go or stay.

Tossing and turning the night before brought no solutions to the problem, and turning to God was a difficult option. Gerald had told her to seek God's will, but that seemed impossible. She hadn't prayed in years. Why would He listen to her now?

God heard your prayer for help in the car, Marti.

The voice was not audible, but it felt so close.

She crawled out of bed and pulled her Bible from the top of the suitcase. Although she'd been a little peeved to find Sandra had tucked it into her suitcase, Marti was happy to have it now. She pulled the Bible to her and felt the warmth of the early morning light as it slid around the thick curtains covering the sliding doors to her balcony. She threw on her robe and opened the drapes. Unlocking the doors, she slid them apart and stepped onto the covered balcony.

Marti's grief was heavy. The loss of her family had been hard, but losing faith in God was devastating. She had nowhere to turn for comfort. She hung her head and let the sorrow roll over her shoulders. Then she opened the Bible to the book of Proverbs.

Chapter three and verses five and six were verses she memorized after she accepted God into her life. She read the verses aloud quietly.

"Trust in the LORD with all thine heart; Lean not unto thine own understanding. In all thy ways acknowledge him, and he shall direct thy paths."

Placing the Bible on the balcony table, she stood to stare over the edge of the railing.

Beginning rays of light filtered through trees on the mountain and shot down to the lake in the distance. Shimmers of light flickered across the surface of the water and highlighted green stems of cattails standing at attention in the shallow end of the lake. The morning mist swirled around them as if an invisible hand stirred the lake.

So peaceful. So serene. It calmed her heart, and she felt her emotions relax for the first time in three years. This place felt like home. She could almost believe God would visit her here. Maybe He brought her here. Could it be God's will that she had come? Was it His will that she stay?

She wanted to ask.

She needed to ask.

Dear God. I know I quit trusting You years ago. To be honest, I felt like You let me down. I was such a new Christian, and You let those horrible things happen. I'm sorry I turned away from You. Please show me now what Your will is for me. Should I stay and see Daniel? Should I go home and forget him? Show me a sign, please?

Beethoven's *Fur Elise* sounded from her room, so she ran inside and unplugged her cell phone from the charger beside the bed. Sandra's name lit up across the screen. She smiled and opened the flip phone.

"Hey!"

"Marti, I've been worried sick. Why didn't you ring last night? I tried to ring your number, but it never connected. I thought maybe there was no phone at your hotel and no cell service up there in the mountains."

"I'm sorry, Sandra. I guess I just got caught up in everything. The new cell I bought for the trip was low in battery when I got here, and I'm not staying at a hotel. I planned on using the house phone, but . . . I guess I got sidetracked." She stepped out onto the balcony and sat down in one of the reclining chairs. "Are you and Wade okay?"

"We're fine, love. How about you? Have you seen Daniel yet? And, what do you mean you're not at a hotel?"

"I'm staying at the house. When I got here, Gerald begged me to stay here."

"He did *what?*"

Marti frowned and explained the situation to Sandra.

A few minutes later, Sandra's voice blared through the phone again. "He did *what?*"

"Shh, Sandra." Marti glanced fearfully at the men feeding hay to horses inside fences on this side of the barnyard. She stood up and stepped closer to the back of the balcony overlooking the stables below.

"You heard me. He lied when he said Daniel was dying."

Marti explained the long conversation she had with Gerald and what he had asked her to do.

Sandra's voice was two octaves higher than normal. "He did *what?*"

"Sandra, you're beginning to sound like someone with a repetitive speech disorder. You heard me. Gerald wants me to pretend I'm here to paint a portrait of Daniel so he'll realize he's not in . . ." Marti stumbled over the word, "love . . . with Veronica."

"How are you going to pretend you don't know Daniel? That'll be impossible. I saw you when you met him at the gallery; remember what a basketcase you were?"

"I know, Sandra. Hashtag: disaster."

"There's no way in this world anyone will believe you've never met him before if they see you together, especially not Daniel. And what about all the other people at the house and around the area?"

"Gerald said if I decide to stay, he'll tell everyone to keep the secret. I don't know how I'll do it either, but I have to try. Gerald asked me to. He actually apologized for sending me away."

"What about Veronica? You know she won't keep it secret. She doesn't want you there stealing Daniel away from her, and I don't have to know her to know she'll fight you with everything she's got."

"I know, Sandra. But, I think Gerald's hoping Daniel will remember me immediately; then that won't be a problem. If she does tell Daniel, it won't be any worse than what she's already told him. Gerald said she made up all kinds of stories about our marriage. Daniel already thinks his first wife was trouble. Hashtag: witch."

The phone was quiet for the space of a minute. "Well, duck, it's your decision to make, of course. If Daniel lost his memory, that means he doesn't remember the accident either. That also means he can't tell you what you went there to find out—what happened the day he threw you out."

"I could always ask Gerald, but I'd rather hear it from Daniel."

Sandra was quiet, but Marti sensed she wanted to say more. "I guess no matter what happens, it can't be any worse than what you've been through already."

"So you're okay with it?"

"You know I'm behind whatever you decide, love."

Marti sat down on the straight chair at the back of the balcony and dropped her head. "I know there's no future for us. If he gets his memory back, he'll never forgive me, and if he doesn't, he'll end up marrying Veronica anyway. But, if I don't help, and they get married, I'll never forgive myself for not trying."

Sandra's voice, uneasy and worried, finally came back across the phone line. "What about your stalker?"

Marti shivered and struggled to keep her voice from giving away the attack she'd had on the road.

"Let's just hope he doesn't find me out here. You and Wade still be careful, okay?"

"We'll be fine, Marti. If this is what you want, Wade and I are behind you one hundred percent. When you left, you went to find out why Daniel threw you out and planned to hightail it back home. Now, you're talking about staying longer. That's a big change of events. Make sure this is what you want to do."

"I don't know what I want to do, Sandra. I'm hoping Daniel's memory will return soon. Then . . . we can talk, and he can tell me why he was so angry over an accident that was surely just an accident. Maybe I won't be here long enough for the creep threatening me to do anything. I just want you and Wade to be careful as long as I'm here. Please?"

Sandra grunted. "Don't worry about us, sweetie. Wade knows how to handle things. He installed a timer on your lamp above the gallery so it comes on at the usual time you have off—just as if you were here. And I think one of his men patrols outside every night."

Marti felt guilty for misleading Sandra, but Sandra couldn't do anything to help now.

Marti pulled at the skin on her chapped lips with her teeth. "Okay, Sandra. Thank you. I've been praying, and—"

"You what? Did I hear you say you've been praying?"

Marti smiled a thin line. "Yes, I've been praying. There's something about this place that draws me closer to God. I asked Him to show me a sign . . . whether I should stay. I think your being okay with it might be what I needed to help me decide."

Sandra's sigh could be heard through the line. "That's jolly good news, believe me. Thank you, Lord. I'm glad something good is coming from this."

Marti smiled. Trust Sandra to speak her piece. "Please pray for me, Sandra. If you do, I promise, I'll hang your next exhibit all by myself."

Sandra laughed. "You've got a deal, but I got a bargain because I've been praying for you for a year. Listen, love, be careful, okay?"

When Marti finally hung up the phone, she shivered and rubbed her bare arms in the cool mountain air. She'd lost the stalker on the road long before she got here, so hopefully he wouldn't be able to find her here—unless it was someone she knew. She couldn't think of a single soul who wanted her to stay out of Texas bad enough to try and scare her away. Except maybe Veronica. No way could Daniel be involved. It had to be someone else. But Veronica? Maybe she wanted Daniel enough to go to such lengths. It could be her behind all the attacks.

Suddenly, the hairs on the back of Marti's neck prickled. A feeling of being watched tingled through her already sensitive emotions. Someone was watching her. She was sure if it. The same feeling she felt in Landeville traveled the length of her spine.

The landscape around the house seemed still, but the trees swayed, hiding the barn's open doors. As the leaves blew with the breeze, she could just make out an orange glow down by the stables.

A cigarette?

There it was again. It looked like the slow steady pull of a cigarette. She edged in behind the large curtains and closed the balcony doors, never taking her eyes from the pulsating glow.

Sliding the lock into place, she checked it twice to make sure it was secure.

A chill traveled through her body as she jerked the curtains closed and peeked through them one more time. The orange glow was gone. Maybe her imagination had switched into overdrive. It could have been a ranch hand taking a break, not even looking her way. She shook her head as she turned away from the doors.

She felt a nervous tingling as she made her bed and prepared for the day. If she was going to stay, she needed to start thinking about the role she would play—a portrait artist who would paint Daniel's portrait.

Before leaving the room, she peeked out the sliding doors one more time. Everything seemed normal, but staying in Texas might not have been her best decision.

What have I done?

TWENTY-TWO

Daniel towel-dried his hair. When he heard his cell phone ringing in the other room, he ran to pick it up and punched the call button.

"Morning, Veronica."

"Hey, darling. When are you coming home? This trip has been entirely too long."

"I'm home. Got home late last night. The rain started the last day of the auction, and we decided to leave a day early."

Veronica's squeal came through the phone. "Oooo, wonderful, darling! I'm coming over as soon as I can. I told the architect to come a day early so I . . . I mean, so *we* could get the project started. Now that you're home, that works even better."

"Dad said Mr. Reimes called this morning and said he couldn't come today. He said he'll be back in this area one day next week and he'd see us then. Something about a new barn going up over in Gale County."

Veronica was silent for a moment. "If he wasn't the best architect in the state, I'd consider hiring someone else. This is the second time he's postponed."

"Well, I guess he thinks remodeling and adding new stalls isn't as important as building a whole new barn. I'm sure he's thinking about his commission."

"Obviously not enough. He has to realize this is a paying job as well. He'll probably work half the time and still charge us enough to build a whole new barn. That's what they all do, isn't it?"

"Now, Nikki—"

"I told you not to call me that. You know I hate it." Her voice was strong, but the pout she thrust into the words hid the anger. "That's upsetting, his not coming today. I had my heart set on getting these stalls built in a hurry and moving Stripes and Narnia over to your barn as soon as possible. Since we're spending so much time together, it'd be nice to have them close."

Daniel waited to see if Veronica was through before he asked, "Hey, you're bringing Chris over when you come, aren't you?"

"I suppose so. Sometimes I think you love seeing him more than me." Her pout could be heard over the phone. "It doesn't matter, darling. Chris is excited to see his new 'daddy' anyway. I think my dad is coming too so he can evaluate the mares you bought last week. He wants to see if you chose wisely."

Daniel's smile slipped, and a frown deepened the lines in his face. "Funny, funny."

"Believe me, darling, there's nothing funny about it. You know how he is about buying mares from a new supplier."

Daniel paced the bedroom floor, trying not to let annoyance creep into his words. "Yeah, but these are *my* choices and *my* mares—not his. It doesn't affect him at all."

The phone was silent for a few seconds. "If it affects me, he thinks it affects him, and it will affect me once we're married. It's his way of coping with his misery, darling. Let him have his fun."

Daniel made a conscious effort to be patient. Shane Duke had been struggling with depression since his wife died last year, and Veronica seemed to use that excuse for her father's behavior more and more lately. "All right, Veronica. We'll see how it goes. I'll see you in a little while."

"By the way, darling, I'm bringing over a new magazine I found yesterday with perfect ideas for our wedding. Some of the decorating themes are gorgeous, and I know you'll just love them."

Something in the pit of Daniel's stomach prickled, but he summoned a hint of enthusiasm.

"Okay, great. I'll see you in a little while."

"You love me, don't you darling?"

"Of course."

"And . . . you're excited about the wedding; I can hear it in your voice. See you soon, darling."

After Veronica hung up, Daniel stood at the window and waited for the mountains to calm his spirit. His father's words about accepting God back into his life came into his thoughts and haunted him. It would be nice to feel God's presence. Nothing felt right in his life. He'd love to rest in the knowledge that there was a God who loved him and was there to guide him. Not being able to remember that feeling of surrender made him uneasy about stepping closer to something he didn't understand.

Thoughts of Chris coming over made him smile. That little kid had worked his way into Daniel's heart. Shane's despondency since his wife's death made him a poor excuse for a father, but Chris always seemed to enjoy the time Daniel and Veronica spent teaching him about horses and ranch life.

He pulled on a pair of jeans and a shirt and combed his fingers through his hair. Then he hooked his cell case onto his belt and picked up his wallet on the way out the door.

As he rounded the corner of his bedroom door, he glanced into the remodeled art studio. A woman stood at the open windows. Her hand covered her eyes as if she were in pain. Skidding to a stop, he glanced back around the doorway and took in the thin form of the woman with her back to him. Her auburn, shoulder-length hair blew in the slight breeze coming in the window and swirled around her face. She was not very tall and looked painfully thin. Her shoulders were rounded in sadness.

As he watched, she turned to the side, staring sadly out the tall windows. A chord of something beat in his heart. Familiarity? Was his memory returning? He studied her carefully.

No. He did not know this woman, but some kind of awareness flitted through his mind, hovering just out of reach. His neck prickled, and he reached back to rub the tickle. That flicker of awareness caught him off guard, and an uneasiness settled on his shoulders. He shook his head. The doctor said it would take time, but it was maddening—not being able to remember. As he stood watching the downcast set of her shoulders, the young woman turned and caught him staring.

TWENTY-THREE

Marti stood at the studio windows, once again studying the distant mountain range. Suddenly she felt something touch her cheek, as if the wind had blown hair across her face. She raised her head and turned.

Daniel stood in the open doorway, looking at her.

He cleared his throat and emptied his eyes of any emotion. "You must be the artist my father hired."

Daniel's deep penetrating voice did funny things to Marti's heart, and surprise rattled her already shaky resolve to remain calm and detached when she met him "for the first time." The unexpected sight of his handsome features and damp hair in the familiar setting nearly brought her to her knees. The room around her faded into waves of shadow, and she grasped the back of the chair close to her.

How could she stay here and come into constant contact with the man whose appearance made her heart turn to jelly? And yet, even as the thought struggled to take root, Gerald's pleading face swam before her, and she knew she would stay.

Lord, help me.

"Are you all right?" Daniel's voice sounded strained.

Marti nodded her head clumsily, her gaze landing everywhere but on Daniel's eyes.

"Yes. You startled me."

He stepped closer but stopped halfway across the room. "I thought you were supposed to be here next week."

Marti was stunned at the irritation in his voice. She shrank inside of herself and tried to think of something to say. Before she could speak, Daniel took another step closer.

"Why are you here early?"

Marti looked at him then. He stood tall and stiff—as if he were angry. Had he remembered who she was then? The thought scared her into silence.

When she didn't answer, he came closer and towered above her. His expression softened, and his stance relaxed.

"Are you all right?"

A nod was all she could manage.

"I'm Daniel Rushing. I'm sure my father has told you I'm the subject of this portrait you're supposed to be painting. To be honest, this is entirely my father's idea. I'm not happy about having my portrait done."

Marti's head lifted. Then he hadn't remembered who she was. Her gaze settled on his chin to keep from looking at his eyes.

Marti smiled shakily, trying to pretend she hadn't felt the strong emotions filling the room. She knew the smile didn't quite reach her eyes, but it was all she could muster.

"Well, truthfully, it won't take much of your time. After the initial pastel study, which takes about an hour, and a short photography session, I work from photographs until the last sitting."

Marti knew in her heart she could paint his portrait from memory without a single piece of reference material, but she kept that thought to herself.

His features relaxed, and flecks of relief sparkled in his eyes. "That's a relief, Ms. . . . I'm sorry; I don't know your name." He reached out to shake her hand.

Relief forced a smile to her lips, and she shyly reached out her hand to shake his. "Marti Rushing."

Shock filled his eyes for a second, and she realized her mistake. She used her married name.

Since leaving here three years ago, she had adopted her maiden name, Ross. Daniel's presence had thrust her into the past, and the name Rushing came easily from her lips.

"The same last name. How odd. What a strange coincidence."

She nodded slowly, her eyes trying not to land on their hands content in the clasp of each other—her thoughts consumed only with the feel of her hand in his.

When he realized he still held her hand, he dropped it as if it scorched his skin. Marti watched a shocked expression darken his features before his other hand rubbed the nape of his neck, as if he were easing a pain there.

She stilled and looked for the first time into his golden brown eyes.

Please remember me, Daniel.

His head tilted to the side as he stared into her eyes. Goose bumps on her arms tingled.

"Do I know you? " His voice was suddenly injected with a tight barrier. "You seem familiar, and yet. . . Did my father tell you I had an accident and can't remember anything during the last few years?"

She nodded silently.

"Yet, you seem familiar." He stared at her, and the furrow between his brows deepened.

The whole room tilted. She clenched the chair tighter with her left hand, trying to stop the world from spinning. Holding her breath, she waited. Would he remember? It was the loudest silence she had ever endured. Her heart was filled with a sense of foreboding—aching for him to remember and yet scared to death he would.

Remembering their life together meant he would recall the accident—the cause of his sister's death—and the other horrible accusations he had hurled at her the day she left. Her soul shivered.

He would send her away again, and her heart would rip into pieces once more.

Marti watched his gaze separate from hers and said, "I know a little about amnesia myself. I . . . I was in a car wreck a few years ago, and I lost several weeks of memory surrounding the accident, so I know how you feel."

She turned away to distance herself from him physically and emotionally when he suddenly pointed one finger in the air.

"Now I remember where I've seen you."

The air was sucked out of her lungs.

"You were the artist at the Landeville Gallery reception."

Slowly she took a breath and nodded.

"But, I don't understand. The artist's name at the exhibition was Ross. Is that you?"

She nodded again, unable to find the words to explain.

"Oh, you must be using Ross as a professional name."

She stood silently, not wanting to lie, but letting him believe the apparent solution.

His eyes opened wide as if he'd suddenly remembered something. "I bought one of your paintings that day. Would you like to see it hanging?"

Her mouth felt parched. "Sure."

Daniel left the room and waited for her to follow. She slowly walked through the door and watched him as he entered the room on the other side of the large hallway.

Sweat popped out on her forehead, and the breath in her throat felt hot enough to burn as it entered her lungs. This was their corner suite. Their bedroom when they lived as man and wife. Her heart ached, remembering his touch ... his devotion ...

His angry words the day I left.

She straightened her spine and made a decision.

I won't let him get to me. I have to be strong. I'll help him get his memory back and leave before he sends me away again.

They could never have a life together once Daniel remembered the accident. And the wounds she carried from his words still throbbed. Trust was necessary in every marriage, and he had stomped all over what little he had in her.

TWENTY-FOUR

Marti carefully entered the suite where she spent four years as Mrs. Daniel Rushing. The décor in the sitting room had been completely changed. It had an almost gaudy look about it. Walls that had been a light blue were now painted a dark green, and even though the wood floor remained the same, new rugs, accented with a hideous orange color that clashed with the green in the walls, were placed in odd spots around the sitting areas. She cringed. *Hashtag: garish.*

Three recliners sat side by side, all covered with various fabrics.

"Excuse the extra furniture. My fiancée is in the middle of refurnishing these rooms. She said the old furniture looked revolting and the blue color reminded her of a typical bachelor's room."

Marti's fist clenched. How dare she! There was nothing wrong with the way Marti had decorated the room. Revolting?—indeed!

She followed Daniel through the ostentatiously redecorated sitting area into the bedroom and gasped.

There, above the gigantic stone fireplace in the center of the outside wall, was the landscape he purchased from her spring exhibition at Sandra's gallery. The colors of blue and gray in the sky and mountains of the painting complemented the curtains and flowers scattered around the room. The aged leather sofa and chairs at the end of the bed brought out the sienna of the trees and lazy cabin resting beside the lake in the painting.

The décor of this room had not been touched. The familiar colors and fabric brought back an onslaught of memories. Even the soft smell of magnolia blossoms tore at her heart and created a longing so strong that she felt her heart was weeping. She struggled to keep her features inert.

Without speaking, Daniel pulled aside the massive curtains to reveal the landscape outside.

She already knew what she would see before he motioned her closer to the windows. The painting on the wall mirrored the mountains in the distance. How could they not match? She had painted the picture hanging on the wall with this particular view in mind.

He looked at her with questions in his eyes. "How could you paint something to match so perfectly when you've never been here before?"

Marti's lips felt numb. Color rose in her cheeks, and she faced the mountains to hide the truth in her eyes. "I've visited this mountain range in my heart many times." It was the truth, and yet it gave nothing away. "I've seen pictures of these mountains before, and their beauty is something you never forget."

Daniel nodded, and his tone softened. "Yes, I know what you mean. Even when I'm away for business reasons, I miss the peace they make me feel. My fiancée wants me to move this painting to a room downstairs, but . . . I haven't given in yet. "

Daniel glanced out the window toward the stable and noticed someone walking there. He stiffened.

"There's my fiancée now, and her brother. If you'll excuse me, I need to go."

"Her brother?"

"Yes, her parents adopted a little boy three years ago, making him her brother." He looked uncertain, but politeness made him continue. "Would you like to meet them?"

Meeting Veronica face-to-face again was not something she was looking forward to.

"Uh, no. I need to get unpacked and get everything set up here in the studio."

He walked toward the door but glanced back at her. The uncertainty of her look made him pause at the door.

"Our cook, Stella, is off this morning, but Anita placed plenty on the breakfast bar, if you get hungry. My dad will be here, but please feel free to scrounge around. I won't be around today—there's an equine exhibit at the Natural History Museum in town. But I'll be able to work with you on the portrait tomorrow if that's acceptable."

Marti nodded. "Tomorrow's fine." She took a step toward the door but had a thought and stopped. "For the portrait . . . maybe you'd like to be holding something in the picture—like . . . one of your wood carvings."

Daniel stopped dead in his tracks and turned to her, a question darkening his eyes.

"How did you know I used to make wood carvings?"

Marti's heart did a flip-flop. "Oh . . . uh . . . your dad must have mentioned it."

Daniel stared at her in confusion for a few seconds before nodding. "I'll see you tomorrow." He turned and left the room.

The air rushed out of her lungs, and she collapsed on the edge of the bed. Bombarding Daniel with memories was going to be harder than she ever imagined because it opened a Pandora's Box of memories for herself as well.

After her heart returned to its normal rhythm, Marti inched over to the window and looked at the redheaded woman standing by the stable. The fashionable riding jacket she wore was a brilliant green, and the tan riding slacks were silky and fit her perfectly. Dressing with flair was one of Veronica's best assets.

A small boy jumped and skipped around her in circles and laughed as he tugged on Veronica's hand—his collar length dark hair blowing in the slight breeze. Laughter trickled through the closed window and tickled Marti's heart. Sorrow for the little boy she lost in the accident drove a knife of pain through her heart.

As she watched, Veronica glanced up and saw Marti standing at the window. She yanked up her designer sunglasses, and her eyes tightened to tiny slits. Marti could see the fury radiating through her features. It was obvious Veronica knew nothing about her coming. Marti's heart trembled, and she stepped back quickly.

What had she gotten herself into?

Veronica took a step toward the house and glared up at the window. Marti was sure Veronica had to be aware of the fact she was standing in her old bedroom. She pulled back further from the window to hide from Veronica's wrathful gaze and peeked through the tiny slit of the curtains. Eventually she saw Daniel hurry out of the back patio door. The little boy launched himself into Daniel's arms. The kiss Veronica gave Daniel was long and meaningful. When she pulled back, she linked her arm in his and raised her head in a victory salute toward the top floor window. Some of the air deflated from Veronica's posture when she saw Marti wasn't standing at the window any longer. She flipped her head with determination and turned to Daniel with a worshipful look. He gazed down into her eyes with a smile.

Marti's soul died a little in that instant. This whole charade was futile. She didn't have a prayer of winning Daniel away from Veronica when his lack of memory prevented him from feeling the connection they shared during their four-year marriage.

Her shoulders were rounded in rejection when she heard a startled exclamation behind her.

"Oh my!"

Marti turned and encountered the scowling face of Parker's' wife.

"Anita!"

"It's you. I thought I was going crazy." Anita's face suddenly tightened. "What are you doing in this room?"

Anita's brows drew together, and Marti could feel the sudden injection of frostiness into her voice. Anita and Marti had always been close, but after the accident, Anita too had scorned their friendship. She mirrored the same aloofness as her husband, Parker.

Marti walked to the door a little shakily. "Didn't Gerald tell you? I'm here to paint a portrait of Daniel, and he was showing me the painting he bought in the spring."

Anita nodded. "Mr. Gerald told me, but I was surprised after . . ." Her voice trailed off, and frigidness filled the air.

Marti looked at Anita carefully and saw dislike flaring out from her eyes. There was nothing else to say. She turned and left the room. As she turned the corner in the hallway, she bumped into Gerald marching down the hall.

"Oh, excuse me, Marti. I came to see . . ." He paused when he realized she had come from Daniel's bedroom.

"Daniel was showing me the painting he bought at the Landeville Gallery this summer . . . my painting," she explained.

A look of surprise flitted across the old man's face. "Then . . . you've seen Daniel?"

Marti nodded. "He came into the studio and introduced himself."

"Did he remember anything?"

"No. He remembers meeting me at the Landeville Gallery, but that's all."

A gleam of hope died in Gerald's eyes. His thin shoulders deflated. "Well, I have faith your being here will eventually help him remember. That is . . ." He lowered his head and looked at her through the top of his lashes. ". . . if you decide to stay."

Marti would be crazy to even think about staying. Not only would her heart take a beating, but she knew Veronica would make life miserable for her. She would be a fool to stay and face such hostility, but rebellion reared its determined head, and she had a sudden desire to fight for Daniel.

A glance at Gerald revealed a softness around his eyes and compassion in their depths. Gerald was a different man. He had turned his life around and was trying to correct his mistakes. She remembered the passion in his eyes when he begged her for forgiveness and asked her to help Daniel find happiness.

In spite of the opposition she faced, she knew what the answer would be even before the words left her mouth.

"I'll stay—even if I don't think this will work and even if I know as soon as he remembers he'll tell me to leave again. I'll stay. I'll do it . . . for you."

Gerald put both hands on her arms. "Sweet Marti. Thank you. And pray, Marti. Pray with all your heart for God to work things out." He kissed her on the cheek and walked back down the hallway.

Marti watched his retreating figure and frowned. God didn't help her keep Daniel before. Would he really help now?

Hashtag: futile?

TWENTY-FIVE

On his way downstairs to meet Veronica, Daniel walked through the spacious den and into the kitchen while thoughts of the artist in the room upstairs marched around in his head. The brief handshake they shared left an indelible impression on his right hand and created goose bumps across the back of his neck. Her outward beauty was obvious, but something made him uneasy in her presence. For some reason, her hand, warm and tender, felt good in his, and that made him angry. His heart did funny things during the short time he was with her—almost as if they'd connected before.

Guilt reared its head at his reaction to a beautiful stranger—because of Veronica. Veronica was his best friend—for as long as he could remember. The bond between them should have been stronger than his initial reaction to a stranger. They were getting married, for goodness sake! Although he tried to feel comfortable in the role of Veronica's fiancé, it still felt strange to think of himself in that way—and that bothered him.

Daniel walked out the patio door to meet Veronica and her father standing beside their Mercedes—close to the stable yard entrance.

Veronica's arms were crossed in front of her, and green eyes flashed from a flushed face. Had he done something to upset her?

The fury changed immediately, however, when she saw Daniel's approach. Little Chris launched himself toward Daniel and into his arms.

"Daniel, sweetheart." Veronica leaned against him and kissed him soundly, glancing toward the second story of the house. When her countenance fell, Daniel was surprised at her reaction.

Chris started squirming when he saw the stable hand leading a white horse from the stable.

"Down, Unc'l Dan'l. Let me down."

Daniel lowered the squirming toddler to the ground and laughed as Chris' legs began pumping before his feet hit the ground.

"Not too close, sweetie. We don't want you to get hurt." Veronica called as the stable hand stopped Chris from getting closer to the huge animal.

She turned to Daniel, eyebrows raised, and a question in her eyes.

"Did I see a woman's face at your bedroom window upstairs, darling?"

Bingo! That's why she was mad. She'd seen the artist upstairs. He hurried to explain. "It's the artist my father hired. Remember? It's an amazing coincidence that it's the same artist we met at the reception in the Landeville Gallery—the one who did the painting in my bedroom."

Fire flashed through Veronica's eyes before she could suppress the anger. "Yes, that is quite a coincidence."

She lowered her eyes and pulled him closer.

"She's not going to take too much of your time is she, Daniel? Because you know we're in the middle of planning our wedding. I don't see why you can't wait until after the honeymoon to have your portrait done. Why don't you suggest she come back in about a month?"

Daniel blew out a troubled breath. "This is my dad's doing, Veronica. After the first session, I won't have to see her at all until she's done. It won't hinder our plans. I promise."

Veronica laid her head on his shoulder and glanced up. "I've missed you while you were gone this week, darling. I hated for you to go to an old auction without me. Being apart is unacceptable this close to the wedding. Your dad said you had a touch of food poisoning. Are you feeling better?"

Daniel looked into her green eyes and smiled. "Yes, definitely back to normal."

Veronica pursed her tiny lips and looked at him through her dark painted lashes. "Will she be staying here at the house?"

"Who? Oh, the artist. Yes. My dad fixed up a studio suite, remember?"

Veronica stepped away as Daniel turned toward her father inspecting the white horse Max had brought out of the stable. She murmured something under her breath that sounded like "I bet he did."

Daniel looked at her with a question in his eyes. "What's gotten into you lately? It's not like you to be so cross."

Veronica didn't answer but lowered her eyes as Mr. Duke turned toward them. Daniel held out his hand.

"Hello, Mr. Duke. It's good to see you again, sir."

His tall neighbor reached over and shook Daniel's hand enthusiastically. "Hello, Daniel, my boy. I came by to see the new mares you brought in this week. This one looks promising."

Tension tightened Daniel's features, and he bristled at the envy he saw in the steel gray eyes. He knew there might be hard feelings after he'd won the bid for the lot of breeding mares belonging to a famous horse breeder in California. Shane had put in a bid for the same horses, but his bid had fallen short. Daniel searched Shane's eyes for a sign of anger but saw none.

"Sure. Most of them are in the stable still getting accustomed to their new home. Come on and I'll show you." He led the way as Veronica forced a laugh and linked her arm in Daniel's.

Shane strode beside them until they stepped inside the barn and let their eyes focus in the dim light. Shane stepped over to one of the stalls and checked out the filly inside. Then he walked down the wide aisle, inspecting each mare.

"They really look good, son. I can tell they have good marketable bloodlines." Shane's voice almost sounded defeated. He walked into the stall with a buckskin mare and ran his hands over her carefully. "This one might give you some trouble. I saw her history sheet, and she hasn't performed as well as the others. You never know, though; sometimes a horse with limited abilities will produce a foal of much better quality."

Daniel propped his legs on the bottom rung of the wooden railing and looped his arms over the top of the stall. Shane was giving the mare a thorough evaluation—almost as if he were thinking about a purchase.

Veronica tugged on Daniel's arm and pulled him into the large storage closet that housed saddles, bridles, and blankets hanging on the walls. She wrapped her arms around his neck and pulled his head close. After a sweet lingering kiss, she looked into his eyes.

"Daniel, wouldn't you like to move up the wedding three weeks? We could get married this weekend instead. I'll even give up the hand-picked white orchids for my wedding flower if you'll say yes." She leaned in toward him and whispered "Please?" with lips that parted slightly.

"What?" Daniel was shocked. After all the preparations Veronica had insisted on handling herself, he couldn't believe she wanted to throw it all away just for the sake of three weeks.

"I know, darling, I've worked so hard to make the wedding a success, but I just can't wait to become Mrs. Daniel Rushing. And, think of Chris—he adores you. It would make him so happy to have a daddy that much sooner."

Daniel shook his head. "No. I don't think that's a good idea. There are many more things to consider than the type of flower you've picked. What about the horse auction next week? I have several mares ready for sale, and next week's auction will bring the best price."

Veronica's shoulders fell. "Oh, Daniel. Which is more important? Selling a few horses for a tiny bit of extra money, or the happiness of your fiancée and her brother?"

A hand was closing around his throat. What was he supposed to say? He had the wedding jitters, and it was still three weeks away.

"I don't know, Nikki . . . I mean, Veronica. In order for things to run smoothly, I think we need to keep things as they are." He flashed her a placating smile. "You know how I am—live by the book and plan everything."

Veronica's lips pushed out in a flirty pout. "Okay, darling, but promise me you'll think about it, anyway?"

Daniel frowned. "I don't think I'll change my mind. Just keep on planning the wedding, and before you know it, it'll be here."

TWENTY-SIX

Later that afternoon, Gerald sat in the recliner watching the local news channel when Parker entered the room.

"Mr. Rushing, there's a woman named Amber Pike in the living room. She says she's an insurance investigator, and she'd like to talk to you about the accident, sir."

"The accident? What accident?"

Parker didn't answer—just raised his eyebrows and looked at his employer.

Gerald sighed and peeled himself out of the chair. "All right, Parker, I'll talk to her in here. Show her the way, will you?"

Parker nodded and left the room.

Gerald took a minute to stare out the window at the clouds rolling overhead. Why would an insurance investigator be checking into his daughter's accident? That had all been settled long ago.

When the investigator entered the room, she clutched a briefcase in one hand and a Providence Insurance bag in the other. Tall and thin with jet black hair pulled up high in a bun, the young woman looked like she stepped off the page of a fashion magazine. Her suit was tailored and well-pressed, and the shine on her black high-heeled shoes would make a sailor proud. She glanced around the room before walking over to Gerald and offering him a firm handshake as she introduced herself.

Gerald nodded and motioned toward the chair across from him as he seated himself. "Please sit down, Ms. Pike. What can I do for you?"

"Please call me Amber, sir. May I call you Gerald?"

When Gerald nodded, she sat down on the edge of the chair, opened her briefcase, and pulled out a yellow pad and a green pen with Providence Insurance stamped on the side. Leaning back in the chair, she studied Gerald for an uncomfortable moment.

"Gerald, I have some information I'd like to share with you eventually, but first I'd like to ask you some questions about the accident that claimed the life of your daughter and son-in-law."

Gerald's insides felt shaky. "What is this about, Amber? I thought all this was covered three years ago, and the case was closed."

"No, not exactly. The case was filed, but not closed. Something came to my attention recently, and I've re-examined the case."

Gerald's eyes narrowed. "Look, that was a horrible time in all of our lives. I don't have any desire to revisit any of those memories. What do you mean, something new came to your attention?"

"We had some new information come to light that forced me to do more investigating and have the sheriff's office run more tests on some of the materials gathered at the accident sight."

"What kind of information?"

Amber leaned forward and stared at Gerald as if she were interested in every move. "The officer working the accident understood that your daughter-in-law—" she looked down at the paper—"Martha Rushing, was the person driving the car. Is that correct?"

"We call her Marti now, but yes, that's what our neighbor, Mary Duke, told the police. She was the first one on the scene. She delivered my grandson. Unfortunately . . . he . . . didn't make it."

"Yes, that's what the report said." Amber tapped her finger on the briefcase cover.

Gerald could stand the mystery no longer. "Look, ma'am, if you have new information—"

Ignoring Gerald's outburst, Amber interrupted. "Mrs. Duke said Mrs. Rushing was driving but was thrown out of the car when the car turned over. Is that correct, sir?"

Frustration made his eyes burn, but Gerald answered the question. "Yes. Mary said when she arrived, Marti was lying on the driver's side of the car, about ten feet from the vehicle."

"*Hmm.* What about seat belts? Do you remember if Mrs. Rushing mentioned wearing a seat belt?"

"No. Honestly, Amber, I never spoke to Marti. She was in intensive care and wasn't allowed visitors. My daughter was in critical condition, and I was with her. I didn't even see Marti again until she came home from the hospital. By that time, my daughter was dead, and—"

"Yes, I understand, Gerald, but I was told Mary came straight to you first when you arrived at the hospital. I was hoping she might have mentioned the seat belts."

"She just told me that Marti had been driving—that she was thrown out when the car flipped over and came to rest upside down. Mary didn't stay at the hospital long. She was upset about the baby. When Mary arrived at the accident scene, Marti was in labor. Since Mary's a nurse, she delivered the baby before the ambulance got there. The storm had washed the bridge out, and the ambulance had to go all the way around by Martinsville."

Amber's eyes lit up. "So Martha was thrown out of the car, and yet the seat belt—"

"Look, ma'am, what's all this about?"

Amber stood to her feet. "I'm sorry, sir. I'm not at liberty to disclose information at this time. However, I'll be contacting you again. Thank you for your time." She leaned over and held out her hand to Gerald.

Gerald's surprise weakened his handshake, and he stood in awe as the woman left the room. What in the world was all that about? What information could she possibly have uncovered to make her re-open the case?

TWENTY-SEVEN

Stella Washington hummed quietly in the Rushing kitchen. She loved her job of twenty years. Feeding the Rushing family and their hardworking hands was a satisfying challenge. Now that Marti was back, there was hope singing in her heart.

Her hand curled around the potholder and pulled the oven door open. She poked the roast beef with a fork and turned down the temperature. Almost done. The vegetables were cooked and simmering on the stove, and all she had to do was toss the salads. She had plenty of time to make a dessert.

She pulled out her recipe file and flipped to the dessert tab.

"Let's see. What looks good?"

"Talking to yourself again?"

Stella smiled at the humor in Marti's voice. "You know what they say, young lady. You talk to yourself when you want intelligent conversation."

Marti laughed out loud. "Oh Stella, I've missed you." She moved toward Stella.

Stella laid down the recipe file she was holding and turned around to give Marti a big bear hug. Stella was shocked at the emotion that one little hug stirred in her heart. She squeezed extra hard and was shocked at what she felt. The poor little thing needed more fat on her bones. Tears threatened to form, but she cleared her throat instead and thrust some force behind her words.

"My word, child. You need to eat a lot more of my cooking. If you get any thinner, you'll have to rent a shadow."

Marti laughed. "I hate to cook for just me, Stella. And, I never was the best cook in the world."

Stella pulled out a four by six card from her file and waved it in front of Marti. "Well, we're going to fix that . . . starting right now. I'm going to teach you how to make your favorite dessert. You go to the fridge and pull out those fresh peaches I've been saving. We're about to make a peach cobbler."

"Really? Do you mind? I've longed for your peach cobbler so many times I can't even count them."

"It'd be a pleasure, child. Now you get the peaches, and bring the milk and two sticks of butter too."

Stella pulled canisters of self-rising flour and sugar out of the cabinet and grabbed a fifteen by ten inch casserole dish from the cabinet beside the stove. Then she opened two sticks of butter and laid them in the bottom of the glass pan and stuck it in the oven, right under the roast beef.

Stella pulled two paring knives from the drawer and handed one to Marti. "Let's get the peaches peeled while the butter's melting, then we'll be ready to mix everything together. We need about six cups."

They sat down on the tall stools behind the bar that divided the kitchen and placed the peeled peaches in a large bowl. Marti worked with her head ducked down, concentrating on peeling with as little peach wasted as possible.

Nostalgia prompted Stella's musing. "Remember how you used to visit with me in the kitchen on rainy days?"

Marti looked up from peeling and smiled. "Yeah, and you always pretended I was in the way."

"Well, you weren't. As a matter of fact, that's what I missed more than anything when you left."

Sadness rounded Marti's eyes, and they filled with tears.

"I'm sorry, hon. I didn't mean to make you cry. I just wanted you to know how much I missed your sweet face around here."

Marti nodded and smiled through her tears. "Thanks, Stella. That means a lot."

When all of the peaches were peeled, Stella told Marti, "Now we need to cut the peaches into thin slices. Then I'll let you mix everything together."

They worked together for a couple more minutes, and finally, Stella pushed the rest of the ingredients toward Marti.

"First, you mix the flour, sugar, milk, and peaches together, and then pour it all into the melted butter. This is the simplest recipe you'll ever find, but since we're cookin' for a passel of folks today, we have to make more than usual. Remember that if you ever decide to cook it just for yourself. Today, we're gonna double the recipe. Mix two cups each of flour, sugar, and milk into this big bowl."

Marti measured out two cups of each ingredient and stirred it together with a wire whisk.

"Do you have to use fresh peaches?"

"Oh no, you can use canned peaches if you like, but they're not quite as fresh. Make sure, if you buy fresh peaches, you get ones that are good and ripe. If they're hard, they won't cook soft enough or have enough juice to make that wonderful flavor."

She watched as Marti mixed the ingredients together.

"Now we just pour the peaches into the sugar mixture and stir it all up."

Stella pulled the pan of melted butter out of the oven, set it on the counter, and watched as Marti poured the peach and sugar mixture into the middle of the butter. "Now, take a spoon and sort of scoop some of the butter in the corners of the pan up onto the middle of the peach mixture."

When they were done, Stella took the roast beef out of the oven, and put the cobbler on the top rack. "Now we'll let it cook for an hour—on three hundred and fifty degrees."

"Wow, that was easy. I wish I'd let you teach me how to cook years ago. Who knows? I could be a famous chef by now."

They both laughed.

Stella heard a strangled *"humph"* from the doorway, and she turned to see Anita standing inside the door.

"Come on in, Anita. Did you need something?"

Anita turned a wary look in Marti's direction and walked over to the cabinet beside the refrigerator. "I just came to get my iron tablets."

Marti seemed to shrink in the seat, and it irritated Stella that Anita acted so ugly. "Anita, would you like to stay and help us set out the good china for supper?"

Marti looked up—surprised. Stella winked.

"Uh, no, thank you. Parker and I have work to do." Anita's emphasis on the word *work* made it clear she thought they were socializing instead of getting supper on the table. "Besides, I don't think Mr. Gerald would appreciate using the good china without a special occasion." She gave Marti a snide look that roamed from her head to her toes.

Marti turned her head and looked out the window.

Stella gave Anita a reproving look. "We do have a special occasion—Marti's visiting."

"I hardly think a *visit* from Marti is something the whole family thinks is a special occasion. Besides, I happen to know that Veronica will also be here tonight. How do you think Mr. Daniel's fiancée will like having his ex-wife here in the same house?"

"Anita!" Stella voice held a touch of censure.

"I'm just saying—Mr. Rushing invited her here, not Daniel. And I don't think Daniel will be at all happy when he finds out who she really is. If I hadn't been ordered by Mr. Gerald not to say anything, I'd have told him already."

She huffed out of the room, and Stella saw the stricken look on Marti's face. "Don't you mind her, child. She's always in a snippy mood lately. Now come on and let's get that china out of the hutch. Tonight we're going to celebrate."

"That's okay, Stella. I think I'll just have supper in my room tonight, like I did last night. It would be better all around." She put her hand on Stella's arm and looked her straight in the eyes. "But, thank you for teaching me how to make the cobbler. I'm going straight upstairs and writing down the recipe. I hope mine tastes half as good as yours when I get up enough nerve to try it."

Marti smiled, but the glow was gone from her eyes. Stella knew why Marti was here, and she was hoping with everything inside her that Mr. Gerald's plan worked. But from the stricken look on Marti's face, Stella could tell Marti had no hope whatsoever.

TWENTY-EIGHT

The next morning Marti checked her image once more in the mirror beside the door and smoothed her powder blue, sleeveless top. The soft collar angled gently to end at the tan buttons down the front of her blouse, and the waistline of the blouse fell just above the identical blue buttons on the pockets of her khaki capris.

She tugged at the band on the capris and adjusted the seams. It was a little big, but it had a special meaning and was perfect for the situation. Daniel gave her this outfit on her twenty-third birthday—the year she left the house. He said he'd searched for the perfect color to match her eyes. It was the best birthday of her entire life. He took her horseback riding to the waterfalls at the back of the property joining the mountain range, and they enjoyed a wonderful day—picking flowers, eating the picnic lunch Stella prepared, and bass fishing in the ten-acre pond.

She sighed. "Maybe, just maybe, this outfit will stir up some of those memories."

Pushing the soft auburn curls behind her ears, she applied extra concealer to the dark circles under her eyes and took a deep calming breath.

"May as well start the day," she said as she headed out her bedroom door and into the light and airy studio.

A few butterflies fluttered in the pit of her stomach as they always did when she contemplated starting a new portrait commission. On one hand, she was itching to get started, but on the other, this portrait would be harder than all the rest.

This was Daniel she'd be painting.

The butterflies became bats, and she clutched her stomach when Daniel's big brown eyes came to mind. The details of this painting would affect her like none she'd ever done.

She walked over to the tall double-paned windows and begged the blue mountains to calm her heart. The sun's rays filtering through the pines vibrated on the red tin of the gambrel stable roof and mocked the peace she was searching for. She turned to the floor-length mirror hanging on one side of the tall windows and noticed the pallor of her skin.

"This not sleeping for a week is for the birds, and it's murder on the makeup." Her nervous laugh frightened even herself. "What am I doing here? This is crazy!" she whispered. "Hashtag: ludicrous."

"Talking to yourself?" Daniel's voice boomed behind her.

Marti jumped and turned. "Oh, you scared me."

Daniel laughed. "I have a habit of doing that, it seems. Did I hear you say something about a hashtag? Do you tweet?"

She grimaced. "I write tweets for the gallery in Landeville. My boss got me started."

Daniel smiled. "I've heard it's good business practice for retailers."

Marti shrugged. "It keeps your name out there."

Daniel smiled. "So, are you ready to do this thing?"

"The portrait, you mean?"

He nodded.

"As ready as I'll ever be . . . I mean, I'm always ready to start a new painting."

"How about we eat before we get started? I heard Stella's making pancakes this morning." His smile transformed the whole room into a ray of light.

"I can see pancakes are your favorite."

"Stella can make cardboard taste good."

She laughed, but her body felt as tight as a drum. Forcing her muscles to relax, she nodded.

He glanced at her attire and turned back toward the hall without making a comment. The hope that he'd recognize the matching outfit vanished into thin air like fog on the mountain when the sun pops out from behind the clouds. Her heart took a tumble but slowly rejuvenated. She hadn't lost the war, only one battle.

He must have noticed her silence because he said, "If you don't like pancakes, you could probably get her to whip up about anything that suits your fancy. I don't know of one thing Stella can't cook."

The smile still clung to his features, and she couldn't help smiling back. "Pancakes are fine, but I'm hoping she'll make triple chocolate gravy and biscuits sometime while I'm here."

Daniel stopped dead in his tracks and turned to her. "What did you say?"

Marti gulped. Should she have mentioned the chocolate gravy and biscuits? It was something Daniel had taught her to love.

"I said I love triple chocolate gravy and biscuits. You know . . . chocolate sauce made into good, thick gravy and poured over hot buttered biscuits. Mmm . . . Hashtag: delectable. The best breakfast in the world—and one of the most fattening too—even if you do eat it with fruit." Her nervous laughter filled the hallway.

Daniel's eyes sought hers and crinkled. "You know, I didn't know anyone else but my family even knew about that recipe. Stella started making it when I was very small. I thought it was one of her own concoctions. Who introduced it to you?"

Marti looked at him out the corner of her eyes. "Uh . . . my ex-husband used to eat it when he was growing up."

Daniel stopped and looked at her. "You were married before?"

She nodded silently, not looking at him.

Daniel stood perfectly still. "I was married before too, but she's been gone three years now." He shrugged. "I can't remember her at all. Of course, that's not saying much." He grinned. "I can't remember anything else either." He raised his arm and motioned toward the kitchen door, indicating she should enter through the open archway.

"Watch out for the wheelchair. My dad bought it for one of the neighbors down the road, I think."

A smile formed inside Marti. She'd thought it was for Daniel.

Daniel led her into the kitchen where she'd spent time with Stella the day before making peach cobbler. She stood just inside the door, noting some of the changes in the room she'd overlooked while cooking the night before.

Everything in the room had been modernized and expanded. State-of-the-art, stainless steel appliances formed a comfortable, triangular work space. And, how had she missed the cute little breakfast nook hiding over in the corner? Pastel blue curtains stretched across the top of the airy space, and comfortable cushions covered a café-style bench seat and several matching chairs.

Stretched out on the bench seat was a white and chocolate colored Snowshoe cat. When Marti walked by the table, the cat scrambled up with a loud meow and launched herself into Marti's arms.

"Princess!" Marti buried her chin into the cat's neck and rubbed the soft fur. Musical purring filled the room as the cat rubbed her head against Marti's neck and curled into the crook of her arm, squirming for more attention.

Daniel stopped, stunned. "How odd. She hates strangers. Sometimes she hibernates for days when we have company, and usually she growls or hisses when anyone gets close. She only barely tolerates me touching her." He paused. "Did I hear you call her *Princess*? How do you know her name?"

Too late once again, Marti realized her mistake. "I've seen her before," she answered truthfully.

Daniel shrugged, obviously satisfied she'd been introduced to the cat when she arrived and the cat had taken a liking to the visiting artist. "That's amazing. She must sense you like animals."

Daniel motioned to a breakfast bar loaded down with pancakes, syrup, muffins, and several different kinds of fruit. "Go ahead and fix yourself a plate. I'll get us some coffee."

Marti washed her hands in the kitchen sink and picked up a plate from the breakfast bar. As she began filling it with homemade pancakes, she watched Daniel fill two cups with coffee before he picked up the sugar spoon. She inhaled sharply when he dumped two scoops of sugar in one cup and enough cream to make the coffee white.

He remembered how she liked her coffee? Would this be the moment he remembered everything else?

Daniel remembering that tidbit from their past had both panic and elation battling inside her. She sat down at the table and waited for him to bring the coffee, barely breathing as she stared at him.

When he turned toward the table, a sudden look of bewilderment filled his eyes, and he looked in a daze down at the cups in his hand.

"What in the world?" he murmured.

Marti held her breath and tried not to move when he looked toward her.

"Did you tell me how you like your coffee?"

Marti's throat was dry so she just shook her head.

"That's weird. For some reason . . ." Daniel sat the coffee down in front of her and looked deep into her eyes. "Are you sure we've never met before?"

Daniel gawked at her—waiting for an answer. She could only stare, hypnotized by the yearning in his eyes. When the cat jumped in her lap for more attention, Marti looked away. She put the cat down, picked up the cup of coffee, and touched it to her lips. "This is perfect. Just the way I like it."

He shook his head. "I don't understand . . ."

Marti looked at him out of the corner of her eyes and grinned. "Hashtag: weird."

He laughed and filled his plate before he joined her. "I must be clairvoyant."

Gerald walked into the room and plopped a black leather-bound Bible on the table. The gleam in his eyes was proof he'd heard their conversation. Picking up a plate at the breakfast bar, he began stabbing pancakes with the fork. The smile he gave Marti was a little like the cat who swallowed the canary—a bit too jubilant. He looked at Daniel as he poured honey on top of his pancakes. "I talked to Max this morning, and he said Abigail's about ready to be exercised. She's probably well enough for a good run. Maybe Marti would like to take her out for a ride." He glanced at Marti and winked.

Daniel looked at Marti with a question in his eyes. "Do you ride, Marti?"

Marti nodded and glanced at Gerald. "I used to ride quite a bit, but I haven't in a while."

Daniel nodded. "Okay. Maybe tomorrow when you get tired of working in the studio, you can come down to the stable and we'll get you fixed up."

Gerald suddenly seemed excited. "That sounds like a great idea, Marti. You should get Daniel to show you the waterfall on the west forty acres. It's a good place to gather inspiration." His smile held worlds of meaning.

She didn't answer but ducked her head. Things were spiraling completely out of her comfort zone. How in the world did she get herself into such a mess?

TWENTY-NINE

Zach Parsons sat on an old stump behind the Rushing barn and took a puff. Smoke curled above his blond hair and disappeared into the tree branches overhead. If he could stay hidden for a few more minutes, Max wouldn't know he'd been gone. The stable manager was a stickler for not goofing off. Even though it wasn't time for a break, Zach had to have a smoke. He'd been smoking since high school, and after ten years, smoking was as much a part of his life as breathing. Cigarettes would probably kill him one day, but right now, they sure did scratch an itch.

He took another puff, laid the cigarette on the edge of the stump beside his set of work keys, and pulled out his new pocket knife.

Max had assigned him another job on top of his daily chores. Anger bubbled up inside of him when he thought about the "easy" job the stable manager wanted done. Max obviously thought his day wasn't complete unless he assigned Zach an added chore—as if he thought Zach's day wasn't long enough.

According to Max, one of the halters Daniel used in training was too large for the smallest of the colts. He was supposed to punch another hole in the leather to make it smaller. It was just his luck he'd lost the leather punch the day before.

He opened his new Victorinox knife and searched for the right tool. The knife was a new toy. It had thirty different tools attached—anything from a blade to a pair of scissors—and the shiny red handle had a gold and yellow flame embossed on the side.

He pulled out the reamer tool and pushed the tip through the leather. Once the tip poked through on the other side, he gave it several twists until the hole opened up and enlarged to the right size.

He twisted the knife out of the oiled leather and stuck the knife blade into the old stump. The prong of the halter buckle slipped into the hole he'd made and held tight. Perfect. Maybe this would get Max off his back.

He picked up the cigarette and took another puff, then glanced around the edge of the barn to see if Max had missed him yet. He didn't see Max, but he did see a tall man walking over from the house garage.

He'd recognize that walk anywhere. Jordan Welsh. Vinny's father. Years ago, Vinny drove a car in the NASCAR circuit, and Zach had been one of his on-the-road truck drivers. Jordan hung around the track making his son miserable—and everyone else as well—until Vinny made him leave. Sympathy surged through Zach for the way Vinny had publicly evicted his father. No one deserved to be humiliated in such a public way.

Zach stubbed out the cigarette in the dirt and rounded the corner of the barn where he stood with hands thrust in his pockets. When Jordan saw Zach hovering around the barn, he walked toward him.

"Zach, what are you doin' here?"

"Workin'."

"I can see. I guess you gave up following the circuit around and found a job you could handle."

Zach bristled for a second. "I did okay working for Vince at NASCAR. Better than some."

It was Jordan's turn to bristle. Zach's jab hit home. Vinny had thrown his father out of the pit before the last race of Vinny's racing career. Jordan had been livid. Vinny yelled at the top of his lungs, "We only need one boss around here, and I'm him. Now, get out!"

There was bad blood between father and son back then—that's for sure.

Jordan swallowed hard and took two steps toward the barn. He eyed the stump and halter but didn't comment. "That's all in the past. I hear you used to work for Vinny and Angela on the other side of the county."

Zach nodded. "Yeah. So?"

"I heard you worked there breaking green horses."

"Yep. Moved everything I owned from California to Texas and broke every horse they brought me for a year, till Vinny died."

Jordan gave him a pointed stare. Turning back toward the mountains, he said, "Are you interested in doing that kind of work again?" Jordan didn't look at Zach but waited for Zach to speak.

"Are you offering?"

"Maybe. If you're interested. I need someone to break new colts. I figure . . . you might be the one to talk to. I hear Rushing also has a successful way of training show horses. Figured you've learned his technique while you've been working here."

Zach's surprise bled into his voice. "Maybe."

"How long you been here?"

"Long enough. You come offering me a job, or did you come for somethin' else?"

Jordan crossed his arms and looked around the yard. "I thought I'd mention the job, but I also came looking for Gerald."

"Not home."

"What about Daniel?"

"Not home either."

"When will they be back?"

"Don't know."

Jordan stared at Zach, waiting for him to say more. When he didn't, he said, "Think about what I said. Let me know if you're interested." He pulled a card from his pocket. "My number's on the card."

Zach took the card and stuck it in his back pocket.

Jordan leaned over the stump and looked at the keys and halter spread out on the stump.

"What's this?"

Zach jerked up the halter. "Haven't you seen a halter before?"

Jordan stiffened his back. "Of course. I just wondered what you're doing with it." When Zach didn't comment, Jordan leaned into his personal space. "I want to talk to Gerald or Daniel. I'm running the Welsh ranch now, and I'd like to find out how they handle certain things on the farm, that's all. Will you tell them I stopped by?"

Zach nodded and pulled on the halter to loosen the hole in the leather a bit more. He tried to ignore the man still standing beside him.

"That's a sharp looking knife you have there." Jordan picked up the Swiss army knife and turned it around in his hand.

Zach took the knife from Jordan and pulled out all the attachments. "Yep. It's a beaut. It has almost any tool you could ask for, and it cost a pretty penny too." Pride filled his voice as he rotated the knife in front of Jordan.

Jordan nodded. "Not exactly what I'd use to poke holes in leather. Don't you have a hole punch?"

Zach closed up the attachments in a few short movements and stuck it back in the stump. "Yep, I'll tell the boss you came by to see him."

Jordan took two steps toward the front of the building. "Would it be all right if I took a look around the barn?"

Zach shrugged. "Reckon it'd be all right. I'll see if Max can show you around." Zach took the halter with him as he stepped into the office. Max was nowhere to be found, so he walked back to Jordan who was standing at the corner of the barn. "I'd better show you around. The boss don't like strangers 'round his horses."

Zach showed Jordan around the place. First, he took him into the training arena and explained how Daniel's training methods were done. He pretended he knew all the steps of training, and pride swelled his voice as he told Jordan he was Daniel's number one assistant.

After Zach showed him around the main areas of the barn, he said, "I better get back to my chores. It'll be dark before I'm done."

Jordan nodded. "Think about what I said, but don't think too long. I have to fill the position soon."

Zach watched Jordan walk away and bellowed out a laugh when the car drove away. Jordan bought his bragging about being a good trainer. He was a better actor than he thought. He grinned. Jordan thought he'd "learned something" while working here, and he'd only been here three months. That was a laugh. 'Bout all he'd been doing in that time was mucking out stalls. If he took that job, he'd have to learn all Daniel's tricks before he left. No sense in throwing in with Jordan if he didn't have an edge.

When Zach turned back toward the old stump, he noticed something shining in the grass. The leather hole punch. He must have dropped it there on one of his smoking breaks. He picked it up and punched through the halter. The hole was more rounded now. Perfect. After checking the halter to make sure the buckle worked perfectly, he went to find Max and show him the excellent job he'd done. Maybe it would earn him points with the boss, at least until he took the other job.

THIRTY

"Turn just a little to the left, toward the light."

Daniel's shoulders shifted toward the windows in the studio, and he raised his eyebrows, asking for guidance.

"Much better. Now just relax and try to stay in that position."

Daniel laughed. "That's an oxymoron, isn't it?"

Her tentative laugh sailed across the room. "Well . . . do your best, okay?"

She stood in front of the easel and tried to ignore Princess rubbing against her leg and filling the room with her purrs. Finally, the cat settled at the base of the easel and rested her head on Marti's foot.

Daniel watched the cat settle in and commented. "I can't believe how friendly that cat is with you. It's not in her character at all."

Marti said nothing but smiled. She picked up a blue-green pastel and began forming shapes of Daniel's face on the sanded pastel paper. After five minutes of uncomfortable silence, and watching his eyes observe her every move, Marti's hands began to sweat.

"You can talk if you like. It'll help you loosen up, and it won't affect my sketch enough to worry about."

"Oh . . . okay. Tell me something about your family."

Hashtag: NotAGoodIdea.

"Uh . . . I'd rather you do the talking so I can concentrate on my sketch. Why don't you tell me about your time in the army?"

Daniel frowned. "Well, I don't remember anything about the army, but I'll tell you about raising horses. I've been doing that for as long as I can remember."

"Okay. That sounds good."

As Daniel launched into the details of breeding, training, and selling prize-winning quarter horses, his eyes glowed with an excitement she used to love to see. Her heart plummeted to the bottom of her stomach. Bringing back those memories was physically painful and made her mouth go dry.

After sketching for twenty minutes, Marti's psyche had taken a beating, and she'd endured all the memories she could stand. She laid the rose madre pastel back in the wooden box and stood back to distance herself from Daniel and the fast growing likeness of him in front of her.

"Okay, let's take a short break."

She nodded her head as she stood evaluating her work. After brushing off the excess dust at the bottom of the paper, she held it up carefully for Daniel to see.

Daniel stood captivated, his eyes traveling over the square piece of paper.

"That's amazing. It must have taken you years to learn that skill."

Marti shook her head, gazing at the portrait to keep from looking at his eyes. "Actually, I've only been painting about two years." She put the picture back on the easel. "I think it's a God-given talent."

"Two years? You're kidding, aren't you?" He moved over beside her and looked over her shoulder at the loose sketch of his face. He leaned in toward her, examining the picture closely.

Marti felt heat travel to her face when he stepped closer—even before she felt the warmth of his arm next to hers. The musky smell of his aftershave sent a ripple of emotion shooting through her veins. Her knees, almost too weak to hold her up, locked into position. Turning her head slightly, she was so close that the image of him blurred. He turned closer toward her and looked into her eyes. The contemplation in his gaze quickly turned to . . . what? Recognition? Familiarity? Longing?

All she knew was that he stilled immediately, peered into her eyes until he found her soul, and held it prisoner. She couldn't move. Something inside her came to life, a longing so strong it consumed her and begged to be set free.

Marti saw the question in his eyes before they moved down to her lips. His hand moved to touch her face then stopped. "I feel a closeness to you, Marti. Are you sure . . ." He stopped in midsentence and moved his head a little closer. From the doorway, someone gasped.

"Daniel!"

Like a horrible reminder of something dead, Marti remembered why she was here.

Veronica.

Daniel jerked away from Marti and took a guilty step backward. He turned toward the angry head of red hair standing in the doorway.

"Veronica, come see the sketch Mar . . . uh . . . Ms. Rushing has done. It's amazing. A perfect likeness so far."

"Ms. Rushing!"

Princess let out a mournful wail and went flying into the bedroom and under the bed.

Furious was a mild word for the emotion Marti saw flash across Veronica's eyes. Livid was closer to the mark.

Veronica's eyes diminished to slits. Her lips thinned to tight small lines.

"Daniel, your father asked me to tell you they need you in the office downstairs. My father is there, and they want to discuss the auction next week."

Daniel glanced at Marti and spoke with an edge of annoyance. "I'll be back later to finish the session."

Marti nodded at him and began sorting her pastels into the proper sections of the box, trying to ignore the foot-tapping, arms-folded, fury-filled woman staring at her from the doorway.

"What do you think you are doing here?"

The first sentence out of Veronica's mouth was laced with a warning that sounded as deadly as strychnine.

Marti raised her chin. "I'm painting Daniel's portrait for Gerald."

Veronica glared at her, doubt filling her eyes and sarcasm lacing her words. "Sure you are."

Veronica took deliberate steps over to Marti and pushed herself into Marti's face. Her voice sounded red-hot—almost enough to sizzle the hair on Marti's forehead.

"Leave him alone, Martha. You had a chance to make him happy, and you blew it. Not only did you hurt Daniel by killing his sister, but you disgraced the whole family with your drunkenness and promiscuity. Don't think for a minute Daniel will ever take you back, even if he does remember your horrible excuse for a marriage."

Marti blanched white at the rage filling that one paragraph and the insecurity Veronica's words thrust through her heart. The air seemed to seep from her like a balloon with the tiniest of holes, but she summoned one last burst of anger.

Through gritted teeth, she said, "My name is *Marti*, and it's none of your business what happens between Daniel and me."

After that fiery statement and before her legs became so weak she couldn't stand, she walked out of the room and into her bedroom, slamming the door behind her. Slumping against the door she bit her bottom lip, trying to hold back the tears that formed in spite of her attempt to keep them at bay.

Remind yourself why you're here, Marti, even if this is crazy.

Veronica would do anything to keep Daniel, even lie if necessary, and there would be nothing Marti could do about it. In spite of all Marti's attempts to make Daniel remember what real love felt like, Veronica might still become his wife. And that filled Marti with a sadness so strong it sucked the life right out of her heart.

THIRTY-ONE

Veronica paced across the stone pathway outside the Rushing ranch, waiting for her father. Anger festered inside her. How dare *Marti* waltz back into Daniel's home and pretend she was here to paint a portrait! *Marti* couldn't even paint—much less a portrait. She was here to cause trouble.

She furiously patted her foot on the sienna stones. "Marti—indeed!"

No matter what she thought of Marti's name change, Marti being here would definitely complicate things. She might even make Daniel think twice about his engagement. She would put doubts in Daniel's head and confuse him about who could truly make him happy.

Daniel belongs to me!

Veronica squeezed her fists and stared at the second story window where she'd seen Marti flirting with Daniel. Fury and fear built inside her until she gave in to the desire for retaliation. What could she do that would hurt the most? Make Marti look inept in front of Daniel? Tell Daniel who Marti really was? That would make him boil. She had exaggerated Marti's character flaws enough that Daniel would be furious when he found out Gerald let Marti slip back into his life.

But . . . telling Daniel that Marti was his wife might blow up in her face.

Daniel already felt a physical pull toward Marti—Veronica felt a chill as she remembered the look in his eyes. When Veronica walked into the studio, their faces had been only inches apart. Marti was batting her eyes at Daniel—pretending to be so shy and feminine—and Daniel was confused, that's all. If Veronica told Daniel who Marti was, he might decide to forgive Marti and give her a second chance. She couldn't let that happen. After all, she would make Daniel happier than Marti ever had, wouldn't she? She was beautiful, a much better horsewoman, and from a wealthy ranching family—an excellent catch in most people's eyes, though she had to admit those qualities hadn't drawn Daniel to her before Marti came along. Marti—a nobody with no family and no future. What had he seen in her?

Veronica shook the memories from her head and focused on the present. Daniel hated confrontation. He wouldn't like it if she acted vindictive by telling him who Marti really was. That would push him away even further. She'd have to act without exposing Marti, but Marti definitely had to be taken care of.

The side door opened, and she turned to see her father walking out the door with Gerald. Daniel followed closely behind. Daniel came over to the truck and grabbed her hand. His face seemed a little pale.

"Veronica, why are you leaving? I thought we were going riding."

A debate went on inside her—should she show him that she was peeved? Or should she act as if jealousy was the last thing on her mind? She decided on the former.

She pasted a little pout on her lips and looked at him through her lashes. "I guess I was a little jealous, darling. It made me feel terribly uncomfortable to see you standing so close to that artist—especially since you know how it feels to have someone be unfaithful."

Daniel's eyes flashed a bright brown. "What do you mean?"

"I felt a little like you probably felt when you heard your wife had been flirting with another man."

Daniel dropped her hands and backed up. He didn't say a word, but Veronica could see the conflict going on in his eyes. Had she chosen the right course of action?

Finally, he spoke. "Nikki, I was just looking over her shoulder at the picture she had drawn with her pastels, that's all. I didn't stand beside her for any other reason. I was looking at the picture."

"Well, how would you have felt if you had found me standing that close to a tall, handsome cowboy? Wouldn't you have been just a little bit jealous?"

Daniel seemed to consider that scenario. He shook his head. "Nikki, I think trust is unarguably the most important thing in a relationship. Didn't I learn that from the mistakes of my first marriage? If I trusted you, it wouldn't make any difference, but I admit, I can see how it might have made you feel a little uncomfortable."

A shiver of uncertainty traveled through Veronica. Had she gone too far? Veronica shook her head. "Okay, darling. We'll let it drop. I do trust you, but I don't like that artist living in this house. Can't you get her a hotel room in town?"

Daniel's expression turned dark, and she decided changing the subject was the best course of action. Insisting on moving Marti to a hotel only accentuated her lack of trust. It was *Marti* she didn't trust, but she didn't want Daniel to think it was him. At least this conversation might give him something to think about.

"Look, darling. It's getting late. Why don't we reschedule our ride for tomorrow?" She kissed him on the lips and gave him a hug. "I love you, Daniel. You know that, don't you?"

Daniel nodded but kept silent.

"I'll be by tomorrow for our ride."

Daniel nodded. "I'll see you then."

Disappointed that he didn't assure her of his love, Veronica stepped past their fathers and climbed into her father's truck to gaze unseeing toward the pasture.

Daniel shook hands with Shane when he approached the driver's door. Shane got in behind the wheel and spoke through the open window to Gerald.

"I'll call the auctioneer next week, Gerald, and see if he'd like to stay at the house. This is the first auction we've had in our county. We want to make a good impression."

Gerald nodded. "I think we'll get one hundred percent participation from the adjoining counties, and I know the Quarter Horse Association is on board. If we keep up our end of the bargain, I think we can be assured of future events being held in our county. I'm glad the path of that doggone wildfire has turned away from the town. Hopefully, they'll have it out soon."

Veronica sat biting her lip. She wanted Daniel to feel her aloofness, but at the same time, she didn't want to make him angry. She wanted to leave him missing her. As her father cranked the truck and pulled away from the curb, she leaned toward the window, smiled, and blew Daniel a kiss. He waved and smiled.

Yes! That was perfect. He loved her. She could tell by that grin on his face. Now maybe he'd think twice about how he acted when hanging around Ms. Portrait Artist.

Veronica sat up straight in the seat and blew out a frustrated breath. She was getting a headache.

"Why are you in such a bad mood, sugar? Didn't you enjoy your visit with Daniel?"

"Ha! What visit?" Veronica tugged on a lock of her red hair and looped it behind her ear. "Martha was there and completely monopolized Daniel. You should have seen her, Daddy. When I went upstairs to get him, Martha was leaning over toward him—laughing and flirting. It was disgusting, especially after the way she ruined his life the first time."

Shane's nostril's flared. "What did he say when he saw you?"

"Oh, he acted like he'd been caught with his hand in the cookie jar. He was contrite and embarrassed. But Martha acted purely smug. If she thinks she's going to win Daniel back from me this time, she's got another thing coming. I won't let it happen. He loves me. I can see it in his eyes. Martha humiliated him when she had him, and I won't let her at him again."

Shane pulled the truck into their driveway and stopped. He turned toward her. "Be careful, darlin'. You might not want to admit it, but Daniel loved Martha once. Just because she did something to turn him away doesn't mean all those feelings he felt for her completely dried up. At this point in time, he can't even remember the pain he felt over what she did, so the anger he feels now won't be as strong as it was when it happened. He might be angry at what she did, but if you push too hard, I'm afraid he might decide to give those loving feelings a second chance. And we certainly don't want that to happen."

"So, do you think I should tell him who she is . . . or was?"

"No, I don't think so." He leaned over and gave her a hug. "Just be your sweet self and win him over that way instead of by making Martha look bad. You attract more flies with sugar than with vinegar."

Veronica glowered at her father. "Oh Daddy. Honestly. Vinegar?"

Shane smiled, put the truck in gear, and drove down the long driveway.

Veronica lounged back in the seat. No way was she going to leave everything to chance. She had to show Daniel how much he loved her. Maybe she'd ask him to take her on a trip to the rodeo in the next county for the weekend. He seemed to be at ease and happier when he was at an event that included horses.

The smile on her face grew wider. She'd keep Daniel away from Marti. Veronica knew Daniel loved her. He just needed to get away from Marti's devious strategies. All she had to do was keep them apart, and she had a perfect idea how.

Marti had crossed a line—something Marti would be sorry for. Veronica would have to take matters back into her own hands. Yep, she knew exactly what to do.

THIRTY-TWO

Marti's subconscious screamed at her to wake up. She struggled out of sleep and tried to put a finger on what was causing her unrest. The room was as black as the deepest section of woods at night and just as scary.

A muffled noise came from somewhere close.

Her eyes, heavy with sleep, struggled to see through the darkness. She sat up in bed and searched her bedroom. A tiny sliver of moonlight shimmered through the opening of the sheer curtains enough for her to see that everything was quiet and peaceful. She must have been dreaming.

She turned over in bed and tried to relax. A muscle in her neck tensed, as if waiting for something to happen.

Another noise.

She turned toward the window again and stared at the place the sound came from. The ray of moonlight coming in the window was broken by a shadowed movement as it moved closer to the bed.

Marti jerked up in bed and screamed as a figure in black rushed toward her. Her screams vibrated through her skull, until they were silenced by a hand clamped over her mouth. She kicked at the covers and pulled at the leather glove keeping her from breathing.

The hand dropped from her mouth as one of her pillows replaced it and was pushed against her face. The power of the blow forced her back onto the bed with bone shaking fierceness and mashed her body into the mattress. Her arms thrashed about trying to defend herself against muscle and strength, and the bedside lamp tumbled to the floor with a loud crash. Her attacker threw himself on top of her, restraining her body under the covers. She kicked at him with frantic jerky movements and tried to escape the covers holding her captive on the bed.

Claustrophobia inched its way into her consciousness.

I can't breathe! I need air!

Marti's hands clawed at the person holding the pillow. The muscles under the material felt like steel. She tore at the pillow covering her face, trying to turn her head and escape the pressure on her nose and mouth. Her head was held in a vise. She felt the gloved hands clinch the corners of the pillow and press even harder. Her lungs cramped, begging for air. She felt the heat of her open mouth in the pillow as she tried to find oxygen to breathe.

God, please help me!

Her internal screams never escaped her throat but were joined by the uncontrollable spasms of her lungs fighting for air. Panic the size of mountains rose in her chest. Her heartbeat hammered in her ears.

She twisted to the side and for a second, the pressure on her body lessened. She coiled her legs up close and gave one kick with every bit of strength she had. The man on top of her was thrown off balance, and she heard him hit the floor.

She clawed at the pillow over her face, but before she could get out of bed, he was on top of her again. This time he showed no mercy. The blow hit her chest with a vengeance that forced the air from her lungs, and the pillow was mashed onto her face with extreme force.

Her arms, clawing at the man on top of her, became weak and ineffective. She tried to think how to get away, but her thoughts became jumbled as she struggled, weakened by lack of oxygen. Finally, strength seemed to ooze from her fingertips. Her hands curled into tight balls and stopped clawing at the pillow. Reality floated around her until finally it faded into the darkness.

THIRTY-THREE

Daniel's head felt heavy on his pillow as he lay in bed, trying to make his tired brain relax. Emotional turmoil was keeping him up at night. The face of the new artist materialized again before his eyes. Marti Rushing. How odd that they had the same last name. Something about Marti suggested warmth and comfort. She was easy to be with. Her cobalt eyes called to his like a shining beacon—drawing him toward something familiar.

He rolled over in bed and punched the pillow. He was exhausted with trying to recall things that seemed just out of reach.

Then Veronica's face took the place of Marti's in his mind. She had right to be angry with him. When she'd walked into the studio, the air between him and the new artist had been emotionally charged. Marti's lips looked sweet and inviting. What was he thinking?

Thinking? Who was thinking?

Some way or another, Marti's magic had taken over his senses, and he reacted purely on instinct. Standing next to her, he almost felt it was where he was supposed to be. How could that be true? The pull toward her was so strong that he'd actually wanted to kiss her. How crazy was that? A stranger, no less.

He had the strong impression he'd seen her somewhere before. Maybe she was an old girlfriend. No, Veronica would have told him. She would never keep something so explosive a secret.

His father had urged him to pray about his situation. Prayers might have been familiar at one time in his life, but now they seemed foreign and unsettling. How could he pray to a strange God? A God he knew nothing about. His loss of memory wasn't selective—not only had he forgotten names, faces, and events, but he couldn't remember trusting a God his father claimed he depended on at one time. It was disappointing. It would be nice to feel comfortable praying to a God who loved him and led him in the right direction. His father claimed the Bible would tell him about God, but after college, he wasn't sure he trusted the Bible either.

He turned over onto his back and tried to push God and both women out of his thoughts. He had to get some sleep.

Relax, Daniel.

The doctor said memory returns easier when you don't try so hard.

He stared at the muted moonlight wafting through his balcony doors. The images faded as he concentrated on the relaxing exercises he learned in therapy.

His muscles relaxed, and his subconscious thoughts were fading until a bloodcurdling scream coming from somewhere in the house jolted him up in bed. Instinct had him tense and ready to spring, and an automatic reflex made him reach for the Glock self-loading pistol he had attached to the bed frame under the bed.

When a loud crash sounded close to his room, he bounded onto the floor and cautiously pulled open the door.

All was still and silent. Army instincts forced him into a low crouch, creeping slowly and checking each shadowed doorway. He made his way into the hallway, alert to every movement.

At the wooden door across the hall he stopped when he heard a muffled scream coming from the room. He turned the knob slowly and pushed open the door. As he entered the moonlit studio, his eyes passed over shadows of the easel and work station then advanced further through the moonlight to the closed bedroom door beyond.

He crept across to the bedroom and listened for sounds coming from within.

"Ms. Rushing?"

Not hearing an answer, he softly opened the door and cautiously peered inside. He was just in time to see Marti thrust the pillow from her and suck in a frantic breath of air. When she saw him standing in her room, a scream burst from her lips.

Daniel quickly flipped on the light switch beside the door, and the lights around the room came to life. Marti jolted up in bed until recognition deflated her tensed muscles and diffused the panic in her flushed face. Daniel stood staring at her.

Marti's breath came in uneven gulps. Then her eyes lowered to the gun in his hand. "Wh-what are you d-doing?"

Daniel pointed the gun toward the ceiling and slowly advanced toward her. "I'm sorry. I heard you scream and I . . ." he lifted a shoulder. "Army instincts, I guess."

He laid the gun on the edge of the dresser and stepped over to lift the bedside lamp from the floor. Straightening the shade, he placed it back on the nightstand.

"Having a nightmare?"

Marti jumped out of bed, but her wobbly legs collapsed against the bed. Daniel reached to steady her, and she looked at him like he was crazy.

"No, it wasn't a nightmare! There was someone in here trying to smother me with a pillow. Didn't you see him?"

Daniel was immediately on alert. He picked up his gun and searched the room thoroughly. Then he glanced at the open balcony door and swiftly moved to search the tiled porch before returning with a shake of his head.

"There's no one here, Marti. The lock's not jimmied. I don't think anyone could have gotten up here from below. You must have been dreaming."

He looked at her doubtfully.

Her eyes implored him to listen. "You . . . you don't believe me?"

Daniel frowned. "There's no way anyone could get through the security of this ranch—at night, everything's locked up tight. You must have been dreaming."

Shock filled her eyes.

"There really was someone here."

"Okay, Marti. I'll check the security tapes in the morning, but for tonight, try to get some sleep."

Marti's eyes brimmed with tears. "I wasn't dreaming. Please believe me." She broke down then and covered her face with her hands.

Something inside him tugged at his heart. He went to her, softly pulled her to his shoulder, and let her cry. Empathy with what she was feeling filled his thoughts. Flashbacks he'd experienced as a result of a war he couldn't remember still left him shaking in terror

"I understand, Marti. I have nightmares from my stint in Iraq." His voice got quiet. "They seem real even when you're in a safe place and wide awake."

His hand draped around her unexpectedly felt hot. The goose bumps once again did a dance across the back of his neck. He could feel her frailness and vulnerability and felt . . . not only compassion, but that illusive sensation. Everything inside of him screamed there was something important to remember about this woman who sent electric currents through his body.

Marti's shoulders shook uncontrollably, and Daniel felt her muscles cramp convulsively. Sobs wracked her body as she clung to him and cried.

Daniel not only felt her frailness through her thin gown but also a familiar sensation.

A strange feeling that he'd felt compassion for this woman before set up camp in his thoughts.

He held her close and rubbed her back. "It's okay," he murmured to her softly, trying to hang on to the familiar feeling. Something inside of him melted as the memory tried to force its way into his thoughts—he was afraid it might just be his heart.

THIRTY-FOUR

The next morning Marti groaned as she pulled the comforter up over her head and rubbed her forehead on either side of her eyes. As a result of the sleepless night, a sharp pain thrummed in her temple and threatened to get worse. The intruder's attack had her lying in tense silence for most of the night—waiting for a figure in black to suddenly appear beside her.

Daniel hadn't believed her. That's what hurt the most. He'd thought she was dreaming.

She knew her attacker was real, and he wasn't threatening anymore. His attacks had stepped up from threatening to deadly. What would happen if she continued to stay in Texas? The Rushing's ranch wasn't as safe as she had thought it would be. Yet, even if she left now, he knew where she lived in Tennessee. She would have to uproot and move again.

That thought made her furious. She would not leave her home again. Her fragile roots had reached deep into the soil of Tennessee, and she didn't want to uproot them. Maybe if she had someone help her? Should she tell someone about the stalker? She couldn't tell Daniel. He thought she was dreaming and probably wouldn't believe her. What a stupid idea to think staying in Texas wouldn't arouse her stalker's anger. Why hadn't she informed the police here in Carson so they would be aware of her problem?

Because he'd threatened her if she told anyone, that's why. Well... she felt threatened anyway. What difference would it make?

Her thoughts raced back to the navy blue truck on the road to the ranch. Was it the same person who entered her room last night? She should have reported the incident. At least she would have proof that someone was intimidating her. How did he get on the ranch? Gerald mentioned they had a state-of-the-art security system.

She closed her eyes against her throbbing temples. The threats were real enough, but the whole situation last night rolled around her head in a fog. She couldn't tell Daniel about the stalker warning her about returning back to Texas because she was here under false pretenses.

I'll think about this later. I can't handle this now.

She shook her head and determined not to mention the attack to anyone. Not until she figured out what to do.

She got out of bed and pulled the sheets over the pillows. When she reached to straighten the comforter, her foot kicked something under the bed.

Ouch! That stung. A tiny ball of blood oozed onto the end of her big toe.

Bending over, she glanced under the bed to see what had caused the cut, and immediately she clenched a section of the comforter between white knuckles. Her knees grew weak, and she slid to the floor—her eyes never leaving the object lying under the bed.

A knife.

A large blade with a red handle covered with flames.

It wasn't there last night when she'd pulled her suitcase out from under the bed to search for a missing hairbrush. The intruder must have dropped it in the night.

Instinctively, she glanced at the curtains covering the doors. No one was there, but her imagination felt prying eyes staring at her from somewhere. A cold wave covered her body, and tears filled her eyes. He could have killed her with the knife.

A shudder radiated from her heart. He knew she was here. Now, he would never leave her alone.

How could she stay?

How could she go?

A knock on the door made her jump. "W-who is it?"

Gerald's voice filtered through the closed door. "It's Gerald, Marti. May I come in?"

Marti ran to the door and yanked it open. "Gerald. There's a knife under my bed. It must belong to the man who tried to smother me last night."

The look on Gerald's face was full of cautious concern, but he walked to the bed and leaned down. Pulling a tissue from the holder beside the bed, he picked up the knife and examined it carefully.

"Marti, this looks like the knife Daniel bought last month in town. He bought it because of all the extra little gadgets. He also told me about your dream and busting in on you. Maybe he brought the knife along with his gun last night."

Marti stared at him with her mouth open.

"I know it spooked you, Marti. Dreams like that would scare anyone half to death." He patted her on the arm. "I'm sure it's Daniel's, but I'll ask him about it and make sure, okay?"

Marti frowned. "You think I was dreaming too, don't you?"

"I don't *not* believe you, Marti. I think your nerves are overly sensitive because of being back here after so long and under not-very-desirable circumstances."

"Gerald, there's something I need to tell you—I should have mentioned it before, but after I left here, three years ago, a stalker started following me. He vandalized my apartments and called me constantly with threatening phone calls. No matter how many times I changed my phone number or moved, he found me. The police couldn't find out who it was or why he was harassing me. I almost went crazy. Then about a year ago, it all stopped. I thought he finally gave up and was going to leave me alone . . . until he started back up a few days before I came here. He warned me not to come to Texas, and he threatened my friends if I did. Now, I'm worried this might be the same person."

Gerald sat down on the over-stuffed red chair. "A stalker? Here? Marti, there's no way a stranger could get on this ranch without keys. You know how much some of my stallions are worth. I have to keep tight security. There's a security guard at the gate all night with sensors and cameras around the perimeter, and they're monitored constantly. Look, I'm not saying there wasn't someone following you around the country, but you're here now, and we have excellent security. No one could have gotten through to your room last night."

"But, someone ran me off the road on the way here, and there was this man who—"

Marti stopped in mid-sentence. Gerald's arms were crossed, and his jaw was tight. He wasn't listening to her, even if he did believe her.

"Marti, dear, you're a beautiful woman. Sometimes crazy people go after women because of their beauty. Surely you don't think someone would threaten you for coming back to Texas. What reason would he have?"

Marti gaped at him.

"To be honest, Gerald. I don't know what to think. He warned me not to return to Texas, and since I'm here, I assumed that might be why he came last night."

"I think the man chasing you, if there was one, only wanted to scare you as a way of controlling you—to get his thrill by making you afraid."

"I don't know, Gerald. He warned me about coming back to Texas from the beginning. I think he meant it."

"All right, Marti. I'll have our police detective, Brent, check into it. If there was somebody here, he'll find out." He put his arm around her. "If you need protecting, we'll protect you."

Marti nodded and tried to feel comforted.

Surely the police could check into everyone in this area and eliminate suspects by their alibis. Couldn't they?

THIRTY-FIVE

Marti slammed the back screen door and turned toward the barn. After limited sleep and painting all morning, she needed something to help her unwind. The stables outside her studio windows had beckoned her all morning. She was dying to smell the scent of oiled leather, sweet feed, fresh hay, and horses—all the smells she spent hours enjoying when she lived here. Even the sharp smell of Absorbine was an odor she remembered fondly. She'd spent lots of time rubbing the medicine into the sore muscles of their best quarter horses.

Out of the corner of her eye, she saw Parker hovering under the tree shading the back of the house. The pungent smell of cigarette smoke burned her nostrils. Parker was smoking? Smoke curled from his mouth when he leaned his head back and blew out a slow breath.

After living through a house fire caused by an employee's cigarette, Gerald made a steadfast rule: No smoking close to the house. Parker was disobeying that order while the boss wasn't looking. He'd been with Gerald for at least twelve years or more—he should know the rules.

Marti's flicker of anger became a flame. She glanced at him when she walked by and was shocked at the disgust in his face. His body language spoke volumes. She hastened her steps. Parker and Anita were friendly when she lived in the house with Daniel, until she'd gotten "religion" as they called it. After seeing her change in lifestyle, they became friendly but distant. However, since she returned to the ranch, they made it clear by their actions—they were no longer willing to be friends.

Remembering the red glow at the barn and the feeling that someone had been watching her on the balcony, she shivered. Parker was smoking. Could he be her midnight attacker?

Averting her eyes, she took a deep breath and walked toward the barn. Surely he wouldn't have attacked her in his own home. Parker and Anita had obviously believed what was said about her, but they had no reason to hate her or want her dead. Still . . . since Parker was in charge of the house, he probably had a key to her balcony door. She glanced back and saw him peek into the windows of the house, like he was worried he might be caught.

Marti shook her head. His cautious attitude didn't seem in character with a ruthless stalker.

The stable had been covered with a fresh coat of red paint, and the open windows at the end of the gable roof were framed with black trim. Water tanks flanked each side of the tack room attached to the east side of the barn, and horses mingled in the various corrals around the barn. The wide center door stood open and inviting. She took a deep breath and moaned in pleasure as the smells mingled and aroused a sleeping awareness.

As she walked across the wide expanse of plush green grass, she saw a man exit the barn with a riding saddle thrown over his shoulder. His hair was a little whiter, but Max Gibson still had the same agile but controlled posture she remembered. The sun had darkened his rugged features and lightened his steel gray eyes, and his white beard glistened in the sun. He always wore his blue tee shirt two times too large, but she could see toned muscles rippling underneath the thin fabric. The man's eyes found hers, and recognition flashed across his face. Marti's hands dug in her pockets, wondering what kind of reception she might receive.

"Well, as I live and breathe! If it ain't Martha Rushing." His Texas drawl was still part of his charm.

Marti's face registered timidity, then pleasure. "Max! Everyone calls me Marti now. Oh, it's good to see you again. How have you been?"

Max dumped the saddle on the green grass and reached to give her a one arm hug.

"I'm just fine, punkin. Gerald told me you was comin'. I'm as happy to see you again as a dog with two tails. You know Apollo near 'bout grieved hisself to death when you left."

An ache the size of Texas grew in her heart. Apollo was a wedding gift from Daniel and one of the things she missed the most about the ranch.

"I missed him too, Max, but . . ." She never finished her sentence and let her gaze drop.

Still holding her hands in his, Max sat down on a pile of square bales of hay and pulled her down beside him.

"Now, munchkin, I never did hold to the fact you were guilty of all them things they said. Don't you think for a minute I believed it."

Tears popped into her eyes, and she smiled through them. "Thanks, Max."

After patting her on the shoulder, he pulled out a white cloth and wiped the sweat off his forehead. "Truth is, I don't trust rumors no way. They always get all mixed up and out of whack, and by the time they land somewhere, it's nothin' like what really happened."

Marti sat up straight on the hay and pulled a piece of straw from the bale. She broke it into little pieces before she answered. "That was a long time ago, Max. We can't turn back time."

Max stole a glance toward the house and leaned toward her. "I heard what you're doin' here, and I want you to know I'm behind ya all the way."

She looked down at the ground. "I hope it works, Max. I'm afraid it's going to backfire in my face."

He studied her for a moment and lifted one thumb in the air. "You go, girl, as all the kids say nowadays." Then they stood up, and he gave her another hug.

"Where is Apollo? Can I see him?"

"Course you can see him. He's around the back of the barn in the big field. I bet he remembers you too."

A tall, sandy-headed man stepped out of the double doors with an overflowing trash can and a bucket of feed. "Max, the new white mare won't eat her feed. I kept pushin' it in front of her, but she got real agitated."

Max looked angry. "I told you, Zach, we don't force new horses to do anything. How many times do I have to tell you that? Now, if you can't listen to what I tell you, maybe this isn't the place for you anymore."

Zach frowned. "Sure, Max. Whatever you say."

"Just hang the bucket on the side of the stall and leave it there. If she gets hungry enough, she'll eat."

Zach lifted the wooden lid of the outside trash container and chucked the trash into the dumpster. Then he turned back toward the barn—his steps making an impression in the dirt with every step.

Max turned toward Zach and yelled, "Hey, Zach. I thought you were supposed to be inspecting the brakes of the backhoe today, not feeding the mares."

Zach ground to a halt. "Warren claims he knows more about brakes than me. He told me to trade jobs." He turned and entered the barn.

Max turned to Marti and frowned. "I guess we'll see, won't we? That man's been here for three months, and I swear he'll never learn to follow orders."

"Who is he?"

"A man Daniel hired a few months ago. There were rumors about him ruining an expensive quarter horse where he worked before coming here, but for some reason, Daniel decided to give him a second chance. He's a little lazy at times. Name's Zach Parsons, but if I didn't know better, I'd say it was Couch Potato."

Marti ducked her head and smiled. Max was the same as ever. Tolerant and patient on the inside, but firm on the outside.

When several loud bangs came from inside the barn, Max laughed. "Well, I had better help Zach see to the afternoon feeding. The natives are getting restless." He heaved the saddle back onto his shoulder. His grin widened his entire face. "It's good to have you home, gal. I'll be seeing you 'round."

Marti smiled her goodbye and headed toward the large field next to the barn.

THIRTY-SIX

Marti stopped at the edge of the field and sucked in a surprised breath of satisfaction. A palomino quarter horse drank water from the large metal tank against the fence about midway down the field. The horse raised his head quickly and smelled the air, turning his head slightly. When his eyes fell on Marti standing next to the fence, he snorted and turned to trot in her direction.

Marti stood still and waited, trying not to hold her breath.

When Apollo neared the fence line, he pushed his head over the top of the planks and nudged her in the chest.

Marti laughed and rubbed the soft place on the horse's nose.

"Apollo. You remember me! Oh, I've missed you so." She climbed over the wooden fence and hugged Apollo's neck. Fire burned in the back of her throat, and she buried her head in golden brown muscle and mane. Apollo nickered and pushed his head against Marti's back.

"He acts like he knows you." Daniel's voice came from beside the barn where he stood, looking pensive. "I guess Apollo and I have something in common. You seem familiar to both of us."

Marti walked toward him, and Apollo followed. "He's a beauty. Did you raise him?" Her voice was hoarse.

Daniel looked at the ground and scowled before answering. "No, actually, he belonged to my ex-wife—so I'm told." The scorn in his words made her wince.

"Then why is he still here if she's gone?" She had to get the jab in.

Daniel's gaze traveled to the thick woods in front of the tallest mountain. His slow answer was steeped in pain. "She left. She destroyed our family and left. I've been told she was a disgrace and embarrassment, and it's good riddance that she's gone."

The anguish in his words took her breath away. His anger chopped at her heart like a knife on a block of cheese. If he remembered her with as much heartache as he expressed, he certainly wouldn't forgive her for what she'd done.

"I'm sorry," she said softly.

Apollo stomped his foot and nudged Marti again on the arm.

"Looks like he wants more attention." Daniel pulled a carrot from the feed box beside the barn and handed it to Marti, the green stems still attached. Marti broke the carrot into large pieces and held it out in the flat palm of her hand. Apollo grabbed the carrot and munched contentedly.

Daniel's face reflected a brooding, almost sad look while he watched her. "My dad and I are visiting customers in the next county, so I guess I better get going."

Marti turned to Apollo. "I'll just stay here a while and get to know Apollo a little more. Maybe I can ride him sometime?"

Shaking his head immediately, Daniel firmly said, "No. He's much too spirited for a beginner."

"Actually, I'm not really a beginner—I just haven't ridden in a while. I used to ride some pretty spirited horses, and Apollo and I seem to have bonded already."

"We'll see. Apollo has a mind of his own. If you're not careful, you'll end up at the falls on the back side of the farm whether you want to or not. That's his favorite place."

Daniel's grin was a little bit contagious, and when Marti remembered Apollo's stubborn streak, she grinned too.

Daniel crossed his arms and continued. "I remember once when Apollo saw a snake in the road—he reared up on his back legs and took off running. Instead of heading back to the barn, he headed straight for those falls." Daniel laughed. "Near about threw his rider off."

Marti choked. She leaned over double, and strangled coughs kept her airways tight until her lungs cleared. Daniel patted her on the back.

"Are you okay?"

Marti's thoughts were running wild. It was *her* riding Apollo that day. She remembered hanging on for dear life until Daniel, who was riding Tornado, picked up the dropped reins and stopped the runaway horse. By the time she came to a stop, the falls were right in front of her.

Marti nodded as tears fell down her face. "I . . . got choked."

Daniel stepped back with a look of unbelief in his eyes.

"I remembered something." His voice was soft and pensive.

Marti held her breath. She stared at Daniel, a frown between her eyes and a knot in the pit of her stomach. If he remembered that ride, would he remember it was her riding?

Daniel stared at the mountains in the distance and rubbed the back of his neck. Closing his eyes, he seemed to be reliving that day.

"I can see Apollo running ahead of me. I was so scared the woman . . . it was a woman . . . I was so scared she would fall off any minute. I remember pushing Tornado as fast as he would go. I grabbed Apollo's reins . . . and turned to the rider."

Suddenly, he stopped and turned toward her, peering deep into her eyes.

He reached out his hand and touched her on the cheek with his fingers. "What is it about you that brings my past so close to the surface of my memory?" His hand dropped, and he studied her.

Marti's cheek burned with the memory of his touch. Her knees wobbled, and she leaned against the wooden corral. "Maybe I just remind you of someone." Quietly, Marti's breathing returned to normal, but her hands still felt wet with sweat.

Daniel shook his head and turned toward the barn. "It must have been Veronica."

"Does Veronica have auburn hair?"

Daniel stared at her. "How did you know the woman had auburn hair?"

"Just a guess. You said I helped you remember in some way. I thought it might be my hair color."

He shook his head and mumbled quietly as he turned. "No . . . Remember? Veronica has red hair. It couldn't have been her anyway. She's scared to death of Apollo."

Tears threatened to fill Marti's eyes as she watched his retreating figure.

She couldn't take this anymore. She had to get away.

She bit her cheek to hold back the tears when Daniel stopped at the barn and turned toward her. "I have to get going. I'll see you around."

Marti kept her eyes averted until Daniel was out of sight. Resolutely, she led Apollo to stand beside the fence. She climbed up on the wooden railing and slid onto Apollo's back. His head shook back and forth, and she could feel his excitement as she pushed his neck to turn him toward the pasture. Tears blurred her vision as she and Apollo galloped through the pasture as one.

THIRTY-SEVEN

Marti stood listening to the crashing of the water on the rocks above her. The falls were always pretty, but something about being surrounded by spring flowers and freshly sprouted ferns made them seem like what heaven would be. She had forgotten what a magical place this was and how much she loved it here.

The sun shadowed one side of the mountain as she sat down beside the lake and listened to the song of the whip-poor-wills. She loved the Texas bluebonnets that were scattered all around the low areas of the valley and the scent of honeysuckle and lavender. The leaves of the cool, green grass felt soft and plush beneath her fingertips. A melancholy sensation came over her when she remembered how close she felt to God up here.

In the last few months before the accident, she had come here to gather strength—strength to fight a family who scorned her new beliefs. This valley had given her strength. She felt God's love so strong it made her ache. Sadness swamped her, and a strong longing to reach out and talk with God consumed her. Staring into the sky, she thought of the reasons why she'd turned from Him. Her newly found faith in God had taken a beating because of the accident, the loss of her newborn son, and Daniel's accusations and eventual divorce.

The verse somewhere in Joel came to her mind. God had promised the children of Israel if they repented, He would "restore what the locusts have eaten." She wondered if He would do the same for her.

She looked up into the clouds and let the vastness of the sky fill her soul with the closeness of the Lord.

"God, I'm sorry for turning away from You. Please forgive me, Lord, and restore what the locusts have eaten of my life. If it's Your will, please restore my marriage. I know you can't give me back my baby, but if You will, Lord, restore my marriage and allow us to have more children."

A feeling of calm and peace flooded her soul and washed away her doubts. No matter what happened now, she knew God was back in control of her life.

She sighed and picked up a pine needle to throw into the water. It swirled around in the rushing stream before settling against a rock along the shore. She sighed and turned back to find Apollo eating the lush green grass.

"You love it here too, don't you, fella?"

After rubbing his nose, she pulled his mane and led him to the stump of a large tree. She stepped onto the stump then froze. A tingling traveled up and down her arms. That same feeling of being watched crept up her spine, and goose bumps broke out on her arms once more. With an anxious eye, she searched the trees around her. Why had she come out so far from the ranch by herself? It was a foolish mistake.

The chirping of the birds stopped. She felt the silence.

Suddenly, she heard a soft *"fffftt"* near her ear. She turned her head and froze. Buried deep in the tree behind her was the shaft of a red arrow.

She jerked her head around to see where the arrow had come from and searched the woods across the creek fed by the waterfall.

Apollo sensed her fear and began stomping around in circles. She grabbed his mane and tried to pull herself up on his back as the frightened horse pulled away and ran down the path.

One leg on his back and the other hanging limply behind her, she struggled desperately to pull herself up onto the pounding animal. His gait was too fast. She couldn't find her balance.

She ducked as he ran up against low limbs of trees and made an erratic path through the woods. The horse was running in the direction of the farm house, but the short cut was riddled with briars that tore through her jeans and pulled at the tender skin on her arms.

Trying to hide her face from the punishing limbs and branches, she heard another *ffftt*, and an arrow tore through the sleeve of her shirt. Panic increased the adrenaline in her system, and with all the strength she could muster, she pulled her body up over the back of the stallion and settled onto his back, keeping her head low. With her feet pressed against his stomach, she kicked Apollo into a full run and tried to keep her head down as they turned toward the ranch. Petrified, she hoped whoever was shooting at her would never catch up with the strong horse.

For the next few minutes, she spent more time looking back to see if she was being followed than looking ahead. The next thing she knew, she felt a hard bump on her head, and she was tumbling to the ground.

For a minute, she couldn't breathe. The fall knocked the wind from her lungs, and she lay on her stomach, struggling to get a breath.

Had she been shot?

Her thoughts were muddled as she finally sucked in a fresh breath of air. When she rolled over, she screamed. Standing over her stood Daniel, staring at her with concern in his eyes.

"Marti? Are you all right?"

Marti gazed into his concerned face. "What happened?"

"Apollo ran you under a low limb. Are you okay?"

Marti slowly sat up, massaging her shoulder. "Yes, but it wasn't Apollo's fault. He—"

"Are you crazy? I told you he wasn't a good mount for a beginner. And bareback? Are you suicidal? You could have killed yourself, not to mention injury to Apollo." He reached out a hand and helped her stand. Her legs wobbled but held.

"It wasn't Apollo's fault . . . it was . . ." Suddenly Marti jerked her head up to stare in his eyes. Doubts crept into her heart. Fear that it was him stalking her the last three years returned, and she stuttered, "I t-thought you were going to see a c-customer."

Daniel looked confused. "He had to cancel, so I'm out here mending fences. One of the men noticed that a tree fell on the fence line last night."

She knew he must be telling the truth because his arms glistened with sweat, and he wore nothing but jeans and a pair of work gloves. His shirt dangled from one of the fence posts. She shook her head. "S-someone was ch-chasing me—with a bow and arrow. He shot at me, at least twice."

Daniel's brow furrowed and turned toward the woods, searching. When he turned back to her, unbelief flashed in his eyes, not guilt.

"Are you sure you weren't imagining it when Apollo took off running?"

Marti stared at him. "No! I'll show you." She held up her sleeve for him to see. A three-inch tear ripped up one side of the material. "Right here, see?"

Daniel frowned. "Marti, your clothes are full of tears . . . probably from the tree limbs you ran through."

Marti looked at her clothes. He was right. Tears in the sleeves of her yellow cotton blouse were minor compared to the rips in the legs of her jeans, and her arms were full of scratches.

"Daniel, please listen to me. Someone was chasing me with a bow and arrow. I promise I'm not making it up. Let's go back to the falls. There's an arrow in one of the trees there."

Daniel shook his head. "The falls! You went all the way to the falls?" He walked away, running his hands through his hair. His anger was evident when he turned back to her. "You are not to ride again without our knowledge. Do you understand? I don't have time for this now. I have to finish this fence before the stallions and mares mingle together."

Dull pains pounded in Marti's chest. Daniel still didn't believe her. Tears filled her eyes. The scenery blurred around her, and she couldn't stop the sobs that bubbled up inside her.

Daniel let out a strangled sigh before he moved to her and nervously pulled her into a hug. His voice was softer and calm.

"I'm sorry, Marti, but you scared the living daylights out of me." He patted her gently on the back. "You're okay now."

Marti's tears slowed, but she still could not think clearly. Terror had wiped away her ability to reason. Danger hovered close, and yet the muscled, rock-hard body of the man she was clinging to stood between her and that danger. A sigh trembled through her body, until her emotions began a fast thaw.

Suddenly, the warmth of Daniel's bare back under her hands brought on an onslaught of memory, and her body trembled for a different reason. She was lost in another world. A world of acceptance, trust, and love.

She knew Daniel felt the change of emotion because his muscles tensed.

The tears in her eyes mingled with the pain in her heart, and in an instant that nonexistent world was turned upside down. Her heart thudded back to the reality of pain and rejection.

Clamping her eyes shut, she slowly pushed back away from him—closing her heart to the memories that threatened to drown her very soul.

Daniel leaned away from her and looked into her eyes. The emotions she saw there were intermingled. Surprise. Shock. Awareness. She could see them all doing battle in his eyes.

His thumb reached up and touched the tears on her face. She stood perfectly still. This had to be Daniel's move. She would not push him. He caressed her cheek and leaned in close. Their faces were only inches apart. Longing turned his eyes a dark chocolate. Then he pulled back and dropped his hand.

When he stepped back, his face was devoid of emotion. His eyes turned hard and unfeeling. "I have to finish this fence. Veronica and I are going out tonight."

He turned his back on her and turned toward the broken fence. A throbbing twisted in her heart, and she knew by the agony she felt that part of it had withered.

THIRTY-EIGHT

Daniel paced outside the brick building—fuming on the inside. Lately, everything about this wedding irritated him. Impatience with Veronica and all her picky details was building inside him. He supposed it was just wedding jitters, but wasn't it the bride who was supposed to have second thoughts? Did grooms ever wonder if they were doing the right thing?

Veronica insisted he attend a cake-tasting ceremony with the top caterer in the city. Cake was one of his favorite desserts, but somehow raspberry-almond angel food cake or hazelnut-banana vintage cake topped with something French—he couldn't quite remember what—seemed a little strange to him. Was it ganak, or ganarce, or ganache? Anyway, it was French, and it tasted funny. It tasted nothing like the chocolate icing Stella made. He didn't understand why Veronica had to make their wedding so ostentatious. A nice quiet ceremony and a plain old chocolate cake with plain old chocolate icing would be okay with him.

He watched through the glass doors as Veronica glided down the long staircase toward him. She stepped through the opening out into the hot air and frowned at him.

"Daniel. You left before Chef Mikael brought out the last cake option."

"I know, Nikki. I tasted so many different cakes, now they all taste the same. I'm done. I'm going back to the ranch. You can come over later with your dad."

"Wait, Daniel, we have one more meeting—with the florist. We simply *have* to keep that appointment. You don't cancel on Melvin Du Bois. We'll be the laughing stock of the whole town if we do."

"No, Veronica. I promised Chris I'd take him on a canoe ride this afternoon, and that's what I'm doing. You meet with Mr. Du Bois yourself, and pick whatever flowers you want. You're the one who's picky about wedding details anyway."

Veronica's lips stuck out in a pout, and Daniel rubbed his face to hide a grin at her melodramatic expression.

"A canoe ride." The way she said it made it sound like a migraine.

Daniel crossed his arms and stood firm.

When she saw he wasn't backing down, her pout turned into frustration. Anger made her voice tight and clipped. "Very well, Daniel, but don't blame me if you hate the flowers I choose."

Veronica huffed off toward the florist downtown and didn't glance back in his direction. He already knew what kind of flowers she'd want anyway—hand-picked white orchids. Rare, showy, and, of course, expensive.

Lately, she'd talked about nothing but the wedding. As a matter of fact, she was obsessed with it. Cakes, flowers, rings, bridesmaids—it all made his head hurt.

He slid into his pickup and slammed the door. He'd pick up Chris at the Duke ranch and take him out on the lake for a relaxing afternoon. Chris had been begging for weeks, and he'd promised to take him sometime before the Quarter Horse Association picnic. Veronica could fend for herself. Daniel pulled out his cell phone and talked to the maid at the Duke ranch. After making sure the young woman packed Chris another set of clothes,

Daniel pulled into the Dukes' driveway and smiled at Chris waiting on the front porch.

Chris jumped up and down when he saw Daniel's truck pull into the driveway, and Daniel laughed at his excitement. Chris had been talking about the picnic for days, but now his one-track mind was on a canoe ride.

When Daniel strapped Chris into his car seat, he noticed the straps were getting tight. Maybe he should warn Veronica that Chris was outgrowing his current seat. Chris might weigh enough now to be switched to a booster. Daniel would enjoy being able to watch Chris's face instead of the back of the car seat.

He waved at the Duke's maid, and pulled out of the yard.

When they arrived at the Rushing farm, Daniel parked in the grass and helped Chris climb out of the truck. He grabbed his tiny hand and walked with him down to the lake. After pulling a child-sized life jacket out of the canoe, he turned to Chris.

"Now, let's put this on."

"What's that, Unc'l Dan'l?"

"It helps you float if you fall in the water."

"Can I go swimming?"

"Not in your clothes. Today we're going riding in the boat."

"But, I have a thing on to help me swim. Why can't I jump in?"

"Not today, buddy. Now come on and get in."

"Why can't I go swimming, Unc'l Dan'l?"

His whiny voice stopped Daniel in his tracks. "Chris, do you want to go swimming?"

Chris' little head bobbed up and down. "Yes."

"Do you want to go ride in the canoe?"

"Yes." Once again his head bobbed.

Daniel placed his hands on his hips. "Well, buddy, one is in the boat, and one is in the water. You can't be both places at once. Which one do you want to do?"

Chris put his hand on the side of his face and looked way up into Daniel's face. "Go in the 'noo."

"So, you want to go for a ride?"

Chris nodded, and Daniel sighed to himself along with a laugh. "Back to where we started."

Daniel got into the boat and helped Chris settle in the middle seat. He picked up the oars and sat down in the back of the boat.

He handed Chris a child-sized oar.

"Want to help paddle?"

Chris lunged at the oar and nodded his head vigorously. After gripping the plastic handle with his small hands, he plopped it into the lake.

Daniel showed him how to push the paddle through the water and hid a smile as Chris's short arms stabbed the water with the oar. Daniel pushed off from the shore, and the canoe glided smoothly through the water. As they paddled along the shoreline, Daniel noticed a woman standing inside the new gazebo skirting the edge of the water. She was wearing a sunflower yellow top with blue jean walking shorts, and the sunlight shining under the edge of the roof highlighted the russet color of her hair.

Marti.

The back of his neck tingled, and he swatted at his hairline to ease the feeling. The same emotional reaction he felt after Marti fell in the woods returned to tickle his stomach. He wished he could figure out why being with Marti brought something inside of him back to life.

"Come on, Unc'l Dan'l. Let's go, let's go." Chris splashed the oar back into the water and tugged it backward, sending a spray of water at Daniel's face and hair.

Daniel ducked and laughed. "Okay, okay. How about we pick up a passenger?"

"A pass-ger?"

"Passenger. That means a friend."

"Okay."

Daniel paddled toward the gazebo and watched the back of Marti's head as she gazed across the lake. Her beauty was obvious, but something else called to him. Her personality? Her character? Something made him long to spend more time with the pretty portrait artist.

The oars made a plop sound as he steered toward the shore—trying to keep in perfect rhythm with the beating of his heart.

THIRTY-NINE

The bench in the garden between the house and the stables was shaded by a gnarled oak tree and was the perfect resting place away from memories rolling over Marti's sensitive emotions. After spending all morning staring at Daniel's likeness on canvas, slivers of memory penetrated her thoughts one after the other. When she felt she could take no more of the emotional roller coaster, she wandered outside to let the beautiful spring weather lighten her mood. Princess followed her outside, and when Marti sat on the stainless steel yard bench, the cat jumped in her lap for nuzzling and a short nap.

Marti sat contented to hold the cat and appreciate the beautiful gardens surrounding the area. A vibrant patch of red salvia was encircled with a thick stand of dusty miller, and around the edges of the small garden were orange marigolds and shasta daisies. Anita's green thumb was evident in the compact flower garden. Anita not only cleaned house but also spent time outside, enjoying her gardening hobby.

When Marti's gaze turned toward the lake, she spotted a gazebo standing a few feet from the boat dock. She set Princess on the ground, walked down to the edge of the lake, and stepped up on the wooden structure skirting the sandy shoreline. It was a new construction Marti had never seen before, but it offered a perfect view of the mountains on the other side of the lake. They were picturesque this time of year—covered with new growth of leaves and foliage but still showing a touch of snow on the tips. Across the lake, wild flower blooms were beginning to pop out next to the water, adding touches of blue, purple, and orange.

She was standing on the gazebo enjoying the peaceful atmosphere when the mood abruptly changed. The air almost seemed charged with an electric current. She turned around and saw a canoe floating toward the edge of the lake with Daniel paddling through the water toward the dock. Daniel waved at her from inside the canoe, and she waved back. The little boy she'd seen the other day sat inside the canoe, trying to help paddle. She smiled at his awkward jabs at the water.

Daniel's rust-color, patterned shirt emphasized his tanned features and coordinated with his knee-length khaki shorts. His hair was tousled from the brisk breeze, but he was beaming. Her heart took a nosedive, and goose bumps broke out on her arms. She would never get over her body's reaction to his presence.

She smiled back and watched as the canoe approached the dock.

"Hey, Marti. Come meet Chris!" Daniel called from the canoe as he pulled it up to the short dock.

Marti crossed the grass from the gazebo and stepped onto the dock. Leaning over, she shook the little boy's hand. "Hello, Chris. My name is Marti." The boy had brown hair and the biggest brown eyes Marti had ever seen. His light blue shirt matched his blue jean cargo shorts, but Marti's gaze was drawn back to the little boy's face. She was startled by how much like Daniel's the little boy's eyes were.

Chris looked up into her face. "Hi." His shy little smile ducked behind the handle of the oar he was holding.

"This is Veronica's baby brother."

"No, Unc'l Dan'l. Brudder. I'm her brudder."

"Oh. Okay." A smile and a wink were aimed toward Marti.

She shivered as a wave of warmth swept over her skin. She turned to the little boy.

"How old are you Chris?"

"Free." He held up three fingers.

A wave of suspicion coursed through her. Veronica's adopted brother? One who looked a lot like Daniel? And he was three years old? Was this the reason Daniel had sent her away?

"Would you like to come with us for a ride?" Daniel waved toward the canoe.

Marti mentally shook herself and stored those thoughts away for later. "Uh, sure. It's been years since I've ridden in a boat. I'd like that."

Chris raised his head. "You can wear a light racket, but you can't swim," said Chris with a serious face.

"A what?" Marti frowned.

"He means a life jacket," said Daniel with another wink as he handed her an orange vest.

"Oh, okay." Marti took the vest Daniel handed her and clicked the locks in place. Daniel braced himself on the dock and held out his hand to assist her into the boat.

When Marti's hand touched Daniel's, a current of warmth spread through her body. She spotted the surprised look on Daniel's face and knew he felt the same sensation. For a minute, the world stopped turning while they stared into each other's eyes and tried to absorb the unexpected responsiveness.

Daniel tugged on her hand. She leaned on his support and climbed into the middle of the boat. She made her way to the front seat and collapsed before her legs could give away. When Daniel turned to push the canoe away from the dock, she took several deep breaths and tried to calm her running away heart.

Chris turned to her shyly. "I'm helping Unc'l Dan'l go." He illustrated the words by placing the oar into the water then turned to her. "Wanna help?"

"Sure, Chris." Marti moved up to sit beside Chris and put one hand on the oar.

Chris moved over and smiled up at her as they pushed the oar in the water together.

Daniel grinned at their awkward partnership. "It's nice to have some help, isn't it, buddy?"

Chris nodded and concentrated on pushing the oar away from the boat.

Daniel looked at Marti with a strange expression on his face. "I have something to show you," he said as he steered toward the other side of the lake. He pointed toward a protruding piece of land across the water in the center of an alcove. "Over there."

Marti tried to recall exploring that area, but she couldn't remember ever being on the other side of the huge lake. "What is it?"

He grinned and put his finger on his lips. "Wait and see."

Marti forced a mock frown and then offered him a smile. "Hashtag: secret, huh?"

Daniel smiled and nodded. "Yep."

When they reached the shore on the other side, Daniel slowed the boat by dragging his oar in the water. "Okay, guys. Pull your oar out of the water and be very quiet."

"Why, Unc'l Dan'l?"

"We don't want to scare the mama."

"What mama?"

"You'll see."

Chris looked up at Marti. "I don't have a mama."

Marti's heart bled. She leaned over and hugged Chris. "I'm sorry, Chris. I didn't have a mama either when I was your age, but I had lots of friends. Don't you?"

"Yep. Unc'l Dan'l, Papa Shane, Ronica . . . and you."

Marti thought the love in his eyes would make her heart melt. She gave him the biggest smile she could muster and a kiss on the cheek.

"Now," said Daniel as he pulled a flashlight from the storage box, "be very quiet."

Chris pushed his lips together and turned to Marti. He put his finger on his lips. "Shhhh."

Marti did the same and smiled at Chris. He was such a precious child. That same longing for a child grew inside her until she had to tamp it down before tears followed. *Not now, please.*

Daniel stepped out of the boat and held out his hand to help Chris. Marti waited until he turned to her. Then she put her hand in his and smiled up at him. The tingling in her hand came back, and she hurriedly stepped onto land.

Daniel pulled the canoe up onto the shore and waved at them to follow. They rounded the point of land jutting into the water and walked about a hundred feet away from shore. Daniel squatted in the shade of a large oak tree and whispered, "Be really quiet for just a minute, then you'll see what I brought you to see. Now, Chris, we have to be absolutely still when the mama comes back, or she might leave. Okay?"

Chris nodded excitedly and squatted with Marti beside Daniel and waited. Chris's excitement bubbled out, and he squirmed and kept grinning up at Marti. After a few minutes, a large brown bird flew around the area and perched overhead on a large tree limb. Chris stopped his squirming and froze.

"That's an owl," Daniel whispered to Chris.

They watched as the mama bird sat on the limb, looking around the area before she flew over to a hole that looked like a tunnel in the ground and went inside. They heard loud twittering noises.

Chris's eyes widened, and his mouth formed an "O." He put his little hand over his mouth and grinned. Daniel smiled back and put his finger on his lips again to indicate silence.

The bird stuck its head out of the hole, looked around the area, and flew away.

Daniel grabbed the little boy's hand. "Come on! Hurry! She'll be back in a minute." He led Chris over to the gap in the ground as Marti followed. Daniel leaned way over to look through the opening. "Look in here and see what you see." He held the flashlight so the beam went directly into the hole.

Chris leaned to peer in and then drew in a quick breath. "Babies! Baby birds."

Marti was amazed. "What kind are they? How did you find them? How old are they?"

Daniel laughed. "You sound like Chris—full of a million questions."

Chris looked confused. "I'm not full of questions."

Marti and Daniel laughed, and Daniel told them, "They're called burrowing owls, and the babies are about three weeks old. I saw them one day while I was over here cutting down a tree the beavers had sawed half through."

"Can I hold them, Unc'l Dan'l?"

"No, Chris. As a matter of fact, we need to leave now so the mother bird can come back to feed them again."

They slipped back over to the tree and squatted to watch. In a few minutes, another brown bird came swooping into the area.

Daniel leaned over to Chris and pointed toward the bird. "I think that's the daddy bird, Chris. See how much bigger he is than the mama? They take turns feeding their babies until they're old enough to feed themselves."

Marti was awed. "I thought owls always built their nests in trees," she whispered.

"Not all of them. Many species of owls build in tall grass, burrows abandoned by other animals—sometimes we've even had them build in the holes of the barn or hay sheds around the place."

"That's interesting," Marti said.

"Most other owls are active at night, but some burrowing owls are out during the day—like today. I guess they catch their prey better in the day time. They eat large insects and small rodents."

"What's a rodun, Unc'l Dan'l?"

"A small animal, like a mouse."

Chris scrunched up his nose. "*Eeeuuuww.*"

Daniel grinned and whispered to Marti, "Hashtag: disgusted."

Marti nodded and hid a smile.

Once the daddy bird left the area, Daniel stood up. "Come on. We need to leave them alone now."

They walked toward the boat until Chris spotted a large bullfrog hopping across a grouping of round lake rocks.

"Look! A frog." He climbed up on the low rocks until the frog jumped back down on the sand beside the water. Chris giggled and hopped down after him.

Daniel laughed and turned to Marti. "Shall we follow and make sure he doesn't get into trouble?"

When she nodded, he took her hand. "The rocks are a little rough here."

He led her across the jumbled group of rocks and helped her down the last one. When she stepped down onto the ground, the sand was soft and her foot twisted. Daniel's hand reached out to help her even as she found her balance. Their faces were inches apart. His eyes found hers, and she stared into them—mesmerized. Her breath was shallow, and Daniel seemed to have frozen in time. His head tilted to the side, and he whispered, "Marti," as he reached up and caressed her cheek. He leaned toward her and touched her lips with his. The kiss was short, yet explosions of magnitude went off in her head. It was even better than she remembered. Even as her heart tried to find its rhythm again, she felt a stabbing pain for the wasted years they'd lost.

Unexpectedly, Daniel pulled away and stepped back. Without his arm holding her up, her knees gave way, and she sat down on the rock behind her.

"I'm sorry, Marti." He turned away from her and looked into the clouds. "That wasn't right. This never happened." He turned toward Chris and yelled, "Chris, let's go!"

When he turned toward the boat, Marti felt a heavy weight pressing on her chest. Daniel could pretend it never happened because he had no memories that once it was so much more, while she remembered in detail the love, passion, and companionship she'd lost. This was breaking her heart, and Daniel was determined to ignore any feelings he might feel toward her. She had to leave—and soon—or there would be nothing of her left.

FORTY

A few days later, Princess jumped into the bed with Marti and began kneading the blanket beside her. Marti jolted awake and sat up in bed, absentmindedly reaching over to stroke the cat's soft fur.

The pounding in her temples reminded Marti why four hours of sleep a night was not enough. Rubbing her head, she got out of bed and walked into the studio. The morning light angled across the room and touched the edge of two portraits sitting on the easel. Daniel's portrait was almost done—just a few last minute highlights. The other project, a surprise for Gerald, still required work but was close to being completed also.

After the intruder broke into her room, sleeping every night was almost impossible. As soon as the sun went down, the darkness made its way into her bones, and closing her eyes was terrifying. So she painted into the wee hours of the morning until the first light touched the edges of the mountains and bathed the lake with fog. Then, while the rest of the ranch awakened and started on chores, she crashed in bed until the bright light of the sun sneaking around the edges of the curtains woke her.

Marti stood back and stared at the picture, making a mental note of the changes she needed to make on the skin of the face. Gerald had been kind to her, and she wanted to give something back when she left . . . hopefully soon. Daniel showed no signs allowing himself to accept any kind of bond between them; instead, he seemed more determined than ever to go through with this wedding to Veronica. Gerald's plan hadn't worked. It was best that she leave and try to salvage the rest of her future—without Daniel. She had to accept the fact. Daniel wasn't meant for her. She would finish Daniel's painting to keep her promise to Gerald, and then she'd wipe the dust of Carson, Texas, from her feet and never look back.

She moved Princess to the foot of the bed and pulled the comforter back over the pillows. She dressed in five minutes flat before she returned to the studio.

Her hands flew as she worked fast and furious—trying hard not to think about Daniel. She hadn't seen him since the canoe trip, but his kiss was on her mind constantly.

The last two mornings, Veronica drove up in her sporty BMW convertible and took him off to who knows where. Yesterday, they went to a rodeo in the next county and returned late in the evening. She thought she heard Anita say they were going shopping for the wedding today. The word *wedding* spread a chill through her bones. What was worse than hearing the word was knowing she could do nothing about it.

She stepped back to critique her work and picked up her filbert brush. After blending the shadows on one side of the face, she put down the larger brush and picked up a detail brush. She blended in a tiny stroke of white highlight on the tip of the nose in the painting, and then she stood back. That one little spot of white paint made the nose pop off the page and looked totally three dimensional. *Wow!* It still amazed her that a tiny bit of paint on a flat surface could make something look so round and so real.

She was rinsing out her brush when someone knocked on the door. "Marti? May I come in?"

"Just a minute." She quickly hid the one painting behind a blank canvas and propped Daniel's painting on the easel.

"Come in."

Gerald stuck his head around the door. "Can I take a peek?"

Marti smiled. Gerald's eyes sparkled like a child waiting expectantly for a trip to Disneyland.

She waved him in. "Certainly. It's almost done."

Gerald walked around the easel and stood in silence. His mouth dropped open. He glanced briefly at Marti before looking back at the painting.

"Marti! I'm speechless. They told me you were good, but I had no idea how good. I'm shocked. This looks exactly like Daniel. I can even see his character and personality in the eyes. Oh, Marti. I love it." His voice broke and she saw tears in his eyes. "I just wish . . ."

Marti went to him then and gave him a hug. "One thing you reminded me when I came here, *Dad*, was to trust God. We have to believe that no matter what happens, God allows it in our lives. There's a verse that my friend in Tennessee reminded me of—Romans chapter eight, verse twenty-eight. It says—"

Gerald's voice interrupted her. "'All things work together for good to them that love God.' Yes, Marti, I know that verse, and it's true. We have to keep trusting—no matter what happens."

He gave her another hug. "And, I love hearing you call me *Dad*. I never appreciated that when you were here before, but it's like music to my ears now. Thank you."

She smiled at him—a sad smile but one filled with emotion. "You're a good man, Gerald. Hashtag: Dad."

"I've heard you use that word before. What does 'hashtag' mean?"

She smiled. "Never mind." If Gerald still owned a cassette player, a dot-matrix printer, and a VCR, he'd never understand about Twitter.

"Gerald, I'm almost done with the painting, and I . . ."

A panicked look filled Gerald's eyes, and they shifted all around the room. "Hey, I came in to ask you two things," he said as a deliberate interruption.

"What?"

"First of all, I usually go to church on Sundays, and I wondered if you'd like to come with me tomorrow. I'm the only one who goes, and I thought it'd be nice if I had some company for a change."

Marti smiled. "I miss going to church. That's tempting. Is Pastor Sammons still there?"

"Yep, and he still preaches a mean sermon."

Marti laughed. "I'd love to go see him again. I'll think about going. Thanks for inviting me. And the second thing?"

Gerald sat down on a wooden stool she used for Daniel's photography session. "Right before Daniel signed up for the Special Forces, I sent an investigator to find you . . . to see if you were okay."

"You did?" Marti was stunned.

Gerald nodded. "Even before I accepted God into my life, Marti, my attitude toward you changed. I realized what a sweet daughter-in-law you'd been. I didn't want to admit it at the time, but . . . I missed you."

Tears filled Marti's eyes, but she blinked them away quickly.

Gerald cleared his throat and spoke with a scratchy voice. "Brady never caught up with you for a long time, but he found a ranch where you'd been a few weeks before. He said you'd been working at a dude ranch in Oklahoma—breaking *wild* horses." Gerald hid a smile by rubbing his mouth.

Marti straightened up, embarrassed. "It wasn't like you think."

"*Hmm*, that's what I heard eventually, but I had to admit, his first report was unbelievable."

"I imagine so."

They both laughed.

"After his report from Oklahoma, Brady said he lost you, and he didn't find you again until last year."

"Yeah, the man chasing me was always one step behind me. I had to keep moving."

Gerald nodded. "Brady told me you had an unusual way of breaking horses at this ranch in Oklahoma and that the owners hated to see you leave."

Marti nodded excitedly. "Yeah. An Indian passing through the area worked on a neighboring ranch for a couple of weeks. Mostly what I did was muck out stalls, but at night, I'd go to the next farm and watch him break horses the Indian way. Before long I combined the technique with some ideas I had and was training horses myself. I use a much gentler approach than the old-fashioned way. It teaches the horse to trust humans and not be afraid, no matter what we do to them."

"That's what Brady said. Do you think you could teach us how?"

Marti shook her head. "Absolutely not."

"Why? Because you don't want to stay around with Daniel, or because you don't want to teach us your secret?"

She felt about an inch high. "Maybe a little of both."

"Marti, you remember how Daniel despised jumping on a green horse and riding him until either the horse's spirit broke or Daniel's did?"

Marti smiled. "I remember. He hated it. He said it didn't agree with his backside, and sometimes it broke the horse's spirit."

Gerald laughed. "Yep. That's what he said, all right." He paused. "Well, he's improved his technique in different ways since you were here, but it only works with horses that are already used to being handled. We have a bunch of horses that need breaking, and they're pretty wild."

An incredulous stare widened her eyes. "Daniel's colts were never wild."

Gerald shrugged. "He bought these colts from a man in Arizona. The bloodlines were excellent, but the owner was too old to deal with them, so he left the colts in the pasture with the mares. You know what that means. Some of these three-year-olds had never been handled until we brought them here"

"That's awful. Daniel was a firm believer of handling them from birth so they were easier to train."

"Yep. And I'm afraid these colts are going to be hard to break. That's why I thought your technique might be easier on both the man and the beast."

Marti smiled. She could see how much this meant to Gerald, so she pushed herself to give it a try.

"Won't Daniel be upset when he finds out?"

"He's not here today. Veronica toted him off somewhere . . . again." Gerald frowned, and under his breath he grumbled, "That's happening a lot lately."

Marti didn't know what to say, so she said nothing.

"Well, what do you think, Marti? Wanna give it a try?"

Marti heaved a loud sigh, trying to put thoughts out of her head and concentrate. "I'll try to help, but it's been a while since I've even been around horses, especially wild ones. And, I'm afraid I might mess things up. Daniel will be mad when he finds out."

"Let me worry about Daniel, okay? Come on. I asked Max to help us. We can work in the new arena—less distractions there."

Gerald had a spring in his step, and Marti was glad she agreed to help. As they walked, he turned to her and asked, "Now, tell me about this technique."

"Well, I'm sure you know that horses are herd animals. They have a strong instinct to be with other horses. In the herd, the leader is usually the one who is most dominant—the one who watches out for the others. In order for us to break a horse, we have to show him we're the boss."

Excitement bled through her voice as she explained how the Indian herdsman taught her the instincts and thoughts of a horse. She had forgotten how exciting breaking horses in this way could be.

When Marti stepped into the new building, she noted how clean and new everything looked. Two rings were in the center of the building—a large one for horse shows and training, and a smaller one for displaying horses to buyers. The ground in both rings was covered with sawdust. Elevated sets of bleachers for visitors stretched across both sides of the building. Marti inhaled the familiar aromas and sighed in satisfaction.

Gerald led her to the smaller ring. "Now, give me a list of what you need?"

"Are the horses used to wearing a bit?"

"Yep. Daniel's been working with them so they're used to a halter, bridle, and bit. They also know how to obey commands while on the lead."

"Great. That will help. I need a couple of coils of rope, an old saddle blanket and saddle, a lead rope, a snaffle bit, and bridle. And horse treats, if you have them."

Max walked into the arena carrying everything she mentioned. "I got it already, Mr. Gerald."

Marti laughed as Gerald helped Max with the saddle and blanket. He slung them up over the ring fence.

"How did you know I was going to say yes, Max?"

"I know you, Mrs. Marti, and I knew you'd say yes. You're just plumb kindhearted. Should I bring in Midnight now?"

A tingly feeling traveled through Marti's stomach. She hadn't trained horses in a long time. Did she remember how?

"I guess I'm ready if you are."

Max came into the barn leading a black horse by a lead rope. Marti let the horse smell her hand then patted him on the head. "Good boy, Midnight. You and I are going to get along just fine." She led him into the smaller ring, unhooked the lead rope, and let the horse go. The young stallion immediately took off at a run, only to stop at the fence then pranced nervously around the circumference.

Marti talked to him softly and then picked up two pieces of coiled rope hanging on the fence.

"Here we go," she whispered to herself more than to the horse. "Here we go."

FORTY-ONE

Daniel walked toward the barn and heard a horse snorting in the new arena.

"What's going on in there?"

He changed his direction and turned toward the building. When he walked through the open door, he was shocked to see Marti in the small ring with one of the colts running around the circumference of the ring. His father and Max both stood watching on the bottom seat of the bleachers. Daniel said nothing but climbed up three rows of bleachers. Taking a seat, he gawked at what was happening.

Marti held two coils of rope—one in each hand. He watched as she raised a coil in front of the horse and turned the colt in the other direction. The horse's eyes were wide and a little wild. He recognized Midnight—one of the more skittish three-year-olds.

Every time the horse turned in one direction to get away from Marti, a coil of rope was waved in his face on the other side of the ring, and he spun in the other direction.

"What's she doing?" Daniel whispered to himself.

"Daniel." Daniel was so astonished to find Marti working with a horse that he hadn't noticed his father move over beside him.

"What's she doing, Dad?" He watched her jump in front of the horse. "She's going to get hurt."

"I think you'll find she knows what she's doing, Daniel. She's using the instincts of the horse to train him. In the wild, if the dominant mare decides a colt is misbehaving, she runs the colt out of the herd and won't let him come back. That shows the young horse that she's in charge. Marti's showing Midnight that she's the boss."

"But these horses aren't wild, Dad—they're just not used to being handled."

"I think all horses have the same instincts, Daniel. Let's wait and see."

Finally, after being turned many times in the opposite direction, Midnight stopped and snorted, breathing hard. He stood still and watched Marti warily.

As he watched, Daniel was surprised to see Marti turn her back to Midnight and slowly walk across the ring, keeping her back to the horse.

"Now, she's showing the colt she's ready to accept him back."

Daniel watched in fascination as the horse stared at Marti for a few moments before slowly walking up to her back. The horse lifted his head over Marti's shoulder and nudged her gently.

"Amazing," Daniel whispered.

"Just wait and see."

Suddenly, his father's knowledge startled him. "How do you know what she's doing?"

His father put his finger over his lips. "*Shhh!*" He pointed toward Marti.

Daniel's gaze drifted back toward Marti. He saw her turn to the horse and rub its neck. She walked to the side of the ring with Midnight following behind and picked up a blanket from the top of the fence. While patting the colt with one hand, she placed the blanket on his back with the other. The colt immediately bucked it off. Marti picked up the blanket and let Midnight smell the blanket. He snorted but stood still. After a minute or two, she rubbed the colt's neck and again placed the blanket back on his back. This time the horse didn't move. His head twisted a little to the side, but he stood perfectly still. While Marti walked around the fence, the colt followed. She stopped in front of a saddle balanced on the top plank of the ring.

Daniel recognized the old saddle as one he used frequently for breaking horses. Marti pulled it down and gently laid it on the horse's back. Midnight snorted and twisted his head around but left the saddle in place.

"She's not going to ride him, is she, Dad? Apollo's already thrown her once."

"*Shhhh*" was his only response.

Marti slowly and gently pulled the girth underneath and tightened it just enough to keep it on. Then she turned and walked away.

Daniel was astonished to see the colt follow her around the ring with the saddle on his back. Midnight acted as if it wasn't there at all.

After a couple of turns around the ring, Marti walked to the middle of the circle and stopped. The colt followed. She turned and patted the horse. Daniel could see her mouth moving and knew she was talking in soft, soothing tones. She reached in her pocket and gave the horse a snack. After a few minutes, she put one foot in the stirrup and put her weight on the horse's back. Midnight shifted to the side but turned to watch Marti as if waiting to see what she would do next.

Marti dismounted and tightened the cinch a couple more notches before she lifted herself up into the saddle.

The colt jumped and pranced around the ring, but he didn't buck or try to get Marti off his back. The easy going but firm tones of her voice reached Daniel's ears as the colt calmed down and settled into a steady walk.

A feeling of wonder swelled inside Daniel. Marti was remarkable. What a special woman. He watched in awe as she led the colt around the ring at a walk. When she pulled back on the reins, the colt acted a bit uncertain but finally stopped. Marti patted him again, talked quietly, and gently prodded him with the heel of her shoe. Midnight jumped and started walking again.

Gerald's chest stuck out as he turned to Daniel and smiled. "Now, what do you think of that? Don't you think Marti's technique is a lot better than needing a chiropractor at the end of a workout?"

"Amazing." Daniel was stunned. "She just did in a short time what takes me much longer to do. It's definitely much easier on the horse."

"And the man's backside."

Daniel smiled. Gerald patted him on the back. "It's all about trust, Daniel. Trust can move mountains. You might remember that, son." Gerald winked and then carefully climbed down the bleachers.

Daniel watched as his father walked from the building and had the definite feeling his dad had been trying to tell him something.

FORTY-TWO

Marti looked up from rubbing Midnight's neck to see Daniel entering the ring.

"Daniel. I thought you were in town."

"I haven't been here long. I left Veronica at the florist. All those wedding preparations make my head hurt."

Marti's thoughts raced back to their wedding seven years ago. Daniel had insisted on attending every aspect of their wedding plans—cake tasting, flower arranging party, and the three showers they were given. His not wanting to be involved didn't sound like the Daniel she knew—or at least a Daniel who was excited about his own wedding.

She waved an arm at the ring. "I'm sorry—"

"That was absolutely incredible."

She was shocked. "You're not angry?"

Surprise turned Daniel's eyes a brighter shade of brown. "Why would I be angry?"

"I was training one of your horses without your permission. I know how important the initial training is to the future behavior of a horse."

"Well, from what I saw, you took the fear right out of Midnight. Anything that gentles a green colt has to make his training a whole lot easier."

"Just because he's wearing a saddle now doesn't mean he'll do it first thing tomorrow. He'll have to get used to the idea gradually."

"Still, that was amazing. I've never seen anyone break a horse that gently. And I thought you were a beginner."

Daniel was paying her a compliment? Marti looked up into his eyes, and her heart stuttered. So many tender memories flooded into the tiny room of her heart. She would drown in the pain if she didn't do something. She looked down at the sawdust and tried to breathe.

Daniel took Midnight's halter and called for Max.

"Take him, Max, and give him a few extra oats. He deserves it."

Max nodded and beamed from ear to ear as he led Midnight back to his reward.

Daniel waved Marti over to the bottom seat on the bleachers, and they sat down together. He lifted her chin so he could look into her eyes.

"Marti, I'm sorry about the other day. It shouldn't have happened. I don't know what it is about you, but I feel this connection. On one hand, I feel like I'm in a tunnel and I want to explore down that pathway. I'm convinced that at the end of the tunnel there will be something wonderful."

Marti's voice was quiet and thoughtful. "And on the other hand?"

Daniel's lips tightened. "On the other hand, there's Veronica. We grew up together, went to school together, learned to ride horses together. We've dated for years."

Marti's mouth opened as if she wanted to say something, but she bit her lip instead.

"Now we're getting married. I can't ignore that part of my life."

Marti sat still for a moment and then whispered, "Do you love her?"

Daniel started and stared at her. "My father asked me the same question."

"What did you tell him?"

For a minute, he hesitated. She could see flakes of indecision in his eyes, but she gazed deeply into the brown spheres, begging him to be honest with himself.

"I'm comfortable with Veronica. I just don't know how I feel about our friendship moving into something more . . . intimate, to be honest with you."

"How did you feel about marriage when you married the first time?"

"That, I can't remember. My dad says it was nothing like this, but look how it turned out."

Marti turned to face him and took his hand in hers. "Daniel, I know you can't remember your wife, and from what you've told me, you don't want to. But, according to your father, you obviously loved her at one time because you married her. If you're uncertain of your feelings, maybe you should at least wait on your marriage with Veronica until you get your memories back so you can remember what love feels like."

Daniel's eyes were sienna brown in the sunlight filtering into the arena from the skylights overhead, but it wasn't the color Marti saw—it was pure, undiluted pain. Concern for him and his happiness burned so bright in her eyes that she knew he couldn't miss what they were telling him.

"Why do you care?"

Marti couldn't concentrate with his eyes boring into hers, so she dropped his hand and walked a short distance away. "I believe God has a perfect plan for our lives—the right place to live, an appropriate job, an ideal mate. When we step outside the plan He has for us, it messes up everything." She turned to him then. "Maybe you should pray about your decision."

Daniel stood up impatiently. "I don't know how to pray, and to be honest, I'm not sure there is a God who answers prayers anyway. My dad told me before my accident I became a believer in God and what the Bible teaches, but I don't feel it in here." He placed his hand over his heart. "My professors in college said the Bible is just a good piece of literature. Do you believe the Bible is God's book?"

"Oh yes. There're too many irrefutable facts that *prove* it's really God's Word."

"That's not what my professors taught. Give me one good piece of evidence that the Bible is God's Word?"

"I can give you several."

"Yeah? I'll listen to one, so give it your best shot."

She laughed. "Hashtag: pressure." She stepped toward him. "Okay. I'll start with one, and then maybe you'll let me tell you the others later?"

He grinned out of the corner of his mouth. "We'll see."

She laughed and raised one finger in the air. "One—there are more than two thousand specific predictions in the Bible that have come true—and not only have they all come true, but a lot of them came true hundreds and sometimes thousands of years *after* the writers of the Bible predicted. They're very specific too—not these general predictions made by palm readers or psychics you hear about today, and they don't contradict each other."

"Is that true?"

"Look in your history books. The Bible predicted the fall of great empires like Rome, Greece, and Babylon. It even predicted the specific circumstances surrounding the fall of Babylon. If you know your history, Babylon was a great city and has affected almost every area of our lives today. They came up with the first algebra equations, baked bricks, even the alphabet. They also, in some ways, influenced our laws, science, art, astrology, and so much more. As great as they were, you would have thought they would still be around today. But the Bible predicted they would fall—with over one hundred specific predictions or prophecies about Babylon's fall that came true *years* after the prophecies were written. There were predictions about Jerusalem too . . . that it would be destroyed and then restored. That also came true."

"That's two reasons," he teased.

She laughed. "Well, maybe, but it's all about the Bible predictions."

"Okay, okay. You're right; it gives me something to think about. You seem passionate about Bible history. How do you know so much about it?"

Marti froze. Should she tell Daniel she was a believer? Would he shun her if she did?

"I believe the Bible is God's book to us, Daniel" she admitted, gazing off into the distance. "I believe the Bible tells us that Jesus came to earth as a baby to be a blameless sacrifice for our sins. He died on the cross for those same sins and rose again to offer us salvation from an eternity in hell."

Daniel was quiet. "I wish I could remember why I believed . . . as my dad said . . . but I'm not ready to step into something I'm not sure about."

Marti turned to Daniel and put her hands on each side of his face. "If that's true about your future in eternity, then why are you willing to step into something as important as marriage when you're not sure about it either?"

Daniel's gaze never left hers. Marti could see in his expression that he got the point. His eyes turned the bright shade of brown that made her stomach tingle. She caressed one check then forced herself to turn around and walk toward the house.

This decision was something Daniel had to settle for himself. Maybe he would listen to her words and give himself a little more time. For the first time since she arrived, she felt a flicker of hope blaze up into a flame of possibility.

FORTY-THREE

Zach Parsons stepped out of the bunkhouse cabin on the Rushing estate and gazed at the morning fog wafting down from the mountains. What a beautiful sight. He frowned as he turned toward the barn. Of all days to wake up late. Today was the annual Quarter Horse Association picnic, and as soon as everyone finished their morning chores, all the hired hands had the rest of the day off. He had plans for the day. Starting late would put him behind. He'd have to wolf down a breakfast bar out of the kitchen instead of a hot meal.

He shrugged into a light jacket and felt something jingling in the pocket. Reaching inside, he pulled out his set of work keys. *That's* where they were. He thought he'd never see them again after he lost them last week. He sure didn't remember slipping them into his work jacket.

Zach shrugged and slammed the door shut. His thoughts wandered to his conversation with Jordan Welsh. Should he leave the Rushing farm and move to the Welsh setup? He'd been promised he'd make more money. He needed to stay here a little longer and learn more about Daniel's training practices; then he'd impress Jordan with his abilities. Daniel's methods didn't seem that hard to copy—being patient was the only difference he could see. If he could learn how to get good results, he'd be popular with all the ranches in the area.

Inside the kitchen, he grabbed a breakfast bar and a honeybun before striding the distance to the barn, eating as he went. At the barn, he opened the small door to the office. Chores for each stable hand were posted daily on the bulletin board right inside the door. Lately, he'd done nothing but muck out stalls. He hated that job. It'd be a whole lot better if his chores were something different today—like feeding hay or sweeping the barn walkway for the visitors coming to the picnic.

His name was first on the list. *Muck out stalls one through ten. Empty trash cans and haul to dumpster. Straighten shelves in storage room. Muck out stalls ten through twenty.*

A groan escaped his lips. He threw his breakfast bar wrapper into one of the empty wheelbarrows stacked against the wall as he slipped the honeybun into his pocket, jerked down one of the flat shovels, and pitched it into the wheelbarrow. Working for the Welsh ranch looked sweeter and sweeter. Maybe he'd take that job, after all. He'd love to chuck this job and move on to better things. His real dream was training show horses, and if he could make Daniel's method work, he'd be able to find a job anywhere—and name his salary.

A bright yellow sticky-note stuck to the wall beside the office door caught his attention. His name was written across the top.

He moaned. Another chore. This had to stop. Max thought he was the owner of the place—adding more chores to the already long list—as if he didn't have enough to do.

Zach stepped back to the office door and yanked the note off the wall. He read the note and frowned. It was signed "Max." Of course.

According to the note, Mr. Rushing wanted him to go to the ravine pasture first thing this morning and check on the four-year-old fillies grazing there for the summer. He was supposed to check the printed list and record each filly's condition and progress. Hot dog! Something besides mucking out stalls. But, it would take him at least an hour to record the information for the four-year-olds.

The rest of the note said he should also take the backhoe and bring back a couple bales of hay. Irritation deepened the wrinkles between his eyes, and he wadded the note up and threw it into the trash. Didn't Max know they were having trouble with the brakes on the backhoe? How was he supposed to feed hay with no brakes?

He stood there and thought for a minute. There was no other way to pick up a bale of hay without the forks attached to the front of the backhoe bucket—the other tractor with the loading fork was in the hay field. He shrugged. The extra weight from the hay bale might help stop the tractor. He'd check it out. If the weight helped, he'd use the backhoe anyway.

He pulled the clipboard with the filly's chart off the shelf in the office and stomped to the equipment shed. After filling the backhoe with diesel, he cranked the cantankerous machine. It spit and sputtered but finally settled into a rough rhythm. He climbed up on the seat and lifted the loader bucket in the front of the machine until it was well above the ground. The dipper bucket in back groaned as it lifted off the hard dirt. When both buckets were two feet above the ground, Zach backed the machine out of the shed and let it slide to a stop in the driveway.

Man! Warren was right. The brakes were as soft as sheep's wool. The pedal went plumb to the floor. He twisted the steering wheel until the machine was turned toward the back pasture. It was a straight shot. If he was careful, he could make the whole trip without brakes.

Humming to himself, he drove the five miles on full throttle and arrived at the ravine pasture in twenty minutes. He slowed the motor and parked it under a stand of maple trees and away from the fence edging the ravine. The fillies were grazing a short distance away, so he stepped down off the backhoe and turned toward the horses. He took his time, marked each mare down on the clipboard, and recorded size and approximate weight.

A bay filly munched on grass a few feet from him. She was as round as a wooden water barrel. He double-checked her records and saw she'd been grazing in this pasture for a while now. Her bloating was probably caused by over-eating. He remembered Daniel saying too much of the fresh spring grass causes bloating. That's a fact he needed to remember if he went to the Welsh outfit.

Yep, this filly needed moving to the corral at the stable so her feedings could be monitored. He noted it on the chart and made one final check of each horse's overall condition. The rest of the horses were active and seemed to be in good health.

He strolled over to the backhoe, propped the clipboard on the seat, and pulled the honeybun out of his shirt pocket. The morning sun had risen just above the ravine and red light shimmering in the morning fog made the ravine look blood red. What a beautiful place.

When he heard the crack of a broken stick behind him, he turned to see who was sneaking up on him. No one was there. That was odd. He was sure he'd heard a footstep.

He took the last bite of his honeybun, threw the plastic wrapper down in the pasture, and stepped over to a wild stand of blackberries. Luscious berries covered the bushes, and he washed down the last bite of his honeybun with the juice from the berries.

When he'd had enough, he wiped his hands in the grass and walked back to the maple trees. He lifted his foot to climb up onto the backhoe when he felt a hard blow to the back of his head.

His last conscious moment was hearing the words, "Sorry about this, man, but you were in the wrong place at just the right time."

FORTY-FOUR

Marti sat down on the metal bench of the portable picnic table and glanced around the ranch. She couldn't believe how the place had been transformed in the last twenty-four hours. Especially for the occasion, square bales of hay decorated corners of the yard, and pots of blooming geraniums and petunias hung from trees and posts located around the picnic area.

Silently, she watched women arrange desserts and salads on the long tables set up for food. Smoke from grills full of hamburgers and hot dogs filled the air with tantalizing aromas and made her stomach growl. Embarrassed, she crossed her arms over her stomach to hide the sound and spoke to Stella standing beside the table.

"Can I help with something, Stella?"

Stella gave her a lost look and grinned. "If I knew what to do myself, I'd be happy to let you help, but since I don't know what I'm doing either, it'd be like the blind leading the blind."

They both laughed.

"Just relax, honey, and let Mr. Gerald be the big boss of this shindig. In the kitchen, he knows I'm the boss, but at this picnic every year, I let him tell everybody what to do, and I stay out of it. It's all right if the women let the men be in charge once a year." She grinned and ambled back toward the kitchen.

Marti caught sight of a golden retriever on the outskirts of the crowd. He lifted his nose in the air, smelling for something familiar. Then suddenly, as if he'd found what he was looking for, he squeezed through the crowd of children and adults and made a beeline for the tables. His tail twirled around in circles in his excitement.

Marti jerked back as huge paws plopped in her lap and a bobbing head propped on her knees.

"Samson!" a woman yelled, running toward them.

Marti stared at the dog. Samson? *Her* Samson? Instantly she rubbed her cheeks in the fur on the dog's face and put her arms around his neck. "Oh, you sweetie. You remembered me!"

She buried her face in the soft strands of reddish-gold and held back the tears. The golden retriever had been a birthday gift from Skyler only a month before Marti left the ranch. The day she left, she called Skyler and left a message on her answering machine to please take the dog home with her to live. Through an abundance of tears, Marti had left him sitting forlornly outside the ranch house, believing she would never see the affectionate pup again.

Skyler, out of breath from chasing the dog, picked up the trailing leash and rubbed her hand on her forehead. "Man! I figured he'd remember you, but I had no idea he'd react that way."

Marti looked up into the face of her friend. Three years had turned her into a beautiful young woman. "Skyler! Oh, it's so good to see you again." She set the dog's paws on the ground and stood up to give her friend a warm hug.

"Yeah. This is great. Cynthia and I saw Gerald in town last week. He told us you were coming for a visit, but he didn't know when or how long you'd be here."

Marti felt a twinge of discomfort. "He told you I was coming? But, I didn't even let him know I was coming for sure. How did he know?"

Skyler's mouth widened into a circle. "Oh, I'm sorry. I wasn't supposed to mention that he told us. He was at the craft store, and the sales lady let it slip that he was stocking an art studio. We were nosy, and I guess we sort of dragged it out of him. But, he gave us strict instructions not to tell anyone, and I promise, we didn't tell a soul."

Marti felt a knot in the pit of her stomach. "We?"

"Cynthia and me. But, don't worry. Gerald swore us both to secrecy."

The revelation that Gerald was so sure she would stay and paint the portrait was something Marti wasn't expecting. He said he'd prayed about her staying. His prayers must have been potent.

She smiled at Skyler. "Where is Cynthia, anyway? Best I remember, you two were inseparable."

"She'll be here in a little while. She's having her hair done. Don't ask me why. It's not like there are tons of men around here to impress." Her laugh tinkled in the morning air. "Oh, there she is now. Hey, Cynthia!" Skyler yelled as Cynthia got out of her car, which she had parked on the side of the driveway. Cynthia waved her hand in greeting.

"Man, I'm glad she's here. We have something we wanna ask you."

Marti tilted her head to the side. She wasn't sure she wanted to hear what the two young women had dreamed up. She had a feeling she wouldn't like it.

Cynthia came bounding over to the table with a brown grocery sack in her hands. "You found her, Skyler. Have you asked her yet?"

Skyler looked guilty. "Not yet. I thought I'd wait on you."

Cynthia scowled.

"Ask me what?" Marti asked warily.

Cynthia dropped her bag on the table. "For the last three years, the Chamber of Commerce has been sponsoring a fundraiser for a deserving orphanage. They charge money for touring the antebellum houses and churches in Carson, and the Carson Artist Group helps out by holding a plein air painting competition. We paint the beautiful houses during the day, and then they hold an auction late in the afternoon and sell the paintings."

"Yeah," Skyler interrupted, "And this year, we were wondering . . . well . . . if you'd be interested. I mean, you're such a good artist and everything. We thought you might like to—"

"Enter a painting in the auction?"

"Exactly. Would you? Please, please, please? It's for a good cause, and if we can get you on board, other artists might join as well. You know, there's nothing like a good friendly competition." Skyler grinned.

"When is it?"

"Saturday."

"I'll think about it, but I can't promise. I might not be here that long."

Cynthia pouted. "You're not leaving already."

Marti shrugged. "I'm not sure. I may have to go back."

"Please think about it, Martha, won't you?" Skyler gave her a hug.

"Okay, I'll think about it, but only if you agree to call me Marti. I dropped the name Martha when I left here three years ago, and, uh . . . it might be confusing . . . if you know what I mean."

Cynthia jumped up. "Yeah, that's right. You mean because of Daniel, of course. Will do. Oh! I gotta run. I promised I'd help slice cakes and brownies, and I can't do that until I get rid of these chips and buns. Come on, Skyler—you can help. *Marti*, I'll get you a copy of the application form, and we can talk to you later about the auction, okay?"

"Sure." Marti smiled and gave Samson one last hug. "See you later, Samson."

Tears burned the back of Marti's eyes. She stood up and walked closer to the water's edge. She'd lost so much when she left here three years ago. She rubbed the tears from her eyes and listened to the ripples of water making splashing sounds when tiny waves washed up on the shore.

"Miss Marti! Miss Marti!"

Marti turned to smile at Chris as he bounded across the grass and wrapped his arms around her legs. She picked him up and leaned back as he thrust something toward her.

"See what I got?" He held several sticks and a colorful wad of paper.

"Hey, Chris. What do you have there?"

"It's a kite. Unc'l Dan'l bought it for me. He's gonna help me. You wanna play?"

Marti looked up to see Daniel standing beside her. Her heart did a little dance in her chest. Man, he looked good. His dark hair ruffled in the cool breeze, and the smile on his face made her heart flutter. She tore her gaze away and back to Chris.

"I'd love to play kites with you, Chris. Thank you for asking me."

Daniel patted Chris on the head. "Let's wait until after we eat, buddy."

"Ohhhkaay."

Marti heard the disappointment in Chris' answer and had an idea.

"Why don't you go see if you can find some unusual pebbles on the beach?"

Chris' head perked up. "Hey, I'm gonna look for shells." He squirmed until Marti put him down, and then he grabbed Marti's hand. "Come help, Miss Marti."

"Well, Chris, I don't think—"

"There's one, Miss Marti. There's one!" Chris pulled his hand out of Marti's clutch and ran to pick up something on the ground. His little face lit up and he ran back. "I found one. I found one!" He showed a dark pebble to Daniel and Marti.

He handed it to Marti. "It's a shell."

Daniel looked at the pebble. "I don't think this is a shell, Chris, it's a pebble."

Chris stood up straight and shook his little brown head. "No, Unc'l Dan'l. It's a shell. I know. Ronica said shells are always on the beach."

Daniel looked at Marti and winked.

"Whatever you say, Chris."

"Look! I see more."

Chris was off running down the beach trying to pick up all the pebbles his tiny hands would hold.

"Don't get your clothes wet!" Daniel yelled.

"He's as cute as a button," Marti said as she watched the little boy kicking at the waves.

"Veronica will kill me if he gets his clothes wet."

"Oh, they'll dry."

Chris' laughter sounded like music, and she sighed. One day maybe the Lord would answer her prayer for a child of her own.

Daniel turned to Marti. "I've been thinking about what you said about why the Bible is God's Word. Are you ready to argue with me a little more?"

Marti laughed. "Okay. Let me tell you another reason we can know the Bible is God's Word. It was written by more than forty writers who were from different backgrounds—anywhere from fishermen to politicians. They wrote the Bible in three different languages, and they all came from three different continents—yet the Bible sounds like it could have been written by the same man. None of their writings contradict each other, yet they were written over a span of fifteen hundred years. Don't you think that's amazing?"

"Yeah, I guess it is . . . if it's all true."

"Of course it's true. Research it for yourself."

"I just might do that." He laughed at the assured lift of her head.

"Marti!" Marti turned to see Skyler run over to them. "Cynthia and I have to go to work at the clinic. There's been an accident on the interstate, and they need our help. We probably won't make it back before the picnic's over. How about we meet in town and have lunch tomorrow? How does that sound?"

"That sounds good, Skyler. I'm sorry you'll miss the picnic."

"That's okay. Not many single men here anyway."

When Skyler left running, Marti and Daniel exchanged a smile.

"Hey, I could take you to town tomorrow. I have to go by the feed store anyway, and—"

"Daniel."

Marti cringed inside. That grating, familiar voice.

Daniel and Marti both turned to see Veronica sashaying across the yard toward them.

"Veronica. Hey."

Veronica slid up beside Daniel and gave him a showy kiss on the lips. "Hey, darling. Did you miss me?"

Marti fumed inside. Her teeth ground together so hard her jaw hurt.

"Of course," said Daniel. "Chris and I bought a kite on the way over, and now he's picking up pebbles. Hashtag: shells."

Daniel looked at Marti and grinned. When she laughed at the private joke, Veronica's eyes turned a frosty shade of green, and her nostrils flared.

"Did I hear you offering to take Marti to town tomorrow? You know we have that meeting with the pastor." She turned to Marti. "I'm sorry, Marti, but you'll have to find your own ride to town. Daniel and I have business to take care of."

Veronica linked her arm in Daniel's. "Come on, Daniel. Let's check on Chris. I haven't seen him all morning, and I've missed him so."

"Okay." Daniel turned to Marti. "I'll work something out if you'd like a ride. Just let me know."

Marti could feel Veronica's protectiveness building and shook her head. "That's okay. I'm not sure how long I'll be. It'd be best if I took my own car."

"Okay, but if you change your mind, let me know. See you later, Marti. I'm sure Chris will come get you when it's time to fly the kite."

"Thanks." Marti's stomach burned inside as she watched Veronica lead Daniel over to the lake. What felt like salt in a wound was the way Veronica stooped down to give Chris a huge bear hug and a kiss on the cheek. Daniel and Veronica each took one of Chris' hands and lifted him into the air. His squeal traveled across the sand and pierced its way right into Marti's heart. Again, she wondered at the similarities between "Unc'l Dan'l" and Veronica's "adopted" baby boy.

FORTY-FIVE

"Mr. Rushing! Mr. Rushing!"
Max ran in the back door of the house and flew right past Gerald and Marti talking at the kitchen table.

"Hey, Max, I'm right here. What's the trouble?"

Max's face was all flushed, and he was out of breath.

"I found this note in the barn, and Zach's missing." He handed an oily piece of paper to Gerald, who took it carefully.

"What is it, Max?"

"Read it, sir."

Gerald glanced at Marti and sighed. After cleaning up from the picnic, he was plumb tuckered out. He pulled out his reading glasses and read the note out loud.

"I'm sorry for the trouble I've caused her all these years. She didn't deserve what I did to her. Guilt won't let me live with what I've done. Zach

Marti gasped.

"Marti? Are you okay?"

Her hands covered her mouth. "Do you think Zach might be talking about me?"

Gerald read the note again. "Well, it does sound like it fits, doesn't it? But, did you even know Zach before?"

She shook her head.

"Max, do you have any idea what he meant?"

"No sir, but the backhoe's gone too. Warren was supposed to work on the brakes this morning, but he came and told me it wasn't in the equipment shed. I thought you or Daniel had moved it for the picnic, so I didn't think about it anymore until now."

"Well, if Zach left on the backhoe, he can't be far. That old thing won't travel more than fifteen miles an hour. Did you say the brakes needed work?"

"Yes, sir. They gave out yesterday. You couldn't stop it if your life depended on it."

"Take the truck and see if you and the boys can find him, Max. Look in the storage shed. Maybe he's stacking the tables from the picnic. And look in the hay pasture—he could be hauling in a load of hay. If you find him, bring him back in the truck. I don't want him driving the backhoe if the brakes are bad. I don't know what that letter's about, but when we find him, we'll ask him."

"Yes, sir."

Gerald patted Marti on the shoulder. "We'll figure out what's going on, Marti. If Zach is the one stalking you, we'll find out why."

Marti's face was pale, but she returned a trembling smile and nodded.

Gerald left his breakfast and went to find Parker. Anita must have started on her spring cleaning projects, because he found Parker hanging up blinds that Anita had washed and dried with a towel. Parker's two-year-old son Gavin was playing with blocks on the floor.

Gerald leaned over and touched the little boy on the nose. "Hello, Gavin. You sure have grown since I saw you last."

The look on Parker's face surprised Gerald. He looked like he'd been caught doing something illegal.

"Parker, have you seen Zach this morning?"

"No, sir. I was in town until about an hour ago. I had to go get Gavin from daycare. I'm sorry, sir." He ducked his head and averted his eyes.

"It's okay for you to have Gavin here, Parker. I know sometimes you and Anita have scheduling problems."

Parker's eyes searched Gerald's. "Are you sure, sir? I didn't want to keep him here, but we couldn't find a babysitter, and—"

"It's fine. Now, if you see Zach, tell him I'm looking for him."

"Yes, sir."

Gerald gave him a calming look and walked out the back door. He was walking to the barn when the old white pickup came rumbling into the barnyard. It slid to a stop in front of Gerald, and Max leaped out—agitated about something.

"Mr. Gerald, Caleb found Zach at the bottom of the ravine in the back forty. The boys are rigging up a rope system to get him out."

"Is he all right?"

"No, sir."

Gerald turned to rush inside. "I'll call 9-1-1."

Max grabbed Gerald's arm to stop him. "No, Mr. Gerald. It's too late. He's gone."

Gerald's face felt cold. "Are you sure?"

"Yes, sir. The backhoe fell on top of him."

"Oh, no."

"I already called 9-1-1, so they'll be sending out the coroner."

Gerald sat down on the chair sitting in the yard. His fists gripped the edge of the seat. "I don't understand. We spent all last summer reinforcing that fence. Why didn't the fence stop him?"

"I don't know. It looks like he ran the backhoe right through the fence and off the cliff. After that note we found, some of the boys are wondering if it was suicide."

"Suicide?" Gerald lowered his voice and leaned forward. "Max, you knew him better than anybody. Do you believe he could have been stalking Marti?"

"I don't know, sir. Zach kept to himself most of the time, but even Houdini couldn't be in two places at one time. I'm not sure Zach was gone enough to stalk anybody. He didn't act like he was planning suicide either, but there were no skid marks on the ground where he went over. It doesn't look like he touched the brake at all."

"You said the backhoe had no brakes. Maybe he tried but they wouldn't work."

"If that was the case, Mr. Gerald, he would have had time to jump off before it reached the edge. Or he could have turned the thing away from the edge when he realized the brakes weren't working."

Gerald's shoulders slumped. "Okay, Max. I'll come out with the sheriff when he gets here. Go back and help the boys rig up the rope, but tell them not to touch anything until the sheriff says it's okay."

"Yes, sir."

Gerald leaned his head back against the seat and closed his eyes. Thoughts of the backhoe going over the edge of the cliff with Zach straddling the seat burned into his thoughts. Max was right. Zach would have known long before he reached the edge that the brakes were not working. That backhoe was as slow as a new born foal rising to his feet. Why didn't Zach jump? Would they ever know the truth of what happened? And what about that note? Was Marti the one Zach mentioned?

FORTY-SIX

Clara Watting leaned her tall body up under the hood of her Tahoe as she watched steam bubble up from the engine. The water hose was still attached at both ends, but a gaping crack spewed steam that quickly covered everything under the hood in droplets of water.

Nothing was turning out as she'd planned. The man she was "requesting" money from—blackmail seemed like such a nasty word—seemed determined to ignore her demands. She'd put a scare into him. Maybe that would light a fire under his dillydallying.

But the bigger problem at the moment was getting to town. Maybe she could wrap tape around the water hose and make a temporary patch. Every good nurse had tape in a first-aid kit, and she just happened to have one in the trunk.

She examined the hose carefully, and what she discovered made her legs weak. The crack was not jagged, but a straight, even cut. The rubber had been sliced by something sharp. Had someone wanted her to run out of water? For what reason?

She lifted up her head and quickly scanned the landscape. The low mountains on either side of the road fell away to rolling hills. Only one area around her gave enough cover for someone to hide.

"Get a grip, Clara. How could he know the hose would break in this exact spot? There's no way he'd know to hide around here. What? Did you think he'd be hiding in the bushes somewhere?"

Talking aloud to the car eased her tension but couldn't take away the knot in her stomach.

Patching the long slit in the hose was out of the question. Now what was she going to do?

She glanced at the road behind her and saw a black truck parked on the side of the road just inside the curve of the mountain she had passed a moment before. That truck hadn't been there when she crossed the mountain, had it? A cold sweat broke out over her large frame. Could it be the same person who booby-trapped her SUV?

She slid around behind the hood—hidden from view of the truck—and leaned against the front of the SUV, trying to think.

As she stood mulling over ideas, the beep-beep of a horn reached her ears. She leaned around the hood in time to see a white car circle the mountain and pass the black truck, traveling toward her. When the car rounded the last curve, Clara leaned around the fender of her car and waved her hands. The white Ford Focus slowed when it came closer, and for an instant, a sliver of fear made her hesitate. But a glance at the black truck still parked in the curve strengthened her decision. Surely the person in the white car would be the lesser of two evils.

The white car slowed and gently pulled off the road in front of Clara and her vehicle. A woman leaned out of the window. "Do you need help?"

Clara did a double-take. Martha Rushing. Before the picnic, she hadn't seen her in years—not since the accident and the scandal. This was the second time in two days.

Clara pushed aside her train of thought, grabbed her purse from the console, and ran to the passenger side of the white car.

"Do you mind taking me to town?" She took one last peek at the black truck and slid into the seat. "My water hose is busted, and the radiator's out of water."

"Sure. I met you at the picnic yesterday, didn't I? Aren't you one of the nurses at the Marvel County Clinic with Skyler and Cynthia?"

Clara sniffed. "I'm the *head* nurse at the clinic, yes."

"I thought I recognized you. I'm Marti Rushing."

"Yeah, I remember who you are." She could tell her short tones surprised Marti. Clara saw the shutters close over Marti's eyes and turned away to fasten her seat belt. After the rumors that circulated around town about the accident three years ago, Marti had reason to be embarrassed.

Marti put the car in gear and pulled out into the road. "I'll drop you off at the garage on this side of town," she said quietly.

"Thanks." Clara pulled the mirror down on the visor and pretended to fix her hair while she looked to see if the black truck was following. She caught a glimpse of a black shadow moving about a mile back, and anger bubbled up in her throat. She would take care of this threat for good—just as soon as she got into town and to a phone.

She turned to Marti. "Are you going all the way in to the square?"

Marti nodded. "Yes, I have a lunch meeting at the Carson Café in an hour."

"Would you mind waiting a minute while I talk to the mechanic, then taking me on into town with you?"

Marti hesitated and then nodded. "I'll wait."

Marti didn't seem too crazy about the imposition, but Clara didn't care. She had several things to pick up in town, but even more important was a certain phone conversation—and it would have to be taken care of immediately.

Clara kept silent while the rolling hills gave way to gradual signs of civilization. The car garage was located on the outskirts of town in an old rundown brick building. Marti pulled into the parking spot directly in front of the door and turned off the motor.

Clara slid out with a promise to be just a minute. She walked up to the door of the office, and out of the corner of her eye, she saw a black truck pull off the road and park. She squeezed her fists together and wrenched open the office door.

"Just wait," she murmured to herself. "I'll take care of you next."

FORTY-SEVEN

The face in the mirror stared back at him. He swore he had more wrinkles around his eyes than he ever had before. It was supposed to be so easy, but things weren't going as he planned. Now he'd have to implement option number two.

He took a deep breath and pulled a number from a tiny slip of paper in his wallet. He picked up the phone to dial, but it rang in his hand.

"Hello."

"Pardner, I have her in my sights. What do you want me to do?" The voice sounded agitated through the phone.

"Do you have that contraption with you?"

"You mean the bomb?"

"Don't say that word over the phone. I've told you before; anybody with a scanner can hear everything that's said on cell phones."

"Nobody's got a scanner around here, and even if they do, they won't have it tuned to this channel."

"The firemen and cops all have one, and I'm sure they know the exact frequency to use. You never know who might be listening. Just don't say anything you shouldn't."

"Okay, pardner."

"I told you to stop calling me that. Now, do you have it or not?"

"You mean the . . . I mean, yeah, I have it."

Okay, then use it, and don't let anyone see you. Do you hear?"

"Yeah, yeah. I hear. I know what I'm doing."

"How will you attach the . . . er, *key holder* to the car?"

"What? Oh, . . . well, it's magnetized. It'll only take a second to attach. It shouldn't be hard at all."

The man slumped down in his seat. "Well, be careful. If you get caught, you're on your own."

"Yeah, I know. Just like always."

When he hung up the phone, he sat back in his chair and felt a heavy weight on his chest. It had to be done. It was the only way. It was his life or hers. She could mess everything up. He should have taken care of it long before this. If he didn't take care of it now, it would soon be too late.

FORTY-EIGHT

Marti sat in the sweltering heat, waiting for Clara to come out of the garage. The sooner she dropped Clara off, the better. The look on the head nurse's face proved one thing—she'd heard and believed all the rumors and accusations hurled at Marti three years ago. Marti could see it in the wary look in Clara's eyes, and it made her uncomfortable. The court case had been in all the local papers. The Rushings were an important family in the community, and according to the rumors, Marti had disgraced their name.

Marti's clothes felt as if they were melting to her skin. It must be over one hundred degrees today. She reached to turn on the ignition and start up the air conditioner when Clara exited the building.

Clara opened the door and settled into the car. "Now, I'm ready to go on into town. You said you have a meeting at the Carson Café?"

Marti nodded and cranked the car. "Yes."

"Abel said he'd go out and replace the hose on my car and then drive it back to the garage. He was pretty sure it would take less than an hour. I have a couple of stops to make in town, so would it be all right if we park at the café, and then I'll meet you there afterwards so you can bring me back here to get my car?"

"I guess that's okay. I'm not sure how long my lunch will be, but you can wait for me in the park if you get through before I do."

Marti drove to the restaurant on the corner of the square. There was nowhere to park in the restaurant parking lot, so she parallel-parked in one of the pay-by-the-hour spaces across the street. They both got out of the car and stepped onto the sidewalk.

Marti watched Clara glance down the road and scrutinize the traffic. A wrinkle appeared between her brows, and Marti turned to see what held her attention. A black truck disappeared around the corner of the next block. She wondered if it was someone Clara knew. It seemed she wasn't too happy to see the truck. Maybe it was someone she was trying to avoid.

Marti stepped up to the antique meter and saw it was empty. She fumbled in her purse for change, but Clara stepped forward.

"Here, let me take care of that. It's the least I can do to thank you for the ride into town. Would an hour and a half be enough, do you think?" When Marti nodded, Clara fed six quarters to the meter. The meter box clanged and registered ninety minutes on the display.

Clara turned to Marti. "Would you mind leaving the car door open in case I get back before you're done with your meeting? It's too hot to sit in the park."

Marti hesitated before digging out the extra set of keys from her purse. "Here, I have an extra key. Take this in case I'm not here when you get back. It's so hot, you might need to run the air conditioner to stay cool."

Clara took the key. "Thanks."

Marti watched Clara strut down the street toward the bus stop and plop down on the bench. Where is she going? Marti shrugged. It was really none of her business.

She turned toward the café and saw a man walking toward her. Stanley Baxter.

"Mr. Baxter! Hey, I thought I recognized you."

"Well, I'll be doggone, if it's not Martha Rushing." He held out his hand, but Marti pushed by his outstretched arm and gave him a sincere hug.

"How are all your family?"

"They're great. Chelsea sure missed you after you left. You should come see her little daughter, Maria. She's a little doll baby, and growing like a weed."

Marti laughed. "Maybe I will. Tell them all I said hello."

"Sure will, Marti. You take care now." He held the door for her as she walked into the restaurant and then followed her in. A man in a tan suit joined Mr. Baxter. The hostess led them to a table in the back.

Cool air hit Marti in the face as soon as she stepped up to the hostess desk, and she took pleasure in the feeling. She had forgotten how hot Texas spring days could be. The large round clock hanging above the cashier let her know she was ten minutes early.

When the hostess returned, Marti asked for a table on the balcony so she could look out the windows to the river running through the mountains. She stopped at the overlook and saw children splashing around in the shallow rocks and jumping from one smooth rock to another. Sounds of their laughter floated up on the humid air and mingled with the conversations of the other customers, adding a hominess to the atmosphere.

Marti glanced toward the street and noticed a man in a jumpsuit and hat lingering around her car. Her heart dropped to her stomach when he turned toward the restaurant and glanced up at the window. His sunglasses made it hard to see his features, but he stared up at the window. She nervously moved back away from the glass. When she inched back up to the side of the window and peeked around the ledge, the man was gone.

She rubbed her forehead. *You're crazy, Marti—looking for trouble when there isn't any.*

With a smile at the lady sitting next to her table, Marti sat down to watch the street below for her friends. Fans whirred overhead, pushing the cool air from the vents down to the tables below. Marti sat back and glanced around the room at the western style décor. She pulled out the plein air painting application Cynthia sent her through e-mail and began filling in the blanks. She was curious which orphanage they were supporting with the fundraiser. Alana had mentioned how important donors and fundraisers were to the orphanage they were connected with in Tennessee. Most non-profits existed only through donations. This was a fundraiser Marti could participate in wholeheartedly.

FORTY-NINE

Daniel threw the fifty-pound bag of horse feed onto the truck and used his shirt sleeve to wipe off the sweat running into his eyes. He stood for a moment and took a deep breath—paying special attention to the odor radiating from the pallet of stacked feed behind him. He walked back through the double doors connecting the storage room to the store section of the building and nodded at Walt, who was helping a customer behind the counter.

"Are you sure this feed's fresh, Walt? It smells off."

"I just got it in this morning, Daniel. They've added some kind of new yeast culture to help with digestion. That might be what you smell. It's not much different than before as far as performance goes."

"Okay . . . just checking. Thanks."

"You got it. I'll help you load that feed as soon as I get done here."

"Don't worry about it, Walt. I got it covered."

"Thanks, man."

Daniel walked back outside and looked at his watch. Veronica wouldn't be done with her hair appointment for a couple of hours. He could pick up his orders in town and have time to spare. Veronica mentioned having his scraggly hair trimmed after meeting the preacher that morning, so a trip to the barber shop wouldn't be such a bad idea.

He pulled a bag of feed from the pallet and started loading his pickup until the truck body was full. Then he went back in the building to sign the ticket. Walt was busy with another customer, so Daniel walked around the store, checking off the list in his head of things he needed to purchase in town. He scrutinized a couple of halters for young colts, swung them over his shoulder, and pulled a bottle of penicillin out of the medicinal refrigerator.

As he made his way to the back side of the store, he glanced out the window overlooking Main Street and noticed Marti walking up the sidewalk in front of the Carson City Café. She was probably meeting Skyler and Cynthia. The tingling sensation returned, and unconsciously he rubbed the back of his neck. Marti had a way about her that made him feel strange.

He watched her walking along, a serious expression on her face until she saw someone coming in her direction. Daniel's gaze shifted to see who deserved the beaming smile that popped up on her face. When he saw a tall man in a blue sports jacket wave and return her smile, he wasn't prepared for the resentment building inside his chest. Who was this man? And why was Marti so happy to see the guy? Although the man's face looked familiar, he couldn't remember anything about the stranger except a feeling of envy. Why did he remember the animosity but not the man?

The man held out his hand, but Marti pushed aside his handshake and gave him a hug instead. A flame started in the pit of Daniel's stomach and grew into a roaring blaze. Marti had lied to him when she said she was meeting friends in town. Instead, she was meeting *a* friend. Maybe a *special* friend.

Why should he care who she met . . . who she knew . . . who she hugged? That was her business, wasn't it?

A slow calming breath escaped between his lips but was replaced with a sigh of gloom when he saw them walk into the restaurant together.

Daniel grabbed one of the hoof picks from the display in front of him and marched to the front desk. He plopped everything on the counter and propped his arms on the countertop—rigid and straight. He tapped his fingers impatiently and waited for Walt to ring up his purchases.

Walt gave him a funny look. "You okay, Daniel?"

"Yeah, I'm fine."

His clipped response had Walt raising his eyebrows.

The bell over the door rang. Daniel and Walt turned to see a tall man with white hair ambling toward the counter.

Walt nodded to the man and said, "I'll be with you in a minute, Mr. Welsh," and then turned back to Daniel. "How many bags of feed did you get, Daniel?"

"Thirty."

"Okay, let's see . . . you have thirty bags of Rouster Performance Horse Feed, a bottle of Procaine Penicillin G, two rope halters, and one hoof pick. Would there be anything else?"

"No. That's all. Oh wait. I need to order a load of Timothy hay, but make sure you get it from Lance Cobb over in Cossio County. He knows I like the second cutting."

The other customer in the store approached Daniel.

"Daniel, how're you doing?"

Daniel looked at him—confusion creased his eyebrows.

"I'm sorry. Do I know you?"

The man raised an eyebrow. "Jordan Welsh. Vinny's father."

"Oh, Mr. Welsh. I'm sorry. I have a case of amnesia and can't remember most of my old friends. I'm sorry I didn't recognize you, sir."

"That's okay, Daniel. I know about your accident. I heard what you said about the Timothy hay and wondered why it's important to get the second cutting."

"Well, sir, the first cutting always has more weeds mixed in with the hay. Second cutting's usually the best quality and the most pure."

"Don't you feed alfalfa hay to your horses?"

"We feed alfalfa sometimes. It has its place, but our nutritionist doesn't recommend it all the time. Timothy hay has the right balance of nutrition and fiber. Plus the protein and calcium levels are lower."

"I see."

"Here ya go, Daniel." Walt handed him the sales ticket.

Daniel took the paper and nodded to both men, then walked toward the door, consumed once again with thoughts of Marti. He climbed into the truck cab and sat motionless behind the wheel. Straightening his back, he thought about what he saw. Was there a connection between Marti and the guy he saw, and why didn't she mention knowing someone in Carson?

He wished he could remember if he knew the man. It was possible Marti knew someone from this area before she came to visit. He needed to get a grip. It was really none of his business anyway.

If it wasn't any of his business, then why did seeing her hug this stranger ruin his whole day?

FIFTY

"What?" Marti's high-pitched question caught the attention of the other restaurant patrons. She blushed and lowered her voice. "Who did you say the fundraiser is for?"

Cynthia's eyes sparkled. "The Tots and Teens Orphanage in Bishop, Tennessee. It's the only children's home in that area, and the owners are great. They love those kids like they were their own."

Marti sank back into her chair. "I don't believe it! I worked with two of the board members of that orphanage, Alana and Jaydn Holbrook. They're starting a new homeless shelter in Landeville, just a few miles from Bishop, and they hired me to paint a mural on the wall for the grand opening. As a matter of fact, I know the orphanage owners too. Shirley and Darrell Hamlin."

Skyler let out a laugh. "You're kidding! Well, now you definitely have to paint with us in the fundraiser. You have an excellent reason to participate if Shirley and Darrell are friends. You wouldn't want to let the orphanage down, would you?" She smiled a *gotcha* smile.

Marti bit her lip. "Alana told me they had supporters all over, but I had no idea they had connections as far west as Carson, Texas. This is uncanny." She laid her napkin on the table beside her plate. "I guess you can count me in. I love Alana and Jaydn too much not to help."

Cynthia and Skyler squealed and clapped their hands.

"*Ooooh*, I just know this is going to be the greatest year ever. With your talent on our side, it has to be a success! I can't believe you didn't know you were an artist when you lived here before. We could have had so much fun." Skyler said.

Cynthia nodded. "Yeah, how crazy is that? I looked up some of your paintings on the Internet, Marti. They're great."

Skyler agreed. "I know. Your work is amazing. To think we have a famous celebrity in our midst."

"Oh, come on, you two. That's enough." Marti's face felt hot.

"So what gives with you and Daniel?" Cynthia leaned forward and played with the napkin on the table, her eyes averted—as if she wasn't happy about prying but couldn't help herself.

"Yeah, Marti, I wondered why you never came back after the accident. I heard you just left with no explanation."

Marti's cheeks burned.

Cynthia stared at the uncomfortable look on Marti's face and gave Skyler a frown. Then she leaned over and covered Marti's hands with hers. "I'm sorry. We didn't mean to pry."

"No. It's okay. You were the best friends I had when I lived here, and I'm sorry I didn't call you when I left. I was just so devastated . . . after the baby . . . and everything. I don't want to go into it all, but Daniel and I . . . we just . . ." Tears filled her eyes, and Marti struggled to keep them from rolling down her cheeks.

Skyler rubbed Marti's arm. "It's okay, hon. We understand. Let's not talk about it now. Maybe sometime later, okay?"

Marti nodded. "Anyway, Gerald asked me to come and paint a portrait of Daniel to hang with the other portraits in the study. He was hoping it might help jump-start Daniel's memory."

"That's neat about the portrait, but I bet it's hard, isn't it?"

Marti didn't answer, but her gaze shifted to stare unseeing out the window.

"Hey, how about we go down and stick our feet in the creek?" Cynthia jumped up and looked out the window at the river below. "I see lots of cute guys down there, Skyler. That should pique your interest."

Skyler stood up and hooked her purse over her arm. "*Ooooh*, that sounds like fun, but, unfortunately . . . I have to get back to work. Dr. Watson gets his dander up when I take too long for lunch."

"I thought you worked at the clinic."

"That's only part-time. Working for Dr. Watson pays my bills, and working at the clinic feeds my addiction . . . me."

They all laughed.

Cynthia stood up as well. "Yeah, she spends all the clinic salary on jewelry. Wait up, Skyler. I'll go with you." She smiled down at Marti. "Dr. Watson's a great boss, but we do have to stay on our toes. Thanks, Marti, for meeting us for lunch. We loved seeing you again, and we're so glad you're on board with the fundraiser."

Marti smiled up at her friends. "Yeah, me too. I'll fill out the application and drop it off at your office before I leave town."

"Would you like us to drop you somewhere?"

"No, I have my car outside, and I'm meeting someone in about ten minutes. You two go on back to work."

Cynthia leaned forward and hugged Marti. "Oh, do you still have that cool Lexus Daniel bought you when you got married?"

"No, unfortunately, I was too fond of eating. I had to trade it in for a smaller car."

They all laughed.

"We sure missed you when you left, but it's so good to see you again, my friend. We felt lost without you." Cynthia's voice was soft and sincere.

Skyler nodded and gave Marti a hug.

Marti could feel her throat closing with emotion, so she just smiled.

After Cynthia and Skyler left the room, Marti leaned back in her chair. Tears tickled the edge of her eyes when she thought about how many friendships she had lost. Now, for some reason God had brought the two areas of her life together for a purpose. Even though she wanted to believe God abandoned her, she knew better. The Bible said plainly that all things work together for good for them that love the Lord. God had allowed all the things in her life. She just had to trust that God knew what He was doing.

After leaving a tip for the waitress, she decided to brave the heat once more and wait in the car for Clara. She thanked the hostess for a delicious lunch and walked out into the sunshine and oppressive heat.

Across the street, she saw Clara unlock the door of her car and get into the driver's seat. Marti waved, but Clara was fitting the key in the ignition and didn't see her. Marti stood beside the blue plastered wall of the restaurant and waited for the traffic to clear before she could cross the street.

She watched the last car roll past her when a horrible explosion blasted her hearing. The air seemed to vibrate around her, charged with current. She instinctively put her hands over her ears and turned away from the blast. The impact of the explosion pushed her backward, and she fell against the building behind her. When she finally raised her head and looked toward the whooshing sound, she was horrified to see her car completely engulfed in flames. It took a few seconds for the sight to penetrate her understanding. Her car had exploded!

"Clara! Oh no!" She heard herself cry the words. She rushed toward her car, yelling as she ran. "Help! Someone help her! She's in the car." A few feet from the car, Marti had to pull up short when heat from the flames burned her face. The entire car was swallowed in flames, and she couldn't see anything but a wall of orange and yellow rising high into the sky. A grim realization hit her in the chest. It was too late.

Marti's hands covered her eyes. Knowing Clara was inside that towering inferno shocked her. If she left the restaurant a few minutes earlier, she would have been in the car as well.

No. Not just in the car, but driving.

Suddenly, her chest pounded with a heartbeat so fast it hurt. Surely only a bomb could have caused such a violent explosion. A cold chill ran through her in spite of the intense heat. Someone had planted a bomb in her car to explode when she cranked the engine. That bomb was meant for her. When the realization hit her, she wrapped her arms around her waist and sobbed.

Zach wasn't her stalker. The note he left was about someone else. Her stalker was still out there, and Clara had died in an explosion meant for her.

Marti's knees buckled, and she sank onto the curb.

People were running all around her. She heard someone call, "Here comes the fire truck!"

Sirens sounded in the distance, but she couldn't move, couldn't think.

She felt someone touch her on the shoulder.

"Marti? Are you all right?"

She looked up into Daniel's face.

"Daniel, Clara . . . she was . . . it was supposed to be me . . ."

"Calm down, Marti. You're not making any sense." Daniel sat down beside her.

"Clara was in my car," she cried in anguish.

"Clara? Clara who?"

Marti didn't answer but turned to him and fell against him in utter horror. She felt Daniel's arms circle her and pull her close. His hands rubbed her back, trying to give her comfort, and his embrace felt like a warm blanket on a winter's day. She had the strange sensation of being home, surrounded by things familiar and comforting.

A fire engine roared toward them and came to a jolting stop in front of the car, blocking the street. Firemen ran to pull hoses from the back of the truck out into the street. A man, obviously the fire chief, yelled orders at the men hooking up the hose to a fire hydrant in front of the restaurant. The hose finally bulged, and water sprayed onto the towering inferno. The hot metal hissed when the water hit, and Marti's heart felt every sizzle.

A police car pulled up and blocked the traffic flow down the street. Two policemen stepped out of the car and began pushing the crowd farther away from the fire. One officer came over to Marti and Daniel and waved them back.

"Step back, folks. Let's give the firemen room."

Marti raised her head and babbled, "But that's my car."

The policeman lifted an eyebrow and came closer. "Did you say that's your car, ma'am?"

Marti nodded. "And . . . a woman was inside."

The policeman jumped to attention. "There was someone in the car?"

When she nodded, he ran to tell the firemen fighting the flames. When they nodded their understanding, the officer returned to her. "Ma'am, I'm Daren Fisher from the Carson City Police Department. Could you answer some questions now?"

Marti sniffed and nodded.

Officer Fisher pulled out a black notebook and a pen. "What's your name, ma'am?"

"Marti Rushing."

"Any relation to Daniel here?"

Marti looked at Daniel and shook her head. "Uh . . . no."

"She's staying at our house, Daren—painting an oil portrait."

"Oh. Well, could you tell me who was in the car?"

Marti rubbed the tears from her eyes with a tissue and answered. "A nurse from the clinic. Her name was Clara, but I can't remember her last name."

"Watting," Daniel supplied. "Her last name was Watting."

The officer wrote down the name in his black book and asked, "Do you know what made it explode? Was the motor hot or smoking when you cut it off?"

Marti grasped at the idea. Maybe it wasn't a bomb, but it exploded too fast to be anything else. "I don't think so."

The policeman left her and reprimanded a couple of boys who were climbing on the fire truck. He spoke to a couple of the eye-witnesses standing around the perimeter and wrote down their answers in the book.

Daniel took Marti's elbow and pulled her back to the curb on the opposite side of the street. "Come back, Marti. Let's move back from the heat."

She let him lead her back to the doors of the café.

Marti looked into his eyes for the first time. The compassion she saw there made her stomach flutter. He helped her sit on the steps of the restaurant and wrapped his arm around her for support.

Officer Fisher came back to Marti and sat down beside her.

"The eye-witnesses confirmed there was a lady sitting in the car when it exploded. They also say it exploded when she turned the key in the ignition. Can you tell me about this lady, Clara Watting, and why she was in your car?"

"She was the head nurse at the Carson Clinic. I picked her up on the road. She had car trouble, and I was taking her back to her car at the garage. I gave her a key so she could run the air until I was done with my lunch meeting. But, I didn't know—" She shook her head and looked up at the officer. "Zach wasn't the one. I thought all this was over, but Zach wasn't the one."

"What do you mean, Marti? What does Zach have to do with anything?" Daniel's voice sounded confused.

"That note he wrote before he died. I thought the woman he mentioned was me . . . that it was me he was stalking . . . ever since—" Suddenly, she realized what she was about to say. She couldn't tell Daniel about leaving here three years ago. "Someone has been stalking me . . . for several years. When Zach mentioned a woman in his note—that she didn't deserve it—I thought he was talking about me. I thought he was my stalker, but now . . ."

The policeman shook his head. "Ma'am, you're not making any sense. I can tell you're hiding something. You'll have to come with me to the station and talk to Detective Simmons. If someone was killed in your car, you have some explaining to do."

Marti's mouth hung open.

"What do you mean?"

"Ma'am, if you asked someone to ride in your car, gave her the keys so she could use it, and it exploded as soon as she started it up, that sounds awfully suspicious. Exactly what did you have against this woman?"

FIFTY-ONE

Marti was appalled. "Nothing! I had nothing against her. I didn't even know her that well. I only met her yesterday."

"That fact will be investigated. As soon as I talk to my partner, I have to take you in for questioning."

Marti turned to Daniel in shock. "Please, Daniel. I didn't do anything."

"Aren't you jumping to conclusions, Daren? You can see she's upset. There's no way she's involved. Anyway, what makes you think a bomb caused the explosion?"

Daren's posture stiffened. "She has to come in for questioning. No arguments."

"Well, at least let me take her to the station. Don't put her in the back of the squad car like a common criminal."

The policeman frowned but nodded. "All right, Daniel, but make sure you go straight there."

The policeman nodded at Marti and turned back toward the fire.

Marti was terrified. She half whispered to herself. "He thinks I killed Clara."

"Don't worry, Marti. It'll all be straightened out as soon as you tell them what happened."

Marti's reasoning took over, and she realized Daniel was right. She had no connection with Clara, and she knew absolutely nothing about building bombs. Anyway, she was sure the bomb wasn't meant for Clara anyway, it was meant for—

All of a sudden the crowds around her became one big face of terror. He might be here—looking at her with murder in his eyes right at this moment.

"Dad said you mentioned a stalker, Marti, but why would he follow you all the way to Texas? And, when did he have access to your car long enough to plant a bomb? Connecting a bomb to explode when you crank the ignition takes time, and it's certainly not something he could do out here on the street with everyone watching."

Marti looked at him in disbelief. He didn't believe her. What could she do to make everyone understand?

"I saw someone standing around my car while I was in the café, but he was there only a minute. I guess he didn't have time to plant a bomb." Her voice oozed defeat.

Daniel put his hands on Marti's arms and turned her toward him. "I don't know what's going on, Marti, but you're obviously upset. We'll talk to the police and see what they say. If someone's after you, we'll protect you. I won't let anyone hurt you. I promise. Don't worry, okay?"

Marti listened to Daniel's words but felt no sense of comfort. Daniel couldn't remember, but what he'd done to her was far worse than any fear she felt from an anonymous stalker.

Daniel helped Marti stand on shaky legs and guided her to his car. Before he pulled out into the traffic, he leaned over and gathered her hand into his and laced their fingers together like the old days. "It'll be okay, Marti. We'll get this figured out."

They drove to the police station where Detective Brent Simmons showed her to an interrogation room off to the side of the reception area. Daniel sat down outside the room in one of the chairs lined up against the waiting room wall.

Once Marti explained everything about the stalker and the situation with Clara to Detective Simmons, he sat across the table from her with a grim look on his face.

"Why didn't you tell me about all this before, ma'am? We might have been able to stop him before Miss Watting had to die."

"He's never been this violent. He only threatened. He . . . he told me he'd kill anyone I told, but I really didn't think he'd follow me here."

"Are you sure you're not just imagining this stalker of yours?"

Marti looked at him, appalled. "The police in Alabama didn't believe me either until he vandalized my apartment, punctured all four of my car tires, and put a bullet hole through the windshield of my car."

"Which city in Alabama?"

"Brettville."

Brent Simmons took in a heavy breath. "I'll call the Brettville police department and see what they found out. For now, go back to the ranch with Daniel. I'll make sure he keeps his security system armed, and you can call me if you feel threatened again. I'll let you know what we find out about your car. In the meantime, stay on the ranch until you hear from me. Don't plan on leaving the state."

His sing-song voice grated on Marti's nerves.

He stood up and waved at Daniel who rose and entered the room.

"Brent?"

Detective Simmons nodded at Daniel and said, "I'm not sure what's going on, Daniel, but you have a good security system on the ranch—keep it activated until you hear from me. We'll get to the bottom of this."

Daniel nodded. He glanced at his watch and turned to Marti. "Come on, Marti. I need to pick up Veronica from the beauty shop."

Marti withered. "Daniel, please, I can find another ride to the ranch."

Daniel blew out a strained breath of air. "There is no other way back to the ranch, Marti. I'll drop you off first. Veronica won't care if you ride with us."

Sure she won't. Marti nodded with a pale face and walked to the truck. She slipped into the back seat of the supercab and stared unseeing at the floor. When Daniel slid into the seat, he turned around and put his hand on hers. "It'll be okay, Marti. Brent's good at what he does. He'll get everything straightened out."

Marti just nodded with a blank expression and rubbed her hand when he took his away. She turned toward the side of the truck and leaned her head against the side. *God, why is this happening?*

Daniel pulled the truck into the parking lot at the beauty shop, and Marti watched Veronica swagger out the door. Her expression froze when she saw Marti in the back seat.

As soon as Veronica climbed into the truck, she turned toward Marti and smiled at Daniel but spoke to Marti. "Marti, what are you doing here?"

Daniel explained about the explosion, but it didn't seem to affect Veronica at all. She rotated around in the seat and turned toward Daniel.

"I thought you were getting a haircut today, darling. You know we don't want it to look like you just got a haircut for our wedding next week."

Marti was sure Veronica emphasized the words *darling* and *wedding* for Marti's benefit.

"I had . . . uh . . . other things to do."

"Oh really?"

Marti couldn't mistake the fury in Veronica's voice—no matter how she tried to hide it—and Marti couldn't resist making it a little hotter.

"I'd be happy to cut it for you, Daniel. I worked at a beauty parlor for a year and probably cut more men's hair than women's."

"Hey, that would be great! It would save me another trip to town."

Veronica's eyes thinned to tiny slits, and she turned to throw eye daggers at Marti.

When Daniel turned to look at Veronica, her lips turned up in a tight smile, and the outrage in her eyes turned to sugar.

Inside, Marti was rejoicing over the small victory, but she was sure Veronica wasn't done yet. Almost assuredly, Veronica would give Daniel a good taste of guilt for even considering Marti's help. He'd probably back out, and secretly, Marti hoped he would. She hadn't thought what it would mean—cutting Daniel's hair. Such a personal, physical service. Yep, she sure hoped he backed out.

FIFTY-TWO

Daniel strolled into the studio where Marti was cleaning her brushes. She had dipped them in pink soap and was squeezing them into shape. Daniel's hands were behind his back.

"Did you mean what you said about cutting my hair?"

"Uh . . . sure, if you want me to. It's the least I can do for making you miss out yesterday."

"Well, I'd love to have it cut. It really is driving me crazy—just don't tell Veronica." He laughed and pulled a clipper box from behind him. When he held it up for her to see, he said, "Will this be okay?"

Marti's heart thumped hard inside her chest. "Where did you get that?"

"It's Stella's. She was going to learn so she could cut hair for all the ranch hands and make some 'mad money.'" Daniel laughed. "But, she couldn't get up enough nerve. Her daughter gave her this for Christmas, hoping it would prod her along."

Marti laughed. "That doesn't sound like Stella at all."

"What doesn't? Her learning to cut men's hair, her backing out, or her needing 'mad money?'"

"All three." Marti grinned.

He pulled a rolling chair over toward her. "Will this do?"

Marti's throat tightened, so she nodded.

When he sat down in the chair and pulled a beach towel around his neck, he held out his hands in front of him. "Okay. My life is in your hands."

"Why? Because I'm wielding a pair of scissors?"

"No, because if you do a bad job, Veronica will kill me."

Marti faked a frown and lifted her hands. They froze over Daniel's thick dark hair. Could she do this?

Before she could pump up her courage, Daniel's cell phone rang.

"Hold on. Let me get this."

He pulled his phone from the holder and answered. "This is Daniel."

Marti moved away from the chair to give him privacy, but the room was not large enough to keep her from hearing his conversation.

"Sure enough? Are there any surveillance cameras around the area that might have captured someone under the car? Uh huh. Marti said she saw someone near the car, but only for a minute. I see. Okay, I'll get her to call you. She's . . . uh . . . kind of busy at the moment." Daniel looked at Marti and winked.

They were talking about her. What was that he said about the car? Had they found out what caused the explosion?

Daniel finally said goodbye and hung up the phone. "That was Brent. He said they're sure now that there was a bomb planted under your car, Marti, probably with a magnet. He also said it was possibly activated by a remote of some kind—most likely a cell phone. The person would have had to have been close and watching Clara get in the car in order to know when to activate the bomb."

"If he waited until Clara got in the car, then it wasn't me he was after. It was Clara." A wave of relief coursed through her. "That means Zach might have been my stalker after all. But does he know what the motive for Clara's murder was?"

"Brent said he had some other information that came to light about her activities, but he wouldn't say over the phone. Anyway, Marti, you can stop worrying that the bomb was meant for you."

She shuddered. "What a terrible way to die." She sat down in the chair behind her. "I guess Zach was the one following me all this time. I just wish I knew why. I didn't even know him."

"There are crazy people in the world, Marti. You may never know why. Hey, are you ready to do this?"

Marti nodded slowly, dread filling her heart. She would pretend she was at the beauty parlor in Oklahoma and Daniel was just another customer. Yeah, right. That would never work. This wasn't going to be fun. Hashtag: torture.

FIFTY-THREE

Marti laid a brand new French easel—perfect for outdoor painting—in the trunk of the rental car Daniel had provided. Then she packed two canvases and a bucket full of paper towels, tubes of paint, and brushes around the easel.

Daniel walked out the door of the house. "Hey, Marti. Would you like some company?"

She raised up and looked at him with a frown. "Isn't Veronica around today?"

"No, she had to take Chris to the doctor. He has some kind of stomach bug. She might not make it until the auction. I know she'd like to be there."

I bet she would. Guilt reared its ugly head until Marti realized it was *her* husband Veronica was after. She silenced the tiny voice of her conscience and savored the time she had with Daniel.

"You're welcome to come if you like, but I'm going to be painting all day. Hashtag: boring."

He laughed. "I'll risk it. I've never seen a real artist at work. Hashtag: educational."

It was her turn to laugh. "Okay, but don't say I didn't warn you."

Outside the Chamber of Commerce, Marti turned her canvas over to the director so she could stamp the back with the date and time. Daniel stepped off to the side when Marti moved to stand with Cynthia and Skyler and listen to the lady in charge explain the rules of the paint-out:

1. Any building or garden in town could be painted.

2. Every canvas had to be turned in before four o'clock.

3. Each canvas had to be stamped, so no one was allowed to switch canvases during the day.

4. The painting had to be signed and temporarily framed before the beginning of the auction at four-thirty.

Marti was standing at the back of the crowd listening to questions and answers when she saw a car pull into the parking lot. The driver's door of the gray Mercedes opened, and a woman in white slacks and a pink top stepped out. Marti eyes widened, and a smile lit her face. She waved at Alana and ran to meet her.

"Alana! Oh, it's so good to see you again." She gave Alana a hug.

"Marti, Sandra told me you were still here painting a portrait. How exciting to go to a horse competition in Vick and end up in Texas with a commission! I'm happy for you. What about this fundraiser? Isn't it a small world? You're painting to raise money for my orphanage, which is in another state with no connection whatsoever. How amazing is that?"

Marti laughed. "I know. Hashtag: coincidence."

Alana laughed. "No, I say Hashtag: God's planning."

Marti smiled. "You're right."

The crowd began to disperse, and Marti touched Alana's arm. "I better get going, or I won't have anything to auction. I'll see you later, okay?"

"I'm sorry, Marti, but I may not see you again. I'm probably leaving before the auction's over. Yesterday, a couple decided they wanted to adopt one of our six-year-olds. That's why Jaydn didn't get to come today. He's at home frantically trying to get all the paperwork ready. Today's the only day the man could get off work long enough to sign all the papers. Since I'm one of the directors, I need to be there to sign papers too. I'm trying to get a seat on the earliest flight out."

"Oh." Mart felt deflated. She was looking forward to talking with Alana.

Alana leaned over for another hug. "I'll see you back in Tennessee for the grand opening though, right?"

Marti sighed. "I'll be there if I can get done with this . . . uh . . . project."

Skyler and Cynthia approached, so Marti introduced them to Alana.

"We met last year at the last fundraiser. It's nice to see you again, Alana." Cynthia and Skyler gave Alana a hug.

"Okay, you three," Alana said with a smile, "I'm expecting high bids on your paintings this year. Go to it, and have fun."

Skyler giggled. "Okay, hon, but don't be too disappointed. I don't even know where to start."

Cynthia picked up her easel and paint. "I know exactly which building I'm going to paint—the new church on Gowan Street. It's modern, and the flower gardens are gorgeous. I'll see you at lunchtime." She waved and walked toward her car.

Skyler frowned. "How can I ever decide? I'm awful when it comes to picking a reference that'll make a great painting."

"Why don't you come with me, Skyler?" said Marti. "I've already chosen a couple of beautiful houses on Watkins Avenue with dramatic lighting."

"Marti, you always were sweet like that. That's a lovely idea. Thanks."

Alana gave Marti one last hug. "I'll see you soon, my friend. Paint well, and take lots of pictures of your commissioned portrait. I want to see them when you get back to Tennessee."

Skyler gathered her paints and canvas and saw Daniel leaning against his truck on the other side of the street with a phone up to his ear. "What's he doing here?"

Marti smiled and said absentmindedly. "He's getting educated."

Skyler tilted her head. "What do you mean—he's getting educated?"

"It's a long story. Come on. I think I have the perfect house in mind."

FIFTY-FOUR

Daniel leaned against Marti's rental car and watched Marti and Skyler paint. It was amazing to see two people paint with such different techniques. Skyler was all over the canvas, but Marti was tight and deliberate with her strokes. Several other artists were set up around the area painting various houses, but they all seemed to be enjoying themselves.

The phone in his leather pouch vibrated.

"This is Daniel."

"Hey, Daniel, this is Brent. I'm afraid I have some bad news. Your hired man, Zach Parsons, was murdered."

"What?" Daniel stiffened. "I thought it was a suicide."

"The coroner said he had a gash the size of an egg in the back of his skull."

"The backhoe fell on him, Brent. I imagine he had several good-sized gashes."

"Yeah, but only one of them was caused by the wrench we found in the tool box."

"The toolbox on the backhoe?"

"Yep. The coroner said there was DNA and hair on the end of the wrench, but the wrench was found in the toolbox—locked up tight. It was wiped clean, but there's plenty of Zach's DNA to prove it was his blood and hair."

"So it wasn't suicide like the note intimated." Daniel ran his hand through his hair. "But why? Do you know what motive someone would have to kill Zach? He was new in the area, and as far as I know, he was a stranger to everyone around here."

"We don't know, Daniel. That's what we're trying to find out. We also found a note in the trash can at the stable telling Zach to check those fillies in that field. Looks like pre-meditated murder. Did you ever see him talk to anybody other than everyone around the ranch?"

"Yeah, I did. Jordan Welsh came by the ranch a few days before Zach died. I saw them out by the barn, and then they walked through the stable. I didn't know who it was then, but I saw him the other day in town and he introduced himself. Jordan's been stocking Vinny's ranch on the other side of town and came over to ask us some questions about boarding horses, when we give vaccines—things like that. I suppose Zach was showing him around. Other than that, I never saw him with anybody. He loved spending time in town, though. We teased him about having a girlfriend. You might check that out. As soon as he was done with his chores, he was gone. Kept pretty much to himself around here. I did see him in the hardware store a couple of months ago. He bought one of those Victorinox knives. As a matter of fact, I bought one as well."

"Is yours like the one Marti found under her bed?"

"What?"

"Gerald brought me a knife a few days ago and said Marti found it under her bed the day after she thought someone broke into her room."

And Daniel had dismissed it as a bad dream. "I didn't know about that, but the knife Zach had is just like mine. It's red with flames on it, and it has thirty different attachments."

"Yep. That sounds like this one. Do you still have yours?"

"It's at the house."

"This one might be Zach's then. Could be Zach's murderer planted it under Marti's bed to make it look like he's the one who attacked her."

Brent was quiet, and Daniel assumed he was writing everything down. "Do you know if Zach had any family?"

"He said he had none. He wasn't much of a hired hand, but I can't imagine why someone would want him dead."

"We researched our database and found out he was married before. Did he ever mention a wife?"

"No. I had no idea he'd been married."

"Well, there's one thing for sure, he couldn't have been Marti's stalker like she thought. He had a secure alibi for the two years Marti says she was being followed. He worked at a ranch in California as a horse wrangler. The ranch owner and foreman confirmed he never left the place. I guess that means her stalker is still at large. Tell her to be careful."

Daniel grimaced. "Okay, Brent. I'll let you know if I think of anything else."

"Thanks, Daniel. There's something else I want to run by you..."

FIFTY-FIVE

The afternoon sun was hot, but the slight breeze kept Marti and Skyler cool for the most part. The umbrella over Marti's painting reflected most of the light away from her eyes, and the cowboy hat she was wearing kept the sun from beating down on her head. She looked toward the light, high in the sky. "It has to be close to lunchtime."

"I know. Gosh, I'm starved."

Marti watched Skyler pull on the chain around her neck and look at the clock swinging on the end. "One o'clock. No wonder I'm dog-hungry. Cynthia's supposed to bring us some vittles, but maybe she's forgotten. I don't know if I can wait any longer. What about you, Marti? You wanna go get a bite to eat?"

"I'll wait on Cynthia a little longer. She said she was bringing something, so I'm sure she will. If she doesn't come in a little while, I might get something. Go ahead if you want to. I'd like to finish this house corner before the light changes."

Skyler leaned over Marti's shoulder and gasped. "Marti! This is a dazzler, hon. You sure can't claim God didn't give you talent. I've been bitten by the green-eyed monster." Her eyes were wide with wonder.

Marti grinned. She'd forgotten what a bigger-than-life character Skyler could be.

Cynthia drove up behind them, parked on the curb, and rolled down her window. She held up a Chick-fil-A sack. "Hey, gals! Let's eat."

"I'm with you, honey," Skyler crooned as she opened Cynthia's door and helped tote the to-go tray with drinks.

"I'm sorry I'm so late. The place was packed. I brought a couple of extra sandwiches in case someone's totally famished. If Daniel needs something, he's welcome."

Marti glanced at him across the street. His back was to them, but she could see the phone held to his ear. "He's on the phone now, but he might want something later."

They sat down on a blanket Cynthia provided and ate their salads and sandwiches. When she was done eating, Skyler looked across the street. "Hey, the ice cream shop's on the next street over. I'm gonna walk over there and get a cone. Would anyone else like something?"

"Ooo, that sounds delicious," said Marti as she swallowed her last bite of salad. "Make mine chocolate."

Skyler hopped up. "Come help me carry them, Cyndi."

The two ladies left as Marti folded the blanket and threw the trash into her portable trash bag. She sat down in front of her easel. The sun's rays were intense, but the slight breeze kept the temperature manageable. She rubbed on another layer of sun block and evaluated her painting. A shadow crept over her and covered her palette. She peered over her shoulder to find Daniel standing behind her.

"Hey, this looks great." He leaned over her shoulder and pointed to a corner of the house that glowed with the morning sunlight. "I love the light in this area."

Marti looked at her painting with a critical eye. "Art is all about the light and shadow. The proper lighting can make or break a painting. I painted that area this morning while the morning light was strongest."

"I can see why. It looks like you'll finish your painting before the auction, but Skyler's looks half done." He leaned his head sideways and stared at the impressionistic image Skyler was in the middle of painting. "Or maybe she's finished."

Marti laughed. "They say art's in the eye of the beholder."

"I guess."

She picked up her paint brush and smeared paint on the only spot left on the canvas without paint—the bottom corner. The unease she'd felt earlier in the day about Veronica's eventual appearance returned. "Was that Veronica on the phone?"

"No. Oh, I forgot to tell you—"

"Hey! Somebody help me." Skyler called from across the street as she balanced three ice cream cones. "Cyndi deserted me and went back to painting."

Daniel went to help her.

"We got a cone and a sandwich for you too, Daniel, but you'll have to eat your dessert first."

Daniel grinned. "Stella would have a fit if she were here."

When Skyler finally popped the tip of the cone in her mouth, she looked at her clock. "Two-thirty. Yikes! I have to get busy."

Marti swallowed her last bite and jumped up. "Me too."

"Oh no! I'm out of red paint." Skyler threw her empty tube in the trash.

Daniel swallowed his last french fry and wiped his hands on the napkin. "I can run over to the gallery and get you more."

"Oh, would you, Daniel? That would be super." She dug into her art bag and handed him a wad of bills. "I need one large tube of cadmium red light."

Marti worked until Daniel returned. He handed Skyler the paint and moved to stand behind Marti while she put the finishing touches on the grass in the front of the painting. His closeness was a touch unnerving, but she tried to think about the auction and how much it meant to the orphanage.

At the end of the afternoon, Marti finished her painting about five minutes before Skyler threw down her brush and yelled. "I'm done."

They all laughed at her excitement, packed up their paints, and walked with Daniel to the auction headquarters where the paintings were turned in and processed for the auction.

After turning in her painting, Marti entered the auditorium. Daniel was already sitting on a chair in the last row of seats arranged for bidders—a white bidder's ticket stuck out of his shirt with the number one hundred forty-six stamped in black on the front. He waved to Marti and pointed at the seat beside him. She noticed there was an empty chair on his other side—probably for Veronica.

He turned to her as she rounded the last row of seats. "If Veronica shows up, I'll probably ride home with her, so you can leave whenever you get ready."

"Oh, okay."

"Good luck with your painting. It deserves the highest price in the auction. It's so beautiful. Hashtag: masterpiece."

Marti laughed and sat down just as the auctioneer began his welcome and introduction of Alana.

Alana walked up to the podium.

"Hey everyone, I can't tell you how excited I am to be here today. I'm afraid I have to leave before the auction is over, so I won't get to thank you all in person. We have an adoption pending that has to be taken care of today. But before I go, I wanted to say thank you and let you know how much this means to all of us in Tennessee. You'll never know what your contribution will mean to my sweet orphans. Not only will they get the new computers they've been dreaming about, but they'll know in their hearts they have friends and supporters who care about them. Thank you all for your time, your prayers, and your financial contribution. We love you all."

The crowd clapped, and the auctioneer stood up on the podium. "Okay folks, let's get started. Dig deep in your pockets, and remember who the funds are for. Bring out the first painting."

Halfway through the auction, a disturbance at the back of the room made Marti turn her head. Veronica had stepped into the doorway and was conversing with the one of the security guards.

Marti cringed and faced the front. Great. Now the fun was about to begin.

FIFTY-SIX

Gerald sat at the barn office desk and watched out the window as Parker stepped onto the patio of the house and turned in his direction. When he trotted across the yard with a determined look on his face, Gerald moved to meet him at the door.

"What is it, Parker?"

"Would it be all right if Anita and I leave early today, sir? We . . . uh . . . have something we have to take care of."

Gerald was surprised by Parker's edgy behavior. Parker's feathers were never ruffled. "Of course, Parker. Whatever chores you have left can be put off until tomorrow if you have somewhere important you need to be. Are you going to the auction?"

Parker shook his head. "No sir." He turned toward the house but then stopped. "Oh, I almost forgot. Amber Pike called and wanted to know if you were here. She and Detective Brent Simmons would like to come out and see you if it's convenient."

"Now?"

"Yes, sir."

Gerald blew out a slow breath. What kind of trouble was he about to wade into? "Okay, Parker. Call and tell them they'll find me in the barn."

"Yes, sir."

Gerald spent the next thirty minutes double-checking records of the horses they were sending to next week's sale. Training schedules as well as learning performance records were updated and included in the packet for each horse. Vaccinations for Western and Eastern Encephalomyelitis, rabies, tetanus, West Nile Virus, and influenza had all been given during the last month and were up to date for the sale. Daniel had checked boxes and signed the certificates of vaccinations. Gerald stapled them together with the vet's overall health report and filed them in a large yellow envelope.

He glanced out the window and saw a man and woman walk around the corner of the house—Marvel County's Police Detective, Brent Simmons, and Amber Pike, the insurance investigator. He closed his files and met them outside the barn door.

"Brent, Amber. Parker said you were stopping by."

Amber Pike spoke first as she raised her head and regarded Gerald. "Sir, I'll get right to the point. I told you I'd let you know when I concluded my investigation of the accident that killed your daughter and son-in-law. I'm afraid I have undeniable evidence to prove your daughter-in-law, Martha Rushing, was *not* driving the car the night of the accident but was instead riding in the back seat."

Gerald's muscles went rigid. "What? But Mary said—"

Amber picked up the thought. "Ah, yes . . . Mary Duke. According to the police report, she was on the scene for some time before the ambulance arrived, and she stated emphatically in the *insurance* report that she found Martha on the ground outside the vehicle beside the driver's door and Vinny was riding in the back. However, in the *police* report, she stated Martha was behind the wheel when she arrived at the scene. And yet, Martha's DNA and blood type were nowhere in the front seat. As a matter of fact, her DNA was found everywhere in the back seat of the car, riding behind the driver. The DNA and blood type of your daughter's husband was all over the steering wheel, floorboard, front dash, and the driver's seat—and of course, the air bag."

She paused and watched Gerald.

Gerald slumped against the bales of hay stacked behind him. "You mean . . . Vinny was driving? But, it was Daniel's car—it was logical that Marti would have been driving. All this time, we thought she was driving . . . because of what Mary said. Why would Mary lie?"

"I don't know, sir. Do you have any idea why she'd want to make it look like your daughter-in-law was driving? Did your daughter-in-law and Mary Duke get along?"

Gerald shook his head. "Not really. I always suspected Mary was jealous of Marti, but not enough to frame her like this. Daniel and Mary's daughter, Veronica, grew up together. We thought they might . . . well . . . get married one day, but the first time Daniel saw Marti, that was the end of that. I can't believe Mary hated Marti enough to blame her for the crash."

"Martha was convicted of reckless driving and vehicular manslaughter, wasn't she?"

Gerald nodded. "Yes, but she was released on probation."

"There was alcohol involved, I believe."

Gerald nodded sadly. "I didn't want to believe it, but according to the officers who investigated, there were open liquor bottles in the front seat. Since they thought Marti was driving, they assumed the bottles had to be hers. But, Marti was pregnant. As far as I could tell, she never drank during her pregnancy, and she had given up alcohol completely right after she . . . found the Lord, six months before the accident."

"I also have concrete proof, Gerald, that the DNA on the open liquor bottles and the fingerprints did not belong to Martha Rushing but to Vinny Welsh."

Gerald shook his head. "But, the hospital said her clothes smelled like liquor, and that she had liquor on her breath."

"Yes, but the blood results showed no concentration of alcohol in her system. Since the bridge was out that night because of the storm, and the rescue personnel spent so much time trying to save your daughter's life, the proper tests to check the alcohol levels in Martha's system were overlooked. That's why the judge only gave Martha probation. Tests were inconclusive to prove she had been drinking at all. Now, since we believe the evidence at the scene was manipulated, we have questions about the verdict. The judge has instructed me to compile the evidence for all the things I've just told you, and it's possible they will clear Martha's name. Unfortunately, Mrs. Duke is no longer with us to question, so the job will be a little harder. But, I assure you, sir, I will be able to prove, undeniably, that Martha Rushing was not driving at the time of the accident, neither had she been drinking. Therefore, we're almost certain to get Martha acquitted and completely exonerated of any fault."

Gerald's heart raced in his chest. Of all the things he had accused Marti of, most of them had just been refuted, and because the other accusations had also come from Mary Duke, those were in question now. His heart quaked when he thought of the awful things he'd called Marti when he ordered her from his house. He moaned and turned to Amber.

"Please, Amber, will you keep me informed, and let me know as soon as the judge makes a positive determination?"

"Of course."

Brent Simmons cleared his throat and nodded at Gerald. "Now, Gerald, I have news that will probably make your blood boil, but I think you should be aware of it. I'll have to ask you to keep it quiet for now—until we can prove what we suspect." He took a deep breath and let it out slowly. "Do you remember the nurse who died in Marti's car?"

"Clara Watting?"

Brent nodded. "Yes. After she died, one of her friends came to see us. She received a letter in the mail that Clara obviously mailed the day before she died. It contained a yellow envelope with instructions to be opened in the event of her death. When Clara died, the friend opened the envelope and found some pretty strong accusations about Mary Duke and an elaborate cover-up of a crime that would interest you."

Gerald waited. Dread made his heart beat faster in his chest.

Brent sat down on a hay bale beside Gerald, pulled an envelope out of his pocket, and handed Gerald three pieces of paper. Gerald took the cream-colored papers and pulled reading glasses out of his pocket. After slipping them on, he held the papers in front of him and glanced at the first one. It appeared to be a birth certificate. The mother's name was Tommi Robbins. The father's name was blank, but at the top of the paper, he noticed the date—the same date as the accident that claimed his daughter's life.

He slid that paper behind the others and glanced at the second paper. It too was a birth certificate, but what caught his eye was Marti's name. Her name was typed on the line that said "mother" and Daniel's name was typed in as the father. The date was the same.

When Gerald looked at the third piece of paper, his hands shook. It was an official fetal death certificate used by the clinic for deceased infants. The date was the same as the other two, but the mother's name was not Marti's as he expected—instead the name *Tommi Robbins* was typed on the line.

Deep furrows appeared between Gerald's eyes. He looked at Brent. "I don't understand. What does this mean?"

A glance passed between Brent Simmons and Amber Pike.

"It means that Marti's baby was born alive instead of stillborn like Mary told the hospital when she arrived with the baby after the accident. Mary filled out a birth certificate at the clinic, which could only mean one thing. In Texas, a birth certificate is not filled out *unless the baby is born alive,* and a nurse or midwife who knowingly falsifies a birth certificate will be charged with a third degree felony. Mary could have lost her medical license if she hadn't filled them out properly, so she completed the form but hid the death certificate somewhere at the clinic."

The confusion on Gerald's face left wrinkles above his eyes. "I don't understand. Are you saying Marti's baby was born alive and then died before they reached the hospital?"

Brent shifted on the hay. "Gerald, I'm saying there's something strange about the whole situation. Mary and Shane supposedly *adopted* Tommi Robbins' baby. The birth certificate filed with the adoption papers—the one Mary recorded—was identical to the one you have there, but there was no record of the fetal death certificate in any of the clinic's papers. The accident that killed your daughter happened right outside the clinic. We suspect Mary hid the original death certificate for Tommi's baby somewhere in her office at the clinic, and Nurse Watting must have found it. She then mailed this copy to her friend the day before she died. Tommi Robbins' baby was born alive, but according to this record here, died shortly after birth."

Gerald shook his head. "I don't understand. What does that prove?"

Brent stood and ran his fingers through his hair. "Gerald. The death certificate is for *Tommi's* baby—not Marti's. And Tommi's baby was supposedly adopted."

Suddenly, Gerald felt as if there were no blood left in his veins. His body felt cold and hot at the same time. Understanding sped through his heart, and he knew why Brent and Amber had solemn stares on their faces.

Marti's baby was alive.

Chris Duke, who had been adopted by Mary and Shane Duke, was Daniel and Marti's baby.

FIFTY-SEVEN

His throat felt tight, but he had to ask the question. He had to hear it for himself. "Are you telling me that the baby Shane and Mary adopted is my grandson?" His voice was rough and scratchy with emotion.

Brent leaned toward Gerald and put his hand on his shoulder. "I'm not one hundred percent positive, Gerald, but it looks that way."

Gerald stood up with as much strength as he could manage. "Then, let's go get him."

Brent put both hands on Gerald's arms to stop him in his tracks.

"Hold on, Gerald. We have to have proof in hand before we go taking someone's legally adopted child."

"Are you crazy? Legally adopted, nothing! If you're right, she stole our baby—my grandson!" His voice broke on the last word. He sank onto the hay and held his head in his hands. "My grandson."

Brent sat down beside him and put his hand on Gerald's shoulder. "I'm sorry, Gerald. I know how you must feel, but we have to prove it first—beyond the shadow of a doubt—so there won't be repercussions down the road. A paternity test will prove what we suspect. Then, I promise we'll make it right. If Mary lied and stole Chris from Marti, Chris will be returned to his biological parents."

"How can you do that? They're divorced." Pain for the things Marti went through—losing her home, her husband, the baby—all raged through him like wind through a wildfire. And Daniel—he lost a sister, a wife, and a son—all in one day.

"If they'd had the baby . . . they might not have—." He turned to Brent. "What are you waiting for?"

"We have to get a court order first, and before we can do that, the judge has to make a ruling about the accident. Once we have the court order, we'll have a paternity test run. We have to go slow so we can find out who else knew about all of this. When we find out, everyone involved will be prosecuted to the fullest extent of the law. Now, please be patient. Give us time to finish the investigation. You want everyone involved to be held accountable, don't you?"

Gerald gritted his teeth and felt a tightening in his chest. He nodded.

"We finished the investigation concerning Marti's car, and I called Daniel and told him. You'll be interested to know what we found. The bomb that blew up Marti's car was activated by remote control. That probably means whoever planted the bomb was targeting Clara, not Marti, and waited until Clara got in the car before activating the bomb—most likely with a cell phone."

"So the bomb wasn't meant for Marti?" Gerald felt numb. Marti wasn't the target after all, but there was so much else to process. "Marti said she was being stalked. Could that have to do with the accident?"

Brent shook his head. "We're not sure, Gerald. I talked to one of the Alabama police detectives, but he said they never followed up on her file. She moved shortly after reporting her tires being slashed, and they dropped the case."

"Why would someone want to kill Clara?"

"Clara mailed a copy of those forms to her friend, so she must have suspected the babies were switched. We think she might have tried to blackmail someone."

Gerald's head jerked up. "Who? Who was she blackmailing?"

"Mary would be the primary suspect, but since she's dead, it has to be someone else."

"Shane?"

"We don't know yet, but he's definitely suspect. There are a couple other people we want to check out as well. One of the nurses at the clinic during that time said there was a male nurse working at the clinic that night who left the day after the accident and never returned. We're trying to find his new address, and we're also checking into the alibis of two other people."

"Who?"

"Parker's one."

Gerald was stunned. "Parker? You're kidding. No way. He and Anita were friends with Marti. They wouldn't have . . . and killing Clara? No. Not Parker."

"Records show that Parker and Anita had been trying to adopt a child for years. On Mary's computer, we found records to prove she arranged an illegal adoption for Parker and his wife. If Clara found out about that and tried to blackmail him, he'd have been worried she might be investigated and they'd lose the baby. I'm sure he would have felt desperate—desperate enough to plant a bomb in Marti's car."

"But Parker—"

"We also want to check out Jordan Welsh."

Gerald didn't know how many more shocks he could handle. "Welsh? How does he fit in?"

"Jordan and Mary Duke were cousins who lived in the same town growing up. They'd been in regular contact over the years. Jordan was convicted years ago and did time in prison for murder one as well as falsifying government documents. He was also the primary suspect in a jewelry store robbery when the security guard was killed, but they had no concrete proof. He has the background and experience to counterfeit the adoption papers for Parker and Anita. He has an alibi for the time when the bomb could have been detonated, but it's weak. His men said he was working with them on the ranch mending fences, but the ranch is right outside the city limits. He could have driven to town, planted the bomb, and been back working on the fences in less than twenty minutes. His men agree he could have been gone that long without them missing him."

"But what would he have against Marti? None of that has anything to do with her."

"We don't know all the answers, Gerald, but we will. Give us a little time."

Brent paused for a minute and watched Gerald process all the information before he continued.

"We still need to check out the male nurse on duty that night at the clinic. Even if he's not involved, he may have seen something. We're in the process of trying to locate him."

Gerald nodded—still staring at the ground.

Amber Pike had been silent, but now she stepped forward and held out her hand to Gerald. "Goodbye, Gerald. Will . . . will you be all right?"

Gerald stood and shook her hand. His nod was slight but firm. Brent shook Gerald's hand and patted him on the back. "Gerald, remember . . . don't mention this to anyone until we have proof . . . especially Marti or Daniel. I wanted to see if you could help us solve some of these mysteries and to ask you to keep your ears open."

Gerald nodded, but wondered how in the world he was going to sit on this powder keg of information.

FIFTY-EIGHT

Daniel turned around and saw Veronica speaking to the security guard. He cleared his throat and whispered to Marti, "Excuse me."

He walked back to the door and put his arm around Veronica's shoulders. He explained to the man that Veronica was with him, and he let her pass. Veronica gave him a warm embrace until her eyes picked up Marti sitting on the back row. She flashed a startled look into Daniel's eyes. Marti could hear everything she said and cringed at the tone in her voice.

"What's she doing here?"

Daniel responded quietly, and Marti heard nothing of what he said.

"What do you mean, she has a painting in the auction? Have you seen her painting? This is just a ploy . . . a trick. She just wants to spend time with a handsome man like you, darling."

Marti imagined the enraged green of Veronica's eyes and gulped, refusing to glance back. Spouting angry words in private was one thing, but within hearing distance of a full crowd was a little embarrassing.

At that moment, her painting was placed up on the easel.

"Here we have a beautiful painting of the Hendrix House on Watkins Avenue by Marti Rushing. Notice the light and shadows that make this painting such a treasure. Who would like to start the bidding?"

A man in a green shirt sitting in the front row raised his hand and bid. "Fifty dollars."

Marti listened with feeble breath as several bidders raised the price of her painting to five hundred dollars. During a short pause in bidding, the auctioneer reminded everyone what a great cause they were raising money for, and someone shouted, "Five hundred twenty-five!" When another pause hushed the crowd, a voice from the back called out.

"Five thousand dollars."

The crowd collectively gasped and turned toward the back to get a glimpse of the person bidding. Marti didn't have to turn around to recognize Daniel's voice. At the same time it registered who the bidder was, she heard Veronica's shocked voice. "Daniel!"

The auctioneer shouted, "We have five thousand dollars. Going once, going twice, sold to bidder number one hundred forty-six for five thousand dollars!"

The crowd went wild. Everyone was talking at once.

Through the uproar, Marti glanced back at Veronica's stunned face. She could feel the electricity in the air, and she didn't want to be around when Veronica blew up. She grabbed her purse from the floor and made her way to the doors on the other side of the auditorium, trying to stay as far away from the arguing Daniel and Veronica as possible. When she pushed the door, she realized it was locked. The only way outside was through the door behind Veronica and Daniel. She saw Veronica stand at full stature and glare at Daniel. Marti spied the restroom sign and crept into the open hallway leading to the restrooms. She could hear Veronica's voice as plain as if she were standing next to her.

"Daniel, what do you think you're doing? You know how I feel about your bidding on a painting *she* created. Why did you do something so offensive—something you knew would upset me?"

"Nikki, I bid on a beautiful painting. It matches the one in my room at home, and I have plans to hang it on the opposite wall."

Daniel spoke to Veronica in strained tones until Veronica straightened her shoulders and looked into his eyes. "We planned on moving the painting in your room, remember?"

"No, *you* planned on moving the painting. I never agreed. I like that painting, and I like this one. I'm keeping both of them—in my bedroom. End of discussion."

"Daniel, either you give that painting right back to the auction immediately, or I'll have to tell my father you're being untrue to our relationship."

Daniel stiffened, and his lips thinned to a tiny line. Peeking around the corner of the open doorway, Marti could see the hesitancy in his stance. He was "between the devil and the deep blue sea," as Sandra always said. Marti actually felt sorry for him.

He put both hands on Veronica's shoulders and leaned in close. "Veronica, compromise is a big part of any relationship. I've let you decorate my bedroom in any way you wanted, but I want this painting. I don't really care who the artist is or how much I had to pay for it. You can tell your father anything you want, but I intend to keep the painting."

Veronica's eyes filled with tears, and she shrugged his hands off her shoulders. In two seconds she was out the door and had disappeared down the hallway.

Marti watched Daniel rub his forehead and turn back toward the crowd. She slipped out of the hallway and through the outside door. Outside the auditorium, she leaned against the wall. Listening to the fight between Daniel and Veronica made her stomach clench. Was she doing the right thing?

FIFTY-NINE

"Listen to me carefully. It has to be done exactly like I tell you so they'll think the wildfire jumped the firebreak and consumed the shed. You'll have to tie her with soft rope that will burn in the fire, and make sure the gasoline starts the woods on fire as well. If the fire works toward the wildfire and toward the shed, it'll look like she got caught in the middle of the fire with no way out. She went to the shed for protection and got trapped. Understand?"

"Yeah, but I thought the wildfire turned away from that shed."

"It did, but if you spread gasoline through the woods all the way to the burned out section of property, they'll think the sparks jumped the firebreak and burned toward the shed. Those old gasoline cans have been stored around that shed for years. They won't think anything about them being there. If there's not enough gas in the old cans, there are more stored at the end of the stable. I saw them the other day. Just don't get caught. Do you understand the plan?"

"Yeah. I understand. How much are you paying me this time?"

"Paying you? I've already paid you more than you're worth. Just do it, and I won't go to the sheriff with what I know about your past."

"Are you blackmailing me?"

"Of course not. It's not blackmail; it's a promise. You either do what I ask, or there's a prison cell with your name on it."

"You can't scare me. If I go to prison, you'll be right there beside me. You forget—I know things about you now as well."

"Yeah? I'd like to see you prove it. It's your word against mine."

"Phone calls are traceable, idiot. All I have to do is tell them you called me, and they'll be able to prove it with the phone records."

"You think I'm stupid? I bought this throw-away phone out of state with cash, and it's not traceable."

The phone line went silent.

"Now, are you going to do what I ask? Or, am I going to make the next call to the sheriff's office?"

"All right. I'll do it, but this is it. After this job, we're through. Don't call me again, or I'll turn you in and hang the consequences."

After that promise, he hung up the phone and balled his hands into fists. If he knew a way to get that lying, greedy, no-good . . . A thought worked its way into his mind. If he planned it right, he could make it look like murder instead of an accident, and he could frame his no-good blackmailer for the murder. Every little detail had to be perfect.

Yeah, he could do this. All he had to do was a little bit of planning, and he'd be able to "kill two birds with one stone," he thought with a chuckle. That not being able to verify their connection worked both ways. His blackmailer wouldn't be able to prove he'd paid him to do his dirty work either.

He threw his phone into his truck and jumped into the driver's seat. If he wanted to catch her by herself, he'd have to get going. He had work to finish before the auction was over. Then he'd have to come up with an air-tight alibi.

He'd have to plan every little detail before he set the fire. Maybe put something incriminating at the scene before the fire was started to make sure his blackmailer was placed at the scene.

What could he plant? Ah! He had the perfect thing. Now to get the shed ready, then on to pick up little Miss Artist.

Everything was going to work out fine.

SIXTY

Marti gathered up her equipment outside the auditorium and packed her paint and brushes into her tote bag.

While she worked, several emotions fought a battle inside her. Tenderness toward Daniel for his five thousand dollar bid on her painting brought tears to her eyes. What a great boost for the orphanage, and how special it made her feel. Then anger at Veronica's ultimatum took over her thoughts. Veronica tried to force Daniel to return the painting or suffer her consequences. How dare she make threats! Tell her father, indeed!

Marti was sticking in the last of her brushes when she heard someone calling her name.

Skyler and Cynthia came running toward her.

"Are you leaving, Marti? We saw you leave the auditorium."

"Yeah. I guess I'm headed back to the ranch."

Skyler leaned her head to the side and gazed into the sky with dreamy eyes. "Wasn't that sweet what Daniel did? Bidding so high on your painting? And he doesn't even remember who you are. I think it's so romantic."

Cynthia nodded. "Yeah, Marti. He must still love you, or he wouldn't have defied Veronica like that in front of the whole town."

Marti leaned against the building. "Listen, you guys. Don't go jumping to conclusions. Just because Daniel liked the painting and wanted to help out the orphanage by bidding so high doesn't mean he still has feelings for me. He's made it perfectly clear—he wants to marry Veronica. I'm going home and finish his portrait, then get in my little rental car and leave." She looked at their sad faces. "I'm sorry, my friends. I know you miss our friendship. I miss it too, but I can't be here for the wedding. I don't think my heart could take it. Now, please, I hate long goodbyes."

"We understand, sugar. But we'll miss you bunches."

Both Cynthia and Skyler gave her one last hug and told her to keep in touch.

When her friends went back into the auditorium, Marti slid the handle of her tote over her shoulder along with her purse, grabbed the handle of the portable easel, and turned toward her car. In her dream world, she was basking in the feeling of joy over the words Daniel had said about her. He had stood up for her. But that's all it was—a dream.

By the time she reached the car, the noise from the auditorium had faded, and she realized how alone she actually was. The hairs on her arm stood to attention.

"Stop being so paranoid, Marti. Zach was your stalker, remember?"

Nervousness worked its way into her heart, and she glanced around her—still not able to shake the feeling that someone was watching her. She fumbled for her keys and tried to find the key that opened the lock. When she realized she had pulled out the ring containing her apartment keys, she scrambled in her purse again for the set of rental keys.

A couple of steps shuffled behind her.

Terror made her heart race and circled in her throat, making it hard to breathe. Before she could turn around and see who was behind her, a hand slipped around her face and pressed a cloth over her nose and mouth. She was pulled against a hard body, and her arms were pinned to her side.

She tried to scream, but the cloth muffled the sound. Even as she kicked and struggled, a sweet smell infiltrated her lungs and everything around her gradually faded into nothing.

SIXTY-ONE

Gerald sat for a long time on the hay after Brent and Amber pulled out in the police cruiser. He felt as if his world had been turned upside down. How could he live with the pain he had caused others? He leaned against the barn and closed his eyes. The warmth of the sun caressed his face while he tried to pray.

"Lord, this is something I can't handle by myself. If all these things are true, then Mary took Marti's baby and left her with one that . . . Please, Lord, help them find the proof they need, and help us show Marti the love we should have shown her three years ago."

Gerald stood up and walked around the exercise path he created for the horses—his mind trying to grasp all the ramifications if these facts were true. Marti's baby was alive and being raised by Veronica and Shane. What about the other accusations Mary had made? Horrible memories exploded in his thoughts of things he and Daniel had accused Marti of on the day she left the ranch.

He had to find Marti. He couldn't tell her what he'd heard until he knew the facts, but he wanted to make sure she knew she was loved and wanted. Daniel might not remember his love for Marti, but Gerald remembered how much she had loved Daniel and how happy she had made him. They were meant to be together and would be together still if evil had not stepped through the door.

Gerald walked back toward the barn and entered the tack room door. When he stepped inside the door, he heard a voice coming from one of the stalls at the end of the aisle.

Was it Daniel?

He turned toward the door that opened into the walkway between stalls when the voice became louder.

"I said I got her. She's tied up in the old equipment shed down by the river. I tied her to some old well pipes buried in the ground. There's no way she can get loose."

Gerald froze.

"Nobody saw anything. I grabbed her as she was packing up her car after the auction. No one else was in the parking lot."

There was a pause in the conversation, and Gerald strained to hear the rest.

"I said, where are the gas cans? The ones behind the shed only held a drop or two. I'm at the stable. Okay. I'll check. As soon as I find them, I'll start the fire. The wildfire's already burned close to that shed, so it'll look like it all burned at the same time. I'll let you know when it's done."

Gerald heard the man close his phone. Footsteps came toward the tack room. Gerald ducked behind the wooden shelf containing salt and mineral blocks and bent low to the ground. His heart was racing.

He heard the outside door of the barn creak open and slam.

Gerald remained still—afraid to move in case the man was still in the stable.

Who was he? His voice was too low to recognize, but it sounded vaguely familiar. And, were they talking about Marti? She had been at the art auction. What was it he had said . . . she was tied in the equipment shed? And he was starting a fire?

Suddenly, all the things Marti had tried to tell him came to mind—the truck following her from Tennessee, the intruder smothering her in bed, the arrows, the bomb—it all made sense now. Brent said Zach couldn't be her stalker, but someone was trying to kill her. Was it because of Chris?

The reason didn't matter. He had to find Daniel. He had to get help.

He reached for his phone, but it wasn't in his pocket. He must have left it in the office. Adrenaline pumped through his legs as he rushed around the shelf to get to the office. In his eagerness, his shoe caught on the corner of the shelf, and he tripped. His ankle twisted, and he fell headlong into a row of wheelbarrows propped against the wall. Twisting his body to avoid a hard fall into the wheelbarrows, he glanced off the first wheelbarrow and slammed against the cement floor. The wheelbarrows toppled like dominoes into the wooden shelf. He turned in time to see the shelf teeter and slowly fall toward him. Mineral blocks sprinkled around him and fell like thuds on his unprotected body. When the shelf was emptied of its contents, it too fell forward and landed in a burst of agony on his legs. Gerald cried out in pain and felt blackness closing in around him.

"Lord, help," he whispered before he lost consciousness.

SIXTY-TWO

Bells were ringing in her head, and when she moved the bells turned into trumpets. She tried to rub her forehead with her right hand, but it felt lethargic and heavy. A hard cold metal strained against her wrist.

Slowly, she opened her eyes.

What she saw made her gasp.

A steel chain was wrapped several times around her hands and connected to another chain binding her ankles together. She could only move an inch or two. The end of the chains holding her was wrapped around a metal pipe that disappeared down a hole in the middle of the floor. The floor underneath her head was dirt, packed with age and as hard as the chains. Waves of panic pounded through her temples, and she fought the sick feeling churning in her stomach.

Someone had brought her here and left her to die. She remembered a voice—a low raspy growl she had heard before—in the alley. The same man had made good on his threat to kill her if she returned to Texas. And, no one could help her. Sweat popped out on her forehead even as a cold chill paralyzed her body.

The realization hit her in the pit of her stomach. No one knew where she was, or probably cared. Gerald was at the ranch. Skyler and Cynthia had long ago said their goodbyes. Veronica could care less, and Daniel . . . Daniel would probably be happy to have her absent from his life—finally.

Tears bubbled up in her eyes and blurred the shivering shaft of light coming in from a crack in the roof. She had run from this man for years. She'd have to run no longer. It was over. Her struggle to win Daniel back. Her fight against evil in the world. Her fight to survive. It was finished.

"God, please forgive me for turning from you. Please forgive my lack of faith. Help me die quickly, Lord."

When she said the words out loud, shame raced through her. Her words sounded so childish, so weak, so pathetic. She was giving up without a fight. The Lord promised His strength in her weakness. Anger fired through her veins.

"Okay, Lord. I'll trust You. I can't even move, much less get out of here, but I know You can help me. Please send someone, Lord."

How long had she been here? Had anyone missed her yet? Surely someone would notice her absence if nothing but as the absence of an irritation. She closed her eyes and prayed silently until she heard a cracking sound outside. Maybe someone was riding by.

"Help! I'm in here! Please help me!" she cried.

More scraping came from outside the shed. Thoughts of her attacker coming back to finish the job ran through her head, and she grew quiet. Listening.

Scratching sounds against the wooden walls sounded faint, but distinct. Could it be some kind of animal? Another kind of fear coursed through her veins.

She lay still and searched the base of the walls around her. The light was dim and made it hard to see, but there was no small foot digging under any of the walls. A silent, hopeful breath escaped her parched lips.

The sounds grew quiet until suddenly, a loud thud banged against one outside wall, then another. Through the crack under the wall beside her, she saw boot-clad feet walking back and forth from the woods to the shed. Should she cry out? Should she beg for her life? Indecision tore her apart. The wrong choice could cost her life.

Each time the feet came back to the shed, there was another dull thump. She saw a small branch poke through the hole at the base of the wall. Someone was piling up branches outside the shed.

While she waited, trying to decide what to do, a strong stench reached her nose—the pungent sharp smell of gasoline.

A flame of fear ripped through her. She looked out under the crack in time to see the whoosh of a fire. Terror made her faint. She strained on the chains.

"Please! Let me out! Please," she cried. Tears rolled down her cheeks and made silent plops on the hard dirt. She watched in horror as fire raced along the bottom edge of one entire wall and crept along the wall toward the door.

No, not the door! There's no other way out.

"Lord, please help me. I am weak, but You are strong."

Smoke began to filter through the cracks of the old shed, and her nose burned with the strength of the smell. The fire had reached the door and whooshed across it to the other side of the wall.

In panic, she watched as the fire crept toward the last wall of the shed. Smoke was filling the building and reached its tendrils toward her. As much as she could, she covered her mouth with her shoulder and tried to have faith. God would save her if it was His will. If it wasn't, she prayed He would be merciful.

A single whiff of smoke penetrated her covered lips, and she coughed uncontrollably. The acrid smell stung her eyes and her throat, and her stomach rebelled against the smell of smoke entering her lungs.

"Lord, please help me."

SIXTY-THREE

Daniel jumped out of his Chevy diesel truck and glanced around. His father's truck was still in the garage. Why hadn't he made it to the auction? And where was Marti's car? She'd left the auction, but no one knew where she'd gone.

He turned toward the pathway from the garage and crossed the yard toward the barn. Maybe his dad was having trouble with one of the horses. He'd check in the barn and see if one of the stable hands knew anything.

The door to the office was closed, but he yanked it open and peeked inside. Max sat at the computer. The horse roster was spread out in front of him, and he was entering the new information concerning each horse into the computer.

"Hey, are you checking the immunization records for the new mares?"

"Yeah. I'm almost done. Mr. Gerald wanted it done by the end of the week."

"Speaking of my dad, have you seen him today?"

"Yes, sir, I saw him this morning. He was vaccinating some of the foals in the next pasture."

"You haven't seen him this afternoon?"

"No, sir."

"If you see him, tell him I'm looking for him. He was supposed to come into town for the art auction, but he never showed up."

Max leaned back in his seat. "Yeah, he asked me this morning if I'd like to go along, but I forgot. He was right excited about seeing Marti's painting. It's odd he didn't show up."

Worry built up in Daniel's thoughts. If Gerald asked Max to go with him, it wasn't like him to forget, and it certainly wasn't like him to ignore something important either. "I'm going to take a look in the barn. If you see him, call me on my cell."

"You got it."

Daniel hurried to the barn and through the stalls where the new horses were stabled. He checked each stall carefully and made sure his father hadn't fallen in the hay out of sight. There wasn't a sign his father had even been in the barn. The feed troughs were empty. He turned toward the storage room.

When he opened the door, chaos met him. The shelf was pulled over onto the floor, and the contents were spread everywhere. Bottles of topical hoof treatment were piled in a heap, and the fluid leaked out of several bottles. He reached to pick up one of the leaking containers, when his eyes caught a glance of a boot under all the supplies.

Worry shot through him as he ran to the barn door and yelled, "Max! Come here!" Hurrying back to the mess on the floor, Daniel began tossing salt blocks into the corner—out of the way. Slowly the boot became more visible, and his stomach sank—a cowboy boot. A hollow moan came from somewhere under the pile of supplies.

"Dad?" His actions became frantic as he jerked on the heavy shelf. It didn't budge.

Another moan—louder than the first—escaped from his father's throat. "It's okay, Dad. I'm here. Just be still. I'll have you out in a minute. Max, get in here!"

Max slid around the corner into the room. "What happened?" he puffed out.

"I don't know. Help me lift this shelf."

Daniel and Max strained to lift the shelf up and over to the side. After the shelf was out of the way, they worked together to move the heavier bags of feed.

"Call 9-1-1, Max," Daniel said. "Dad's going to need an ambulance."

Max left the room to make the call. Daniel pulled salt blocks, paper towels, and plastic bottles of soap from off the top of his dad. "Dad? Can you hear me?" His words were tight with panic. Daniel knelt beside his father's head. Gerald was lying on his back, his eyes were closed. His leg was twisted at an odd angle. "Dad, can you hear me?"

Gerald's eyes opened slowly. His pupils looked even but dazed. "Son . . . Marti—"

"It's okay, Dad. Max is calling 9-1-1."

Gerald reached up and grabbed Daniel's arm. His grip was surprisingly strong. "Marti . . . help Marti."

"Marti doesn't need help, Dad. You're the one who needs help. The ambulance is on its way."

"No, Daniel. He will . . . kill her." Gerald dropped back and struggled for breath.

"Who are you talking about, Dad?"

"Marti . . . help Marti. Equipment shed . . . fire."

Daniel struggled to understand. What was his father trying to tell him about the equipment shed? Was Marti at the old shed? His dad must be worried about the wildfire.

"First let me help you, Dad. Then I'll check on Marti, okay?"

"No, Daniel. Leave . . . me. Go to Marti. He's going to . . . kill her . . . build a fire. She was right."

He felt like ice water had been thrown in his face. "Someone is trying to kill Marti?"

Gerald nodded jerkily. "Help her, son."

Max ran back into the room. "The EMT's are on their way, Daniel."

Gerald pushed Daniel's hand. "Go!" He had a panicked look in his eyes.

Daniel stood up. "Max, take care of him. I have to go check on Marti. My dad says someone's trying to kill her at the equipment shed. I don't know if he's talking out of his head or if there's something to what he's saying, but I'm gonna check it out. Call the sheriff. When the ambulance leaves with my dad, get the sheriff to come out to the old shed."

"Yes, sir. Don't you worry none. I'll take care of your dad."

Daniel ran to his truck. As he backed the truck down into the barnyard, he saw the tip of a red ax handle propped against a tree where one of the men had been splitting firewood. He jumped out of the truck, grabbed the ax, and threw it into the back of his truck on top of a pile of log chains. He barreled down the gravel road toward the back forty acres as fast as the gravel would permit. About a mile from the equipment shed, he saw dark gray smoke billowing into the air. It was too concentrated to be the widespread smoke of the wildfire.

Fire! There was a fire. His dad was right.

Sweat popped out on his forehead, and he pushed the gas pedal to the floor. His heart sank as he sped to the scene. If his dad was right, Marti was in the shed. Was someone really trying to kill her? She had tried to tell them someone had been stalking her, but they wouldn't listen.

In spite of the unsettling way she made him feel, he cared for her. Her sweet, innocent personality had worked its way under his skin. He fought the attraction, but he couldn't deny one was there.

Guilt raised its head. He shouldn't be thinking about another woman when he and Veronica were getting married in a week.

When he turned the last curve, his heart pounded. Flames rose high into the sky above the shed, and the wall that contained the only door was completely engulfed and hidden by flames and smoke. Marti's car was parked outside the engulfed building, and the driver's door stood wide open.

"God I don't remember ever praying to You, but I could sure use some help now. Marti loves you, God, so will You please help me find her?"

He rushed out of the truck, grabbed the ax, and headed toward the inferno.

SIXTY-FOUR

Even as Marti tried to have faith that God would send someone to rescue her, she heard a pounding on the only wall not consumed by fire. The ground shook with the force. She saw a small hole splinter at the base of the wall. With every crash, the hole opened a little more. Through burning and teary eyes, she watched a man force his way through the opening. An old rag was tied around his face, and his other hand held an ax. When he saw her, he rushed to her side and dropped to the floor beside her.

Daniel! His eyes were the only thing she could see through the smoke, but she recognized them well.

"Marti!" he screamed. He jerked the rag from his face and laid it over her mouth and nose to protect her from the smoke before he tugged at the chains near the ground. When they wouldn't give, he grabbed the ax and began pounding on the chains. His muscles rippled as he lifted the ax way above his head and struck the chain with full force. The chains were strong and seemed untouched by the tremendous blows.

Marti's heart sank. He was here, but he couldn't help her. He would die trying. She knew that. That was the type of man he was.

"Go, Daniel. Leave me. Please!" Coughing weakened her voice. Smoke burned her eyes. Tears of pain rolled down her face—mingled with tears of fear.

Coughing thwarted Daniel's movements, but he covered his mouth with his sleeve, patted her arm, and then pushed his way back out the opening in the wall.

The feeling of abandonment numbed Marti's limbs until she saw Daniel climb back through the hole. Behind him he dragged another chain, larger than the one around her arms and legs. He wrapped the chain around the pipe sticking up out of the ground and hooked it together with the hook on the end of the chain. He disappeared once again through the opening in the wall.

Through the popping and cracking of the burning building, she could hear the noise of a diesel motor revving up. Slowly the chain tightened until the pipe strained against the dirt edge of the opening in the floor. The chains around her legs tightened, and pains shot through her ankle.

Even as the chains played tug-of-war, a large portion of the roof on the far side of the shed cracked and fell inward—falling a few feet from Marti. She screamed in terror. Ambers flew through the air and landed all around her and on her clothes. She shook her elbows, trying to dislodge them from her blouse. She watched in horror as they left tiny burn holes in the sleeves of her shirt. She rolled on the floor to mash the smoldering embers and felt the chains tighten again.

By this time the fire had consumed the supports of the far corner, and the wall behind her gave a shudder and broke apart. Burning pieces fell on the floor behind her. The room became a blistering inferno, and her skin felt as if it were being roasted.

Once again the chains around her ankles clenched even tighter, and the pipes anchored in the ground exploded out of the floor. The chains fell off the bottom of the broken pipe.

Another fit of coughing brought tears to her eyes, and she covered her face with her shoulder, trying to summon faith that God would give Daniel the strength and knowledge to save her.

"Lord, please help us." Her throat was hoarse and almost silent, but she knew God heard. He would answer in His will. She laid her head closer to the dirt floor and tried to breathe in the fresh air flowing through the cracks under the walls. The fresh air from the hole in the floor fanned the flames, and the smoke and fumes filled her lungs.

Confusion laced her thoughts even as she saw a blurry Daniel push back into the burning inferno.

No, Daniel. Go back. Save yourself.

She was so sleepy. She lay her head down on the floor and prayed. Lack of oxygen made her dizzy, and without being able to stop it, the world around her slipped away.

SIXTY-FIVE

Daniel stood up as his father came out of the examining room at the emergency wing of the hospital. Gerald was walking on crutches, and a furrow creased his brow.

"Are you all right, Dad?"

"The doctor said it's not broken, just severely bruised. Have you heard anything from Marti yet?"

"Not yet. The nurse said the doctor's still with her."

"Did she ever wake up?"

Daniel shook his head. "I don't know. They had her in the ambulance before I could find out."

"What did she look like when you pulled her out? Was she conscious? Was she still breathing?"

"Yes, Dad, she was still breathing but unconscious. She was pale, but the nurse seems to think she will be okay. She said the oxygen levels in her blood are good, but they want to do more blood tests and a chest x-ray to make sure there's no lung damage."

The double doors of the emergency room exit swooshed open. Brent Simmons walked in. He saw Gerald and Daniel in the corner and headed toward them. Then the doors opened again, and Shane Duke hurried in. Both men joined them in the corner.

"How's Marti?" Shane asked. Concern wrinkled his brows.

"The nurse seems to think she's going to be okay."

"Great. That's good news."

Gerald blew out a breath of relief. "Thank the Lord you got there in time, Daniel."

Daniel nodded. "I wouldn't have known about it at all if you hadn't told me, Dad. How in the world did you know?"

"I overheard somebody talking in the stable. Max was feeding hay, and I was the only one there. Whoever it was came looking for gas cans. At first I thought it was you, Daniel, but when I heard him say something about a woman being tied up and unable to get loose, I knew it wasn't. He also said something about starting a fire where she couldn't get out, and I had a gut feeling they were talking about Marti. I got worried, and in my haste to get help, I knocked over the supply shelf right on top of myself."

Shane leaned forward. "Who was it talking in the barn? Do you know?"

Gerald shook his head. "No. The voice was too muffled."

Brent crossed his arms. "We've confirmed it was arson. Empty gas cans were spread all over the woods, and the county investigator said there's no doubt the shed was doused with gasoline. We also found a body."

Daniel stiffened. "What? Who?"

Brent nodded. "Jordan Welsh."

"Jordan! I don't believe it. Why was he even around that shed?"

"That, we don't know, but it was probably him that tried to kill Marti. He had gas all over his clothes, and his fingerprints are on the gas cans. I guess the smoke got to him, and he died before he could get away."

Shane crossed his arms. "Jordan Welsh. Do you think it had something to do with Marti's accident? Vinny's death hit him hard. After all, it was Marti's fault."

Brent cleared his throat and gave Gerald a strange look. "Could be. Hopefully we'll know more after the investigation."

Gerald leaned his crutches against a table and sat down. "Could he have been the one stalking her?"

"Someone's been stalking Marti?" Shane was surprised.

Daniel just nodded.

Shane sat down in the seat next to Gerald. "No kidding. Why?"

Gerald spoke up. "She doesn't know why, Shane."

"I doubt Jordan was the stalker," Brent said. "He's been too busy whipping Vinny's ranch back into shape. We have a couple more suspects we'd like to talk to." Brent said.

"Well, if he's not the stalker, then don't you think she still needs protection?"

"I do, Daniel, but you know we don't have the manpower to provide protection round the clock. Especially since Jordan died, and we believe he's the one who tried to kill her."

Gerald spoke up in a firm voice. "If you can't provide her protection, Brent, I'll hire a bodyguard myself. Somebody's got to protect the child."

Shane leaned forward. "Gerald, my cousin Ralph is a bodyguard who's looking for work. He has three kids, and I know he'd appreciate a job. He got laid off when his company was down-sized."

"Thanks, Shane. That sounds like a good idea. Do you have the number?"

"It's out in the truck. I'll get it for you."

Gerald stood up. "I'll walk out with you. I need to exercise this leg before it gets so tight it won't move at all."

Brent shook hands with Daniel. "I'm gonna head back to the station. Daniel, if we can do anything, let us know. I'll be in touch."

Daniel nodded and watched the three men step through the automatic doors.

As soon as they left, a nurse came around the corner. "Mr. Rushing, you can go in and see Ms. Rushing now. She's sedated, but she's going to be fine."

Daniel stood up quickly and followed the nurse. He glanced back at the emergency room doors as he walked by them. His dad would wonder where he was, but the nurses would tell him.

SIXTY-SIX

The phone in the holder on his belt vibrated and filled the truck cab as Shane watched Gerald hobble back into the emergency room exit.

"Hello."

"Would this be Shane Duke?"

"Yes. Who is this?"

"My name is Agnes Miller. My husband used to be a nurse's aide at the Marvel County Clinic with your wife."

"Yes? What can I do for you, Mrs. Miller?"

"Well, sir, I always thought the world of your wife when my Geoffrey worked there with her. She was most kind and caring. That's why I felt like I should give you warning. I've been questioned by the Carson City Police about what my husband told me concerning a death certificate your wife filled out three years ago."

"A gift certificate?"

"No, sir. A death certificate. A young woman named Tommi Robbins had a baby who died, and Ms. Mary filled out the death certificate. My Geoffrey was there that night and came home telling me about how strange it was. He'd come home during his shift to check on me 'cause I had the flu with a high fever, and he was worried. When he returned to the clinic a couple of hours later, he said the baby was alive. Your wife told him she'd performed CPR and brought the child back to life."

"Yes, I think I remember her mentioning that. We all thought it was a miracle."

"Well, sir, I had to tell the police today what my husband told me about that night. My Geoffrey died about a year ago, but I remember how upset he was about that night. He said there was something suspicious about that baby's miraculous recovery and about the baby itself."

"What are you saying, Mrs. Miller? What do you mean, *suspicious*?"

"For one thing, the little tot that died had red hair—just like his mama. But the baby Mary insisted was Tommi's baby had black hair—as black as soot. Geoff said he didn't think too much about it at the time, because what with the uproar about the mama dying and fighting to keep the baby alive, he thought he was just mixed up. But after talking to the detective there in Carson yesterday, I've remembered a few other things he said too. Geoffrey said the baby that died was a tiny little thing—skinny and bony. And he was lethargic, like he was sleepy. Geoffrey said he never did cry out when he was born. The baby Mary had when he got back was chubby and full of life, and Geoffrey laughed about the strength of his lungs—they were good and healthy. When he got back to the clinic, that baby was squalling bloody murder while Mary was giving him a bath. Now, he didn't know what made all them changes, but I thought it would only be fair to warn you about what I told the detectives—Ms. Mary being your wife and all."

Silence reigned for the space of a full minute. "Are you saying that my Mary lied, Mrs. Miller?"

"No, sir. I'm saying I told the judge and the detective that there were unusual things my husband told me about that birth, that's all. But, since it concerned your wife, and since I thought so much of her, I wanted you to know."

"Thank you for calling, Mrs. Miller."

Shane hung up the phone as if in a dream.

Suddenly his stomach churned, and sweat popped out on his forehead. All his hard work was about to unravel. This woman knew that Mary had switched babies.

And she had told a judge!

Flashbacks of that night filled his thoughts. Mary came home from the clinic the night of the accident with a baby in her arms. She said the mother had died, and Mary wanted to adopt the sweet little thing. He wasn't too keen on raising another child so late in their lives, but Mary insisted for Veronica's sake. Veronica had been to the doctor that week, and he'd told her she could never have children. It was devastating to both Veronica and Mary. He thought at the time that adopting the baby was Mary's way of taking care of Veronica's future.

Shane climbed out of the truck and lifted the back seat. He pulled out a scrapbook, sat back down behind the wheel and flipped through the pages. He stopped at a well-worn section of the book that contained newspaper clippings. Articles about the accident that killed Daniel's sister filled several pages and brought back tender memories. Mary had been praised and called a hero for saving Marti's life by delivering her baby after the accident.

Mary told Shane on her deathbed what she'd done—switching the babies while the aide went home to check on his sick wife. Mary tested the blood types, and they were a perfect match—both O negative. That way, if for some reason they took a blood sample of the dead baby, it would match Marti's blood type as well.

Chris was Marti's baby.

And this woman had told a judge?

That meant Daniel would find out Marti was his wife. Then Marti would take Chris away, and Daniel would want to be with his son. He would leave Veronica.

"No!" The agonized cry burst from his lips. "I won't let it happen. Not again."

Something had to be done and done right away. If the judge ruled that Chris be given back to his parents, Veronica would lose the chance of raising a child. Her not being able to have children was why Mary had done what she did.

Shane firmed his jaw and pounded his fist against the steering wheel. Marti was the problem. If Jordan had done his job like he'd told him to, everything would be okay. But Marti had been rescued. If she disappeared, Daniel would stay with Veronica, and they could raise Chris together. Marti was the one thing standing in the way of Veronica's happiness.

SIXTY-SEVEN

Daniel quietly stepped through the curtains of the ICU and stopped just inside the partitioned room. The smells . . . the sounds . . . the slight figure of Marti lying in the bed hooked up to an IV tube and oxygen mask—it all circled around him like smoke from a campfire, smothering his thinking. His mind was blank until his emotions took over. Suddenly, he felt as if a door to the past had opened in his mind.

Sometime in the past, he had been here. Here in this room. Here beside an injured Marti—exactly like now. The memory was on the edge of his thoughts like the name of a person he was trying to remember but couldn't.

He took a tentative step closer to the bed and stared down at Marti—the bruises on her face, the bandages on her arms. Her hands lay limp on the sheet.

Something around her neck caught his eye. A chain hung around her neck; at the edge of the hospital gown was a small wooden object. He stepped closer, and it became clear. A horse's head.

He lifted his head quickly, and a cool feeling traveled across his face.

A wooden horse?

One more step brought him within two feet of Marti. He could see the horse clearly now. It had an emerald embedded in the horse's mane.

Then he knew. This horse was the missing horse from the set at the house.

He stared at the sunshine filtering into the room, dividing the wall into disorienting stripes. The memory of that horse—belonging to Marti—stirred a chord that had been dormant for months. Immediately, he was transported back in time. Back to another day, years ago. Back to a time he had forgotten until now. Instantly, the memories came flooding back, like horses running from a wildfire, and he couldn't hold them captive any longer.

Marti was his wife.

No. Ex-wife.

He had been with her, here in this room, when the state patrol came and told him Angie had died and that Marti was responsible. Mary Duke had been here also, and the horrible things she had accused Marti of came crashing back into his thoughts. He remembered the anger—the feeling of humiliation and disgrace. While Marti lay in that bed unconscious, his faith, his trust, his love for her had died a quick death. Even the pull of his heart toward accepting Marti's religion and her God suffered a beating as a result of those accusations. How could he accept her trust in God as real when she was totally a different person than the one he had fallen in love with and married? So . . . he had left an unconscious Marti to go to his mourning father.

It all made sense now. His father had brought Marti here with a purpose in mind.

Suddenly, all the air in his lungs escaped with a deep moan. Painful memories and accusations sucked the life from his being. He turned and stumbled down the hospital hall to the elevator.

When the doors opened, his dad hobbled out on crutches. Gerald took one look at Daniel's face and turned white.

"Daniel . . . is she—?"

"You knew all this time, didn't you?"

"What do you mean?"

"You knew she was my ex-wife. You brought her here . . . knowing how I felt about her when she left." He stepped into the elevator.

Gerald touched Daniel's arm. "Wait, son. Listen to me for a minute."

"Why should I listen? You've done nothing but lie and hide the truth." He waved off Gerald's outstretched hand and pushed the elevator button.

"Daniel, wait! It wasn't true. What we were told—"

The doors closed as Gerald's sentence was left lingering in the air. Daniel's heart hurt so that his legs could hardly hold him up.

The elevator bumped to a stop, and Daniel dragged himself out the door and down the hall to the mass of people sitting in the waiting room. He didn't see any of them. All he could think about was hiding away somewhere. A place where there was no one to ask him questions or remind him of the past. A place where he could think and relive things he vowed he'd never remember again.

Daniel stormed out the emergency room exit but stopped when he heard someone calling his name. He turned around and saw Veronica running toward him from the double doors.

"Daniel, wait! Where are you going? Daddy told me you were here."

"Not now, Nikki. I can't talk now."

"Wait, Daniel. Let me come with you."

"No."

She stiffened and stared at him. "What's the matter?"

Daniel turned his back toward her. He ran his fingers through his hair and turned to face her. Fury flushed through his face. "I remember everything—that's what's the matter. You lied to me, Nikki. You said we've been dating—since high school. You even said we dated regularly during college and made plans years ago to get married. None of that was true. I feel like a fool."

Veronica's face looked like a statue, but fear flickered in her eyes. She pushed her way into his personal space and lifted her head to bat her eyelashes up at him. "Oh, Daniel, I wanted to help you heal. I started telling you those things, thinking you'd remember the truth if I shocked you, but when you didn't . . . well . . . I guess I started believing it all."

"You knew Marti was my ex-wife too, didn't you?"

Veronica nodded. The beginnings of tears pooled in her eyes. "She wasn't right for you, Daniel, and she proved it by the way she acted. I . . . I didn't want you to make the same mistake twice."

Disbelief bubbled up inside him. "Like that was your decision, Veronica. Give me credit for being able to make my own decisions."

"Well, you sure didn't make the right one the first time, and look what she did to you. I didn't want you to get attached to her again."

Behind her, Daniel saw Shane walking toward them from the parking lot.

Daniel looked back at Veronica. "Well, you've got your wish. I'm not attached—to Marti or to you. We're done."

Veronica clung to his arm. "No, Daniel, please. Think about Chris. Sweet, little Chris. Think about what this will do to him. Please think about that. We can make it. I know we can. I'll change. I'll do anything you want me to, just please don't turn away from us."

Daniel looked at the tearful, hurt expression on her face, and pity bubbled up inside him. "There is no 'us,' Veronica. There never has been." He turned her around and handed her into the arms of her father. Her tears fell then, and she slumped into her father's embrace.

Shane's eyes were full of hatred, but he said nothing.

SIXTY-EIGHT

Daniel parked his truck halfway in the driveway and halfway in the barnyard. The back bumper hogged most of the driveway, but he didn't care. All he could think about was solitude—to sort out all the pain and memories overwhelming his thoughts. To pray to a God whom he now remembered. A God who gave him peace and comfort after Angie died. A God who loved him and wanted the best for him. A God he had forgotten for months.

He strode into the house and sought the privacy and quietness of the downstairs study where he closed the door firmly. The leather chair faced the floor to ceiling windows and had a perfect view of the mountains. He slumped in the seat and turned toward the sky.

All the memories came flooding back. The cute little barrel racer at the rodeo. Their first date. His proposal after the quarter horse picnic. Four wonderful years of marriage. He hung his head in his hands—remembering the feeling of devastation when Marti had gone three years ago. He'd turned to Marti's God for comfort and guidance. Where was God now? Was He with him the whole time he had amnesia? Was he still able to call on Him for help, comfort, and guidance?

"God? Are you there? I remember trusting you now. I remember turning to You for help. I gave You my life, Lord. I knew then, like I know now, that I'm a sinner. I've broken your commandments. But, Lord, I repented of my sins. I accepted the fact that you died for me, and that you were buried and rose again as a sacrifice for my sins. I remember accepting you as my Savior so You would save me from an eternity in hell. I'm sorry I forgot you, Lord. Please help me. Please give me strength to know Your will for me now. Only You can help me, Lord."

Despair and confusion filled the air circling his head. He was oblivious to the world around him until he heard a soft click.

He looked up to see his father limp into the room—the crutches awkward and cumbersome. Daniel sat up straight in the chair—still angry at the manipulative actions his father had taken and yet anxious about his condition after the accident in the barn. He wrestled with both emotions, unable to speak.

Gerald stopped beside the chair where Daniel sat and put his hand on Daniel's shoulder. "Son, I know you're angry with me, but I have some things that need saying." Gerald propped the crutches on the edge of the couch and gingerly sat down on the soft cushion.

"Yes, son, I brought Marti here on purpose, hoping she would help stimulate your memory. Marti didn't want to stay, Daniel. She knew you would hate her if you remembered why she left in the first place. But, she stayed for *you*. Even though you hurt her—"

"Hurt *her*! She's the one who—"

"Stop, Daniel. Please. Let me finish. Marti . . . uh . . . she came here under false pretenses. I have to confess, I told her you were dying and wanted to see her one last time."

Gerald looked chagrined.

Daniel sucked in a quick breath then blew it out in frustration. He didn't reply, and Gerald continued.

"Now that you can remember your marriage to Marti, you have to admit the deep love you felt for each other. I was hoping you would remember the closeness between the two of you and not the unpleasant last few days."

Daniel wasn't prepared for, nor did he welcome, the compassion he saw in his father's eyes. Daniel raised burning eyes and looked out the window.

Gerald continued. "But there's something I need to tell you now that has nothing to do with why Marti is here and has everything to do with why she left in the first place. We were wrong, Daniel. Marti wasn't the cause of the accident that killed your sister."

The anger in Daniel's eyes made them burn. "What do you mean? She was drinking and driving, and—"

Gerald shook his head. "No, Daniel. That's what I'm trying to tell you. An insurance investigator named Amber Pike came to see me about discrepancies in the accident report from your sister's accident. According to their re-opened investigation, Marti could not have been driving that night. Her DNA was all over the back seat of the car, and . . . Vinny's DNA was found on several places in the front seat area . . . and on the bottles of whiskey."

Daniel was stunned. "What?"

Gerald nodded. "She wasn't driving, Daniel, and she wasn't drinking."

"Then why did Mary—?"

"We don't know, and we'll probably never know. Mary lied. Ms. Pike says the ambulance driver told her that when he finally arrived at the accident scene, Marti was on the ground outside the driver's door. Mary had already delivered the baby, and Marti was unconscious. Mary had the baby wrapped in a blanket and took it to the hospital herself."

A tear formed in the corner of Daniel's eye, and he brushed it away.

"Listen, Daniel. The other things Mary told us may not be true either. We don't know that Marti—"

A knock sounded on the library door and interrupted Gerald's speech.

Daniel walked to the door and opened it to a surprised Parker.

"I'm sorry, sir. I didn't know you were in the house. Ms. Pike and Mr. Simmons are here to see Mr. Gerald."

Daniel turned to Gerald. "Brent Simmons? The police? Why, Dad?"

Gerald turned to Parker. "Bring them in here, Parker." To Daniel he said, "I hope they're here to clear up some things."

SIXTY-NINE

Shane peeked around the stairwell door leading from the basement of the hospital to the information desk. He glanced both ways before quietly opening the door. He stepped into the reception area with a paper bag in his hand. An orderly pushed a lunch cart toward the other end of the hallway with his head hung low, but the information desk was empty.

What luck.

He slipped over to the desk and touched the mouse to activate the screen. Quickly, he typed in Marti's name and made a mental note of the room number.

Voices echoed down the hall as he heard the receptionist give visitors directions to the cafeteria around the corner. He exited the patient screen—so the busybody wouldn't know someone had fooled with her computer—and headed toward the elevator. A voice bellowed from inside the elevator. The doors slid open as two nurses who were dealing with a troublesome patient pushed his wheelchair into the hall. Shane skirted around the group and pushed through the door marked "Stairs."

Marti was on the third floor, and if he remembered right, it would be on the front side of the building. On the third floor, he opened the stairwell door an inch and peeked through the opening to see if there were nurses at the desk. The stairwell was fifty feet from the nurse's station, but only one side of the desk was visible behind the hall wall. One black-headed nurse bent over a patient report in front of her with her back turned to the exit.

He glanced down the hall and saw his cousin Ralph standing outside Marti's room.

He left the door open an inch and sat down on the top stair. From inside his backpack, he pulled out a throw-away phone. He punched in a phone number and covered the phone most of the way with his shirt. Trying to disguise his voice, he spoke when he heard Ralph's "hello."

"Ralph Dell, this is Detective Smith at the Carson City Police Station. Detective Simmons asked me to call and let you know we've arrested the man stalking Marti Rushing. She no longer needs a bodyguard. Gerald had to return to his ranch, but he said if you come by, he'll write you a check. He also wants to thank you for your services."

"Oh, great. That's good news. I know Marti will be relieved."

"I'm sure she will."

Shane hung up the phone and peeked again around the stairwell door. He saw Ralph stick his head inside the door and say something to Marti, then close the door and walk down to the elevators.

When he had gone, Shane opened the door quickly, and slipped into the hall. He walked briskly toward the absorbed nurse and stopped at the fourth door from the stairs. He turned to glance both ways and make sure no one had seen him.

He squared his shoulders and lightly knocked on the door.

"Come in." Marti's voice sounded weak.

He pushed through the door—glad to hear the weakness in her voice. "Hey there, Marti. How are you feeling, child?"

Marti scooted up in bed and scratched around the bandage on her ankle. "Hello, Mr. Duke. I think I've had better days."

"Did you hear? They've arrested your stalker!"

"The guard just told me, but he didn't say who it was. Do you know?"

"Uh . . . no, I don't."

"I'm relieved. I hope they find out why he's been after me all this time."

Shane scooted up beside the bed. "Daniel said the doctor called and is letting you go home finally."

Marti's eyes lit up. "That's wonderful. I'm ready to get out of here."

Shane handed her the paper bag. "Daniel's parking the car at the check-out exit and sent these up. He said if you go ahead and get changed, he'll pick you up there in a few minutes."

Marti looked confused. "The nurses didn't say anything about me leaving tonight."

"I just saw the head nurse at the nurse's station. She said she has the paperwork just about ready."

"Okay," Marti said with a shrug. She crawled out of bed and hobbled with the bag to the bathroom.

Shane tiptoed to the hallway door and peeked at the nurse's station. The black-headed nurse was still poring over the patient reports, concentrating on the computer screen. A second nurse had her back turned to him. She had a sandwich, chips, and coke spread out around her and a paperback novel in front of her face.

Perfect. He could make this work. All he had to do was get Marti out the door.

When Marti opened the bathroom door, she was dressed in jeans and a white knit sweater. Confusion drew her brows together. "Whose clothes are these? Why didn't Daniel bring some of my own things?"

Shane's composure slipped a little. "Uh, I don't know. Maybe he borrowed those from somebody. You know how men are. We don't think too clearly."

Marti sat down on the edge of the bed.

Shane's gaze bounced back and forth from the bed to the door. "Uh, are you ready to go?"

Marti leaned back against the pillows. "I think I'll wait for the nurse."

Shane cleared his throat. "I told the nurse I would help you out. Daniel can't park at the pick-up entrance too long."

Marti sat up in bed. A frown etched her features. "I think I'd better wait on the nurse."

Shane blew out a labored breath. "You just had to make it difficult, didn't you?" He pulled a tiny pistol from his pocket. "Now get up. And don't make a sound or my friend who's with Daniel right now will kill him immediately."

Marti's pale face turned ashen. "Mr. Duke? W-what are you doing?" She stared at the gun in his hand.

Shane's anger felt like a volcano inside him. "Look, we either get moving or we stand here and answer questions while I call my buddy and tell him to shoot Daniel and throw his body in the lake. Which do you want?"

"You . . . you have Daniel?" Marti stood. "I'll go with you, but please don't hurt Daniel." Her legs wobbled as she crept to the door.

Shane grabbed her arm and pointed the gun at her temple. "Now, this is how we're gonna do this. We're going out this door and to the left, down the hall and into the stairwell. If you make one sound to let the nurses know something is wrong, I'll shoot you. Do you understand?"

She nodded. "Where is Daniel?"

"I'll take you to him right now. Just don't make me mad."

Shane opened the door, peeked at the nurses still sitting in the same positions, and pushed Marti out the door. He poked the gun into her back and walked behind her as she made her way to the stairs.

Shane let out a shaky laugh when the stairwell door closed behind them. "That was easy." He poked the gun into Marti's ribs. "Now when we get down to the basement, there's an exit to the right. A black SUV is parked in the parking deck, right beside the door. You get in and drive. If anybody asks, we've been visiting a friend. Do you understand?"

Marti stared at him. "Why are you doing this?"

"Just shut up and walk."

Marti limped down three flights of stairs to the basement. When they opened the door into the parking garage, a security guard slammed his car door three cars over from the entrance. He balanced a McDonald's bag in one hand and a cup holder full of drinks in the other and walked toward them.

Shane pushed the gun into Marti's back. "Remember Daniel," he said. He pointed toward the black vehicle parked in the second parking spot. Marti walked that way and smiled shakily at the policeman as he came toward them.

"Evening, folks."

Marti nodded at him and kept walking.

Shane heard the security guard stop for a second before moving on. If the guard recognized Marti and questioned her, he'd have to think of something. He couldn't let anyone stop him. He had a promise to keep.

When they reached the black SUV, Shane stole a glance at the guard. He was still looking in their direction but the elevator door was closing. Shane opened the door, pushed Marti through the passenger side of the SUV into the driver's seat, and climbed in beside her. He opened the glove compartment, pulled out a large black pistol, and tossed the one he was holding into the back seat.

He grinned at Marti. "What? Did you think I could sneak a real gun into the hospital?"

His maniacal laughter filled the confined space.

Marti shuddered. "I th-thought you said Daniel was here."

"Just drive. You didn't really think I'd let him wait in the car, did you?" Shane laughed again. The sound made him relax. "This is going to work. Mary's memory as a qualified nurse, a good mother, and a loving wife will be intact."

SEVENTY

Marti's breaths came in rasping, choking gulps as she drove the SUV out of the hospital parking lot and onto Park Avenue.
He's not taking me to Daniel. Where is he taking me?
"Turn right at the next light."
The gun was still in his hand and glimmered in the street lights as they flashed by. Farther out on the road, the city lights grew dim, and the row of street lights ended. Still she kept driving.

Shane sat so still that she wondered if he had gone to sleep. She drew her body in as tight as she could. If she made herself small enough and quiet enough, maybe he would forget she was there and take a nap. Then she could find a place to stop the car and escape. Just about the time she gathered enough courage to turn and see if he was asleep, he lifted the gun toward her.

"Turn right at the next driveway."

Marti's heart thumped in her chest. The next driveway was the county's cemetery. The SUV crawled into the turn and slowed almost to a stop.

Marti looked at the ground outside her window. If she slowed the car enough, could she jump before he shot her? Maybe if she pushed the arm holding the gun up into the air and jumped at the same time, it would give her enough time to get out of the car. By the time he got the car stopped, she could be hidden in the trees on the left side of the road. There was a house just about a mile from the cemetery. If she could make it there before he did, she could call for help.

"Go to the end of this road and park, and hurry up. You're driving too slow."

Shane turned his head to look into the cemetery, and Marti knew this would be her last chance. With all the strength inside her, she lunged for his hand with the gun and pushed it toward the ceiling. The gun went off, and the bullet made a tearing sound as it entered the roof of the car. At the same time, Marti shoved open the door and tried to crawl out the opening, but she couldn't move.

She forgot about the seat belt.

Before she could reach to click it open, Shane pushed the gun into her face. His voice fried the air. "Don't do that again. Next time I'll shoot. Close the door and drive."

Marti's hands were shaking so hard she could hardly hold the steering wheel. The car crept up to ten miles an hour then twenty. "Wh-where are we going?"

"You'll find out soon enough."

When the paved road ended at the grass, Shane leaned over and turned off the engine. With a quick movement, he jerked the gear into park and pulled the keys from the ignition. He pointed the gun at Marti. "Get out."

"Where are we going?"

"I said *get out*."

Shane's words were slow and raspy. His voice boiled over with anger.

It took four attempts at unfastening her seatbelt before the lock clicked and went slack. Should she run as soon as she got out of the car? Or, should she wait until he wasn't looking and then try to escape? She opened her door and peeled herself out of the seat. Before she even stood straight, Shane was standing outside her door—the gun pointed at her head.

It was too late. Running was not an option.

SEVENTY-ONE

When Amber Pike and Brent Simmons entered the room, Daniel indicated two chairs opposite the couch, but he remained standing. Amber and Brent sat down on the chairs and looked at each other. Brent nodded at Amber, who leaned forward. Her face was serious and full of worry wrinkles. She pulled out a single sheet of paper from her case and laid it on her lap.

Gerald shifted in his seat and spoke—a touch of impatience in his voice. "Do you have more news of the investigation?"

"We do have news, sir." Amber took a deep breath and exhaled it slowly. "The suppositions I mentioned to you a week ago were correct. Martha Rushing was definitely not driving the night of the accident." Amber continued. "All the evidence proves that Vinny Welsh was driving the car. His wife, your daughter Angela Welsh, was riding in the passenger seat, and Martha Rushing was riding in the back, behind the driver. We also know Martha was not drinking. The blood tests run later the next day showed no signs of alcohol in her system."

"Wait a minute." Daniel interrupted. "They said at the trial it was too late to conduct blood tests for the alcohol levels."

Amber nodded. "Yes, that's what we were told, but blood tests can be conducted for some time after an accident. Her blood was tested at the hospital and turned over to the investigating officer.

Unfortunately, the results were filed in the wrong office. One of the lab technicians remembered running the tests but couldn't find the results when we asked for them. He found them stuffed in the back of the cabinet behind the set of drawers."

Daniel rubbed his forehead with his hands.

Amber cleared her throat and continued. "We also confirmed that the baby brought to the hospital that night and passed off as Martha's baby was, in fact, not hers at all."

Daniel stiffened and walked closer to the couch. "What?"

"Sit down, Daniel, and let them explain," his father said as he indicated the seat beside him on the couch. Daniel slowly sat down.

Brent leaned forward and took over the explanation. "Daniel, we asked your father not to mention it to you until we had proof, but now we do. The baby Mary brought to the hospital that night as Marti's baby was born to a young woman named Tommi Robbins. She died immediately after the birth—preeclampsia, I believe. The baby was born alive the morning of the accident, but died later that afternoon. It seems that Mary switched the babies at the clinic across the road from the accident and took the dead baby to the hospital. She told the nurses it was Marti's baby."

Daniel was shocked. "But why? And how can that happen? What about blood types and DNA tests?"

"The babies had the same blood type, and because of the accident, there was no question about it not being Marti's baby, Daniel. We all just assumed . . . since Mary delivered the little boy and brought him in . . ."

Daniel's face turned white. He stood up and paced the floor. Suddenly, he came to a dead stop. "If that baby wasn't Marti's baby, then what happened to Marti's son?" His voice was hoarse and cracked.

Brent cleared his throat. "You know him, Daniel. I'm afraid he's being raised by Shane and Veronica Duke."

"Chris? Chris is Marti's baby?" Daniel voice broke. "Her baby didn't die?" Daniel sank into the chair in front of him—the paralysis of unbelief frozen on his face. "Are you sure?"

Brent nodded. "Yes. The DNA test proved it. There's no question."

Daniel slumped farther down in the chair. His face was cold, as if the blood had all rushed to his heart to keep it pumping.

Gerald leaned forward. "When can we have him back?"

Daniel heard the control and roughness in his father's voice. His father was accepting this much better than he was. If these things were true, his father had a grandson. Chris was stolen from them. His heart couldn't wrap around that fact.

Brent stood up, and the firmness of his expression spoke of determination. "We've already talked to the judge about a court order, Gerald. As soon as that's done, probably in a couple of hours, we'll pick up Chris. But until that happens, don't mention this to anyone. We don't want the Dukes to get word of the judge's order and run with the child. We have men watching the house, but a police chase could injure Chris if Shane or Veronica panics."

"Veronica? Veronica knew?" Daniel's voice was raspy.

"We don't know for sure, but we're taking every precaution." Brent paused a moment before getting to his feet. "Tell me you'll wait on the department and not take matters into your own hands, or I'll have to leave one of my men here."

Gerald grabbed his crutches and made an effort to stand. He hobbled to stand directly in front of Brent and looked him in the eye. "We'll wait, Brent, but not for long and only because I can't get around very well right now. But I'm telling you, we won't wait long—guard or no guard."

Daniel stood beside his father in complete agreement.

"Understood."

Amber stood, and they both shook hands with Gerald. When they turned to Daniel, he reached out his hand, but his fingers felt numb—as if he were in an alternate universe watching his life unfold through a window. He still couldn't take it all in.

Brent and Amber walked to the door. "We'll be bringing the boy by as soon as we have the court order, Daniel. In the meantime . . ."

Brent was interrupted by the beeper hanging on his belt. He pulled out his cell phone and dialed a number. "Simmons. *What? When?* Seal all the exits and search the hospital. Have Tom block the exit to the parking lot, and get Ronnie to start reviewing the last hour of security tapes. I'll be there in ten."

While he was talking, Daniel's heart dropped into his stomach. Something was wrong at the hospital. Was Marti okay? Did this involve her?

Brent turned toward them. "Marti's gone from her room at the hospital. She left her gown and walked out. There's no sign of a struggle, but no one saw her leave either. She must have gone down the stairs to the basement. The receptionist downstairs says she didn't see her leave through the lobby."

"What about the bodyguard?"

"The nurse said he told them someone from the station called and said they had the suspect in custody and his job was over. So, he left."

Daniel felt a cold wave travel through his limbs. "Let's go." He stepped toward the door.

Brent grabbed his arm. "Daniel, wait. Did she have friends who might have picked her up?"

Daniel shook his head. "She's been talking to Cynthia Morrison and Skyler Rountree, but she wouldn't leave without checking out or telling the nurses. She has no place to go, except here."

"We'll give them a call and find out. Stay here, Daniel, and let me know if you hear from her."

Daniel shook Brent's hand from his arm. "Brent, I have to look for her."

"We'll find her, Daniel. Stay here, and if she comes back, call the station. Amber, we're out of here."

SEVENTY-TWO

"When Brent and Amber left, Daniel moved to the windows to stare at the mountains, seeking some kind of peace. Calmness eluded him like his memory had for so many months.

"Chris is Marti's son. I can't believe it. Do you think Veronica knew?" Fury blazed in his eyes. "You were right, Dad. I don't know her very well. All those things she told me about how close we were—she lied. I should have believed you when you told me so. I thought you were exaggerating because you didn't like her. Do you think she knew Chris was Marti's baby?"

Gerald wore a pained expression. "Daniel, why do you keep calling him 'Marti's baby,' instead of 'our' baby?"

"Because, Dad, that day at the hospital, Mary told me the baby ... wasn't mine. She said Marti had been seeing a man in the next county." Daniel's back stiffened, and he felt nauseated.

"Son, Mary lied about everything else. What makes you believe she was telling the truth about that?"

Daniel sat down in the chair and rubbed his forehead. "Because, Dad, I saw her with him—in town the other day. She was laughing and talking—right outside the café. They hugged each other and went into the café together. She lied about meeting him. She told me she was meeting her friends for lunch. That's one accusation Mary made that I think ... might be true."

"I don't believe it. There must be an explanation, Daniel. Marti would never—"

"Enough, Dad. Maybe you're right, but right now I'm concerned about Marti."

"But Daniel, she never acted like she was unhappy being with you. Don't you think you might be jumping to conclusions like we did with everything else?"

"I don't know, Dad. I just know I saw them together the other day. That's all."

"What did she say when you confronted her with it three years ago?"

Daniel hung his head. "I didn't ask her about it."

"You pursued divorce without asking for her side of the story?"

Daniel nodded miserably. "My pride was hurt. I just wanted to hurt her back."

Gerald moaned and rubbed his eye. "I can't throw the first stone. You weren't the only one who sent her away. I had plenty to say on the subject as well." His face twisted with emotion. "Son, what have we done?"

Daniel sank back down on the couch, a look of utter agony on his face. When he looked at his father, tears filled his eyes. "Poor Marti. What she went through. I have to find her, Dad. I have to say I'm sorry . . . ask her to forgive me. I said horrible things to her . . . all because of my pride. She'll probably never forgive me, but I have to say I'm sorry. I can't stay around here and wait. I have to go find her."

"Go, son. I'll stay here. If she comes back, I'll call you."

The doorbell in the hall chimed, and the sound vibrated through Daniel's heart.

"Marti!"

He ran to the front door and jerked the door open. On the porch stood a man instead of Marti.

Daniel's heart slowed to a crawl. "Yes?"

"My name is Ralph Dell. I'm Shane Duke's cousin. I was told to stop by here to get my check."

"Check? For what?"

"For guarding Marti at the hospital. Detective Smith from the police department called and said they caught the stalker and to stop by here for my check."

Daniel ran a hand through his hair. He had forgotten. The stalker must have made the call. He turned to his dad, whose face was as white as a sheet.

Gerald said only one thing. "Go."

Daniel pushed past the guard and ran toward his truck. He turned his truck toward town with dread filling the cab like a fog. "Lord, please let Marti be okay. Protect her from whomever this is, Lord. Please."

He was reaching for the phone to call Brent when his phone rang. "This is Daniel."

"Daniel, I didn't know who else to call. I need help."

"Veronica?"

"I'm worried about Daddy. He was talking out of his head. He was furious and raving about some nurse and Marti, and he never came home." She broke off in a sob. "I'm scared, Daniel."

"Wait a minute, Nikki. You're not making sense. Start over."

"When I left Daddy at the hospital, he was ranting and raving about some phone call he received. He said it was Marti's fault. Daniel, he was so angry. I tried to stop him, but he left. At first I thought he was going home, but he jumped in his pickup and took off in the wrong direction. He rushed out of the parking lot so fast, he left skid marks all over the driveway. He was saying crazy things like 'he was going to make Marti pay' and 'Marti should keep Mama company.' Now I'm scared, Daniel, because he hasn't come home yet. He was furious, and I don't know what he might do—to himself or someone else."

When the meaning of what Veronica was trying to tell him penetrated his understanding, sweat broke out on his forehead. Shane? Shane was the one after Marti?

"I need to tell Brent what you told me, Veronica. We'll find your dad."

He ended the call and rushed into the station. Brent was just inside the door.

"Any word?"

Brent shook his head. "No. they found her phone and purse still at the hospital. They're in the process of checking the security tapes."

"Veronica called and said her dad was acting crazy. Ranting and raving about Marti. She said he left the hospital in a rush and hasn't returned home."

While he was talking, Brent's phone rang. "Simmons. He did? I'll put out an APB. Finish searching the hospital, question all the staff, and I'll let you know where to go from there."

Brent looked at Daniel.

"What?"

"Shane was on the security tape. He left with Marti in a black SUV."

Daniel's pulse raced. "Shane has Marti."

"Daniel, get Veronica on the phone. I'd like to ask her questions about what Shane said exactly. It might give us a clue where he took her."

Daniel punched in the speed dial number for Veronica with shaky hands and handed the phone to Brent.

Daniel stumbled over to chairs lined up against the wall and fell into the seat. He held his head with his hands and prayed. "Lord, please help us find her. Please let her be okay." What was it

Veronica said she heard Shane say? Make Marti pay. Marti would keep Mary company.

Suddenly, he stood up. "Brent," he yelled. "I know where he took her—the cemetery. Let's go, and I'll explain on the way."

Brent and Daniel got into the patrol car and sped down the road.

"I hope this isn't a wild goose chase, but yesterday, Shane said he goes to Mary's grave every day to keep her company. He thought Mary might be lonely out under those trees all by herself so far from town. He said Mary never liked being by herself, and he wished he could find someone to visit her every day. And tonight, Veronica said Shane thought Marti would keep Mary company." He glanced at Brent.

"You think he took her to the cemetery?"

Daniel shrugged. "Your guess is as good as mine . . . but yes."

Brent got on the radio and ordered every available unit to the cemetery. "Be on the alert for a black SUV. Go in from different directions, and let's make it a silent run, boys. No lights, no sirens."

Brent hung up the radio. "All we can do now is pray."

SEVENTY-THREE

Shane had a rope in one hand and the gun in the other.

"Lay down on the ground," he told Marti.

Marti's stomach clenched. "Please—"

"Lay down!" Shane gave her a shove. "I don't want to hurt you, Marti, so just do as I say."

Marti lay down on the ground. Shane pulled her hands behind her and tied them with the rope. Then he tied her feet together as well. She bit her lips when the ropes cut into the skin around her bandage, but she didn't want to make him mad by whimpering.

Shane stepped to the SUV and opened the back door. He pulled out a long piece of thick plastic and set it on the ground. When Marti saw him pull out a shovel, her pulse pounded in her ears. Was he going to shoot her and bury her? Through dim vision, she saw him pull out a large battery-operated spotlight and a bouquet of flowers. He positioned the spotlight so it would shine toward a tall gravestone.

Marti turned her head to the side and read the inscription.

Mary Duke—Beloved Wife and Mother.

Shane walked to the gravestone and propped the flowers against the grave.

"Hello, Mary. I'm sorry I haven't been to see you lately, but I brought you some flowers and some company. Maybe Marti can keep you from being lonely."

Marti was scared to make a noise, but a scream grew inside her head. Shane was going to bury her in the grave with Mary. He was mad.

Shane picked up the shovel and started clearing off the grass on top of the grave. After a minute or two, Marti heard the shovel hit dirt. He worked quietly and piled the dirt on one side of the grave.

Marti felt faint, like her brain was wrapped in cotton. Mentally, she shook herself. If she didn't think of something, she was going to die. She needed to think—to plan.

Lord, please help me think of something.

She'd heard that by talking to their abductors, other kidnapped victims were able to talk their captors into letting them go. Would it work with Shane?

"Mr. Duke?" Her voice was too shaky. He couldn't hear her. She took a deep breath and tried once again. "Mr. Duke?"

He looked at her but kept shoveling.

"Why have you brought me here?"

Shane stopped then and held the shovel just above the hole. "I brought you here to keep Mary company."

"But, Mary's dead, Mr. Duke. She doesn't need company."

"Yeah, she's dead, but she still gets lonely, and it's your fault she died." When Shane started back digging, she felt the ground shake with the force he was using.

"M-my fault?"

"If you'd just stayed away, everything would have been okay." His voice was loud and angry. "Daniel would have married my Veronica. She can't have kids, but they would have had Chris. Mary made sure of that. All of us would have been happy. Mary too." His voice broke. "But, Mary worried herself sick thinking you were coming back. Now she's gone. And, I'm going to make sure my Veronica has what Mary wanted her to have—a family." He stopped digging long enough to wipe tears from his eyes.

Marti's skin prickled. She felt cold and clammy. *I'm fine. Everything is fine.*

She was *not* fine. She was about to be shot and buried in a shallow grave.

Think, Marti! Think!

"Daniel and Veronica are getting married this Saturday, aren't they, Mr. Duke? Veronica will have what she wants. You didn't need to bring me here. Why don't you untie me now and let's go back home to see Veronica, okay? I won't tell anyone what's happened. We'll just forget about this, and I'll move back to Tennessee. You and Veronica and Daniel and Chris can be one big happy family."

Shane put down the shovel, and Marti was scared to breathe. He walked over beside her. His face was covered with eerie black shadows from the spotlight shimmering across his face.

"You think I'm crazy. You don't understand, do you? I have to do this. I've already done everything I can think of to keep you away. It didn't work. And, there are people who know what we've done."

Marti's throat tightened. He would not be swayed. A sob hung in her throat.

Shane walked over beside the SUV and picked up the plastic bag. When he got closer, Marti felt her whole body go numb. It was a body bag—exactly like the coroner used.

Shane laid it down beside her and unzipped the bag. Then he picked up her feet and stuffed them into the bag.

"No! Mr. Duke! No!"

"Shut up, Marti. This will be easier. It won't hurt like a gunshot would."

"No! No!" Marti kicked and struggled. She hit at Shane with her head and legs until he exploded in anger. He balled his fist and slugged her in the jaw. Her world turned black, and stars appeared around her. She fought losing consciousness even as Shane stuffed her body into the black bag. A piece of duct tape ripped as he tore it from the roll and placed it over her mouth. She heard the zipper in the plastic as it worked its way around to the end of the bag, but feeble resistance was all she could manage. Her head felt as if it had exploded. The tape pulled at her mouth and pinched as she tried to yell.

Marti felt herself being dragged a short distance then she tumbled into a hole. She tried to move, but her head ached, and she couldn't remember what to do. The pitch blackness enveloped her, and dizziness made her stomach roil.

The air around her was hot and suffocating. She struggled to get enough air through her nose, but panic had her hyperventilating. There was little oxygen in each panicked breath. Sweat rolled down her face and into her eyes and mingled with tears.

Lord, please help me.

She felt something light hit her from above.

Dirt! He was burying her alive!

Air! I've got to have air!

She struggled against the plastic and knew it only made things worse. The more she struggled, the more oxygen she used up. When she stopped struggling she immediately felt sleepy. Being sleepy was the last stage before death, wasn't it?

God please help me. She tried to poke through the plastic with her fingernails. It was too tough. She tried kicking with her feet, but the bag was too large. Her feet weren't touching the bottom.

She felt the heaviness of the dirt as Shane threw more in on top of her.

Was this the end?

Thoughts of Daniel and their life together flashed through her head, and a great sadness filled her heart. At least she knew when she woke up, she'd be in heaven, and Daniel would eventually meet her there. She felt so sleepy. If she could rest a moment, she might be able to think of a way to save herself. She'd shut her eyes and rest—just for a minute. Marti closed her eyes and remembered no more.

SEVENTY-FOUR

"We've located the SUV, sir."

The radio in the police cruiser blared out the good news. Daniel's heart breathed a tentative sigh of relief.

"Do you see anyone around?"

Brent's voice was steady and calm. How could he be calm at a time like this?

"It looks like Mr. Duke might be digging up his wife's grave."

A stab of pain pierced Daniel's heart. Had he killed Marti already and was burying her body?

"Don't let him see you. Fan out. Surround the area and wait until we get there. Turn your radios down so he won't hear."

"Yes, sir."

"Dispatch. Get Richard out here now and EMS."

"Ten-four."

Daniel turned to Brent. "She has to be alive."

Brent didn't answer. His mouth formed a tight line.

Daniel splayed hands on the dash. His knuckles turned white with the pressure. "She has to be alive, Lord, please let her be alive."

"Amen." Brent jerked the steering wheel to the right. He stopped on the edge of the road and spoke into the radio. "Is everyone in position?"

"Yes, sir. Tailor and Camden have positions in the back, and Don and I are on each side of the gravesite."

"Okay. We're coming in."

Brent plowed forward with sirens blaring. He slid the car to a stop, parallel to the gravesite.

Each policeman around the cemetery flashed spotlights at the grave and bathed the area with light. Daniel saw Shane squint at the police cruiser and take off at a run.

When he saw he was surrounded, he slid to a stop between two tall headstones.

Brent and Daniel slid out of the driver's side door and crouched behind the vehicle. Brent reached into the cruiser, pressed a button, and picked up the microphone. "Shane Duke. Throw out your weapons and come out with your hands in the air." His voice boomed across the cemetery.

Daniel waited. Before Brent could say more, two shots rang out. Daniel ducked but at the same time heard the impact in the trees overhead.

The scanner blared. "Should we engage, sir?"

"Hold your fire. He shot into the air." Brent peeked over the top of the car but stayed hidden behind the vehicle.

"Shane. You're a respected man of the community. Don't make us shoot you. You're surrounded. Give yourself up."

"Go away, Brent! I have to finish what I started."

A car pulled up behind them, and a man wearing a bullet proof vest got out and ran up to the cruiser. Richard Darnell. The department's negotiator. Daniel's faith took a nose dive. Richard was just out of the academy. How could they place Marti's life in the hands of someone so green?

Brent turned to the young man and nodded.

"What do we have, Chief?"

"Shane Duke—a murder suspect. It's possible he has a woman as hostage."

The man nodded and waved away the microphone Brent handed him. Instead, he raised his voice so Shane could hear him. "Mr. Duke. This is Richard Darnell. I remember you from the Cattlemen's Association. You and I are members of the same group, I think. Isn't that right?"

No answer.

"Mr. Duke. I'm here to help you. Will you let me do that?"

At first, Daniel thought Shane wasn't going to respond, but finally he yelled, "I don't need help. I just need everybody to go away and let me finish what I started."

"You know the police aren't going to do that, Mr. Duke, but I'll try to help you if you'll let me. The policemen out here aren't thinking about what you want, but I'm here to listen to *you*. So will you let me help you?"

"It's too late. I've gone too far. There's nothing you can do."

"There's always hope, Shane. Do you care if I call you Shane? We'll just leave the police out of it, and you and I can talk. Now, would you come out so we can talk—just the two of us?"

"Don't you understand? It's too late. I've already killed somebody."

Daniel's face went hot then cold. *No! Not Marti! Please, God, not Marti.*

"It doesn't matter what you've done, Shane. There's always hope. Let's forget the past and start over right now so no one else will get hurt."

The silence smothered Daniel's optimism.

"It's too late for me . . . and Mary too. We both . . . did things."

"What things have you done, Shane? Maybe I can help you fix those things."

"No. It's too late for Mary." Daniel could hear Shane crying. "She just wanted to help Veronica. Since they were little, Daniel belonged to Veronica. Then that hussy came along and took Daniel away." Rage forced Shane's voice to swell in volume. "But, Mary knew how to fix it. She knew if Marti was convicted of a crime, she'd go to prison. Then Daniel would fall in love with Veronica, and everything would be okay. But they let Marti go. And Mary was afraid she would stay around because of the baby. So she took the baby too. And, that stupid nurse. She just had to stick her nose in."

Brent looked at Daniel. "He killed the nurse," he whispered.

Daniel backed up against the car and pressed both hands to his head. *Lord, please help us find Marti, and please protect her.*

Behind them, the ambulance pulled up to the scene a short distance away and stopped.

"So you love Mary, don't you, Shane?"

Shane's cries filled the air. "She was everything to me. That's why I had to do it. I had to make everybody see what a good person Mary was. I couldn't let Marti go on chasing after Daniel. I had to make her go away. So . . . I brought her here. Mary would know what to do. When I'm done with her, you can have me."

Daniel's head jerked up. He looked at Brent, and his eyes told him they were thinking the same thing. "Marti's still alive, but that's her grave he's digging," Brent whispered.

Daniel jumped to his feet, and Brent wrestled him down. "No, Daniel. Wait. If you go out there, he'll shoot you. That won't do Marti any good. We still don't know where she is."

"I have to find out what he did with her." Daniel's voice broke on the last word, and he slumped against the car.

Richard continued. "Do you think Mary would want you to kill anyone else, Shane? She's such a sweet person. Do you think she likes murder?"

"No. I know she doesn't." Shane's voice grew quiet. "And, I've already murdered two people."

"Two people?"

"Jordan was stupid. He was so scared he'd be convicted of stalking Marti that he stole Zach's knife and left it under her bed so they'd think it was Zach trying to kill her. Zach gave Jordan the keys to Marti's balcony door, and Jordan framed Zach. Then he murdered him so he couldn't squeal. He also tried to leave my shoe prints at the shed with an old pair of my shoes he found in the trash—to make it look like I started the fire. The fool. I told him to make it look like an accident."

Daniel's heart sped up. He didn't mention Marti. Maybe she wasn't dead yet.

"Ask him if Jordan was the one stalking Marti," Brent whispered.

"Was Jordan the one stalking Marti, Shane?"

"Yes. Mary had proof he robbed a jewelry store years ago when the security guard was murdered. Jordan did time in prison for murder when he was younger, so the courts would've given him the death penalty if they could prove he was the one who killed that guard. Mary held that over him to force him to keep Marti away from Texas. Then when Mary died, I offered him half of her insurance money to scare Marti away, but Marti came back anyway. She had to die. And Jordan was stupid, so I took care of him at the shed. Everybody thought I was at the horse auction because I registered to bid."

Daniel could hear him sobbing.

"But, Mary doesn't like murder. Mary won't like what I did. She'll be angry, and I don't want her to be angry. I want her to know I'm trying to help her. It's too late though, isn't it? My Mary."

They could hear his sobs, and his words got progressively softer. "There's no hope."

"There's always hope, Shane. Come out so we can talk."

"No. It's too late. I've already done it. There's no hope now. Marti's dead. I'm done."

They had to strain to hear Shane's last words, so they all jumped when the piercing sound of a shot rang out from behind the gravestone. Daniel jumped in horror. Had he shot Marti? He strained to see Shane and was shocked to see Shane's body slumped down beside the gravestone.

"Who fired that shot?" Brent demanded into the radio.

"He did, sir. He shot himself." There were a few minutes of agonizing silence while the men hurried closer to check on Shane. "He's dead, sir."

When Daniel heard their words, he rushed to the grave. He fell on his knees and began tearing at the dirt with both hands. "Marti! Marti, I'm here!" One of the other officers found the shovel and began digging as well. "God, please don't let her be dead."

Brent came over to help. "Be careful, she may be right under the surface."

It seemed to take an eternity before they hit something besides dirt. They quickly uncovered the black plastic and Daniel jumped into the shallow hole beside it.

Daniel tore into the plastic with his bare hands and cried when he saw Marti's face. Her eyes were closed, her face was cut and bruised, and her hair was matted with sweat. He gently tugged the tape from her mouth and pushed the hair out of her face. He leaned over and kissed her cheek. "Marti. Wake up, sweetheart."

Brent pulled him back. "Let the EMT's work on her, Daniel."

Daniel squatted back on his feet, breathless. The EMT moved up beside him and put his fingers on Marti's neck. He looked up at Daniel. "She has a pulse."

A wave of thankfulness washed over him. "Thank you, Lord. Thank you."

Daniel and the EMT worked to open the plastic bag and gently lift her out onto the ground. They placed an oxygen mask over her face as Daniel knelt beside her and caressed her cheek. In a few minutes, she opened her eyes in panic and moaned. He leaned in and whispered. "It's okay, honey. You're going to be okay." He hugged her. "I love you, Marti."

When her eyes found his, her struggling stopped, and her body relaxed. The deputy cut the ropes around her hands and she reached for Daniel. He leaned over and pulled her to him tightly. "I thought I'd lost you, but I prayed to God, and He answered."

Marti leaned toward him and melted in his arms. Daniel held her and prayed out loud. "Thank you, Lord, for saving my wife. Thank you."

SEVENTY-FIVE

Every muscle in Marti's body ached, but she wasn't going to complain. She was thankful to be alive. She moved slowly in the bed and cringed when her sore muscles cramped. One eye was still swollen, but she could tell the swelling was down from last night. She hated to look in the mirror—afraid she might look even worse than she felt.

"Take it slow and easy, Marti, and you'll be as good as new." That's what the doctor said late last night when she arrived at the hospital.

She pulled the sheet off her body and slid to the edge of the bed. Rain outside the window made pinging noises on the window ledge, so she hobbled across the room to glance at the gray clouds in the sky. Dawn was just beginning, and the faint light over the horizon was barely visible behind the rain-drenched clouds.

Thoughts of Shane entered her head, and instead of anger or fear, she felt only pity. His life had been filled with one catastrophe after another. No wonder he snapped. "Lord, forgive Shane. I want to. He was trying to be kind in his own way. And, thank You, Lord, for sending Daniel to save me. You answered my prayer. I'm sorry for doubting You."

She didn't know what to think about what she'd heard last night. She was so sure she heard Daniel thanking God for saving his *wife*. Yet, that couldn't be right. If Daniel had known she was his wife, he wouldn't have been holding her and carrying her to the ambulance. Maybe he said "life" instead of "wife." She must have misunderstood.

She still shuddered when she thought about that black plastic bag, but God's peace was slowly taking away the feeling of terror when she thought about the graveyard and that shallow grave.

A candy striper came through the door with a hospital tray in her hands. "How about some breakfast, Ms. Rushing? I know it's a little early, but you're the first on my floor and the only one awake."

Marti ran her fingers through her hair. "Thank you. I'll try to eat something."

The volunteer smiled. "I'll put it right here beside the chair if you'd like to sit here and eat. I'll come back for the tray." She laid the tray on the bedside table and pulled out a large ice pack from her cart. "Your young man asked me to bring this for that eye. A young rascal might be happy with that shiner, but a nice lady like you probably wishes it would go away."

"My young man? Do you mean Daniel?"

"I mean that tall, handsome fella who stayed by your bedside all night, that's who I mean. He got a phone call about thirty minutes ago and said to tell you he'd be back soon. I think it was a police detective—something about a woman named Veronica and a little boy named Chris."

Marti's heart sank. She gave the volunteer a trembling smile as she left and tenderly sat down in the chair beside the bed. Daniel had gone back to Veronica.

"Lord, I failed. What would you have me do now?"

Trust me.

"All right, Lord. I'll try."

She sighed and lifted the lid off the plate. The smell of eggs, grits, and toast made her stomach growl. The last meal she'd had was the afternoon before in the hospital. She took several bites of eggs and closed her eyes in appreciation. When she opened them again, Pastor Sammons was walking by her doorway. He glanced in the door as he went by but took a step back and stood in the doorway.

"Marti! What are you doing here?"

She smiled. "It's a long story, Pastor Sammons. Are you here visiting someone?"

"Anabelle Struthers finally had her baby—a girl."

Marti grinned. "Hallelujah for her—after all those boys."

The pastor came and sat down beside her. "That's quite a shiner you got there. You didn't fall off a horse again, did you?"

Marti grimaced. Gossip sure flew around this town. "I'll explain sometime," she said with a smile.

Pastor Sammons grinned. "Hey, I wanted to come to the ranch and see you before you left. I know Saturday will be hard for you, and I thought you might be planning to leave before then."

Marti leaned her head to the side. "Oh really?"

The pastor lowered his head and studied his shoes. "With the wedding and all."

Marti's chest heaved up and down. The wedding? Daniel and Veronica? Was it still this Saturday? A wave of cold shivered through her body, and she couldn't think what to say.

After Daniel's attention last night at the cemetery, she wasn't ready to accept his getting married. "I thought . . . I mean . . . he hasn't mentioned . . ."

Pastor Sammons patted her hand. "I'm sorry, Marti. Maybe I shouldn't have mentioned the wedding."

"I really thought he'd called it off."

"Called it off? No, not that I know of. I haven't heard anything different from Veronica, and I just saw Daniel early this morning. He didn't say anything about calling it off."

"Oh." The pain in her heart got stronger and squeezed the breath out of her lungs. She had to think about something else before she fainted. "Is it supposed to rain all day? Do you know, Pastor Sammons?"

He looked at her and searched her eyes. "Are you okay, Marti?"

"I'm fine, sir. Thank you for stopping in to see me. It's been good seeing you again. I'll let you know before I leave Texas."

The preacher looked surprised, but stood and patted her arm. "Goodbye, Marti. I'll keep you in my thoughts and prayers."

"Thank you." She knew the words were mumbled and insincere, but it was all she could manage at the moment.

After he left, she sat looking at the meal in front of her. It smelled like burned rubber, and she pushed it away.

She'd been so sure she heard Daniel say he loved her at the cemetery. The way he kissed her and held her—happy to find her alive—she thought he cared about her a little—at least enough to call off the wedding. Maybe he remembered the accident and wasn't willing to forgive.

All the work she and Gerald had done to help Daniel remember what happiness and love felt like—none of it had worked. Gerald told her that Daniel's memory had finally returned, but being able to remember had not changed his mind about love. He would marry Veronica and be miserable, and there was nothing she could do about it. She'd run out of time.

"Lord, what am I going to do now?"

Trust me.

There was that sense of a presence again. Marti felt sure it was God's answer. She needed to wait on His guidance. In the meantime, she wasn't going to be depressed. Life was too short to sit around whining because she couldn't have a certain man out of one hundred and fifty million plus men in America.

That realization triggered a decision. She was going home. She'd throw herself into her life at the gallery in Landeville and lose herself in her art. She'd let God take care of Daniel.

She picked up the phone and called the ranch. Luckily, she hadn't brought too many things to Texas. As unfriendly as Anita had been, Marti was sure she'd be happy to pack her things if it meant Marti was leaving the ranch for good.

After Anita reluctantly agreed to have them ready to go, Marti called Skyler.

"Marti, are you okay, sugar? We've been praying for you."

"I'm fine, Skyler. Just a little sore. I was wondering if you'd do me a big favor."

"Sure would, sugar. Shoot."

"Would you run by the Rushing ranch, pick up my things from Anita, and then come by the hospital and drive me to the bus stop?"

"You're not leaving us now, are you, hon?"

"Please, Skyler. Don't ask questions. I promise, I'll e-mail you and even call to explain when I get back to Tennessee, okay? Just don't make me explain right now."

"Okey-dokey, sweetie. I'll be there as soon as I can. We're sure gonna miss you when you go, though. I wish I could talk you into staying longer, but I promise not to ask questions."

"Thanks, Skyler. You're the best. And don't mention it to anyone."

She hung up the phone and looked around desperately. The clothes she had on last night were folded on the window sill. They were wrinkled and covered in stains, but they had to do. She could change into something clean once she got her things from Skyler and was out of the hospital. Skyler would be here soon, and if she hurried, she'd be out of here long before anyone missed her. She hated to leave Gerald without saying goodbye, but she couldn't stay—not now.

She peeled herself out of the chair, picked up the clothes, and limped across the room to the bathroom. She looked at herself in the mirror and cringed at the bruising and swelling. Was she doing the right thing? Traveling all the way back to Tennessee on a bus? By herself?

She laid the clothes on the side of the tub and lifted her blouse to shake out the wrinkles. The horse-head necklace fell on the floor. One of the nurses must have taken it off while she was asleep. She picked up the horse, and memories popped into her head. The emerald shone in the bright bathroom light. Daniel told her the day he gave it to her that the green color was a symbol of forgiveness. He promised to always be forgiving, no matter what she did. Tears blurred her vision. She laid the necklace on the sink and tugged the shirt on.

She had to go. And she had to hurry before she changed her mind.

SEVENTY-SIX

At the bus station, Skyler hugged Marti goodbye at the door. "I know you hate long goodbyes, so I'll just say so long here. You're going to write, aren't you?"

Marti smiled. "Of course, and maybe you and Cynthia can let me know if you visit the orphanage again. We'll have a slumber party in my tiny little apartment."

They both giggled and hugged each other again. "I'll miss you, my friend."

Marti nodded and held back the tears until Skyler left the station and got back in the car.

"Lord, am I sure this is the right thing to do?"

The verse in Proverbs popped into her head.

Trust in the Lord with all thine heart, and lean not on thine own understanding. In all thy ways acknowledge Him and he shall direct thy paths.

He shall direct thy paths. He shall direct thy paths.

Warily, she sat down in the waiting room and tried to be patient for two more hours until the one-fifteen bus left for Landeville. Her suitcase sat on the floor beside her, and her purse was propped beside her on the bench. No one was in sight. Even the station manager had gone to a late lunch, though he told her he'd be back long before her bus arrived. She sat staring out the tall windows at the distant mountains and clearing sky. The sun was beginning to peek out from the rainclouds. Rays of light broke through the clouds and shone on the landscape below, spreading the earth with its warmth and light.

She closed her eyes and tried to pray. *Lord, I think this is right—what I'm doing, but I have this feeling that something is wrong.*

It felt as if an electric current started at her hairline and worked its way down to her toes.

She looked up and found herself looking into startling brown eyes.

"Daniel! What are you doing here?"

He sat down beside her. "You first. What are *you* doing here?"

She looked down at the bench and twisted her fingers together. "I'm . . . uh . . . done with your portrait, and since I had no reason to stay longer, I . . . decided it was time to go home."

Daniel put his finger under her chin and lifted her head until she looked into his eyes. He moaned and gently caressed the bruised side of her face. "If Shane were here today, I'd give him a lickin' for what he did to you."

Marti held her breath. A tingle started in the pit of her stomach and worked its way up her chest.

Daniel continued. "I shouldn't be the one throwing stones, since I've hurt you far worse than Shane ever did."

She couldn't look at his eyes. She was afraid of what she might see.

"Marti, can you ever forgive me for what I've put you through?"

Marti looked down at the floor. Tears blurred her vision, and the tiled floor looked like a puddle of brown. "How . . . how did you find me?"

"Skyler. She said we needed to talk." Daniel touched her on the arm and took a deep breath. "Marti, please come back to the ranch. We have so much to say to each other. Won't you please come back for today . . . so we can talk? Then if you still want to go back to Tennessee tomorrow, I'll put you on a plane."

"What about . . . your wedding?" she whispered.

Daniel blew out a quick pained breath. "There is no wedding."

Marti lifted her head. "What?"

"Veronica and I will never get married. We're not right for each other—never have been. Besides . . ." He lifted her chin again and made her look him in the eyes. "In God's eyes, I'm already married."

Marti felt a warmness spreading over her—like basking in sunshine. Daniel's eyes darkened and strayed to her lips. Their faces were only inches apart, and Marti leaned toward him.

A group of children came running into the waiting room, and Daniel pulled back. He closed his eyes and a moan rumbled in his throat. Two adults were trying to corral the group of rambunctious kids and keep them together. Children were screaming and chasing each other all around the seats.

"Come on, Marti. Let's go home so we can talk in private, please?"

She nodded her head. He picked up her luggage and led her around the rowdy children and out of the building.

The ride home was silent. Marti didn't know what to say, and she imagined Daniel felt the same. When they arrived at the ranch, Max met Daniel at the car. "Mr. Daniel, Lucky Lady's foaling. I called the vet, but he can't be here for another two hours."

Daniel turned to Marti. She didn't even hesitate when she pointed toward the barn. "Go."

"Are you sure?" When she nodded, he said, "I'm sorry, Marti. Go inside and wait . . . please? I'll be back as soon as I can." He softly touched her cheek with his fingers.

She nodded and watched him hand her luggage to Max. "Max, will you take this in for Marti? Then meet me at the stable."

"Yes, sir." Max took the suitcase into the house.

Marti watched the back of Daniel as he ran toward the stable tack room to get supplies for delivering a new foal. Suddenly, everything hit her. Daniel wasn't going to marry Veronica. He remembered being married, but did he remember her? He wanted to talk to her. Of course, that didn't mean he loved her.

Pain tightened her stomach, and she wished she could get away and think—maybe to the falls. She'd spent many hours sitting in front of those falls with Apollo—sorting through the trials life had thrown at her before she left Texas. It would probably be the last time she'd ever see Apollo again.

When Max came out the door, she stopped him.

"Max, would it be all right if I took a ride on Apollo?"

"Why sure thing, Miss Marti, but he's been neglected lately. He's all keyed up like a spring wound too tight. Are you sure you can handle him?"

Marti tilted her head to the side and frowned. "What do you think, Max?"

Max chuckled. "I reckon you can, punkin. I'll get him saddled for you."

"Don't bother, Max. I can do it. You go help Daniel."

Max grinned. "Yes, ma'am."

Marti walked around the barn to the back door and slipped inside. She could hear Daniel talking quietly to Lucky Lady, so she silently gathered the riding tack and turned toward the outside corral where Apollo was grazing.

It was time to think, to pray, and for the first time in a long time, to hope—for her and Daniel.

SEVENTY-SEVEN

Later that afternoon, Daniel saddled Tornado and rode out to the waterfalls. There, he found Marti at the very end of the valley, huddled on the ground in the midst of the bluebonnets and daffodils. He wondered at her beauty—not only her physical beauty, but her loveliness of character and personality as well. In spite of his behavior, she'd been willing to help his dad keep him from ruining his life with Veronica. How had he ever scorned such a lovely person? She sat staring at the waterfalls as if the spray might carry her away to a land devoid of accusations, censure, and pain.

His heart had never been so burdened before. Not only was he angry at himself for forgetting his vow to love, honor, and cherish until death parted them, but he had forsaken his trust in her—something that was unforgiveable. And, it was all because of his pride. The back of his eyes burned when he thought about the pain she must have suffered.

He stepped close enough for her to see him. When she realized he was there, she turned back toward the falls.

"Is Lucky Lady okay?"

"She's fine. She had a little filly."

"That's wonderful." Marti smiled but didn't look at him.

"Marti, can we talk now?"

She clutched her stomach, but she nodded.

He walked toward her, stopped six feet away, and sat down on the grass facing the falls.

"Marti . . . I have several things to say, but the most important thing I have to say is . . ." he turned toward her then, and looked into her eyes. "I'm so sorry. I'm sorry for the pain I put you through—for not believing in you, for not waiting to hear all the facts before I judged you, for not honoring a wife as a husband should . . . for letting my pride get in the way of the truth."

Marti lifted her head. He saw shock in her eyes.

"Did you say wife?"

His belly knotted, but he nodded. "Yes, I said wife. I know who you are. My memory returned when I saw you at the hospital after the fire. I remember . . . everything—you . . . our marriage . . . the accident. I remember the horrible things I said to you, the unforgivable names I called you." He scrubbed his face with his hands. His voice broke as he said, "And I slapped you. Oh, Matty, I'm so sorry for that." He shut his eyes and let the tears fall.

"Did . . . did you call me—"

"Matty. My sweet, wonderful Matty." His voice broke with emotion.

"Daniel, did you say you remembered . . . the accident?"

Daniel looked at her then. "I remember everything, sweetheart. Your smiles, your funny faces when you eat persimmons, your love of horses, your love of books, but most of all, I remember you captured my heart."

"Daniel, I don't understand. After the accident you said—"

He put his finger over her lips. "I don't want you to remember what I said after the accident. I was a fool. No matter what I said then, I don't believe it now."

"But Daniel, you'll never be able to really forget what I did—"

"No, Matty, listen to me; there's so much you don't know. First of all, you weren't driving the car the night Angie and Vinny were killed. Vinny was driving that night, and he'd been drinking."

Marti's face turned white. "I wasn't driving?"

"No. They found Vinny's DNA on everything in the front seat, even the liquor bottles. It was his fault Angie died, Matty—not yours."

"But Mary—"

"Everything Mary said was a lie. Vinny and Angie were in the front seat, and you were riding in the back behind Vinny. Don't you remember?"

Marti shook her head.

"Mary lied, Matty."

"Why? Why would she do that?"

"According to what Shane told us last night, it was because she wanted you to go to prison—to be convicted of causing the wreck. So that . . . so that Veronica and I . . ."

Marti shook her head. "I don't believe it. She hated me that much?"

"No, I don't think she hated you; she just loved Veronica more. Right before the accident, they found out Veronica couldn't have children, and Mary thought if you were in prison . . ."

Marti looked confused. "What would Veronica not being able to have children have to do with me being in prison?"

Daniel blew out an uneasy breath. "That's something else I need to tell you, Matty, and I'm afraid it's going to hurt. Mary Duke lied about your baby. The baby she delivered . . . your baby . . . didn't die. She switched him with a dead baby at the clinic and told the hospital it was your baby that died."

Marti's chest rose and fell in rapid succession. Her eyes reflected her unbelief. She jumped up and stumbled ten feet away, then stopped. Her hands went to her chest, and she swayed.

"I'm fine. Everything is fine."

Daniel felt as if he'd been punched in the chest. The pain radiating from Marti was a silent wave of agony. He could sit still no longer and watch the pain tormenting her. Tears blurred his vision, but he went to her and gently turned her around to face him. She buried her head in his chest and sobbed. Years of regret, loss, and sorrow filled her sobs. Tears filled his heart as well for the sorrow she had endured, and the pain in Daniel's heart moaned in rhythm with her own.

"Matty, listen to me. You lost so much time with your baby, but there's something to be happy about. Your baby is alive."

Marti's knees gave away, and she sank to the ground. Daniel sat down with her.

"My baby? My baby is alive? You know where he is?"

"It's Chris, Matty. Chris is your little boy."

The air left her lungs in a single breath. "Chris? Veronica's brother? Chris is *my* baby? But I thought—"

"The night of the accident, Mary took your baby to the clinic and switched him with a baby who died that day."

"Can I have him back?"

She looked so pitiful that Daniel pulled her into his arms again. "Yes, Matty. We'll get him back. Brent's already promised."

"But, where will he live?" Marti's voice broke. "You sent me away. You called me a—" She choked on the word, but Daniel put his finger on her lips.

"Shhh." He breathed in the cool mountain air and hoped it would infuse him with strength to say what he needed to say—in a way Marti would understand, in a way she could forgive him. *Lord, please give me strength and the words to say.*

He gently let her go and twisted to look at her, holding both her hands in his.

"Matty, when I heard you were in an accident, I was frantic. I caught the first flight home, rented a car at the airport, and drove to the hospital faster than I've ever driven in my life. When I saw you in that bed, all hooked up to tubes and machines . . . then I thought how it was going to kill you to hear we had lost our baby." His voice broke, and he cleared his throat to continue.

"All I could think about was how you were my life. You meant everything to me. I vowed then to protect you, to help you through it all, to love you, to give you another child."

He paused and rubbed his eyes with his hands. "Then the state patrol officers . . . and Mary Duke . . . walked into the hospital room. They told me you were responsible for the wreck. That you'd been drinking. That Vinny was dead, and Angie probably wouldn't make it through the night. I couldn't believe it at first, but the officers said they had an eye witness who said you'd been drinking and that's what caused the accident. I was devastated. They told me they'd have to take you into custody when you were well enough to leave the hospital. When they left, Mary stayed. She pretended to comfort me through the pain, but when I told her you and I would get through it together, that's when she told me she had proof that the baby wasn't mine . . ."

A sharp intake of breath made Daniel look at Marti's face. Wide eyes stared back at him. She tore her hands from his and placed them on her pale cheeks. Tormented eyes met his. "What?" That one word was barely above a whisper. She didn't wait for him to answer. Sobs shook her body, and she turned away from him. "No, no, no." Every word bled with pain. She stood up and shuffled back a step. "That's not true."

As quiet as her words were, Daniel heard them as if they had been shouted at the top of her lungs. He stood up beside her and continued, hesitant because of her gut reaction. "She said she had a witness who said you'd been spending time at . . . a man's house in Cossio County. She said you had a blood test at the clinic and that he was the father."

Marti seemed to gasp for air. "Who? Who did she say?"

"She didn't say, at first. Then right before she died, she named Stanley Baxter."

"Stanley Baxter? The carpenter in Pike?"

Daniel nodded. "She said she saw you in town with him at the café and that you were at his house at least one afternoon each week."

"Of course I was—but with his sister, Chelsea. She was unmarried and pregnant. She was taking Lamaze classes here in Carson and needed a coach. Don't you remember, Daniel? I told you about it. And I was in town at the Lamaze classes with his sister. Stanley drove her there. He picked her up at the café every week after Chelsea and I had lunch."

"But, I saw you with him in town the other day. You had lunch with him."

Marti shook her head. "No, Daniel. I ran into him there and asked him about Chelsea and the baby. He told me what she's doing now, and we walked into the restaurant together, but I ate with Skyler and Cynthia. He had a business luncheon with a client."

The air escaped Daniel's mouth in one lung-collapsing breath. He stared at her, and the truth hit him like a blow to the chest. Mary had lied about this as well. All the pain he had inflicted on Marti because of Mary's accusations. No, he couldn't blame Mary. It was because of his own bull-headedness and pride and willingness to listen to gossip. He'd been embarrassed to find out that he'd been scorned by Marti in front of the whole town. He should have talked to Marti first—let her have a chance to refute the accusations. And Chris. All this time, and he hadn't known Chris was *his own son*.

He raised his eyes to hers but dropped his gaze to the ground when he saw the pain reflected in her eyes like blue pools of crystal clear water. The horrible things he had said. Anguished moans tore through him, and his stomach roiled with nausea. He turned away from her then, too full of shame to face her. He turned his back on her and walked toward the falls, staring at the mountains. What kind of person would listen to gossip and not even ask his wife for her side of the story? Marti had endured such agony because of him. She was so special. He didn't deserve her.

There was no physical touch, no sound, just a sense that she came up behind him, and when she spoke, her voice was close and soft like an angel's voice. "Daniel? It's okay, Daniel. It's all in the past. We can forget it now and get on with our lives."

Daniel turned around then. He took her hand in his and captured her gaze. Tears blurred his vision and spilled onto his cheek.

"I have no life without you, Matty. I know I have no right to ask you, but I don't want to live without you. All this time when I couldn't remember who you were, I still had this feeling, this closeness, this longing to be with you. Now that I remember what we had, I can't face giving it up."

Unexpected tears filled her eyes, as they searched his for truth. "What about Veronica?"

"Veronica has always been . . . just a friend. I'm not even sure she's that anymore. I don't know why she told all those lies, but I never felt the same way about her as I did you. Even when I couldn't remember you, Matty, I couldn't put my finger on it, but deep down, I knew the relationship between Veronica and I wasn't what it should be." Daniel softly rubbed her cheek with his thumb. "I gave my life to God, Matty. Not long after you left, I turned to your God for comfort. Dad kept telling me to pray about the marriage to Veronica, but after the accident, I couldn't remember how to pray. Now I see why my dad wanted to bring you here. He knew if you were around, I couldn't help falling in love with you again. And, he was right."

Marti rubbed her cheek against the palm of Daniel's hand. "Maybe this was God's way of bringing you and your father to Him."

Marti stilled when Daniel reached inside his pocket. He pulled out the wooden horse-head necklace she'd left on the sink at the hospital.

"Matty, my sweet Matty. I love you, sweetheart. Can we put the past behind us and make a whole new wonderful future together? If you can show me the forgiveness that the emerald in this necklace represents, I'll spend the rest of my life making you the happiest wife in the world."

Marti laughed. "I always loved you, Daniel. I'd feel honored to be your wife."

Daniel looked at her eyes and saw the unexpected compassion, the complete forgiveness. She leaned toward him.

This kiss was the sweetest he'd ever remembered. The love of her heart spilled into his with that kiss, and he knew everything would be all right. She pressed her cheek against his, and the tears running down her face mingled with his. They held each other and cried together—their hearts blended into one for the first time in three years.

EPILOGUE

Two weeks later

"I now pronounce you husband and wife. Daniel, you may kiss your bride."

Daniel leaned toward a beaming Marti and kissed her deeply. Marti heard hoots and hollers from among their friends and family, but what broke them apart was Chris pushing between them.

"Mama and Daddy. That's enough kissin'. Can I have some cake now?"

Everyone laughed, and Marti leaned down to kiss Chris on the cheek. "In a minute, sweetheart. First let's give Grandpa his present, okay?"

Chris jumped up and down. "Yes, yes, yes!" He ran to the corner where a large object was hidden beside the huge fireplace in the den of the ranch house. There, Chris stood beside the object, which was draped in black velvet, and held the cord as he had been assigned.

Daniel and Marti each grabbed one of Gerald's arms and led him to the velvet-draped object.

"What's this?" Gerald protested.

Marti turned to Gerald and gave him a kiss on the cheek. "Dad, this is for you." She nodded to Chris, who pulled the golden cord hanging from the velvet. One tug slipped the velvet off to reveal a portrait displayed on an easel. The wedding guests gasped collectively.

Gerald remained frozen. His stood transfixed by the gorgeous face of his daughter, Angie Rushing Welsh. Tears formed in his eyes and rolled down his cheeks, and his face twisted with strong emotion. He pulled Marti to him and squeezed her tightly.

"Oh, Marti. My sweet Martha. It's beautiful, and it's exactly like her. How can I thank you? You are so special to me and so sweet to think of painting this for me. I love you, Marti." He pulled out a handkerchief and wiped his eyes. "Now I have a portrait of each of my children, but my collection is not yet complete. I need one more painting of one last family member."

Marti's brow drew together in a frown. "One more? Who?"

"You, of course."

Their friends standing around them were moved.

"*Awww.*"

"How sweet."

"Isn't that special?"

Marti didn't know what to say.

Stella walked up to her and gave her a hug. "I agree, Gerald. She has to do a self-portrait to hang with the rest of the family."

Gerald hugged her again. "You're my daughter, Marti, and your picture should be on the wall with the rest of the family."

Now tears formed in Marti's eyes, and her throat felt tight. "Thank you, Dad. Thank you."

Daniel wrapped an arm around Marti and kissed her on the cheek. "I agree, Dad. The family wouldn't be complete without my Matty."

Sandra stepped up and put her arms around Marti. "Well, love, it looks like the Lord gave you your 'amigo del alma' after all."

Marti hugged her tightly. "Thank you, Sandra, for nagging me back into God's arms. You're so special. I'm going to miss you."

"I might be around more than you think. I'm moving the gallery to Carson. Running a business in a big city is running me ragged. I'd like to settle down in a nice little town like Carson. Would you be interested in helping me get it started? I seem to remember a promise to hang my next exhibit if I prayed for you, and you know I've been doing that for years."

Marti giggled. "Would I! Oh, Sandra, how wonderful. I'd be able to see you and Wade often, and I'm so happy you're moving."

Sandra gave her another hug.

"Wow, Marti. I'm so happy for you," Alana remarked with a hug as she and Jaydn walked over to the group.

Jaydn shook hands with Daniel. "Congratulations, my friend. You married a very talented young lady. Looks like we both lucked out in the wife department. They're both pretty special."

"You're right, Jaydn. They are. Hey, let's keep in touch."

"Most definitely. Alana will miss having her new friend around, so we'll be visiting back here often. Marti's got her hooked on horseback riding now. We may get some advice on buying horses for the orphanage."

Marti sucked in an excited breath. "That's a great idea. Horses are therapeutic—especially for children."

Brent Simmons and Amber Pike walked over to offer their congratulations.

"I'm glad everything worked out, you two," said Brent. He nodded toward Chris, who was patiently standing beside the cake table. "He seems to have adjusted quickly enough."

Daniel nodded. "He's doing great. We redecorated the bedroom next to the master suite, and he's thrilled with the choo choo trains Marti painted on the walls."

Amber laughed. "It must be nice—having an artist in the family."

Daniel smiled and gave Marti a kiss on the cheek. "I wouldn't have it any other way."

Marti touched Brent's sleeve. "Brent, what about Parker and Anita's little boy, Gavin? Daniel told me that Mary arranged an illegal adoption for them at the same time she adopted Chris and that Parker and Anita were afraid they might lose their son."

"No, everything turned out okay for them. When Parker found out about Mary's deception concerning Chris, he had a lawyer check into Gavin's adoption. The lawyer was able to legalize Gavin's adoption, so Parker and Anita have nothing to worry about."

"So that's why he acted so strange. I guess he was worried sick."

Brent nodded and leaned in. "I also wanted to tell you that we're positive Veronica had no knowledge about her parents' activities concerning Chris. We conducted an extensive investigation and confirm that she was completely innocent of the whole thing—had no idea Chris was your son."

Daniel looked at Marti. "That's good to know. Poor Veronica. I actually feel sorry for her. First she lost her mother. Now she's lost her father and Chris all at the same time. She has nothing and no one."

Marti leaned close to Daniel and looked into his eyes. "She can visit Chris anytime she wants."

"I love you, darling. Did you know that?"

Marti nodded and kissed him again, reveling in the wonderful, joyful emotion filling her.

"Nuff kissin', Mama. Nuff kissin', Daddy. I want some cake!"

Everyone laughed.

Marti leaned over and touched Chris on the nose. "All right, sweetie. Let's go get cake." Daniel and Marti each took one of

Chris's hands. As Chris walked between Marti and Daniel, Marti's heart was completely full—full of acceptance and love. The Lord had indeed "restored what the locusts had eaten" . . . over and abundantly. What a wonderful ending for a new beginning.

Hashtag: HappilyEverAfter.

For more information about
Joanie Bruce
&
A Memory Worth Dying For
please visit:

Web Site: *joaniebruce.com*
Email: *joaniebruce@gmail.com*
Twitter: *@joaniebruce*
Facebook: *https://www.facebook.com/joaniebruceauthor*

For more information about
AMBASSADOR INTERNATIONAL
please visit:

www.ambassador-international.com
@AmbassadorIntl
www.facebook.com/AmbassadorIntl